Grave Allegations

Daphne Neville

Copyright © 2015 Daphne Neville

All rights reserved, including the right to reproduce this book, or portions thereof in any form. No part of this text may be reproduced, transmitted, downloaded, decompiled, reverse engineered, or stored, in any form or introduced into any information storage and retrieval system, in any form or by any means, whether electronic or mechanical without the express written permission of the author.

This is a work of fiction. Names and characters are the product of the author's imagination and any resemblance to actual persons, living or dead, is entirely coincidental.

The views expressed in this work are solely those of the author and do not necessarily reflect the views of the publisher, and the publisher hereby disclaims any responsibility for them.

ISBN: 978-1-326-42914-0

PublishNation, London
www.publishnation.co.uk

Other Titles by this Author

The Ringing Bells Inn
Polquillick
Sea, Sun, Cads and Scallywags
The Old Vicarage

Chapter One

1976

The summer of 1975 was long, warm and dry, hence by September the word drought was frequently mentioned in numerous conversations.

The long, dry summer was followed by a very dry autumn and then an exceptionally dry winter, therefore in the spring of 1976 no-one was surprised when the Government informed the nation of impending difficulties and a summer during which they would inevitably suffer the consequences of severe water shortages.

The residents of Trengillion, as in the rest of the British Isles, braced themselves for water rationing and if the worst came to the worst, the installation of standpipes. However, for Trengillion, a fishing village tucked neatly in a valley on the south coast of Cornwall, there were at least benefits to be had. For as with all seaside resorts stretching around the country's long, curvy coastline, long, dry, hot sunny days and constant blue skies meant holiday makers would inevitably flock to the seaside in large numbers, thus by doing so help to sustain an otherwise impoverished economy.

Anne Stanley paused beneath the overhanging branches of a tall sycamore tree and buried her face deep into the bunch of bluebells she clasped in her hands. She took a deep breath for the pungent scent of the flowers was a firm favourite with Anne and many other inhabitants of Trengillion who rambled at least once through Bluebell Woods during the month of May to marvel at the indigo carpet which covered the woodland floor. For indeed the bluebells were a spectacular sight and a pleasing colour contrast to the tiny lesser celandines growing in clusters alongside the bluebells in shallow soil, and the large, bright yellow marsh marigolds which flourished on the banks of the meandering stream.

When her bunch of flowers was large enough to fill a vase, Anne continued on her way through the woods, carefully following the well-worn path to avoid treading on the flowers. After passing a large horse chestnut tree she reached a clearing where the sunlight peeped through the tree tops and cast dappled shade on the lumpy woodland floor. Here she veered off to the right towards Penwynton Hotel and finally emerged into the open through rhododendron bushes, dense with a multitude of flowers in shades of purple, pink and white.

On the gravelled driveway, stretched out along the front of the large impressive building, which once had been the home of Trengillion's prosperous Penwynton family, she stopped and cast her eyes across to the car park where the windows of numerous vehicles glinted in the morning sunshine. The sight of Danny Jarrams' white MGB parked on the tarmac caused her to squeal with delight. She had not expected him to have arrived so soon.

Anne ran up the steps, two at a time, through the large double doors and into the vestibule where a middle-aged woman sat at the reception desk scribbling notes into an open jotter.

"Bluebells," smiled Mary Cottingham, raising her head. "How lovely."

"I picked them to put on the desk. I hope you don't mind but I just couldn't resist them this morning. The scent was overwhelming because of the drizzle we had last night and I do love them as they remind me of when I was young."

Mary Cottingham threw back her head and laughed. "Surely you don't consider yourself to be old at the tender age of twenty. God, what I'd give to be your age again."

"Well, yes, I know I'm not old but I was referring to my childhood. We had such great fun when we were kids, you see, and sometimes it's nice to pretend those days are still with us." She sighed. "Oh dear, I know they're gone forever and everything's changed ever so much, but, well, oh, you must know what I mean."

Mary smiled as she closed the notebook. "Yes, of course I do, and I think you miss Elizabeth far more than you'd ever admit. I know I never liked it if my sister was not within striking distance." She reached out and took the flowers from Anne's hands. "I'll go and pop these in water and make you a coffee while you get settled in."

Mary turned and walked off towards the hallway and Anne crossed the vestibule to a small cupboard tucked beneath the staircase. There she kicked off her flat shoes, slipped on her platforms and returned to the reception desk. Through the Hotel's open doors, the rhododendrons on the edge of the woods were clearly visible. Anne leaned on the desk, resting her face in her cupped hands and wistfully thought of her sister.

Elizabeth Stanley, a newly qualified primary school teacher, was very glad she had chosen to follow in the footsteps of both her parents and plump for a career in teaching. She did, however, miss her home in Cornwall, her friends and especially her little sister, Anne. And although she was happy with the school in Sussex in which she taught, she had her fingers firmly crossed that her application to teach in a school nearer to home would be fruitful. Hence, every day she was eager to get back to her lodgings, hopeful that a letter congratulating her on her success might be waiting. It seemed a little uncanny therefore that at the very same time that Anne sat reminiscing at the reception desk in the Penwynton Hotel, the postman delivered the hankered for envelope through the letterbox of the house where Elizabeth had a flat.

Anne smiled as Mary returned with a vase of bluebells. "You're right about Elizabeth, I do miss her, but I saw Danny's car when I arrived just now so he can be my soul-mate for the next few days."

Mary put down the flowers on the reception desk. "Well, you won't see him for an hour or two yet. He drove down overnight and was pretty shattered when he got here. But I know he's looking forward to seeing you. In fact I think half the time it's you he comes to see and not Heather and Bob."

The Penwynton Hotel was owned and run by Mary Cottingham, her husband, Dick, Mary's sister, Heather and brother-in-law, Bob. Mary and Dick's daughter, Linda also helped out although she had no financial interest in the business. Danny Jarrams was Heather and Bob's son. They also had a daughter, Penny, who was a nurse, but she visited Cornwall only once or twice a year, for she was married to a doctor and the couple had two children, hence free time was usually spoken for before long before it occurred. Danny, however, made frequent short visits to the Hotel. In moderation he enjoyed the peace and quiet having spent several years on the road racing around the country playing bass guitar with Gooseberry Pie, a 1960s pop group with whom he had found fame and a relatively modest fortune. The group, however, disbanded in 1974, when the vocalist and the lead guitarist both decided to make solo careers for themselves. Danny on the other hand, tired of the high life and weeks on the road, chose to take a more menial path and pursue the occupation he had chosen on leaving school before fame had knocked on his door and now ran his own successful photography business in West London.

The Cottinghams and Jarrams bought Penwynton House in the autumn of 1967 following the death of the last of the Penwyntons, Charles, who, to the surprise of local people, left the entire estate to a distant cousin living in Canada. The house, following its purchase, underwent laborious, detailed planning and finally, after eighteen months of upheaval and refurbishments, the huge transformation to change its usage from a large family home into luxury five star hotel was finally completed.

Anne had worked as a receptionist at the Hotel ever since she had left school. It was a job she yearned for and no other would suffice; for she loved Penwynton Hotel and had done so since she had first encountered the building as a run-down, neglected house during her childhood. And never once since she had left school after taking her GCEs had she regretted not continuing her education and taking her A-levels as had her sister, Elizabeth. For Anne enjoyed the diversity of hotel work, the ever changing faces of guests, the difference in the seasons, and the arrival of seasonal workers. She was also very fond of her employers who treated her in high esteem for her knowledge of the area and dedication to their business.

As Anne checked out and chatted to the first of the guests due to leave that day, Mary returned with the promised coffee and a slice of Madeira cake which she slid onto a shelf beneath the counter, indicating her actions to Anne by means of hand gestures and mime. Anne nodded her thanks as she left, and then turned to wish the departing guests preparing to leave the vestibule with Eric, the porter, carrying their luggage, a pleasant journey. When she was alone she sipped her coffee and read through the departure and arrival list for the day.

"Cor, they were generous," said Eric, as he returned, beaming from ear to ear. "They left me two quid. The miserly Barnetts who went home yesterday, only left me a mingy tenpenny piece and I had to work bloomin' hard for that."

"That's very kind of them," said Anne, as the porter tucked the two one pound notes into his wallet. "Would you like this piece of cake, Eric? I'm not too keen on Madeira but I wouldn't like to say so to Mary and I've not long since had breakfast anyway."

"Cor, yes please, miss. I got up late this morning so I've not eaten anything yet. I didn't even have time for a cuppa, no wonder the old tum keeps rumbling."

Anne smiled. "So what time did you start this morning?"

"Half seven," said Eric, swallowing a mouthful of cake, "and I didn't finish last night 'til eight. Still, I've got tomorrow off so I can have a nice long lie in then."

He finished off the cake and as he wiped his hands and mouth on a handkerchief from the pocket of his uniform, the internal phone rang on the desk. Anne answered it and then informed Eric the Simpsons in room sixteen were ready to leave.

"Blimey, they're all eager to get off today," said Eric, straightening his tie. "I'm on my way."

Anne watched as Eric walked towards the staircase whistling as he went in his usual cheerful way. She liked working when he was on duty; he amused her and his presence created a pleasant atmosphere which was appreciated by most of the guests, whatever their ages.

In his absence Anne prepared the Simpsons' bill, checked everything was included and then totted up the final figure. As she laid it on the counter for the inspection of the departing guests a breeze from an open window sent a waft of perfume from the bluebells in her direction.

Anne closed her eyes and breathed in the strong scent. "I must pick flowers for Grandma when I finish work today and drop them into Rose Cottage before I get home. I've not done so yet this year; she'll think I'm neglecting her."

Chapter Two

Molly Smith said goodbye to her husband, the major, who was reading the daily newspaper at their home, Rose Cottage. She then picked up her straw sunhat, placed it over her blonde curls and set off through the village carrying an empty basket to call for her friend, Dorothy Newton.

When she arrived at the Newtons' bungalow on the outskirts of the village, she found Dorothy and her husband, Frank, both in the garden watering neat rows of green seedlings standing in regimented stripes across the dry, brown earth of the vegetable plot.

"Coo-ee," called Molly, as she raised the latch on the garden gate. "Our garden could do with watering too. The rain we had last night didn't soak down very far, did it?"

Dorothy shook her head. "Sadly not. In fact it did little more than wet the leaves and even that evaporated the minute the sun came out."

Molly closed the gate and put down her basket on the path. "I've come to see if you'd like to come with me to pick some elderflowers, Dot. There's a lovely crop of them this year."

Frank chuckled as he bent down and tweaked a clover leaf craftily hidden amongst the lettuce plants. "You'd better not pick 'em all, Moll. Doris won't be very pleased if there are none left to fruit. We all know what a fusspot she is when it comes to making her elderberry wine in the autumn."

"Oh, there'll be plenty left for Doris," said Molly, dispassionately. "The hedgerows are brimming with flowers this year. You must have noticed, they're a picture and the scent is breath-taking."

Dorothy stood the empty watering can beneath the outside tap. "I did notice when I cycled down to Home Farm to see my big brother. Are you planning to make elderflower wine then?"

Molly shook her head. "No, elderflower champagne. I haven't made any for years because last time I did the bottles weren't strong enough and they burst all over the pantry floor. The major went on about the mess for ages and for that reason I've avoided making it since then. But I had a word with Mary Cottingham at Christmas and she's been saving me proper champagne bottles, so I should be alright this time as long as I can cork them properly."

"Hmm, champagne," grinned Frank. "Are you expecting something to celebrate?"

Molly wrinkled her nose. "No, not really, but then you never know just what the year might hold. On the other hand, we know of one momentous occasion. Ned'll be fifty in August. Ridiculous! How can I possibly have such an old son? Anyway, it'll be good enough reason for a knees-up, but I expect the champagne will be gone long before then. It's really more of a refreshing drink than anything else though as the alcohol content is very low."

"I've often thought about trying to make wine," mused Dorothy, "but I'm a bit nervous cos you and Doris have it off to such a fine art, and I'd probably get shown up."

"Nonsense," said Molly, modestly. "It's really very simple, Dot. You must give it a try. There's something very satisfying about hearing the plop-plopping in the airlock. I'll bring you round a few recipes and some spare demi-johns to get you started. It's the ideal time of year with the promise of summer produce ahead, although of course lots of goodies are available all year round. In fact, on second thoughts, if you come with me for elderflowers, we'll pick you some dandelions at the same time. I've already made mine, cos dandelion's the major's favourite, but there are still plenty of flowers around to make more. What do you say?"

A wide smile crossed Dorothy's face. "Well, yes, why not? There's no time like the present. I'll just pop indoors to spend a penny and change into my old shoes and then I'll be ready."

"And grab a bag while you're in the house," called Molly, and a bit of paper too, then I'll write down your instructions for the first stage before we go."

"Righty ho," shouted Dorothy as she disappeared through the kitchen door.

Molly sat down on the garden bench. "It looks like we're in for another nice summer if this weather holds, doesn't it, Frank? Although last year will take a bit of beating. I hope it's not too hot though. It's frustrating when you can't get outside to do jobs cos you risk being burnt to a cinder and if there's no wind the washing dries in a flash, as stiff as a board and crumpled. Being a man you wouldn't understand that, but it's a nightmare trying to iron things if they're too dry and I can't get on with these steam irons: they always dribble in the wrong places."

Frank chuckled. "Well, it makes a change from hearing you moan about the cold, Moll. I know nothing used to get you more fed up.

"Hmm, well, of course I can't stand being cold either. I reckon the winters are far too long. Having said that, I do like to see snow in the hedgerows and on the trees." She took off her sunhat and looked around the garden. "Your lilac's looking lovely, it's much darker than mine. Does it have a very strong scent?"

"Dunno," said Frank, glancing at the tree. "The blooming flowers are so high up, I can't tell. Dot said we need to cut it back hard so that it'll shoot from the bottom. It's been overgrown all the years we've lived here, you see, though o' course it's even bigger now."

"I know, that's the trouble with lilac. Buddleia too. In fact lots of shrubs need pruning hard. I never like to do it though. It seems sacrilege to cut off healthy growth."

Frank sat down beside Molly on the bench. "I can't see anyone growing record breaking veg this summer, size wise that is."

Molly sighed deeply. "Hmm, the major was saying the same thing only yesterday. He does love growing his veg. Still, hopefully some things will grow alright. It would be a shame if the Village Show was cancelled as a lot of folk look forward to it."

"When is it? I looked at the calendar the other day and there's nothing written down."

"It's always the third Saturday in August, and so this year it'll be the twenty first. Sounds a long way off but it'll be here before we know it."

Molly and Dorothy left the bungalow and walked back into the heart of the village. When they reached the village school they turned into the lane which ran between the school and the School House, where Molly's son, Ned, lived with his wife Stella and two daughters, Anne and Elizabeth.

The lane was narrow with insufficient room for two cars to pass except in field gateways, but as it led to nowhere in particular it was seldom used by traffic so was usually quiet except for the occasional tractor going to or from Long Acre Farm.

"The major tells me that Frank's golfing skills are getting quite the talk of the club," said Molly, offering Dorothy an Everton Mint. "I'm so pleased. I used to worry that he'd have trouble settling down after all those years at the Inn, but he's proved me quite wrong, I'm pleased to say."

"Thank you. He loves the golf club," said Dorothy, unwrapping her sweet. "In fact, I think he's quite happy with his lot in life. It's a shame they lost poor old George Fillingham though, isn't it? I know he was in his eighties, but somehow he never seemed that old, did he?"

Molly nodded in agreement. "Hmm and poor Bertha's taken it very hard, so I hear. It's a shame Sea Thrift Cottage is in such a remote spot, because she could do with being more in the village now she's a widow. Have you seen her lately?"

Dorothy shook her head. "Not for a couple of weeks. I really must get up there. I bumped into May Dickens last Tuesday though and she said she goes round to see her most days."

"Good, they always were the best of friends. By the way, is it true Pat and May have Higher Green Farm up for sale?

"I believe so," said Dorothy, "at least if they haven't yet they soon will have. It's getting too much for them now, milking and suchlike, and I know May is keen to get one of the new houses being built on the new development. Have you been up there for a look? I have."

Molly shook her head. "No, I keep meaning to but it always slips my mind. I hear it's going to be called Penwynton Crescent and that meets with my approval. I mean, now that Charles has gone and the family have all died out it'll be nice to have something to remember them by. I know there's the Hotel but that's not in the heart of the village, is it? Anyway, I'm rambling, what's it like, the new housing thingy, that is?"

"Very nice. They've finished the first row of smaller, two bedroomed houses and they're ready to move in to, so I believe. They're working on the bungalows now. I've seen the lay out and it looks as though they'll all have good size gardens. It's lovely and quiet there and such a nice spot."

Molly pulled a red campion flower from the hedgerow and placed it beneath the ribbon around her hat. "Every bit of Trengillion is a nice spot if you ask me. I can understand why so many holiday makers come here, and many of them year after year too. It beats going abroad where everyone's foreign. Which reminds me, Harry Richardson was telling the major that they're going to rent out the Old Police House on a long-let because doing holiday bookings is getting too much for Joyce since she's been having trouble with her back. So if you know of anyone looking for a place to rent, tell 'em to jump in quick."

"I'm not surprised," tut-tutted Dorothy. "Personally, I think they were a bit daft ever to buy the place. Poor Joyce had enough on her hands with bed and breakfast at their own home without having somewhere else to worry about. You'd think now that Harry's retired they'd both want to wind down a bit, wouldn't you?"

"Well actually, I heard they are giving up the bed and breakfast at the end of this summer, and I suppose if you've always been busy then it's bound to be more difficult to slow down. I can see why they bought the Old Police House though. I mean to say it was a damn good investment and ten thousand pounds was a very good price. The major reckons it was giveaway."

"Yes, I suppose so, but it was a backward step the day we lost our village policeman. I know Fred was due to retire anyway, but it would have been nice to have a replacement. I hear most villages have lost their bobbies now and the police houses have all been sold off. It's such a shame. Such a shame."

"And it's not just a bobby the village has lost," said Molly, her voice rising in anger. "I think it's a disgrace that the church are going to sell off the Vicarage. I don't know what the world's coming to."

"Well, I'm not so sure that I agree with you there. The Vicarage did cost the church a lot of money to maintain and it's not needed now that we share our vicar with other villages in the parish."

"Humph! I don't agree with that either. Every village should have its own vicar and he should live in the village. I don't go along with all these new-fangled, money saving ideas. Call me a Luddite if you want, but I don't like change and what's more I don't think it's right that any Tom, Dick or Harry as can afford it will be able to buy and live in a holy place like the Vicarage."

Dorothy smiled. "But the Vicarage isn't holy. It's not consecrated like the church, it's just a house."

"Well, you know what I mean," tut-tutted Molly, flustered by her vexation. "It's had holy people in it and should be treated with reverence.

"Aren't the hedgerows looking a picture in spite of the lack of rain?" Dorothy said, thinking it wise to change the subject. "I think they're at their best this time of year. Such a lovely array of colour."

Molly laughed. "You're quite right and it's far too nice a day to get all het up over things that cannot be changed."

At the bottom of the hill the two ladies stopped.

"Now, which way shall we go?" asked Molly, sitting on the stone wall beneath which the stream ran under the road. "We definitely don't want to go through the woods cos even though it'll be nice and cool, there are no dandelions there, although there is an elder. So we can either go across the fields here and walk alongside the brook on the other side, or carry on up the hill and go across Penrose land towards the cliffs. Whichever way we go there are plenty of dandelions and elderflowers. So what do you think?"

"Let's carry on up the hill," said Dorothy, without hesitation. "I know it's daft but I don't like the look of those cows over there by the brook."

"But you grew up on a farm," laughed Molly, much surprised. "You should be used to cattle and animally things."

"I know," muttered Dorothy, sheepishly, "and don't ever tell my brother, Albert, but I never could get on with the cows. I've been scared of them since I was a nipper. I know they won't hurt me but it's just the way I am."

Molly stood up. "We better trudge on up the hill then. I'd rather do that anyway because it's often muddy alongside the stream, especially where cows have waded into the water for a drink. Their big feet always leave damn great holes behind."

They carried on up the hill and just before they reached Long Acre Farm, they climbed a gate which led onto a bridle path crossing land belonging to the farm.

I hear young Gregory Castor-Hunt is doing well with his training to be a solicitor," said Molly. "Anne was telling me he's just finished doing a legal practice thingy which is something he had to do on top of his law degree. Now he just has to do a two year apprenticeship in a solicitor's office and then he'll be qualified. Something like that anyway. It didn't all sink in properly as I can't take in education mumbo jumbo."

"Absolutely, neither can I," said Dorothy, shaking her head in agreement. "We didn't have stuff like that when we were young, did we? The three 'R's were enough for us. Is Greg's little sister, Lily, still nursing? She's always struck me as such a nice girl. So polite, and a credit to her parents."

"Yes, she is and it was Lily who told Anne about Greg. They've been friends since they were tots and are always writing to each other. Anne and Lily, that is. I don't think Greg writes much, although if I know what my instincts tell me, then Elizabeth must jolly well wish he did."

Dorothy's eyebrows rose. "Hmm, I see, so you're up to your old match-making tricks again and you think Elizabeth and Gregory are well suited."

"I don't think, Dorothy, I know. I wasn't a fortune teller for no reason. I can see a lot that others can't and I'm seldom wrong. Anyway, that's enough chat for now. Look at all those beautiful dandelions; time to get picking while they're still in the sun."

They filled Dorothy's bags with flower heads until no more could be squeezed in and then continued on into the next field where elderflowers hung in profusion from bushes in the hedgerows.

"Hmm, don't they smell lovely?" said Dorothy, as she helped Molly fill her basket, and they're so pretty too, so delicate. I can't believe some people consider them to be a weed, but they do."

"Philistines," said Molly, with vehemence. "The elder is a magical tree and its fruits have healing qualities like no other. Folks that don't appreciate Mother Nature's gifts are philistines, Dot. There's no other word for it. They're philistines."

"Talking of philistines," said Dorothy, ceasing to pick flowers and placing both hands firmly on hips. "Have you heard what happened to the plates we used to have hanging in the snug bar at the Inn?"

"Well of course. That dreadful Raymond Withers man took them down and replaced them with horrible guns," said Molly, shaking her head. "Everyone knows that. So what on earth makes you bring them up after all these years?"

"Because I'm told by the milkman's wife, who does the cleaning there, that after he'd taken them down, which as we know was close on the heels of changing the name from the Ringing Bells Inn to, well, I can't even say it. Anyway, after that, he put all the plates out the back in the garden shed. And then last week, when one of his boys was tidying it out, he, the son, came across them. So, what do you think he did? Raymond that is, not the son."

Molly shrugged her shoulders. "I don't know. I dread to think."

"Well, I'll tell you. He stood them on the wall out the back in the old vegetable patch and used them for target practice with his beastly gun and blew the whole lot to smithereens. Now, doesn't that take the biscuit for philistinism?"

Chapter Three

"I think next winter we'll give this place another coat of paint," said Raymond Withers, standing in the kitchen of the Sheriff's Badge Inn and buttoning up his waistcoat ready for lunchtime opening. "I noticed yesterday morning when I opened up that it's getting quite shabby in places, especially round the doors, and we can't have folks thinking we're not making enough dosh to keep up with the maintenance."

Gloria, his wife, stepped forwards and removed a grey hair from the collar of his red, check shirt. "Oh, that'll be nice and perhaps we could have a complete overhaul and go more for a nautical theme. You know, crab pots, fishing nets, sea shells, framed glass wall cabinets full of knots, and so forth. The visitors would like that as they always like to chat to the fishermen and join in with the singing on Friday nights."

"What!" spluttered Raymond, dramatically stepping backwards to ensure Gloria could fully observe the genuine look of astonishment and disapproval on his face. "Over my dead body. This Inn's popular because of me, Gloria, and the Wild West theme. Fishing's old hat. Let the other unimaginative pubs go down that road."

"But, Raymond, we've a beautiful coastline here and we overlook a picturesque fishing cove with lots of boats so it makes sense to…"

"…that's enough, Glore. Christ, you'll be wanting to hang more bloody plates on the beams again next. Now where's my holster? What have you done with it?"

Gloria sighed and nodded in the direction of the fridge. "It's up there, where you left it."

Raymond reached for the holster, hung it round his waist, fastened the buckle and then gave his two pistols a twirl.

"You see, folks like something a bit different, Glore and that's what I give 'em. Now come on, cheer up, you know I'm always right." He sniffed the air. "And you'd better take them pies out of the oven before they get burnt to cinders cos they smell like they're done to me."

With his back straight and his head held high, Raymond left the kitchen and strutted into the bar, while Gloria, as instructed, crossed to the Calor gas cooker, pulled her oven gloves from a large brass hook fixed to the wall, and opened the oven doors.

As she placed the tray of pies onto the kitchen table she heard the side door of the Inn creak open followed by the tuneful notes of someone whistling. She was surprised, for the choice of melody suggested Roger was home.

Grinning, her son peeked around the kitchen door. "Those pies smell good, Mum. Any chance of me having one cos I'm starving?"

"Yes, yes, of course," said Gloria, transferring pies onto a cooling rack. "But how come you're home so soon?"

"Lunch break," said Roger, pulling back a chair and sitting at the kitchen table. "We're working in the village for a while now doing electrical work to some of the new houses going up, so you'd better make lots of pies because I'll most likely pop home every day while we're up there."

"Oh, that's nice and handy," said Gloria, always glad to know her sons were safe and close by. "It'll save you a lot of time not having to travel back and forth."

"Yep, and it means I can have a lie in every morning. Where's Dad?"

Gloria placed the empty hot baking trays on the draining board and returned the oven gloves to their hook. "In the bar of course. Why do you ask?"

"I need to speak to him. He wants me to work on Friday night, you see, but there's this really nice girl staying at Sea View Cottage with her family and Friday will be her last night. You must have seen her; the family are in most nights. It's just that we seem to have hit it off and I'd like to spend the last evening with her."

Gloria nodded approvingly. "You do that then and Colin can work instead. Your brother's managed to avoid all his shifts for a week now and it's not good enough. If he doesn't soon do a night he'll have forgotten all the prices, although having said that I think your dad's going to put them all up again soon because of soaring overheads and this damn inflation."

Roger took a pie from the cooling rack and bit into it. "Thanks, Mum, you're a treasure, and your pies are the best in the world. Better than a pasty any day. In fact you ought to put up the price of them cos you can't make much profit at fifteen pence each."

Gloria took a plate from the cupboard. "Here, put the pie on here, cos you're dropping crumbs on your lap."

"Thanks."

"Anyway, if they don't show much profit, it's because you, your dad and our Colin keep scoffing them. Still, I don't mind, if the truth be known, I'm flattered. I think it's a bit unfair of you to say they're better than a pasty though because some of them are mouth-wateringly delicious." She reached for the kettle. "Would you like a cup of tea or coffee while you're here?"

Grinning, Roger rose from the table. "Coffee, please. And while you make it I'll just go and check with Dad that's it's alright to swap with Colin on Friday. You know what he's like if he's kept in the dark."

Raymond and Gloria Withers had two sons, Roger, aged twenty five, an electrician who was very musical and played the piano by ear, and Colin, a car mechanic, aged twenty three, whose hobbies were amateur football and doing up old cars. The family had moved to Trengillion in October 1967 having bought the Inn from Frank Newton around the same time as the Cottinghams and the Jarrams were in the process of buying Penwynton House, now Penwynton Hotel.

Back in 1967, on the first evening of opening after the change of ownership, Trengillion's inhabitants had flocked to the Inn in droves to scrutinise the new licensees. Their verdict was that most agreed Raymond Withers, while seeming efficient, appeared to be an arrogant bully who seriously lacked the gift of genuine charm. Gloria, however, won their instant approval. And as regards the fact they were a family, it was unanimously agreed that for the couple to have two, at that time, teenage sons, would inevitably bring a breath of fresh air to the village.

Their views regarding Gloria still held good nine years on. Likewise, Roger and Colin's presence had proved, as anticipated, an asset as they mixed with and became good friends with the youngsters in the village.

Raymond, however, divided opinions in two. For the changing of the Inn's name from the Ringing Bells Inn to the Sheriff's Badge Inn and then replacing the plates which had adorned the snug bar's beams for many years, with guns, within days of the new ownership, was a bitter pill to swallow for even his most ardent followers.

Frank Newton, in the absence of his wife, Dorothy, finished watering the vegetables and then went indoors to make a mug of coffee and fetch the *Daily Telegraph*. When the coffee was made, he took a handful of rich tea biscuits from the barrel on the shelf, picked up his pipe, matches, tobacco and newspaper and returned to the garden.

At first he sat on the bench but decided the spot was too warm, for the sun had gone round and the seat was fully exposed to its rays thus meaning the glare of the white paper pages would make reading an unpleasant pastime. Wearily, he put down the mug of coffee, smoking devices and paper; the biscuits he tucked into his pocket. He then went over to the shed and pulled out a deckchair which he carried to a shady spot beneath an old pear tree. Glad to be out of the sun, he drank his now lukewarm coffee and ate the biscuits. After reading the newspaper he dropped it onto the grass beside his empty mug. Finally, he lit his pipe and laid back his head on the colourful striped canvas, a much contented man.

In the many years that Frank had owned and run the Ringing Bells Inn he'd had no time for hobbies. The sole purpose in his life was to make the Inn pay for itself and keep his customers, many of whom were also his friends, happy. It was not until his retirement in 1967 that he had found there was so much more to life than work.

On the insistence of Major Smith he had joined the golf club and become a competent player, although he attributed many of his winning strokes to beginner's luck rather than skill. He'd also learned to enjoy watching tennis and eagerly looked forward to Wimbledon fortnight each year when he followed it through with dedicated enthusiasm equal only to his passion for cricket. Furthermore, he took up gardening, the result of which, much to everyone's surprise, soon earned himself the nickname, Green Fingers Frank. For over the years many of his vegetables won prizes in village shows, not only in Trengillion but at other locations also.

But in spite of his hobbies he missed the conviviality of the Inn and wished he had sold it to someone other than Raymond Withers so that he might go there still and enjoy a pint with old friends. Not that his contemporaries still drank at the Inn. Many vowed to boycott the premises on the day Raymond Withers changed the name to the Sheriff's Badge Inn, and much to Frank's surprise they had kept their promises and if they fancied a drink went to Polquillick, where time stood still and the landlord did not inflict his bizarre flights of fancy, whims, and odd behaviour on his patrons. But for all his misgivings, Frank expressed his gripes only to Dorothy and close friends, for he was well aware that the younger generation of the village liked Raymond Withers and his Wild West Nights, and he deemed it would not be right to deny them a bit of fun and enjoy their local hostelry as his friends and customers had done in days gone by.

From inside the house Frank heard the telephone ringing. He cursed; it always seemed to ring when he was outside and every time it could be relied on to stop just as he reached out to lift the receiver.

"Sod it," muttered Frank, "let it ring. If it's important then whoever it is will ring back."

He laid back his head in the chair again and thought about the major. It had crossed his mind that he might drop in for a visit whilst the ladies were out picking elderflowers and dandelions. For Jeremy Thorpe, leader of the Liberal party, had resigned the previous day amidst rumours of scandal and Frank felt sure the subject was something the major would inevitably have strong opinions on, just as earlier in the year when he had talked for days on end about the sudden resignation of Prime Minister Harold Wilson and the whys and wherefores thereof. Frank glanced at the front page of the paper lying on the grass beside his chair. Without doubt, the Thorpe resignation bore all the hallmarks of an equally debatable subject.

Damn," said Frank, slapping his thigh. "That might well have been the major ringing just now to see if I were in. What a fool! I should have nipped in and answered it."

Hoping his suppositions were right, he dropped his pipe onto the grass alongside the newspaper and his empty coffee mug and then marched into the house to phone the major on the off chance he might want to visit for a chat.

Chapter Four

Ned Stanley, headmaster of the village school, tucked a dozen exercise books into his briefcase to take home for marking; he then straightened his desk and left the classroom. In the cloakroom, the caretaker was changing the bag in the vacuum cleaner. Ned bade her farewell and left the school building by way of the main entrance.

Along the road he met Dorothy Newton carrying two bags of sugar purchased at the post office, a necessary ingredient for the making of her dandelion wine. Ned chatted with her briefly and then continued on his way to the School House. Once inside he wearily sat down at the kitchen table. He sighed deeply as he removed his brown, suede shoes.

His wife, Stella, cast a quizzical look. "What's the matter, Ned? Why the big sigh?"

"Oh, I don't know. I suppose I'm just getting old, love. Would you believe it, but I'd completely forgotten there's a meeting tonight to organise the school jumble sale and I wouldn't have remembered it at all if Meg hadn't mentioned it during break this afternoon."

Stella passed Ned his slippers. "Well, you do have rather a lot on your plate and it is nearly the end of the school year so naturally you're feeling a little weary. But it wouldn't have been a catastrophe if you had forgotten, would it? Besides, I'm fully aware of the meeting because I'll be going anyway."

"Yes, I know, but that's not the point. What if it had been something really important and I'd not had you reliable females to remind me. I'll land myself in deep trouble if I'm not careful."

Stella smiled. "All you have to do is check your diary every morning. Surely it can't be that difficult."

"I do check it daily, but in this case I'd failed to write it in in the first place. Do you think I'm getting senile, Stell?"

As he spoke the telephone rang in the hallway. Stella left Ned with his head in his hands and went to answer it.

"Mum," squealed a voice on the other end of the line. "It's me, Liz. I've got the job. Can you believe it? I've got the job. There was a letter waiting for me when I got home today. I start in September. I'm so excited. I can't stop jumping for joy."

"Wow, that's wonderful, Elizabeth," said Stella, thrilled at the prospect of having her elder daughter back home again. "Our congratulations, dear. Anne will be so pleased when we tell her and we're delighted too of course. So can we expect you back home at the end of term?"

"Well, no, not straight away. I'm going away on holiday with Gabby first. She's my teaching friend and flatmate. We're going to Majorca. We've been talking about it for absolutely ages and we're planning to go to the travel agents and book it up this weekend. Up until now I've not been able to raise a great deal of enthusiasm, you see, because of the job, that is. I've been so on edge wanting to know whether or not I'd got it, but now everything's sorted we can make proper plans and it should be great fun. We'll only be away for a week though, so I'll still be home by the end of July or beginning of August at the latest. Is everyone okay?"

"Hmm, yes, we're fine, although your dad reckons he's getting senile. He forgot there was a meeting on at the school tonight cos he hadn't written it in his diary."

"What! Well tell him not to worry, I frequently forget things. Why only yesterday I forgot to take my handbag to school with me and had to walk because I didn't have my purse and any money for my bus fare. But then I suppose that was because I had a bag full of magazines to carry for the children to cut pictures from, so my subconscious must have told me I had everything I needed, if that makes sense."

"Yes, it makes sense but if you left your handbag behind how did you get back into your flat without a key?"

Elizabeth giggled. "Gabby came to the rescue. We usually walk home together anyway, but yesterday she had an appointment with the dentists and so she gave me her key so that I didn't have to hang around. Anyway, is Anne there?"

Out of habit, Stella shook her head. "No, she's not back from work yet. She said Danny was coming down today so I expect she's still at the Hotel chatting to him."

"Oh bother," said Elizabeth, a hint of both disappointment and annoyance in her voice. "Oh well, perhaps I'll ring back later then. I must go now anyway as my money's about to run out. Bye Mum."

"Bye love, and congratulations again."

"So how's the painting coming on?" asked Danny Jarrams, as he and Anne sat on the lawn in the garden at the back of the Hotel after Anne had finished work for the day.

Her smile was an impish grin. "Which one?"

"Christ, Anne, how many are you doing? I mean the one you're doing of the cove looking down from the cliff tops and aided by the fantastic photo I took for you at Easter."

"Oh, that one. I finished it some time ago and it's with the picture framers at the moment. Mum and Dad love it and want to hang it on the wall above the fireplace in our front room, which means Mum's painting of the old mine will be relegated to the hallway, so that's a compliment indeed. Both my parents love Mum's picture, you see. So do I for that matter."

"That's great news. You must show it to me next time I'm down."

Anne cast a sideward glance. "But it'll be ready in a couple of days; surely you won't have gone back by then."

Danny nodded and smiled apologetically. "I'm afraid I will. I did plan to stay for longer, maybe even a week, but a job's come up that I really want to do. I promise I'll be down for longer soon though. In fact I'll definitely come down for a whole week when our Linda gets married. I mean, it's not long 'til then, is it? And hey, it means I'll be able to see my big sister too. I've not seen her for ages. I take it she'll be at the wedding."

"Of course she will," laughed Anne, amazed by his lack of knowledge regarding the family wedding. "Her two little girls are bridesmaids. Linda went up to see them last week to sort out the dresses and so forth; she said they looked ever so sweet, like two little angels."

"Really! They don't take after their mother then. She's never looked angelic as far as I can remember. Anyway, that's brilliant news, because it means all the family will probably be coming down and I've not seen lots of them for simply ages. But while we're on the subject of bridesmaids, do you know if there are any older ones?

By older I mean eighteen plus, attractive, slim, with long legs and curves in all the right places."

Anne threw back her head and laughed. "Yes, but sadly for you, they're just me and Jamie's sister, Sally. We're the older bridesmaids and your nieces are the younger ones. But Sally's definitely not your type anyway. She's clever and wouldn't stand for any nonsense from the likes of you. What's more she's a police constable."

Jamie's face broke into a broad lecherous grin. "Really! I like to see a woman in a uniform. What's her name again?"

Anne giggled. "Sally, but don't get excited about a uniform. She'll be wearing a frilly frock for the wedding and have flowers in her hair like the rest of us."

Ben Gross, one of the two chefs working at the Penwynton Hotel, entered the kitchen at the end of the morning shift with two pints of ice cold shandy just as Bob Jarrams was leaving the room.

"Ta, Ben," said the other chef, Bill, taking his drink. "The boss has just been telling me that the Old Police House in the village is coming up for rent on a long let. I'm thinking of going to see the builder chap that owns it because I rather like the idea of living there, and it's very handy for the pub. Would you fancy coming in with me and sharing the expenses? According to Bob, it's got four good sized bedrooms and quite impressive sea views."

"Well, it might be worth a look," said Ben, scowling as one of the kitchen staff dropped a plate which broke into a hundred small pieces. "I can't say that I'm too happy about living here above the shop, so to speak, and the close proximity of the pub certainly appeals. Any idea how much the rent's likely to be?"

Bill drained his glass and placed it on top of the dishwasher. "No, but let's face it, we earn well here so whatever it is we'd be able to afford it. What do you say?"

"Yeah, count me in. When are you planning to go?"

"No time like the present," said Bill, looking at his watch. "I think we ought to strike while the iron's hot and arrange a viewing as soon as we knock off, and we're nearly done now anyway."

Trengillion consisted of one main street which ran off a trunk-road and wound its way between cottages and houses of various shapes and sizes on its way down to the cove. The Old Police House lay on the left hand side, towards the end of the road and about twenty yards or so before the Inn which stood on the right. It was detached, built of granite, had gardens all around and a small porch on the front.

Following a telephone conversation, Harry Richardson agreed to meet the two chefs by the wrought iron garden gate at the front of the house around midday, hence the chefs made a point of arriving early in order to take in the location and count the number of strides needed to walk from the house across the road to the Inn. Harry arrived in due course and showed them around. Both chefs were impressed, especially by the sea views visible from the upstairs bay window, where, with a pair of binoculars they estimated it would be possible to see if there were any promising females sunbathing on the beach.

Bill addressed Harry. "So how much rent are you asking?"

"Seventy pounds a month and that includes rates and water rates so all you'll have to find is money for electricity."

Bill nodded his head approvingly. "Sounds good to me. What say you, Ben?"

"Yeah, count me in. Are there any rules and regulations?"

Harry laughed. "No, you can do what you like within reason as long as you pay the rent on time and o' course don't wreck the place."

"Brilliant," said Bill, rubbing his hands with glee. "So, when can we move in?"

"Well, we've a couple of holiday bookings we must honour in June, but after that it can be yours. How about if we say the first of July?"

Bill nodded. "Yeah that's fine, and will you be leaving the furniture in?

"Yes, unless you'd rather have it unfurnished."

"No, no, please leave it all," said Bill. "I don't know about Ben, but I don't have any possessions other than clothes, shoes, a stereo and my records."

"Snap," said Ben, "though I do have my coloured telly too. I wouldn't be without that."

"Ah, so would you like me to take the old set away?" said Harry, glancing at the wood cased television attached to its own stand. "It's black and white and as old as the hills. Having said that, the picture's not too bad."

"Up to you," said Bill. "We could always have it in one of the other rooms, that's if there's an aerial."

Harry nodded. "There is. Both sitting rooms have one."

"Great, leave it then, not that we'll have much time for watching the telly."

Harry glanced at the old television set standing in the corner. "It's funny to think that until a few years back I used to watch snooker on a black and white television and somehow knew which coloured balls were which, but I did, and so did everyone else."

"Coloured telly's best thing since sliced bread," said Ben.

"Ah, there is just one more thing," said Harry, as they all shook hands to cement the deal and headed down the passage towards the front door. "Will you keep the grass cut and the garden tidy or would you rather I came and did it?"

The two chefs looked at each other and shook their heads.

"We'd like you to do it," said Bill, "if that's alright, cos we really don't have much spare time."

Ben grinned. "Or a lawn mower."

"No problem," said Harry, chuckling as they went outside. "Although if we have a summer like last year, then the grass won't want cutting much anyway."

The three men shook hands again and then the chefs went over the road to the Inn for a pint to celebrate their good fortune.

"So what did the chefs think?" asked Joyce Richardson, when Harry returned home. "Did they like it?"

Harry removed his shoes, reached for his slippers and sat down. "Yes, I think they were very impressed and they're moving in on July the first. They seem a nice couple of lads and I know Bob Jarrams is pleased with them both. You know, they work well, are reliable and all that, so getting the rent shouldn't be a problem."

Joyce frowned. "Good, but do you think the kitchen will be alright for them? After all it's a bit small and they're used to lots of room and so forth."

Harry laughed. "I don't expect they'll do much cooking there. They no doubt eat at the Hotel, at least the old chef used to, you know, what was his name, the French bloke?

Joyce shook her head. "Can't remember."

"Oh well, it doesn't matter, does it?" He stood up. "Fancy a coffee? I could do with one."

Joyce started to rise to her feet. "I'll make it."

Harry gently pushed her back in the chair. "No you won't, I will. It's time you did a bit less and you need to rest that back of yours, and then when it's better we'll have a nice little holiday and celebrate our retirement properly. How do you fancy a cruise?"

"A cruise," gasped Joyce, her mouth gaped open with surprise. "What a lovely thought. It's something I've always rather liked the idea of. What an old romantic you are."

Harry grinned: he had never been called romantic before. "Right then, Mrs Richardson. A cruise it is."

Molly arrived back at Rose Cottage to find the back door locked and the key hidden beneath a flower pot. Inside, she found a note from the major on the kitchen table saying he had gone to see Frank for a natter.

Molly kicked off her shoes, put on her slippers and filled the kettle. A cup of tea was urgently required for she felt shattered by the heat, the walk, and the lengthy conversations with Dorothy.

When the tea was made she wandered into the living room where it felt a little cooler. She sat down on the settee, rested her feet on the pouffe and enjoyed her tea in peace. But as she drained her cup, she knew there was work to be done. She rose, went outside and from the shed fetched her fermenting bucket. She washed it thoroughly beneath the outside tap and returned to the kitchen where she poured in cold water with the aid of a jug. She then added sugar and stirred it until it dissolved. From her basket she took the elderflowers and gently shook each to remove any insects that may be hidden amongst the petals. She then dropped the flowers into the sugary water and when all were submerged, added the juice of a lemon. After another stir, she put on the lid and pushed the bucket beneath the kitchen table. With the job done she sat back down and wondered how Dorothy was getting on with her dandelion wine. But she knew

Dorothy was a sensible woman and her instructions had been quite clear, so there was very little doubt that she would be able to cope. Nevertheless, she decided to ring and make sure all was well; it would also give her a chance to speak to the major and see if there was anything in particular he fancied for dinner.

Anne, with her arms full of bluebells for the second time that day reached the village at the top of the hill where she walked past her home, the School House, and carried on along the road until she reached Rose Cottage. Once through the gate, she walked up the path casting her eyes over her grandmother's immaculate garden, where red and yellow tulips dominated the borders, mounds of blue aubrietia cascaded from granite stones on the rockery and the scent of mock orange filled the air as she brushed against it. She did not go to the front door as it was seldom used. Instead she walked around the side to the back where she found the door wide open. Delighted with the knowledge someone was home she peeped into the kitchen. Standing at the table, her grandmother was piling mashed potato onto a dish of steaming minced meat.

"Hi, Gran. Something smells nice."

"Anne, hello dear. It's shepherd's pie. Funny you should call because I was just thinking about you and wondering if you'd ask Mary Cottingham if sometime soon I can have some of the champagne bottles she's been saving for me. I'll need them soon, you see, because I've started a batch of elderflower champagne."

"And it's funny you should say that, Grandma, because she asked me the other day when you wanted them, but I forgot to tell you. I'll sort it out tomorrow. Anyway these are for you." She proffered the bluebells. "I picked them on the way home today. Aren't they simply gorgeous?"

Molly leaned forward to smell the flowers. "They're beautiful, Anne. Would you be an angel and put them in water for me? There's a vase under the sink. I'd do it myself but I must get this shepherd's pie in the oven and prepare the vegetables because Granddad will be home in less than an hour."

Anne did as she was asked and then carried the vase of flowers into the living room where she placed them on the sideboard.

"Are you busy at work?" asked Molly, as her granddaughter returned to the kitchen.

"Yes, but we're not full. Mary says they're thinking of diversifying a bit and opening up the dining room to non-residents now they have two chefs. For a start it would only be in the evenings and reservations only. Do you think that's a good idea?"

"Well, yes I do," said Molly, placing the shepherd's pie in the oven. "It would be nice to have somewhere local to go for special occasions. Granddad and I usually go into town for a meal on our wedding anniversary, but I'd much rather go to the Hotel and I'm sure Granddad would agree."

"Good, I'll pass that on then," said Anne. "Anyway I'd better be getting home or Mum and Dad will be wondering where I've got too."

"Yes, you get along cos there's good news waiting for you at home."

"Good news?" asked Anne, puzzled. "What sort of good news?"

Molly pulled a face and bent to take a bag of peas from the freezing compartment of the fridge to hide her embarrassment. "Sorry, Anne, I shouldn't have blurted it out like that. I wasn't thinking straight, but your dad phoned this afternoon to tell me. You pop along home so that your parents can tell you themselves. I don't want them to think I'm an old busy-body."

"It's Liz isn't it?" said Anne, her face a picture of excitement and hope. "She's got the job in Polquillick and she's coming home, isn't she?"

Molly nodded.

"Yippee," shouted Anne, jumping for joy. She kissed her grandmother hastily on the cheek and then ran home to the School House without stopping for breath, to hear more of her big sister's return.

Chapter Five

Standing back from the main road running through Trengillion, lay a row of four houses built in the 1950s and known as Coronation Terrace. Originally it was the intention of the local authorities responsible for their construction, to name the row Trevithick Terrace after the Cornish inventor Richard Trevithick who built the first full scale working steam locomotive. But the sudden death of King George VI in February 1952 changed their decision and they named the row Coronation Terrace in honour of the new Queen whose coronation took place in June the following year; for it was unanimously agreed by all concerned, there was no shortage of places commemorating the name of the Cornish hero in his home county.

The three bedroomed, pebble dashed houses, were identical in design and stood two on either side of a covered entry. All had fenced front gardens with central paths leading to small rain porches protecting blue front doors from the elements. The iron framed windows were generous in size, making the rooms feel light and airy. Around the back, good sized gardens shared panoramic views over the rolling countryside and glimpses of the sea were visible from upstairs windows.

Inside number two lived fishermen Percy Collins, his wife of twenty five years, Gertie, and their three grown up children: twins, Tony and John, and daughter, Susan. The family were the only occupants that particular house had ever known, for Percy and Gertie had moved in shortly after their marriage when the houses had first been completed early in 1953.

As he sat down at the kitchen table with a mug of coffee, Percy heard a cry of delight emanate from the bathroom above, immediately followed by the thumping of feet descending the straight, carpeted staircase.

"I've lost another three pounds," squeaked Gertie, gleefully patting her stomach as she rushed into the room, wrapped only in a bath towel. "Yippee, aren't you proud of me?"

With his mouth full of coffee, Percy attempted to stifle a yawn. "Yes, so does that mean we can start eating proper food again now?"

Gertie's jaw dropped. "Good heavens, no. I've another stone to lose yet. But you see, it'll all be worth it. I bet you can't wait to have a thin wife."

"If I'd wanted a thin wife then I'd have married one," Percy wearily responded. "You're fine the way you are, Gert, and you always have been. Who wants to snuggle up to a beanpole? Certainly not me, and neither would any man if he's completely honest."

Gertie frowned. "Oh, Percy, you're just saying that because you want me to make stodgy puddings again, but you know I can't do that because I like eating them too much." She sighed. "Oh dear, I must admit it's a terrible shame that all nice food is fattening and I'm sure there can't really be as many calories in a little piece of chocolate as my book says. Anyway, losing another stone won't make me a beanpole. I'd need to lose at least two to get anywhere near that category. Gosh, look at the time I'd better get dressed, it's nearly time for work."

Gertie ran up the stairs while Percy finished his coffee; minutes later she returned wearing a thin cotton dress. In the kitchen she slipped on a pair of leather sandals and quickly brushed her hair.

"Your lunch box is in the fridge, Percy." She blew him a kiss. "I must dash. See you later. Bye."

She left by the back door which led into the garden where her bicycle was propped up against a wooden shed. Percy waved through the open window and then went to the fridge, removed his lunch box and peeped inside. Just as he had anticipated there were a couple of rounds of sandwiches made with paper thin, sliced bread, each filled with ham, mustard, and lots of lettuce. There was also an apple but not a hint of any cake or anything sweet or sugary. Percy closed the lid, tossed the box into his bag. He then left the house for the cove. As he passed the Inn, the smell of apple wafted across the path from the extractor fan in the kitchen. Percy rubbed his hands. With any luck he was just in time for one of Gloria Withers' homemade individual apple pies. He crossed the cobbles, went into the Inn where Raymond, having just opened up, beamed from behind the spotlessly clean bar. He grinned. "Your usual?"

"Yep," said Percy. "The wife's still on her silly diet and I'm starving."

Raymond walked to the end of the bar and called through to the kitchen. "One apple pie to take away, Glore, and make it snappy."

Within a minute Gloria appeared with a small package wrapped in greaseproof paper.

"I'd have a meat pie too," grinned Percy, taking the package, "but that'd be really greedy and I'll have to leave a bit of room for Gert's sandwiches. You're a treasure, Gloria. I'd don't know how I'd have survived this dieting fad without you."

Gloria beamed. "The pie's nice and fresh cos I make them daily so it's been nowhere near the microwave. How's Gertie's diet going? I've not seen her for a while."

"Humph! Alright I suppose. She informed me this morning that she's lost another three pounds, so she's over the moon. You won't see much of her for a while though because she's off drinking now. I tried to get her to come out the other evening but she wouldn't hear of it. She says according to her book there are far too many calories in alcohol."

"Three pounds," mused Gloria, nodding her head. "Very good."

"Too many calories in alcohol!" spluttered Raymond. "Whatever next!"

Percy ate the warm apple pie as he walked down to the cove, happily licking his sugary fingers after each mouthful. On the beach he found his friend and fishing partner of thirty one years, Peter, waiting for him beside their new fibreglass boat. Fishing had been good during the early seventies. A boom in the mackerel industry meant the fishermen were able to fish during the winter months as well as the summer, so instead of the crabber's boats being laid up for the winter, they were able to put to sea all year round and make a decent living; and in just few years, many men made a substantial amount of money. But whereas the young, unmarried fishermen spent most of their hard earned cash in the pubs, the older, more responsible family men invested their money wisely. Percy, after discussing the windfall with Gertie, opened a savings account for a rainy day, and Peter and his wife, Betty, who was a hairdresser with a salon in their home at Fuchsia Cottage, paid off large amounts of their mortgage and modernised the hairdressing salon.

Percy and Peter had been fishing together since they had saved enough money to buy their first second hand boat, having learned many skills from Percy's father and other fishermen from the cove. The mackerel boom, however, was as new to the older fishermen, as to the younger ones, hence all learned together the best techniques and ways of locating shoals of fish with the use of echo sounders, instinct, and for the part-time amateurs, following the most successful boats. For the boom in its wake brought in men from all walks of life, postmen and taxi drivers, school teachers and builders, many of these men left their professions to take advantage of the profitable situation and endeavoured to get berths on boats whenever and wherever the opportunity arose. But by the mid-seventies warning signs of the boom's demise were evident for all to see, in spite of Government officials declaring that the mackerel stocks were substantial and sustainable. For the men in the centre of the industry, the fishermen, knew instinctively that fish numbers were dwindling and the bubble was about to burst. Hence, fishermen's wives took jobs to help maintain the family income and pay everyday necessities ready to face leaner times ahead.

Gertie cycled out through the village and onto the road leading to the Penwynton Hotel where she had a part-time job as a chambermaid. When she reached the main entrance, she turned right and cycled between two tall, granite pillars, onto which hung large, black wrought iron gates. She then peddled down the drive and past the Lodge House, where Annie Stevens stood on a stool busily cleaning downstairs windows.

"Morning, Mrs Stevens," called Gertie, swerving to avoid a tabby cat as it dashed in front of her wheels. "Beautiful day again."

"Morning, Gertie," replied Annie. "Yes, isn't it? Come here, you gormless cat."

Gertie continued down the long and winding drive until the Hotel's tall chimneys were visible over the trees and eventually the large building itself came into view. Once her destination was reached, she dismounted, wheeled her bicycle round the side and leaned it against a wall in the stable yard.

Inside the Hotel, the process of cleaning up after breakfast, and vegetable preparation for the evening menu, was underway. Gertie greeted the kitchen staff, relaxed in their work, the stress of a hot kitchen having subsided with the departure of the two chefs. She then went to the laundry room where Heather Jarrams handed her a list of rooms needing her attention.

As she began to climb the staircase, Gertie saw Danny Jarrams in the vestibule, elbows on the reception desk, chatting to Anne Stanley. She waved and they waved back. Gertie grinned; she always thought it rather peculiar that someone whose face had once taken pride of place on posters plastering the bedroom walls of her daughter, Susan, should be a regular visitor to the Hotel, and his presence seemed perfectly normal.

The Hotel gardens, landscaped after the renovations by professionals, were maintained by proprietors, Bob Jarrams and Dick Cottingham. The layout was quite simple: wooden tubs and hanging baskets, each filled with flowering annuals, added colour to the granite building and gravelled driveway around the front during the summer months. Lawns, interspersed with flower beds and borders ran along both sides. And around the back, leading down from the original steps was a terrace which led onto a long, rectangular lawn, where benches were symmetrically placed on all four corners of the grass, each overhung with scented climbers, twisting through the lattice slats of rustic wooden arbours. Beyond the lawn was a wild flower meadow where guests were free to stroll. But the walled vegetable garden, marked *Private*, was for the use only of family and Hotel staff.

Bob Jarrams and Dick Cottingham ambled around the gardens weighing up tasks to be tackled in the coming week.

"Dear, dear, the lawns are starting to look a bit careworn, aren't they?" said Bob. "You'd think it was September rather than late May. If we don't have rain soon then they'll have no colour at all, except scorched yellow, that is."

Dick pulled up a stinging nettle seedling and threw it to the back of the border. "Ah, but at least it's the same all over the country, so anyone arriving here won't be surprised and it's not much different in some places abroad, so I hear."

Bob stopped walking and scratched his chin. "Hmm. What do you think about putting in summer bedding plants? I mean to say, if it's going to be another dry summer then we might as well leave a few bare patches to save watering. Better that than wilting plants looking stunted and neglected."

"I agree with you there, it'd save a few bob too, not to mention the work. We must still fill the hanging baskets and tubs though, cos it'd look very bare without them and they usually have to be watered daily anyway unless we have a wet summer and that's unlikely this year."

Bob nodded. "I agree, but perhaps this summer we could try and find something a bit more drought tolerant than the usual hardy annuals."

"Yeah, good idea," said Dick. "I think a trip to the nursery's called for. We need to get some more watering cans anyway since we can't use the sodding hoses now."

Bob groaned. "Humph, don't remind me. Come on then, but let's pop indoors and have a coffee first. I'm parched and it'll get us out the sun for a while."

"I got a letter from Mum this morning," said Stella to Ned, when he arrived home from school. "She said they'd like to come down for a week this summer if it's alright with us. Will that be okay?"

Ned slipped his shoes beneath a chair and reached for his slippers. "Of course. I'd much rather they came down here than we had to go up there. When do they want to come?"

Stella shrugged her shoulders. "Any time, I guess. They've no commitments now Dad's retired and they've got very good neighbours to keep an eye on the house and water the greenhouse. But I was thinking perhaps I might suggest they come down on Monday the twenty first of June for a week. That way the wedding will be over and done with, but you'll still be at school and Elizabeth won't be back, so we'll not be under each other's feet."

Ned removed his tie and dropped it over the back of a chair. "Sounds good to me. It'll be interesting to hear just how bad the water situation is up there cos according to the News it's pretty dire."

"Hmm, yes," said Stella, absently. "I think I'll give Mum a ring rather than write, but I'll wait 'til after six. Would you like tea? I suppose that's a silly question really as you always say yes, so I'll put the kettle on."

"Did you want to have a holiday this year, Stell?" asked Ned, watching his wife take mugs from the cupboard as he sat down. "I know it was mentioned after Christmas but we never decided one way or the other, did we? And now I suppose it's a bit late to book anything."

Stella dropped teabags into the mugs. "No, we had a nice holiday last year, so I'm more than happy to stay put, especially if the summer's likely to continue like this. Anyway, Elizabeth will be home in a couple of months so there's no incentive to go away. What's more, the interest on our mortgage might well go up again soon with this rising inflation, so we mustn't be tempted into living beyond our means."

"You don't regret taking out the mortgage to buy this place, do you?" grinned Ned.

"Oh, come on, Ned, you know very well that I don't. It makes much more sense to own it than rent it, and it means that now we won't have to worry about where we'll live when you retire. I think the day the authorities offered us the chance to buy this house was one of our luckiest."

Ned unbuttoned the cuffs of his shirt and rolled up the sleeves. "I knew you'd say that. Nevertheless it's always good to have my thoughts endorsed. And as regards your views on a holiday that's good too, cos I can't be doing with all the hassle of going away. Besides, there's no place like Cornwall when the weather's fine and I do like to sleep in my own bed at night. Oh dear, do I sound a bit of a fuddy-duddy?"

Stella nodded. "Yes, but then you are nearly fifty."

Chapter Six

May was a beautiful month with lots of warm, dry weather and plenty of sunshine, and although on some days the wind was quite fresh, the women of Trengillion did not complain, for the conditions were prefect for drying their washing.

Much to the delight of Linda Cottingham, the month of June began on as beautiful a note as May had finished and she prayed that it would continue; for on the nineteenth of June, she and Jamie Stevens were to marry in Trengillion's picturesque village church.

As Linda sat on the front steps of the Hotel, hugging her knees and watching a cluster of fluffy white clouds float over the fully-leaved trees in Bluebell Woods, her thoughts drifted back to November 1967 and the day when she had first encountered Jamie. He was standing outside the Lodge House with his father, Fred Stevens, who at that time was the village police constable. Linda's first thought was that Jamie was very handsome and she was convinced the rapid beating of her heart meant it was love at first sight. It was inevitable therefore, that she was bitterly disappointed to hear that he had a steady girlfriend whom he had been dating for a considerable time. Nevertheless, that unwelcome piece of information did not deter her from daydreaming and fantasising that one day he would be free, thus enabling her to step into the erstwhile girlfriend's place. And as luck, or perhaps even fate, would have it, her dreams eventually came true. For in less than six months after Jamie and Linda's paths had first crossed, Jamie had a bitter disagreement with his girlfriend, who wanted him to give up his hobby as a disc jockey and spend more time with her. Foolishly, she gave him an ultimatum; he was to choose between herself and the time-consuming pursuit of a part-time DJ. Jamie stood firm and without hesitation chose the latter. Never once after the break-up did he regret his decision.

The couple were properly introduced to each other shortly after that. For Linda's parents had struck up a mutual friendship with Fred and Annie Stevens as both couples were often in each other's company during the refurbishment and modernisation of their respective premises, the Hotel and the Lodge House.

Linda and Jamie's engagement had been a long one, almost six years, for they had agreed it was necessary to own their own place before they tied the knot; hence both began to save hard until they had enough money for a deposit on a house. This goal was finally reached in March, thus enabling them to purchase a modest semi-detached property on the new development called Penwynton Crescent, situated in a field which ran off a lane behind the village hall.

Linda looked at her watch; only half an hour to go until it was her turn for a stint on the reception desk, but as she was ready for work she decided to go back inside early so that she could chat to Anne Stanley about the wedding.

To accommodate the ever growing number of graves, the churchyard boundaries had extended over the years and now stretched partway out into the field, once property of the Inn, but donated to the village back in the sixties by Frank Newton, landlord at that time. The purchase of said land by the church was achieved after several meetings between the Parochial Church Council and the Village Field Committee, where it was agreed that a large area at the top of the field alongside the graveyard, become the property of the church thus enabling those wishing to be buried in the village so to do.

In the new stretch of field, Bertha Fillingham sat on the bench she had bought for the churchyard in memory of her late husband, George. But she was unable to appreciate the tranquillity of the setting; her mind was in a quandary and she was undecided as to whether or not she should move from her remote current home into the heart of the village. For Sea Thrift Cottage, the property she and her late husband had bought on their retirement, lay on the outskirts of the village on the cliff tops, and although Bertha felt quite safe and happy, it being summer time, she was a little apprehensive about being away from any living soul in the depths of winter.

Her nearest neighbours were the Castor-Hunts at Chy-an-Gwyns, and May and Pat Dickens who lived and worked on Higher Green

Farm. Bertha was very friendly with May, but she and her husband had the farm up for sale as they wanted to retire into one of the new houses being built in the village and May had suggested that Bertha do the same. For some of the properties would be two bed roomed bungalows, ideal for a widow living alone. Deep down, Bertha knew to move was the sensible thing to do. It was what her children advised and George had expressed similar sentiments when they had briefly discussed the inevitable, that one of them would be left alone at some point. But she had lived in Sea Thrift Cottage for twenty five years since the summer of 1952 and the thought of leaving the home where she had spent so many happy years filled her with dread. For she could not bear to think what might happen to the garden she and George had created and tended over the years. She also found it difficult to accept strangers living in her house and possibly knocking the place apart to modernise it. At the same time, the prospect of living in a brand new bungalow with neighbours nearby appealed to her greatly, hence she was perplexed and had no idea what to do for the best.

As she sat deep in thought, Meg Reynolds, daughter of Trengillion's retired vicar, walked into the churchyard to put flowers on the grave of her late mother, Pearl. Bertha waved and then watched as Meg discarded faded wallflowers and artistically replaced them with fresh Sweet Williams. Once the task was accomplished, Meg crossed the churchyard and sat beside Bertha to enquire as to her wellbeing. Bertha, glad to have company, told Meg of the dilemma she was in and asked for advice.

Meg sighed, sympathetically. "Oh dear, I can see the problem. Sid and I have been in our house for nearly twenty five years now and I often think it's time we bought our own place instead of renting, but it's our first home, where the children were born and so forth so it would be a very big wrench to move. You, on the other hand have the isolation to contend with, so I think if I was in your shoes, as hard as it might be, I would move. At least you wouldn't have to get used to a new location if you went for one of the new bungalows, and as for neighbours, well, many of the houses are being snapped up by local people anyway."

"You're right dear, deep down I know you're right. So how do you think I should get things going? George always took care of financial things, you see, so I've no idea what to do when it comes to buying and selling houses."

"Would you like my son Graham to come up and see you? He works for Pennard and Rowe Estate Agents and although he's only a trainee he knows the basics. He wouldn't put pressure on you either. In fact I'd ask him to see you as a friend and not in an official capacity, and then afterwards you can decide what you want to do in your own good time."

"I think I should like that very much, if he wouldn't mind," said Bertha. "I'll give you my phone number and then he can ring me to say when he'd like to come."

Bertha scribbled her number on the back of an old shopping list she found tucked in the bottom of her handbag. She handed it to Meg. "It'll be nice to have a visitor, so when I know when he's coming I'll bake a cake."

The major dropped Molly off at the top of the driveway leading to the Penwynton Hotel on his way into town. He had offered to run her to the front door but she had insisted on walking; for the driveway's winding discourse through shrubs and bushes was very attractive and although the hydrangeas were not yet in flower, their rotund shapes and large leaves were still pleasing to the eye.

Molly arrived at the Hotel, climbed the steps and walked through the open front doors into the vestibule. Inside she was greeted by Eric the porter, who nodded politely and raised his cap.

"Hello, Eric, I've come to see..., ah, there she is," said Molly, seeing Mary Cottingham at the reception desk.

"Mary beckoned Molly to the counter from beneath which she lifted eight empty champagne bottles.

"I got your message from Anne. Are you sure this is enough? There are plenty more if you want them as we get through quite a few."

"It's enough for now," said Molly, slipping the bottles into her empty basket. "But I may make another batch or two later on and if I do I'll need some more then, if that's alright."

"Of course," said Mary. "They're all in the cellar and you can have as many as you want. What is it you've made again?"

"Elderflower champagne," said Molly, proudly. "I'll send you in a bottle with our Anne when it's ready."

"That'll be very nice, thank you. It sounds lovely." Mary eyed the basket. "Are you sure you can manage them all at once, they'll be quite heavy?"

"Yes, I've plenty of strength left in my arms still," laughed Molly, flexing her flabby biceps. "Although my knees are not as good as they used to be, but then it's hardly surprising is it? I'm seventy two now and I don't care who knows it, cos to be perfectly honest I don't feel a day over thirty."

Mary smiled. "Good for you. I hope I look as good as you when I'm your age."

Molly left the Hotel with the bottles rattling in her basket and set off back to the village by way of the woods. Once deep inside she stopped to rest for the bottles were heavier than she would ever admit and her arms both ached from constantly moving the basket from one hand to the other.

On an old tree stump she sat to get back her breath and recuperate her strength. Her basket she placed by her feet on the green seedpods of bluebells which littered the woodland floor. She glanced up to the trees swaying beneath the blue sky and watched as birds sang and fluttered amongst the leafy branches.

Molly loved the woods as much as her grandchildren did. She loved the peace, the scents, the sound of trickling water from the stream and the feeling of being hidden away from the busy world. Yet at the same time she never felt alone. The rustling trees sang and whispered; they alerted her senses to days gone by and she came to regard them all as friends. She glanced around. All of the trees seemed to be thriving, except of course the poor ash on whose stump she sat. For the ash tree had been felled in the winter after suffering damage during a ferocious storm and Molly very much lamented its passing.

Near to the ill-fated tree stood a tall, beautifully shaped holly, which had flourished much since the demise of the ash. Also nearby, Molly was delighted to see that an unlucky elder, which had lain in the path of the falling ash and consequently suffered partial damage, was now prospering and bore a vigorous head of new growth. For the warm weather had helped mend its wounds and both elder and holly were now able to enjoy the extra space created by the removal of the ash, thus enabling them to spread their branches and lap up what little sun reached the smaller trees in the woods.

Molly smiled, for although she grieved the passing of the ash, she appreciated its stump, for it provided her with a resting place where she could sit between her two favourite trees, the elder and the holly, the latter of which for some reason unbeknown to her, Molly regarded as Mattie's tree.

Chapter Seven

"When do the students arrive, Anne?" asked Tony Collins, as he, his twin brother, John, his younger sister, Susan, and several friends lounged on the beach, sunbathing, one Sunday afternoon in early June. "We could do with a bit more talent down here. I hope your bosses have lined up a cracker or two."

Anne turned towards Tony and peeked at him beneath the brim of her sunhat. "They'll be here at the end of the month when the universities break up. You ought to know that by now, Tony: it's the same every year."

"Yeah, I know, but not being the brainy sort I've never been acquainted with a timetable for swots."

Roger Withers turned onto his side and rested his head on his hand. "Well, I hope they're better than last year's batch. They were pretty grim, weren't they? In fact a right load of smarty pants and not a pleasant face amongst them."

"Oh, I don't know," said Susan, dreamily. "I thought that Welsh bloke, Dave, was rather cute and his deep voice was really seductive."

Jane giggled. "Oh yes, and Phil was a hunk too. Gorgeous eyes. Such a pity he was so boring though. I mean to say, a girl can only listen to so much about archaeology, can't she? And most of what he said went right over my head anyway."

Roger frowned. "But Dave and Phil were both blokes, you numbskulls. I'm talking about girls. It's them as were grim. I must admit all the blokes were alright, except for Poncey Pete. He was a right pain in the arse."

Anne laughed. "Well, irrespective of what you might have thought of them, they all worked well, very well in fact. But I don't think any of last year's batch are due to return this season, more's the shame, eh, girls?"

The girls groaned in unison.

"I hear your two chefs are moving into the Old Police House soon," said Diane. "How much do you reckon they're paying for that?"

Anne shook her head. "No idea, but I suppose it would have to be around forty pounds a month."

"And the rest," said Graham, emphatically. "I think it'd be more like sixty or seventy. Whichever, they'd be better off with a mortgage and be buying their own place."

"Yes, but to buy a house you need a substantial deposit," said Diane, who worked for a building society. "So if you don't have that sort of money, renting is the only option."

"Well, I know that, don't I? That's why I'm saving hard," snapped Graham, her brother. "But what I'm getting at is, if you're paying out the sort of money the chefs are likely to be paying, then it's sickening to think they could have a mortgage for a similar amount, but as it is, with a hefty rent like theirs, they'll never be able to save, so it's catch twenty two really. I've no intention of leaving home until I can afford to buy my own place."

Diane sat up and glared at her brother. "They wouldn't be able to buy a house the size of the Old Police House though for the same amount on mortgage, would they? And not in such a good location either, so I can't see that there's anything wrong with renting if you can find a place you like. Having said that, I'd be out of a job if everyone shared my sentiments."

"Yes, but renting's so unproductive," said Graham, obstinately. "It's so fruitless. You spend years shucking out money to some dodgy landlord and then at the end have nothing to show for it. I think it's a mug's game."

"Yes, but a lot have people have no choice," said Diane, adamantly.

"Will you two stop bickering about money things," said Susan, peering over the top of her sun glasses. "It's very boring for us simple folks."

"You're not simple, Sue," said Graham, patronisingly. "It's just…"

"…shut it," interrupted Diane. "I agree with Sue, it's too nice a day to argue. Anyway, aren't you supposed to be going to see Mrs Fillingham this afternoon?"

"Yes, but not until five o'clock, so there's plenty of time yet."

"Why are you going to see Mrs Fillingham?" asked Susan.

"She wants some advice about selling her house," said Graham. "Apparently she doesn't know whether or not to move. I think she's a bit lonely since Mr Fillingham died. Mum said she's confused too, poor old soul."

Anne sat up. "Oh dear, that's really sad. It must be horrible to lose a partner when you've been married for most of your life."

"I can't imagine being married to someone for most of my life," said Susan. "I mean, how can you be sure the person you go for is compatible enough for a lifelong commitment?"

"You can't," said Diane. "So it's all a bit of a gamble."

Jane nodded thoughtfully. "Absolutely. But going back a bit, what are these two chefs Jane mentioned like, Anne? Young and gorgeous by any chance?"

Anne giggled. "Well, I'm not sure of their ages but I would guess around thirtyish and although I wouldn't call either of them remotely gorgeous, they're both nice blokes and I get on well enough with them. Not that our paths cross very often."

Colin tilted his head to one side. "You must have seen them, Jane. They're often in our pub. One's tall with fair hair and freckles and the other is short with a beard and bald patch."

"That's not a very flattering description of either of them," laughed Anne. "I can assure you, Jane, they're much better looking than Colin's miserable portrayal. They both have a nice temperament too, except, I'm told, when they get all hot and bothered in the kitchen, and that's understandable. But fortunately I'm never around to witness that."

A broad grin crossed Jane's face as she digested information received. "Hmm, I see, so either of them might be a good catch, and as they can obviously cook, it means a dutiful little wife might be spared the monotony of cooking dinner every night."

Tony poked Jane in the ribs. "You lazy moo. That's what women are for, cleaning, cooking and looking after the needs of their men. Anyway, if they're both thirtyish they're too old for you."

"Don't be daft, you male chauvinist pig," said Jane, indignantly. "I'm twenty one, so that's only a nine year age gap. My granddad is fifteen years older than my granny and they've been married for donkey's years and get on fine."

"Where's Matthew?" asked Susan, glancing around the gathered group. "I've only just noticed he's not here. I suppose he's working."

Jane nodded. "He is. That's the trouble with being a fisherman, you work when your friends have time off and vice versa. Still he likes it, so that's the main thing."

"Is he still going out with Trevelyan's daughter?" asked John. "I haven't seen him for ages, though I often hear him go roaring by on his cool bike."

"Yes, it's quite embarrassing that my little brother has a girlfriend and I don't have a boyfriend. It makes me feel unwanted and unloved."

"Oh, poor you," scoffed Tony. "We're all unattached at the moment, so join the club, and roll on summer when we pray some decent talent might arrive."

"Hear, hear," said Colin, raising his can of lager. "I'll drink to that."

Chapter Eight

On the Friday morning before her big day, Linda Cottingham looked from the window of her room at the back of Penwynton Hotel and clapped her hands with glee, for the weather was fine and the sun was shining brightly, a stark contrast to the previous day when it had been dull from dawn until dusk. The sun, however, stayed only for a few hours and in the afternoon rain clouds appeared and it began to drizzle.

Hoping the rain would pass through quickly, Linda put on a brave face and went downstairs to join the rest of the family making last minute preparations for the wedding reception. In the function room she greeted family members who had travelled down from up-country for the celebrations, hoping her smiles successfully concealed her heartfelt disappointment regarding the weather.

The following morning, she woke to find substantial rain had fallen during the night and the wind was blowing fresh to strong. Feeling in desperate need of happy, lively music to alleviate her dejection, she turned on the radio, only to catch the end of the weather forecast which predicted gales for the South West later in the day. With an air of disgust she threw the radio onto the bed, crossed to the window and watched as the raindrops trickled down the panes. She shook her head in disbelief. What rotten luck! How was it possible to have a miserable wet and windy wedding day in the middle of a drought?

Dick Cottingham looked up as his daughter joined the family in their living room, her face stained by tears. "Don't look so glum, love. It's only water and we really do need it. The reservoirs are very low. Remember that programme we watched on television last month about the severe water shortage?"

"I know," choked Linda, attempting to dry her eyes. "But if only it'd waited just another twenty four hours then it wouldn't have mattered. I'm just so unlucky."

"But then it would spoil the plans of someone else," said Dick, logically. "Someone somewhere will always be praying for sunshine and it's not possible for everyone to have their prayers granted. Anyway, at least your reception's here, so once we're back we can shut out the weather and it really won't matter."

Linda sighed. "But what about the photographs? It won't be possible to take any outside the church because even if the rain stopped for a while it'd still be too windy for us to look happy and normal, and muddy too of course."

"We'll have pictures taken of you on the grand staircase instead and you can tell your children and your children's children that we did so because of the dreadful weather," said Mary, compassionately. "Come on, Linda, cheer up. You're not the first bride to lament rain on her wedding day and you'll not be the last either. Now, have some breakfast and let's go down and see how things are coming on in the kitchen."

In the kitchen, the staff and two chefs were bustling around. Bill was overseeing breakfast for the guests and Ben was busy with preparations for the wedding reception menu, for after much deliberation the family had opted for a three course, sit down meal, rather than a buffet and proposed to keep it as simple and stress free as possible, hence for hors-d'oeuvres the choice was between French onion soup and crab cocktail, the main course, salad with a choice of prawns, crab or ham, and a selection of cheeses, and for dessert, knickerbocker glory or lattice apple and raspberry tart with clotted cream or custard.

"The cake's just arrived," said Heather, putting her head around the door. "Do you want it put straight in the function room?"

"Yes, please," said Mary, delighted with progress in the kitchen. "We're on our way there now. How's the decorating going?"

"Lovely," said Heather. "Danny is busy taking pictures of everyone. He proposes to take hundreds to make sure there are plenty worth keeping. He'll have one of you in your curlers, Linda, so be warned."

Linda laughed as they made their way to the function room where aunts, uncles, cousins and even grandparents were busy getting the room ready for the one hundred and twenty guests.

"Ah, here comes the blushing bride," shouted Danny, from the top of a step ladder. "Smile sweetie."

After a series of rapid clicks, he jumped down and gave Linda a hug. "Shame about the weather, cousin. Still, it could be worse, I suppose."

"Could it?" questioned Linda. "Pray, what could be worse than heavy rain and gale force winds in flaming June?"

Danny wrinkled his nose. "Whoops, hmm." He quickly changed the subject. "I say, have you met Carol? No, of course not, you had already gone to bed to get your beauty sleep when we got here last night, not that you need it, I might add. Look she's over there talking to my old man."

"And who might she be?" asked Linda, glancing towards a tall, glamorous blonde. "Yet another girlfriend, I assume."

"Yes, and isn't she a cracker? Mind you there's nothing much up top with her, and when I say, up top, I'm referring to her head not her..."

"...yes, yes, I get the picture," interrupted Linda. "Really Danny, it's time you thought about settling down, you'll be thirty soon."

That same morning, because of the inclement weather, Ned drove Anne to the Hotel to join the girls for dressing and beauty preparations prior to the wedding ceremony. He would have let her take the Escort herself, but as he and Stella were to be guests at the wedding, he knew the car would be needed later, for even the hardiest of folks would not choose to walk in such unpleasant weather.

Ned dropped Anne at the front of the Hotel. She ran up the steps two at a time and slipped into the vestibule without getting too wet. As many of the rooms were occupied by family and friends, no-one was on the reception desk, but there was a brass bell on the wall should any other guests require assistance from a member of staff.

"Morning, sweetheart," chirped a voice from nowhere. Anne jumped; she had not seen Eric hidden behind the huge arrangement of flowers he was placing on the marble column outside the function room door.

Anne hastily slipped off her coat. "Good morning, Eric. Although it isn't, is it? It's really dreadful. I hope Linda's not too upset."

Eric nodded towards the function room door. "Doesn't sound like it to me. Just listen to that din. Sounds like a kindergarten."

From inside the function room, rang the sound of jovial chatter and cheery laughter. Anne, eager to join the merrymaking, hastily hung her coat in a cupboard beneath the stairs, and felt a pang of excitement when she recognised Danny's voice. For he had told her that when down for the wedding, he would stay for a whole week and Anne relished the idea of enjoying his company.

She straightened her hair in the mirror by the desk and then walked along the hallway and peered into the function room. Mary, her face flushed, saw Anne, rushed forward, took her hand and asked if she approved of their combined efforts.

"It looks beautiful," said Anne, stunned, as she moved aside to allow kitchen staff to carry in tables from the dining room. "I don't think I've ever seen quite so many flowers together other than in a garden, that is. It's breath-taking and the scent it gorgeous. It makes up for the dreadful weather."

"Don't mention the weather to Linda;" whispered Mary, glancing heavenwards. "We're trying to keep her spirits up and fortunately Danny's doing a very good job for us there. Oh, but you've not have seen him since he arrived last night, have you?"

She called to Danny. "Look who's here. Aren't you coming to say hello?"

"Anne," shouted Danny, advancing and taking her hand. He kissed her cheek. "It's brilliant to see you again. But come with me, there's someone I want you to meet."

Gripping Anne's hand tightly he led her across the floor to where a Barbie doll-like blonde was watching Dick Cottingham and Bob Jarrams hoist a garland of flowers and ferns up to the ceiling.

"Hey, Carol," said Danny, patting her shoulder. "This is my old friend, Anne. You know, the one I told you about who does the paintings. She's going to be a bridesmaid."

Anne felt her heart thump loudly. Goose pimples shot up her arms and she prayed Carol was another cousin or a distant relative, but then she heard the dreaded words. "And, Anne, this is my girlfriend, Carol."

Tears welled up at the back of Anne's eyes. She tried to smile but was conscious the corners of her mouth could not be coerced into curling up. She tried to speak, but the sudden sensation of a lump at the back of her throat prevented her from doing so. She had often heard Danny speak of his numerous girlfriends, but she had never supposed he would ever bring one to the Hotel, especially for a whole week when she had a painting to show him.

"Are you alright, Anne," asked Mary, alarmed by the lack of colour in Anne's face. "I think you ought to sit down, dear, you don't look at all well."

"I'm fine," whispered Anne, managing a half-smile. "Really, Mary, I'm fine. I just feel a little too warm that's all. I'll think I'll go back out into the vestibule for a minute. It's cooler out there."

She ran from the room as the first tear rolled down her cheek and dripped onto her dress. Depressed, dejected, sad, and grief stricken, she sat on the cold floor and tried to adjust her mind-set to enduring a whole day and then the whole week with Danny flaunting the unwelcome Carol. She gulped. It was a very bitter pill to swallow.

Inside the Lodge House, Annie Stevens neatly pinned pale yellow carnations into the buttonholes on the lapels of Fred and Jamie's suits, while upstairs, Sally, home for the wedding and chief bridesmaid, applied make-up prior to slipping on her primrose, satin dress. When she had finished her toiletries, her hair, and was dressed, she went downstairs to join the rest of the family.

"Blimey, Sal, I haven't seen you look this feminine since you were May Queen," laughed Jamie, lifting the hem of his sister's very full skirt and letting it fall. "Bit of a change from the old police uniform or jeans, eh."

Sally slapped his hand. "Don't remind me. I feel most uncomfortable and I'm having to wear a grotty girdle cos I'm having a fat day."

"Oh dear," sympathised Annie. "What a nuisance. Still, if you want to, you'll be able to pop back and change after the meal. That's the beauty of living so close to the Hotel. We can all change if we choose to."

Sally scowled at her reflection in the mirror over the fireplace and turned away. "I can't wait, and I'll feel even worse when I get to the Hotel looking like a drowned rat."

"You shouldn't get wet, there'll be brollies galore," smiled Fred. "Come on, Sal, I'll run you up to the Hotel now and then you can share your wows with the other females, who'll no doubt be in a flap too."

Jamie's best man, his work colleague, Desmond, picked him up from the Lodge House half an hour before the wedding ceremony was due to commence and drove him to the church. As they left the car parked on the kerbside and ran beneath the lichgate the rain was falling heavily and the westerly wind had strengthened considerably.

Inside the porch, they each combed their hair and then stood waiting to greet guests beside a colourful array of umbrellas which had created a small pool of water on the grey, flagstone floor.

Because of the atrocious weather all formality was dropped and arriving guests exchanged banter with the groom and best man as they endeavoured to regain their composure before taking their seats, as allocated by the ushers, inside the church.

Shortly before it was time for the bride to arrive, Jamie and Desmond went inside the ancient building and walked up the aisle where they stood and waited at the chancel step for a nod from the vicar to say all was well.

Linda found it hard to see a funny side to the weather as she stood between the open double doors of the Hotel and watched the rain drops splashing heavily onto the steps.

"I can't walk through all that water in satin shoes," she hissed, tears again welling in her eyes. "They'll be ruined before we even get to the church. Oh, what am I going to do, Dad?"

"Ah, my wellies," said Anne, standing in the in the vestibule with the other bridesmaids. "I always keep a pair in the cupboard in case it's muddy when I walk home through the woods. What size are you, Linda?"

"Six," said Linda, a look of horror on her face.

"That's perfect," said Anne, dashing to the cupboard beneath the stairs from which she pulled her shiny black Wellington boots. "They're clean because I always wipe them over if they get muddy. I'm very fussy about my footwear."

"But...but, I," stammered poor Linda, as a tear trickled down her cheek.

"Put them on," said Dick, offering his arm for support. "And when you get to the church you can change into your shoes in the porch. Come on, chop, chop or we'll be late, love."

Danny, still at the Hotel with Carol so that he could take pictures of the bride and bridesmaids leaving for the church, hooted with laughter at the sight of his cousin clutching her long white, satin gown, thus revealing the cumbersome Wellington boots.

"These photos will be far better than the usual run-of-the-mill wedding pictures. Quick, get the brolly Carol and hold it over me so that the camera doesn't get wet."

"But I'll get wet," she whimpered.

"Doesn't matter, it's only water, for God's sake, girl," he hissed. "You'll soon dry out."

From the foot of the steps Danny's camera rapidly clicked as Linda ran down the steps holding her dress and bouquet beneath an umbrella held by her father.

Anne smiled as she climbed into the bridesmaid's wedding car waiting on the driveway. Once seated she peeked from the back window and watched Danny and Carol climb into his MGB. She smiled, for in all the years she had known Danny he had never spoken to her in such an aggressive manner. Hence his little display of annoyance with Carol pleased her greatly.

By teatime, as forecast, the wind was gale force, as observed by Linda and Jamie who stood, arms round each other, by one of the large function room windows watching the trees in the wood opposite the Hotel lean and bend in the squalls. In the room behind, Best Man, Desmond, enthusiastically played records to suit all tastes, as guests let down their hair, the meal and formalities of speeches and cutting the cake having long since passed and the tables returned to the dining room for the Hotel guests' evening meal.

Anne, still wearing her lemon bridesmaid's dress, felt a little happier than earlier in the day when she had first encountered Carol, for it was plain for all to see, that Danny was not smitten by his young girlfriend to the degree where he had time only for her and no-one else. In fact quite the opposite seemed to prevail. Danny mingled with everyone as though she did not exist and to Anne's surprise, Carol's attention seemed to be taken by Disc Jockey Desmond, at whom she gazed adoringly, apparently quite oblivious of Desmond's wife close by his side.

At half past six, Linda changed from her bridal gown into her trousseau, she and Jamie then bade farewell to the guests and left for the two hour drive to Plymouth, where they had a hotel room booked for the night prior to taking the ferry across the Channel the following day to begin their honeymoon touring Europe.

Before their departure, Linda climbed on a chair and threw her bouquet into the crowd where eager young females jumped and stretched desperate to catch the flowers. Anne's netball skill proved very helpful and she caught the bouquet in mid-flight. She beamed, much surprised by her good fortune as the crowd clapped and cheered. And when Danny slapped her on the back, winked and said. "Well done, Anne, looks like you'll be next." She blushed.

The departure of the bride and groom did not put an end to the merrymaking. Wine and champagne flowed like water and much to the amusement of the more bashful well-wishers, singing broke out as uninhibited guests danced and sang along to the Wurzels number one hit, *Combine Harvester*.

Meanwhile, in a car bound for Plymouth, as thudding windscreen wipers dispersed heavy raindrops and wheels splashed through deep roadside puddles, Linda leaned across from the passenger seat and kissed Jamie's cheek.

"Mum and Dad were right," she whispered. "I did make too much fuss about the weather this morning, because in a funny sort of way the rain and the wind have both made a memorable contribution to what really has been the happiest day of my life."

Chapter Nine

The morning of June the twenty first began with cloudy skies but by lunch time the grey clouds had given way to the sun which rapidly raised the temperature and thus created a hot summer's day.

Stella, in preparation for the arrival of her parents, cleaned the School House from top to toe, she then took a cool bath, made a salad sandwich for her lunch and sat down in the front room ready to watch the first day's play from Wimbledon. Before the first tennis match had finished her parents arrived, having made an early start from their home in Surrey. Stella turned down the sound on the television and went out to greet them just as Ned arrived back from school.

"Perfect timing, Ned" said Stella, after hugging her parents. "Now you can help Mum and Dad in with their luggage while I make us all a cuppa."

Ned shook hands with Tom Hargreaves and kissed Connie on the cheek. "Did you have a good journey?"

"Fine thanks, Ned," said Tom, glad to stretch his legs. "It's a bit too hot for my liking though and the sun's glare puts a strain on the poor old eyes."

Connie tut-tutted. "I did say you ought to wear your sun glasses, dear. They'd have made the world of difference, but you wouldn't listen."

Tom turned up his nose. "I don't like sun specs. I think they dim the vision too much and when you're on unfamiliar roads it's imperative to have your wits about you. Anyway, it's lovely to see you again, Ned, and you're both looking extremely well. Must be the sea air."

Inside the kitchen Stella put on the kettle whilst Ned took the suitcases up to the spare room.

"Would it be alright if I popped in the sitting room to watch the cricket?" asked Tom, sheepishly, after eying the clock.

"Of course," said Stella. "The telly is on cos I was watching the tennis, so you'll need to swap channels, but please, help yourself."

Tom raised his hands. "No, no, I wouldn't hear of it. If you were watching the tennis I'll not…"

"…Dad, please, go and watch the cricket. The match I was watching was nearly finished and so it's bound to be over by now. Anyway, I'd like to sit in here with Mum for a chat and Ned will want to see the cricket score when he comes down, cos he's nearly as fanatical about the game as you are. I'll bring your tea in to you when it's ready. Now off you go."

Tom did not need telling twice to leave the room and within minutes he and Ned were sitting in comfort, drinking tea, eating sticky ginger cake and watching their beloved cricket.

Tom kicked off his sandals and rested his feet on a round, leather pouffe. He sighed, a contented man. "This is the life, eh, Ned? This is the life."

Stella sat with her mother at the table in the kitchen and each, when asked, communicated the well-being of various relatives and associates; however, during Connie Hargreaves' report on the health of her brother, whom she had recently visited, Stella could see that she was not at all focussed and seemed strangely agitated.

"How are Ned's parents?" Connie asked, with equal distance. "We must get round to see them soon."

Stella frowned. "His father's fine as far as we know. Sadly we seldom see him and he has never once been down to visit us here, I'm sorry to say. His mother on the other hand is a frequent visitor and she's remarkably well, and so is the major."

Connie smiled. "Silly me. I always forget the major is not Ned's natural father. Such a shame, we've only ever seen him once, his real father that is, and that was at your wedding; he was with his young wife. Oh dear, I can't remember either of their names."

"Ned's father is Michael," said Stella, aware of the lack of eye contact, "and his step mother is Marilyn. But let's not bother with all this trivia; there's something on your mind. What is it?"

Connie looked at the floor, clearly flustered. "How perceptive of you, Stell. You're quite right of course, there is something on my mind. I know it's silly, but I'm a little apprehensive about bringing it up. I don't want you to think we're being pushy, you see. I mean, everyone needs their space, don't they?"

"Space! For heaven's sake, Mum, what on earth are you talking about? Your hesitance is really beginning to annoy me."

Connie looked at her daughter in alarm. "Oh dear, that's the last thing I want to do, so I'll come out with it in a nutshell. The thing is, we, that is your father and I, would like to come and live down here, not under your feet of course, we'd settle for anywhere as long as it's in Cornwall. It's just we see so little of our grandchildren and in a few years' time there might even be great grandchildren and it's so nice down here, so pretty and we..."

"...Mum," interrupted Stella, laughing. "We'd love to have you living down here. In fact I can think of little I'd like more."

"Really?" The tortured look on Connie's face broke into a rapturous smile. "Oh, that's such a relief. I'd convinced myself you'd be horrified, you see. Your dad was right though. He said you wouldn't mind at all. I suppose I'm just a bit of a fuss-pot, but do you think it will be alright with Ned?"

Stella nodded. "Ned will be pleased. In fact delighted because he has said on several occasions it's a shame you're so far away. And you mustn't even think of looking further afield than Trengillion. You must definitely come and live here in the village, so let's have no more nonsense. Now, when do you want to make the move? I think the sooner the better."

"In that case we'll put the house up for sale as soon as we get back," said Connie, as she rose from her chair. "And then with any luck we'll be here for Christmas. I'm just so excited, Stell. I must go and tell your dad right this minute. He'll be dead chuffed too."

Gertie sat wearily down in the laundry room on Friday afternoon and wiped her glowing brow.

"All done," she said, fanning her face with a Cornish tourist guide leaflet. "I must admit I'll be jolly glad when the students arrive. The other girls and me could do with some help."

"Oh, Gertie, you know I've always said that I'd give you all a hand if you felt under pressure," tut-tutted Heather Jarrams, re-arranging stacks of bath towels in floor-to-ceiling cupboards. "You really shouldn't get yourself all hot and bothered like this; it can't be good for you."

Gertie grinned. "Ah, but working up a sweat and all the stretching and straining must be helping me lose weight and the other girls don't want to be beaten by the workload either. Besides, you're our boss, we can't expect you to do the beds, clean loos and so forth, it wouldn't be right. What's more you've had your Danny here this week and you don't see a great deal of him."

"Danny and Carol went back this morning and I'm your boss in name only. We're a team here and we're all as valuable as each other. Now you put your feet up and rest while I go and make you a cup of tea, or would you prefer coffee?"

"Tea please. I can't drink coffee without sugar, it's ghastly, besides tea's more refreshing."

In Heather's absence, Gertie kicked off her flip-flops and rested her feet on the basket of dirty bed linen awaiting collection by the laundry. In the distance, the hum of a vacuum cleaner on the first floor indicated that the rooms in which she had just changed the beds were in the process of being cleaned.

The last week had been very busy at the Hotel, with family and friends of the proprietors down for the wedding; for as well as the rooms they had occupied in the main part, several had stayed in rooms at the back of the Hotel, which in the days of the Penwynton family would have been the servants' quarters. Hence the use of additional accommodation had made extra work, for all rooms had to be kept clean, the guests had to be fed and then on their departure it was necessary to prepare the back rooms ready for the students due to arrive at the weekend for their summer's working holiday, as well as prepare the main guest rooms for new arrivals.

As Gertie rested she heard footsteps on the tiled floor of the passage off which stood the laundry room and she knew the appearance of her tea was imminent. For without doubt, the footsteps were those of Heather, who always wore high heels whatever the time of day, unlike her sister, Mary, who wore flatties and only changed her style of footwear on special occasions or if she was going out.

"That was quick," said Gertie, removing her feet from the laundry basket.

"Well, as luck would have it the kitchen staff were just making a brew so I didn't have to hang around. I hope it's not too strong for you."

Gertie took the mug from Heather's outstretched hand. "No, that's fine. Thank you."

Heather sat down in a chair opposite Gertie and drank the tea she had brought in for herself. She sighed. "I can't believe we're on the brink of the height of the holiday season again already, it seems like only yesterday it was Christmas. I don't know where all the time goes, but then I suppose we've been pre-occupied a lot of late with the wedding."

Gertie smiled, dreamily. "I'm so glad Linda and Jamie are married. They make such a lovely couple and they've been really sensible saving for a house before taking the plunge. I can't see my boys settling down for ages though. They don't seem to look any deeper at a girl's assets other than eying up her legs and boobs, especially Tony."

"Typical males," said Heather, with a laugh. "I wonder if this year's students will live up to expectations. One of the bar staff asked me only yesterday when they were due to arrive. It seems to be quite an event from what I can make out."

Gertie nodded vigorously. "Oh, it is, believe me. My boys keep going on about it, but I think the girls also quite look forward to a bit of new male talent around. I know there are always plenty of holiday makers, but they're never here for more than a fortnight, so any girls, or chaps for that matter, available for wooing are usually packing their bags ready to go home before our kids have got to know them. Whereas of course the students are here for a couple of months so it gives them a bit more time. Anyway, how many do you reckon will be coming this year?"

"Eight, the same as last year," said Heather. "That is to say, the same in number not the same students, although I've a feeling one of them has been before, but I'm not really sure. Mary handles that side of the business, as you know."

Gertie chuckled. "I'd laugh if they were all boys."

Heather shook her head. "No, they won't be, I do know that. Apparently, there are four of each, so hopefully that'll keep everyone happy."

The following day the students arrived by various modes of transport and at different times of the day. First to arrive was an attractive redhead, Suzie Pilkington, who was dropped off at the main entrance from her father's chauffeur driven car. Next, drama student, Malcolm Barker arrived driving his own Mini Cooper. After him, Dilys Lee arrived in a taxi along with Jack Smeaton, the couple having alighted from the same train at Redruth station where they'd agreed to share a taxi on realising the Hotel was their mutual destination. Crystal Hart arrived on foot following a walk from the village bus stop. The major part of her journey had been by coach which had dropped her in Helston where she caught a service bus to Trengillion. And finally, much to the amusement of Anne on the reception desk, Poncey Pete sauntered through the large double doors having parked his red Ford Corsair in the car park. The other two students had still not arrived by nightfall, much to the annoyance of Mary.

"This happened a few years back," she grumbled to Heather. "If the other two haven't turned up by lunchtime tomorrow, I'll put an advert in the post office window. "We'd probably be better off with local people anyway, at least that way we might possibly know something about them. The trouble is most of them are tied up one way or another at this time of year."

Chapter Ten

"How's the wine coming on?" Molly asked Dorothy as she filled the kettle for elevenses on Wednesday morning in the kitchen of Rose Cottage. "I meant to ask the major to find out when he popped in to see you other day but I completely forgot."

"Still plopping away in the corner, but much slower now and I think it's beginning to clear a bit," said Dorothy, with pride. "Does that mean we can rack it soon?"

Molly nodded. "Probably. I'll pop round later in the week and take a look. Mine's getting quite clear now, but then I did make it a month before you. Would you like a slice of lemon cake, Dot? It's quite fresh as I only made it yesterday."

"Oh, yes please. I don't eat cake very often because Frank's not too keen on it, although he does like a bit of fruit loaf now and again and he eats biscuits by the packet."

Dorothy had walked into the village to see Molly because Frank and the major had gone to the golf club as spectators for a tournament of some note.

"I hear the two chefs from the Hotel are going to rent the Old Police House," said Molly, sitting down at the kitchen table opposite Dorothy. "Have you met them? I've not, but I'm told they like their beer."

"No, I can't say that I've come across them, I met their predecessor though, the French chap," said Dorothy, with a twinkle in her eyes. "I liked him; the tone of his voice was very seductive and his manners were impeccable."

"Oh yes, I agree with you there. He could charm the birds out the trees. Anne told me he'd left at Easter to open his own restaurant in Newquay. If it wasn't such a long drive I'd ask the major if we could pop over there some time."

Dorothy broke off a piece of cake. "Well, it shows how good he was then if they've needed to take on two chefs to replace him. Mind you, I would imagine cooking breakfast and evening meals for guests is pretty time consuming. I know I found it quite hard work with just a handful of guests at the Inn."

"Well, according to Anne they took on two chefs because there was nothing to choose between them and they liked them both, and two would also give each a chance to have the occasional day off. They have lots of other staff in the kitchens as well of course and so there's always someone to do the chores. I've just remembered, Anne also told me the other day that they're thinking of opening up the dining room to do meals for non-residents too, but I don't know whether or not that'll come off."

Dorothy raised her eyebrows. "Really! Now that is a good idea, and I hear the basket meals Gloria Withers does at the Inn are very popular too." She sighed. "I suppose if we were still there then we'd be doing that sort of thing now, but I'm not sure whether I like the idea. I feel a pub should be somewhere to drink, relax and meet friends; a restaurant or café somewhere to eat, and never the twain should meet."

"Hear, hear," laughed Molly, gently banging her fist on the table. "Mind you, there are times when I've walked past the Inn and the smell of food cooking has been very enticing. But I'd never go in; it would be disloyal to Frank. Anyway, I couldn't because when he changed the Inn's name I told Raymond Withers in no uncertain terms that I'd never set foot in the place again as long as he was there, so I can't weaken and let him get the better of me. Besides, he's such a nut, he'd probably chuck me out if I did anyway."

Dorothy giggled. "Just as well everyone doesn't think like you or the place would be empty."

"Hmm, and if it was it would serve him right. Having said that, Ned and Stella go in from time to time and the youngsters think Raymond's a laugh, but then they laugh at him, not with him, and what's more they didn't witness the good old days when you and Frank ran the place."

"That's very sweet of you to say so," said Dorothy, with modest pride, "and a lot of our contemporaries feel the same. Still, things will change again one day, though the way the world's going, probably not for the better."

"Hmm, oh and before I forget, I must give you a bottle of elderflower champagne to try." Molly left the table, disappeared into the pantry and returned with a bottle in her hand. "If you like it then next year you must make some too. It's still quite lively but it's ready to drink."

"Have you found anything to celebrate yet?" smiled Dorothy, taking the bottle and reading Molly's homemade label.

"No, nothing except the fact I'm still alive," laughed Molly, sitting back down. "Having said that I've a sneaky feeling something intriguing's going to happen in the not too distant future. I don't know what, but I see a puzzling occurrence on the horizon and I've had a few unexplainable visions, but it's probably wishful thinking and my imagination forever in search of a challenge."

Dorothy picked up the remaining cake crumbs on her tea plate. "Well, perhaps something queer will happen at the barbecue thingy whatsit tonight. I don't really get the gist of what it's about. I mean to say, it seems most odd having stalls out on the beach at night and as for eating stuff cooked outdoors, that seems most peculiar unless of course you're in the middle of a field, camping."

Molly sighed deeply. "Well, it seems it's one of the new trends. Anne's quite excited about it; not that she'll be there because she works on Wednesday nights. She's tried hard to raise some enthusiasm in me, but I don't know, I'm inclined to agree with you, the notion's a bit too unconventional for my liking and I reckon in spite of the warm weather folks are likely to get a chill parading around on the beach at night."

The idea of barbecues on the beach was brought about by the prospect of another hot, dry summer, the notion of which inspired the villagers to get together once a week during the holiday period so that different organisations could make necessary preparations in order to benefit from any profits likely to be made from the events. Wednesday was the nominated day, it being mid-week, thus ensuring all new crops of holiday makers would be aware of the activities which they would hopefully attend in large numbers.

The first barbecue was scheduled to take place during the last full week of June and was in aid of the Village Church Clock Fund. For the old clock had stopped in early May and was greatly missed by most of Trengillion's residents; especially insomniacs who lamented not hearing its melodic chime as they lay awake in the small, dark hours.

The Parochial Church Council had received an estimate for the repair work and to their dismay it would cost considerably more money than funds could stretch to, hence they were only too happy to throw all their efforts into making their barbecue a huge, and they hoped, profitable success.

The evening was warm when Ned, Stella, Connie and Tom walked down the road to the beach, and into a gentle wind blowing off the calm sea which caused a stretch of bunting draped between the winch-house to a telegraph pole, to flap and flutter in the breeze.

On a stall tucked alongside the winch-house, Molly and Dorothy endeavoured to sell raffle tickets to the considerable crowd, a not too difficult task since the first prize was a weekend stay at the Penwynton Hotel, donated by the proprietors, a prize which appealed to holiday makers and inquisitive local people alike.

Molly waved when she spotted her son's in-laws and beckoned them to her stall. "Connie, Tom, how lovely to see you both. I was going to pop round and see you this morning but then Dot dropped in. How are you both, you're looking well?"

"We're fine," said Connie, giving Molly a hug, "and it's lovely to be here again. Shame we won't see Elizabeth though, but Anne's made such a big fuss of us so she's made up for the loss."

"She's a lovely girl," said Molly. "Nothing's too much trouble for her and she certainly has your Stella's gift for painting. Have you seen her latest? A water-colour of the cove. It's quite superb. How long are you down for?"

Connie nodded. "Yes, we have seen the painting as it does have rather a prominent position over the fireplace, and to answer your second question, we're here until next Monday."

Tom winked at Molly. "That means we'll have plenty of time to pop round and see you and sample your cherry cake again."

"Tom!" said Connie, shocked. "Where are your manners?"

Feeling flattered, Molly laughed. "Pop round tomorrow afternoon unless you've made other plans. The major will be in then and I know he'd like to see you both. He would have been here tonight but unfortunately this event coincides with his golf club's Annual General Meeting."

"What a shame," said Connie.

Molly sighed. "Yes, well, these things happen. Anyway, if you do come, I'll definitely make a cherry cake."

Tom rubbed his hands together. "Tomorrow it is, then, and we'd better have fifty pence worth of raffle tickets while we're here. I miss the old clock already and we've only been here for a couple of days."

The six students who had turned up on the appointed day, quickly settled into their jobs at the Hotel and worked well, although some showed more enthusiasm than others.

Suzie Pilkington was beautiful and she knew it, but nonetheless, she did her work conscientiously and without fault.

Dilys Lee on the other hand was a plain Jane, who seemed to lack even a modicum of common sense; she was also clumsy, and although seemed willing and polite, it frustrated Mary that she was unable to follow even the simplest instructions, hence she was put under the supervision of Gertie in the capacity of a chambermaid, where it was hoped she would be able to cope with the work load.

Crystal Hart was very pretty, and although shy, was capable of extreme patience and politeness; therefore she worked on the reception desk with either Anne or Mary during the busy times of day.

Jack Smeaton let it be known he was the outdoor, sporty type, so he was allocated a job in the grounds doing general repair work and maintaining the gardens with Dick Cottingham and Bob Jarrams.

Malcolm Barker, the drama student, whose parents were also theatrical and in whose footsteps he hoped to follow, was put on the bar in the lounge, where he could charm guests with his wit, good looks and gift of the gab, and finally, Poncey Pete returned to the position of waiter as in the previous year.

At her home in Coronation Terrace, Meg Reynolds rushed in from the garden where she had been hanging out the washing, because the phone was ringing. On lifting the receiver she found Bertha Fillingham on the other end of the line.

"Meg, I'm so glad to have reached you," she said, a hint of excitement in her voice. "I've been thinking long and hard about moving since your lad, Graham came to see me and I've decided that to sell up and buy somewhere on the new estate is the right thing to do."

"Oh, I am pleased," said Meg, genuinely delighted. "You'll be so much happier here in the heart of the village and nearer to all the activities too."

"Precisely," agreed Bertha. "Now, the thing is, my daughter rang last night and she insists I go up and spend a couple of weeks with her for a little holiday, so naturally I don't want to put the house up for sale before I go. So if it's alright with you I'll give you a ring when I get back and Graham can come and see me again or send someone from his office to get it valued and so forth."

"That's fine. I'll pass your message on, and as I really can't see that you'd have any problem with selling your cottage, you could well be in your new home by autumn."

"That'd be wonderful," said Bertha. "Oh, I must go, Meg, there's someone at the door. I expect it's May. Goodbye, dear and thank you."

"Okay, goodbye, have a nice holiday and I'll speak to you soon."

Chapter Eleven

In response to the Hotel's advertisement in the post office window regarding vacancies for additional staff following the non-appearance of two of the students expected, Mary took on Gertie's daughter, Susan, who would be free to work at the weekends and in the evenings. Susan had a full time job; she worked in an office as a shorthand typist but needed some extra money as she was saving up to buy a car. No other person responded to the advertisement until the day after the first barbecue, when Anne, working alone on the reception desk, encountered a scruffy, unkempt boy in his late teens, who timidly walk into the Hotel with a large rucksack on his back.

To Anne's dismay, Eric was nowhere to be seen, so she reached for her handbag, on the surmise he was a beggar, in order to give him some money and quickly hasten his departure before he was spotted by guests or her employers. When he reached the desk, however, he did not ask for money but made a soul searching plea.

"I've come about a job, miss. I saw an advert in the post office window." Anne's heart sank. "Oh, please don't be put off by my appearance," he begged. "I clean up nicely, really I do. I've been sleeping rough, you see. I lost my job in Cambridge when the firm I worked for went bust. I came to Cornwall last week thinking I'd be able to do casual work and have a holiday at the same time. You're the first place I've asked for work and I really would be reliable. I'm honest and trustworthy and I promise I won't let you down."

Anne's instinct told her she could trust him implicitly, but she knew if she were to leave the desk to find Mary and something were to go missing then she would be in grave trouble. However, there was no need for her to leave her post because right on cue Mary Cottingham walked into the vestibule with a batch of papers tucked beneath her arm. When she saw the boy she stopped dead in her tracks; before she could speak Anne sprang to his defence and reiterated his request.

Mary noted the pleading tone of Anne's voice and her expression softened. "As a matter of fact we do still need someone," she said, looking him up and down and trying not to scowl. "Would you want to live in, I wonder? I think under the circumstances, should I deem you suitable, it would be for the best if you have no other accommodation."

"What live here?" said the lad, glancing around the large vestibule with mouth gaping. "Wow, yes please. And I'll do anything you want, miss. Clean the toilets, sweep the floors, empty the rubbish, peel spuds. I'll do absolutely anything."

Mary acknowledged his enthusiasm with a nod. "Come with me then up to my office and you can tell me a bit about yourself and then providing I'm satisfied with the interview I'll introduce you to the others, after you've cleaned yourself up, I might add. I don't want anyone to see you in your current state. Do you have any other clothes?"

Grinning, the young man held up his rucksack. "Yes, in here but I'm afraid they're a bit grubby. In fact they're probably worse than the ones I'm wearing."

"Oh dear," sighed Mary, forcing a half-smile. "Never mind, we shall have to find you something else to wear until your own clothes are washed. You look about the same size as my nephew, Danny. He always keeps a few bits here. I'll get my sister to look something out for you."

"Wow, thank you miss. You're really kind. You won't regret taking me on, I promise."

Mary placed the papers she had tucked beneath her arm on the counter. "My name is Mrs Cottingham and I hope you are as good as your word. Come with me, please."

Anne giggled as Mary led the youth away, very much amused by thoughts of Danny's reaction when he discovered that such an urchin was to be kitted out in some of his expensive items of clothing.

"So what does your old man do?" Chef Bill asked student Pete, as he made himself coffee after the breakfast shift.

Pete paused from stacking dirty dishes beside the sink. "He's an antique dealer in Brighton. Got his own shop and so forth. I'm glad you asked cos that's reminded me, he told me to look out for anything that I might think of any value while I'm down here, so I'd better take a rummage through any junk shops in town soon, before I forget."

"Are you planning to go into antiques then?" asked Bill. "I bet it's quite a lucrative business to be in if you've got the knowhow."

Pete shook his head. "No, it doesn't appeal to me at all. I mean to say, yes, there's plenty of lolly to be made but it's not really my cup of tea, I think there are too many crooks involved. I must keep on the right side of the old man though because he pays my bills and so forth. I'm hoping to go into property development eventually and make myself a fortune, but of course I'll need financial help from the old man to get me started for that, so I gotta keep him sweet."

As he spoke, Suzie walked into the kitchen with the last of the dirty dishes. "All done," she said, "but a couple of cloths want changing. I'll do that and you can load the dishwasher?"

"Okay, Sue," said Pete, with an over accentuated smile.

"The name's Suzie," she snapped, haughtily throwing back her head. "I don't answer to Sue, it's too common." And with that brief statement she flounced off.

Bill scowled. "I hope she doesn't speak to the guests like that. She's a proper little madam, that one."

"I'll say," grumbled Pete, annoyed that she had made him look foolish. "She's alright with the guests though; in fact she's almost nauseatingly charming, especially with the ones she thinks might be worth a few bob."

Bill's eyebrows rose. "I see, you think she's a gold-digger then."

"Well, I don't know about that," said Pete, opening the dishwasher. "She claims Daddy is loaded and I'm told she arrived in a chauffeur driven car, so I suppose she just thinks she's better than anyone else. I'd love the opportunity to take her down a peg or two though."

In one of the larger guest rooms, Gertie and Dilys finished making the double bed and then proceeded to clean the en suite bathroom. When all glass was sparkling and the white suite gleaming, Gertie went to hang the towels on the rail only to find they had omitted to bring the royal blue towels required for that particular room. To Gertie's surprise, Dilys offered to go to the laundry room to fetch them, and so in her absence, Gertie, aware that Val with the vacuum cleaner was close on their tails, went into the next room and changed the bed in there on her own. When she had finished she crossed the floor to the bathroom, passing by the only original piece of furniture in the Hotel from the days when the Penwyntons were in residence. The chair, a Queen Anne, had been re-upholstered in its original colours, rich turquoise flecked with gold brocade, which matched the new décor of that particular room. The chair stood in a corner near to the window, but much to Gertie's mystification, since the arrival of the students, it had frequently changed its position. For Gertie was very particular about the correct location of all furniture and was punctilious that every item should look neat and straight. The chair in question, she deemed, should face out into the room and not look towards the window. Gertie tut-tutted and pulled the chair round to its correct angle, she then went into the bathroom to give it a quick wipe over. She was very surprised therefore, when she returned to the bedroom, to find the chair facing the window again. Knowing she was alone in the room, she went to the door and looked into the corridor just in time to see Dilys slip into the next room with the royal blue towels. Annoyed at the lackadaisical attitude of her colleague and the time taken to do a simple task, she forgot all about the wandering chair and instead reprimanded Dilys for her overlong absence and precious time wasted. Not that any of her harsh words sank into the student's head, for Dilys had her own schedule each day, hence, before she had collected the absent towels, she had peeped into the kitchen hopeful of seeing her idol, Poncey Pete. Thus when she saw him in the kitchen peeling potatoes for the evening meal, she seized the moment and took an impromptu tea break, during which she chatted non-stop to the unsuspecting apple of her eye.

"So, what's the water situation like up your way?" the major asked Tom and Connie Hargreaves as they sat in the living room of Rose Cottage, while Molly made tea and sliced her homemade cherry cake in the kitchen. "Probably worse than down here I should think, cos we have at least had the odd spot of rain."

Tom nodded. "I should say you're about right there. Your grass is a bit greener than ours back home. Well, ours isn't green at all, it's yellow. Yellow interspersed with green where deep rooted weeds like wretched dandelions have managed to get down far enough to find a bit of moisture. Some of the streams in the South East have completely dried up as well and the reservoirs and rivers are in a bad way too. They're so shallow in parts that fishing's a complete waste of time, I regret to say."

"I've heard mention of that," said the major. "So how exactly does drought affect fishing then?"

"Well, there are several reasons really," said Tom, warming to his favourite subject. "Fish aren't daft and they avoid shallow water because it means they'd be exposed to airborne predators if they ventured into it. Then on top of that, with less current in the rivers, any waterborne sediment drops down and is filtered by weed; that of course means the water is much clearer so the fish can see not only the end of the fisherman's rig, but the perishing fisherman too. We could do with a damn good downpour to stir everything up a bit."

"We need more than a downpour," said Connie, trying to stifle a yawn. "We need several weeks of constant rain to get things anywhere near like back to normal."

"Yes, I know that," said Tom, annoyed by his wife's contribution for stating the obvious. "But I was speaking from a fisherman's point of view. A downpour would stir up the water thus making it more difficult for the fish to see. Anyway, with any luck I'll be able to try my hand at sea fishing soon. Did you know we're hoping to move down here, Ben?"

"We're not hoping to, we're going to," said Connie, emphatically. "We have Stella and Ned's blessing so there's nothing to stop us."

"We've got to sell first."

Connie half-smiled. "Please don't be negative, Tom."

"It's about time you moved down here," said the major. "There's no place like Cornwall, I'd recommend it to anyone. Do you play golf, Tom?"

Tom wrinkled his nose. "A little, but I'm not much cop. I like anything that gets me outdoors though as I'm a great believer in lots of fresh air."

"Brilliant," said the major. "You'll have to join our club then. We could do with a few older members as at present we're overrun with youngsters showing us pensioners up."

"Has anywhere down here taken your eye yet?" asked Molly, as she poured tea into bone china cups laid out on her new hostess trolley. "There are some lovely houses going up in Penwynton Crescent."

"Not yet," said Connie, "but then we're not really looking at the moment because we feel we ought to get our own place sold first. I'd hate to find somewhere and not be able to do anything about it cos we didn't have a buyer. Not that I think that'll happen as our house is in very good order, thanks to Tom, and it's in a popular area too."

"I assume your new housing estate is called Penwynton Crescent after the bigwigs who once lived here," said Tom, taking a cup from Molly's outstretched hand.

"Yes, and rightly so," said the major. "Trengillion wouldn't exist at all if it wasn't for the Penwyntons. All the old buildings at one time belonged to the estate. I think it's a damn shame the family died out, their presence added a bit of class to the place and I rather liked the late Charles, even though he was a bit odd.

"Oh, before I forget, you won a prize in the raffle last night," said Molly, nodding towards the sideboard. "It's over there by the lamp. The streptocarpus. Isn't it a beautiful rich colour?"

"How lovely," exclaimed Connie, putting down her teacup and rising to look more closely at the plant. "I admired it when we came in but I'd no idea it was ours. Thank you."

"We left the barbecue early cos Connie had a bit of a headache," said Tom, his face beaming as Molly handed him a generous portion of cherry cake. "She's okay today though, aren't you, love? We think it was just too much sun yesterday because we sat on the beach for a couple of hours in the afternoon. It was nice though, in spite of the crowds. In fact I don't think I've ever seen the beach as busy as it was yesterday in all the years we've been coming down here."

"The phone hasn't stopped ringing this afternoon," said Anne to Mary Cottingham, as she prepared to go home. "It must be the weather. Suddenly everyone wants to come to Cornwall and we're fully booked now right through 'til the end of September."

"Excellent, I thought that would soon be the case. I hope we don't run out of water down here with the huge influx of holiday makers. The reservoirs really are alarmingly low."

"I know," said Anne, slipping on her flat shoes. "Grandma and Granddad Hargreaves say they'll be having to use standpipes soon unless they get rain. I've never known a period of time like this when the weather crops up in every single conversation. Everyone's talking about it, young, old, and even kids."

"Where do your grandparents live?" asked Mary.

"Horley in Surrey. It's really nice up there cos they live near the railway, and when Liz and I went there as children we used to play guessing how many coaches the next train might have and then we'd sit and wait to see who was right. Sounds a bit daft now but we loved it at the time and it kept us quiet for ages. We used to go in August too, when the rowan trees were smothered in orangey red berries; so rowan trees always remind me of Horley."

From outside, Eric the porter came in fanning his flushed face with his cap. "Cor it aren't half hot out there, especially in this uniform. I don't suppose there's any chance of you finding me a summer outfit, Mrs C? Shorts and a T shirt perhaps."

"Oh, poor you," sympathised Mary, trying not to laugh at the image conjured up in her mind of Eric in shorts. "But I don't really think your request would emit the right impression, do you? I tell you what though, you can take off the jacket and the hat, but you must put the hat back on when you're called to help the guests. How does that sound?"

"Very good, Mrs C," grinned Eric, "it'll please the wife too. She says my shirts are horrible and smelly cos I get so sweaty under the jacket."

"Yes, I can understand that," said Mary, wrinkling her nose, "and talking of the heat reminds me. Chef Ben has made lovely lemon ice-cream for tonight's menu. I've tried it and it's quite delicious, but he's worried that by the time it gets to the dining room it'll just be a splodge on the plate. I don't envy tonight's waiting staff. He'll expect them to move faster than lightning, so I suggest you steer well clear of the kitchen this evening, Eric."

"I'll have gone by then Mrs C," grinned Eric, removing his jacket. "I finish at five today, so it'll be poor Wesley who'll have to watch his step."

"And I'm off now," laughed Anne, rolling up the sleeves of her blouse. "At least it'll be quite cool for my walk home in the woods.

It's a shame the stream is little more than a trickle though, as I miss the sound of it splashing along its pathway like it does when we've had heavy rain. By the way, did you take that lad on? I do hope so because I thought he was very sweet."

"Yes, I did," said Mary, with a bemused frown. "I meant to tell you that. I'm a bit miffed by his name though and I'm not sure whether or not he's having me on. On reflection though I think he must be kidding because the family has now died out. He says his name is Grenville Penwynton."

Chapter Twelve

"Grenville Penwynton!" gasped Stella, as Anne sat down at the kitchen table and told her the news on her return home from work. "Surely not. I mean to say it's not possible. There aren't any Penwyntons now and Grenville Penwynton went missing donkey's years ago; so even if he had any descendants I'm sure they'd have turned up long before now."

Anne shrugged her shoulders. "Well, that's what he claims to be called. Mary thinks he might be pulling her leg but judging by what little I saw of him I got the impression he was rather earnest and not the type to tell tales." Anne removed her shoes and pushed them under the table. "Have Grandma and Granddad gone out? I see their car's here but the house is very quiet."

Stella nodded. "Yes, they've popped round to see your dad's mum and the major and then they said they might go for a walk."

Anne stood, walked over to the sink and filled the kettle. "I see. Anyway, can you tell me exactly what the story behind Grenville Penwynton is? I remember there was a lot of talk about it a few years back, but I was quite young then and I can't really remember any of the details. I suppose it didn't interest me at the time either, I'm sorry to say."

In a state of bewilderment, Stella ran her fingers through her hair. After a brief reflection, she shook her head. "No, I don't see how he can be...oh dear, let me think." She sat down. "Hmm, yes, you want to know Grenville's story. Right, I'll do my best." She clasped her hands and rested them on the table. "It was Jim Hughes who told me about him. You obviously know Jim, don't you? Grandma's next door neighbour."

"Of course," said Anne, "he gives me peppermints every time he sees me; in fact he's done so for as long as I can remember."

"Does he? Bless him, he's a good sort." Stella unclasped her hands and rested her elbows on the table. "Anyway, it would've been back in 1967 when Jim told me of the Penwyntons' history cos it was the year that Maggie Nan went missing, but I've never forgotten the story because it fascinated me at the time, and Jim and I have often chatted about it since then. In fact I've written down most of what Jim has told me because I thought it would be a shame to have it forgotten when we're all dead and gone."

"Would you like coffee, Mum?" asked Anne, as the kettle boiled.

"Tea, please," said Stella, brushing a crumb from the tablecloth.

Anne made the tea and coffee and then sat down opposite her mother. "Right, off you go."

"Thank you." Stella picked up her mug of tea and thoughtfully took a sip. "I think I'd better start at the very beginning, that's if you really want to hear it, but I'll only go back as far as George Penwynton who was Grenville's father, otherwise without my notes I'll get completely lost."

Anne smiled. "I'm all ears."

"Right. Well, George Penwynton was born in 1820 and married Charlotte Grenville. They had two sons, Grenville born in 1850 and Cedric born in 1852 and during the birth of Cedric, his poor mother Charlotte died. Anyway, a couple of years later, George married again and his new wife was called Talwyn Nancarrow. She came from down Penzance way and in 1854 she produced a son who they named, Gorran. And then a couple of years later they had a daughter who was christened Kayna. I think that's rather a pretty name, don't you?"

"Hmm, it is, but I can't say that I'm too keen on Gorran. Anyway, please continue."

"Well, Jim worked as gamekeeper on the Penwynton Estate, and that's where he met his first wife, Flo, who worked in the kitchen back then, but I don't expect you remember her, do you?"

"Vaguely, but does she have anything to do with the story?"

Stella shook her head. "Actually, no, as you've noticed, I digress easily, sorry. Anyway, the story handed down through two generations of employees says that Talwyn, the second wife, didn't like Charlotte's boys, especially Grenville who would inherit the estate on his father's death, him being the elder of the two. And because of this, they, the staff that is, thought it odd that he, Grenville, suddenly, out of the blue, went off without saying goodbye. Apparently, he did leave a note though, explaining he wanted a less complicated life and asking his father not to try and find him. According to Jim, George, the father, did try and find him, but he had no luck, so to this day his fate is a complete mystery. Though it's considered perhaps Talwyn knew the truth, because she had money of her own, though no doubt peanuts in comparison with the wealth of the Penwyntons, and because of that, rumour of the day had it that she gave Grenville enough money to start a new life elsewhere, and if that was the case, then his contemporaries concluded he would've been only too glad to accept the bribe because she made his life miserable."

"Miserable!" laughed Anne. "In what way?"

"Well, apparently she was cruel, not physically, but mentally," said Stella, "which is pretty harsh considering the poor soul lost his mother when he was just a tot."

Anne looked puzzled. "That's horrible! But why didn't Grenville tell his dad that his stepmother was bullying him. I mean, it sounds a bit odd if his dad didn't know what was going on."

"Well, we can only surmise, but according to Jim, Grenville wasn't his father's favourite; Cedric was. Grenville didn't like, hunting or shooting, you see; he didn't like riding either and what's more he was afraid of horses. They say he was a bit frail too, like his poor mother. On the other hand Charlotte was considered to be a fine horsewoman so she couldn't have been that frail."

"Can you remember in which year Grenville disappeared?"

"Yes, it was 1876. Good grief, that makes it one hundred years ago now."

"Wow! So it does. How strange."

"You mean strange because of the Grenville who has arrived at the Hotel?"

Anne nodded. "Yes. Anyway, what happened when George died? Did the estate go to Cedric?"

"Well yes, but it's said that before that Talwyn actually tried to get Cedric to leave as well, but that obviously never came about. I suppose he had too much to lose, so nothing she could do would drive him away. Anyway, much to Jim's disgust, Talwyn got her wish in the end, because although her own offspring didn't inherit the estate, her great grandson did. You see, because Cedric's son, the late Charles Penwynton, had no descendants and neither did his late sister, who incidentally was his twin, everything went to a second cousin living in Canada. It's a bit complicated, but Talwyn's daughter, Kayna, married a London banker, whose name was something or other Reeves. They had a son called Geoffrey who moved to Canada and naturally married a Canadian girl. That union produced a son who they christened, Bernard, and he, who must be in his sixties now, inherited the lot. Not, I suppose, that that side of the story is really of any relevance to Grenville's plight."

"Hmm, so what happened to Kayna's brother, Gorran then? I mean, didn't he have any family?" asked Anne, confused. "Because if he did, then surely they should have taken precedence over Kayna's descendants when it came to inheriting the estate."

Stella laughed. "Well, that's another story. Gorran died in his early twenties, you see, in a shooting accident on Penwynton land. Actually, I think it might even have been in the woods, I can't remember for sure."

"What Bluebell Woods?" said Anne, horrified. "You mean that Gorran might have been accidently killed in the woods I walk through every day. That's a bit unnerving."

"Well, they claimed it was an accident, but many tongues expressed their doubts at the time."

"You mean it might have been deliberate! Why?"

Stella drew in a sharp intake of breath. "Because when a young girl who worked at the house as a chambermaid discovered she was pregnant and claimed Gorran was the father of her unborn child, Talwyn instantly sacked her. Apparently, Gorran was callous just like his cruel mother and he denied having had anything whatsoever to do with the poor girl, who needless to say was broken hearted. I can't remember her name but I'm sure it had something to do with food."

"Hmm, actually that sounds vaguely familiar," said Anne. "I remember Liz telling me about the chambermaid, but I was rather young and I can't remember any of the details. So you believe that Gorran was deliberately shot."

Stella nodded. "Well, yes, if the rumours are true. You see, it appears that the girl's father was a fisherman from Polquillick and he was also a poacher. Everyone knew he had a rifle, so they put two and two together, and in the eyes of many made four. But of course we may be doing Gorran an injustice, although many said at the time that the child the girl bore had Talwyn's eyes."

Anne nodded thoughtfully. "So do you think there's any chance that the Grenville who turned up at the Hotel today might be a descendent of that child or even of Grenville who vanished into thin air? I can't believe he was. He didn't look as though he had two ha'pennies to rub together. I wish Elizabeth was here. I'd love to hear what she thinks."

"I don't know about him being a descendant of Grenville, but he certainly can't be a descendant of Gorran's offspring because that child died in infancy. It's far more probable that he called himself Penwynton just to raise curiosity and secure himself a job at the Hotel."

"Well, he's certainly raised curiosity," giggled Anne. "But surely he wouldn't have chosen the Christian name Grenville, without foreknowledge, would he? So there must be more to this than meets the eye. I shall investigate further. I'm doing the evening shift tomorrow and Susan will be working too, so I'll see what she makes of it."

"Ham!" said Stella, gleefully slapping her hands on the table. "

I knew it had something to do with food. The chambermaid's name was Florrie Ham."

Chapter Thirteen

Before dawn, on the first day of July, Chef Ben was woken by a loud clap of thunder. Bleary eyed and sleepy, he slipped from his bed, pulled back the curtains and stood by the window to watch the passing of a short, light storm. Minutes later, disappointed that it developed into nothing more than a few half-hearted rumbles, he drew the curtains, yawned, climbed back into bed and slept for another hour.

Later in the morning, while clearing up after breakfast was in progress, another storm sent hotel staff dashing towards the windows hopeful of witnessing a significant downpour of rain. The rain, however, just as observed by Ben earlier in the day, did little more than wet the ground and the rumbles faded away as quickly as they had begun.

"I hope that's not an omen," laughed Ben, as he removed his chef's clothing and tossed them into the laundry basket. "I'm referring to the rumbling weather. I hope it doesn't mean our occupancy of the Old Police House will encounter sinister happenings."

"I dunno, I rather hope it does," chuckled Bill, buttering a spare slice of cold toast. "We could do with a bit of excitement round here, especially if it might involve the Powers of Darkness."

"I take it you've started reading that Denis Wheatley novel then?" said Ben, clearly delighted. "I told you you'd like it."

Bill reached for the marmalade pot. "Like it! I love it and I can't believe it's got me looking under the bed before I climb in each night. I reckon by the time I get to the end I might well be a quivering wreck."

When Bill had finished his toast, the two chefs left the kitchens in the hands of students and other employees to be cleaned and tidied. They then went to their respective rooms, collected their belongings and prepared to move into the Old Police House, with the knowledge that on their departure, Jack, Pete and Malcolm, who had since their arrival, temporarily shared a room, would be gathering up their own few possessions in order to spread out and have a room each.

As the chefs drove away from the Hotel, all traces of the storms had passed; the ground was dry; the sun was shining brightly but to the relief of many, the temperature was a little lower than the previous day's.

"Do you know what the students call us?" laughed Ben, as they began to unload their possessions from the back of his van and take them into their new home.

"No idea," said Bill, puzzled. "What?"

"Big Ben and Old Bill," said Ben, with an uproarious laugh. "I heard that lad Pete telling stuck-up Suzie this morning that Old Bill and Big Ben were moving today and he's dead chuffed cos it means he'll be getting a room to himself. Cheeky little bugger."

"But I'm not much older than you," said Bill, deflated by his nick-name. "It must be because of my bald patch. Big Ben's a good name for you though. I mean to say, how tall are you? Six one, two, three?"

"Six two, so I'm glad we're not renting one of the fishermen's cottages with low ceilings and wretched beams or I'd have a permanent sore head. But out of curiosity then, how old are you?"

Bill rubbed his hand over his bald patch as he looked in the hall mirror. "Thirty one, so I'm not exactly on my last legs yet. How old are you?"

"Twenty nine, so really there's nothing much between us. You know, it must be the beard as well as the bald patch. I think beards always make blokes look older."

"Hmm, perhaps you're right. Fancy a beer? The Badge should be open by now, then I think we ought to take a walk down to the beach, cos I'm told there are a couple of unattached females staying at Cove Cottage this week and you never know, they might fancy a couple of good looking chefs to knock 'em up a cordon bleu meal."

"Now the Badge is a good idea and I want to sample one of the landlady's pies," said Ben. "I've heard several people raving about them, so I'd like to try one to analyse just exactly what she puts in 'em. As for chasing a couple of birds, that sounds good too, but bagsy mine's the one with the biggest knockers."

They finished unloading the van, carried Ben's television set into the corner of the main living room and then each took their possessions up to their chosen rooms on either side of the stairs on the front of the house where they had views of the sea stretching out towards the Witches Broomstick. When their rooms looked as homely as possible and their clothes were put away in drawers and wardrobes, they changed into shorts, T shirts and flip-flops, left their new home and crossed the road to the Inn.

In the afternoon, Linda and Jamie returned from their honeymoon. Anne was the first to know when she answered the phone at the Hotel to hear Linda speaking from their new house in Penwynton Crescent. For Linda, having been away for two weeks, was eager to hear all the latest gossip, hence Anne was able to tell her with unbridled enthusiasm the most newsworthy events, namely: the arrival of a lad who called himself Grenville Penwynton, the chefs having finally moved into the Old Police House, and the arrival of the students. Like Anne, Linda was amused to hear that Poncey Pete had returned

"I'll pop up this afternoon to see everyone," she said, her appetite whetted by Anne's tittle-tattle. "I have little gifts for you all too, but don't get too excited."

"Okay, but whatever it is you shouldn't have."

"Nonsense, Anne. You're a good friend and you saved the day when you loaned me your wellies for the wedding, and I sincerely mean that, even if I didn't appear very enthusiastic at the time."

Anne giggled. "You're welcome. So, what time will you be up?"

"Hmm, well I really ought to unpack and put the washing machine on but that can wait 'til tomorrow, so I'd say about half an hour. Oh, and before I forget, has Danny sent down the wedding photos yet?"

"No. Your mum rang him a couple of days ago to see if they were ready. He said they were but he wouldn't put them in the post 'til you were home because he wants you and Jamie to see them first."

"Ah, that's so sweet," said Linda. "Anyway, I'll see you all in a minute. Jamie's just putting the kettle on so we'll be with you as soon as we've drunk our tea."

"Fancy going down the Badge for a pint, later?" Tony Collins asked his twin brother John who had just returned home from work.

"Yeah, alright. I am feeling a bit dry. What time are you thinking of going?"

"Eightish, after *Top of the Pops*. I want to see if Queen are on first. I rather like their new record and I've only heard it a couple of times."

John nodded. "Okay, I think I'll have a bath then as I'm feeling rather grubby. We've been pulling old lathe and plaster off stud walls today and the muck gets everywhere."

"I can see that, you've left dirty great footprints all the way along the hall. You'd better get that cleaned up before Mum sees it."

"Sod it. Where is Mum?" asked John, glancing back and forth. "The house is quiet so she must be out."

Tony looked heavenward. "According to Sue, she's gone for a brisk walk cos she ate a slice of coconut cake today when she went to a coffee morning at the Village Hall. Apparently coconut is quite high in calories but Mum didn't realise and so she had a real shock when she got home and looked in her book."

John groaned. "Mum and her sodding book."

"Yeah, absolutely. The brush and dustpan live under the sink, by the way, just in case you didn't know."

John removed his boots and brushed his trousers with his hands sending clouds of dust into the air.

"Ay, be careful," shouted Tony, taking a step backwards, "or you'll have to find a duster too."

"Bloody hell, this is ridiculous. Where's Susan?"

Susan called from the top of the stairs. "I'm up here. Do you want something?"

"Yeah, I want you to clean up this mess, Sue, before Mum gets back. You'd be so much quicker than me."

"What! But I'm off to work in a minute, waitressing at the Hotel. You'll have to do it or I'll be late."

"I'll pay you," pleaded John, in desperation, "every penny helps when you're saving for a car, my dearest, favourite sister."

"How much?" asked Susan, brushing her hair as she leaned over the banister, obviously tempted.

"Fifty pence," said John, hopefully.

"Make it a pound and I'll do it."
"You greedy bugger, that's daylight robbery."
Susan shrugged her shoulders. Tony laughed.
"Alright, but you'd better make a good job of it."

John pulled a pound note from his wallet, laid it on the hall table and went up the stairs in a huff. When he came down, however, he was surprised to find the hallway clean and the pound note where he had left it and beside it was a note saying:

Keep the pound but you owe me a favour.
Sue x

Graham Reynolds was working on the bar when the twins arrived at the Inn. As he poured them each a pint he nodded to the Wild West Night posters plastered over every wall in both bars.

"Are you coming down tomorrow?" he asked. "Looks like it'll be a good night again as there's been a lot of interest from holiday makers."

Tony sat down on a bar stool. "I expect so. It's always good for a laugh." He looked around. "Where's Dead-eye Dick tonight? Out target practising?"

"No, he's actually taken poor Gloria out for a meal. Roger told me that she said to Ray, that she wouldn't sing tomorrow if he didn't take her out. I must admit I'm rather impressed with her taking a stand like that. He walks over her far too much. My mum would never stand being treated like that."

"Blimey, neither would ours," said John, in agreement. "Dad likes to think he wears the trousers in our house but we all know it's really Mum. I mean, can you imagine Raymond Withers having to live on rabbit food if Gloria went on a diet?"

Graham shook his head. "Not likely. I take it your mum's still slimming then? I heard Susan telling Diane she had started a diet but that was weeks and weeks ago."

"Oh yes, and to us it seems like years," said Tony, as Graham put the second pint on the bar. "The latest weight loss is three pounds, so goodness knows how much longer this will go on for. I suppose if I listened I might know, but I'm inclined to switch off as soon as diets, weight and slimming are mentioned".

John pulled change from his pocket. "Since we're half starved, we'll have a couple of packets of crisps too, please. Salt and vinegar, if you've got 'em."

"Two pints and two crisps, that'll be seventy six pence, please," said Graham, laying the crisps on the bar.

John counted out the correct money and dropped it in Graham's outstretched hand. Graham put the money in the till and then turned back to the twins. "Do you think there's any chance of the Hotel's female students coming in for the Wild West Night tomorrow? I've heard one of them is a real beauty but haven't actually clapped eyes on her yet. Although Poncey Pete and another chap have been in and of course the two chefs treat this place like their second home."

"Fingers crossed," grinned Tony, as Graham moved on to serve another customer. "We saw her the other day coming out of the post office and she is gorgeous, so if she does come in tomorrow and our little sister's here too, then Sue can do us a favour and introduce us."

When Susan finished waitressing she went to the reception desk where she knew Anne would be on duty.

"What's all this they're talking about in the kitchen about a young male Penwynton being on the scene?" she asked. "I mean to say, aren't they all supposed to be dead and buried?"

Anne laughed. "I was hoping to see you tonight so that I could share your thoughts. Yes, we do have someone working here with the Penwynton name but he probably isn't the real thing. No-one knows for sure, but it's rather intriguing all the same. You'll no doubt see him soon, though I'm not sure what he'll be doing cos he doesn't actually start work 'til tomorrow. You'll like him, he's very sweet and when you do meet him, you can judge whether or not you think he has any link with the Penwyntons from here."

"Hmm, but is he handsome? That's more important than being a Penwynton," said Susan, eyebrows raised with anticipation. "I mean, do you think he's my type?"

Anne laughed. "I'm not really sure what your type is, Sue. Most of your boyfriends have been chalk and cheese."

"Fair enough, but do you think we'd make a nice couple? To look at, I mean."

"Well, our new chap has a very nice face. He's about five nine in height and he's pleasant to talk to. You'd look alright as a couple but I think he might be a bit too meek for you."

Susan roared with laughter. "Meek! Oh, definitely not my type then. How about that Jack bloke? I saw him in the Badge the other night and thought him rather dishy, but he's got a silly accent. Where on earth is he from?"

Anne smiled. "Loughborough apparently, but we all think he's trying to talk posh to impress snooty Suzie and instead of sounding upper class he sounds like a moron. You should see the way the blokes flock around Suzie, it's quite nauseating."

"Humph, you don't need to tell me, I see it all the time when we're working together, and as for Jack, we'll have to get him drunk so we can see what he really talks like. In fact, I might give that a try as soon as the opportunity arises. Anyway, where is Loughborough?"

"Leicestershire. Are you going to the Wild West Night tomorrow? I've got the night off so I think I might go."

"Well, yeah, if you're going then I will too, definitely, and I'll ask Di if she wants to join us."

"Ah, I've just remembered, I knew there was something I had to tell you," said Anne, excitedly. "I heard this morning that Steve Penhaligon is going to start working for Dave Richardson soon. You really do fancy him, don't you? So you might get the chance to meet him properly through your John as they'll soon be working together."

Susan's jaw dropped. "Really! You bet I will then. Steve's a real hunk and John owes me a favour anyway, so he can definitely introduce us. But it'll have to be when I'm dressed up. I shall have to put my thinking cap on and plan when that might be. Brilliant! It's always nice to have something to look forward to, and as for Jack, well, he's history already."

Chapter Fourteen

Fancy dress was optional on Raymond Withers' Wild West Nights at the Sheriff's Badge Inn, therefore for many it was an invitation too good to miss, and the majority of the Inn's local, male clientele spared no expense when it came to choosing their costumes; for each was eager to re-live childhood cowboy fantasies and imagine themselves with the prestigious reputation of being known as the fastest gunslinger in town.

The women on the other hand seldom dressed up and invariably looked on with pitying glances at the men folk with whom they shared their homes: each amused that their girlish, long forgotten dreams of romantic rescues by knights in shining armour could not possibly be re-enacted in a similar manner to the men's fantasies due to a severe shortage of eligible gallant knights.

Outside, around the picnic bench, the younger generation, not bitten by the cowboy bug, sat together enjoying the jovial ambiance created by their elders.

"Mind if I join you?" asked Jack Smeaton, fanning his flushed face with a cardboard beer mat. "It's far too hot in there."

"Of course not," said Anne, moving along the bench to make room for him. "We're all out here for the very same reason."

Jack sat down between Anne and Susan and introduced himself to those in the small gathering around the table with whom he was not acquainted.

"I'm Jack Smeaton," he said, offering his hand to each person in turn as they recited their names. "I'm a student working at the Hotel for the summer. You've a great set-up here and your landlord's an absolute nutcase."

"Yes, he does get a bit carried away on Wild West Nights," said Diane, glancing heavenwards. "Having said that he's much the same every night which is a bit of a pain when you just want to come here for a quiet drink."

Jack nodded. "Yeah, I know what you mean. I came in the other night with Pete and we got a lecture on guns. He told us he was a brilliant shot and we weren't quite sure if that was his way of warning us he didn't want any trouble or if he was just boasting."

"He was boasting," said Susan, emphatically, making comparisons between Jack by her side, and Steve Penhaligon. "That's his speciality."

Tony picked up his cigarette packet and offered it around. "It's a pity you didn't bring some of your fellow students with you tonight, Jack. Female ones, I mean. We've noticed there's a right cracker at the Hotel this year."

Jack grunted. "Humph, yeah, that'll be Suzie Pilkington. She's a beauty alright but I don't really think this would be her sort of thing. Besides, she's a waitress and the kitchen staff don't usually finish much before nine. I'm lucky though, I work on the grounds so I have every night off."

Susan, still comparing the looks of Steve Penhaligon and Jack, leaned forwards. "You've got gorgeous eyes, Jack. They're real green, almost emerald. I don't think I've ever seen any quite that bright."

Jack fluttered his eyelashes and laughed. "Wow, thanks. I'm often referred to at university as the green-eyed guy."

Diane leaned across the table so that Tony could light the cigarette she'd accepted. "So, what are you studying at university? Anything interesting?"

"History," he promptly replied. "Which reminds me. What's all this I hear about someone called Grenville disappearing and a chap called Gorran being shot dead by his lover's father from Polquillick or some such place. It's not the sort of thing I'd expect to have happened in the back of beyond like this, but I heard the Pots talking about it yesterday when they were out in the garden having a crafty fag and I couldn't make much sense of what they were saying."

John's eyebrows quickly knitted into a confused frown. "Who the devil are the Pots?"

Anne giggled, amused by the look on John's face. "Our two chefs. Unfortunately they're called Bill and Ben. Pete started the craze off by naming them Big Ben and Old Bill, but now Malcolm's gone one step further and named them Bill and Ben the Flour Pot Men and the students call them the Pots for short."

"Oh, and I thought students were supposed to be studious, brainy and sensible," laughed John. "Silly me."

"We are, but that doesn't mean we don't have a sense of humour," smiled Jack. "Anyway, is anyone going to tell me about the historic murder or not?"

Anne briefly sketched out the history of the Penwynton family, Grenville's disappearance, and the demise of Gorran after his alleged liaison with Florrie Ham.

"Oh, I see," said Jack, turning over the facts I his mind. "So all this happened at the Hotel when it was a house and is topical at the moment because of the arrival of the mysterious Grev Penwynton. Brilliant! It sorta makes sense now you've explained it."

It was Jane's turn to frown. "Who on earth is Grev Penwynton? I thought the family had all died out."

Anne shrugged her shoulders. "We don't really know. He's just a young lad who turned up at the Hotel the other day looking for work and he says his name is Grenville Penwynton, but he insists we call him Grev because he thinks Grenville sounds dreadfully old fashioned and pompous."

John laughed. "I bet Poncey Pete wishes he was called Grenville. Snooty bugger!"

"Who's Poncey Pete?" asked Jack.

"Your fellow student, Pete Pritchard," smiled Anne. "He was here last summer too and he didn't go down too well with this lot because he looked down his nose at them. Although I must admit he seems a lot less bumptious this year."

"Oh, I see," said Jack slowly nodding his head. "Pete didn't tell me he'd been here before. How odd, but that'll explain why he got to know his way around before the rest of us. Going back to the Hotel's history though, Anne. Do you know if the place has changed much since it was the family home?"

"Oh gosh, yes, it's been fully refurbished since the death of Charles, although the layout of the rooms is much the same. None of the furniture is original though. The trustees had a big auction sale when we were kids, and Mum and Dad, like everyone else in the village, bought a few bits. Our treasures include a desk which my sister used to hate but she now likes, and a luxurious chaise longue. The paintings weren't sold at the auction though; they were all donated to an art gallery, but Mary is negotiating with the gallery to see if we can get one or two back, especially one of the front of the house which is a couple of hundred years old. I've not seen it but I hope we can get it."

Jack grinned. "You're very dedicated to the Hotel, aren't you, Anne? I've noted before that you always speak of it with unbridled reverence."

"I've known the place since I was a child when we used to play in Bluebell Woods; in fact we had a den there. I loved the house then and still do. I sometimes think it has bewitched me. It's silly, but I feel at home there."

"Actually, there is one piece of furniture that's original," said Diane, thoughtfully. "The chair Granddad bought and then sold back to the Hotel when he left the Vicarage. Don't you remember, Anne? Granddad bought it at the auction sale but didn't have room for it when he moved into his little bungalow, so to help him out, Mum put an advert in the post office window offering it for sale, and Mrs Cottingham bought it."

Anne nodded. "Of course, you're right. It's been re-upholstered since then but in its original colour because Mary thought it would be sacrilegious to do it differently. It has pride of place in one of the blue rooms now. I'd forgotten all about it, but then I very seldom go up there."

"What are the blue rooms?" asked Jane, intrigued.

"Guest rooms," smiled Anne. "The Hotel has its rooms graded by colours. There are four blue rooms, each decorated predominantly in white with accessories in various shades of blue, for example turquoise, royal, sky and navy. They're the biggest and most expensive rooms. After that we have the green rooms, then the pinks, followed by the yellows and the smallest most economical of all are in shades of mauve. Does that make sense?"

"I see," said Jane. "How clever. That's rather an interesting way of doing things. You're really lucky working at the Hotel, Anne, it sounds quite fascinating."

"Right, my glass is empty and if you'll let me I'd like to buy you all a drink," said Jack, rising to his feet. "But I'll need one of you to come with me and help me carry them."

Susan jumped up and volunteered before anyone else had a chance to respond. "I'll help because I know what everyone's drinking. We need three dry Martinis, two lagers, a rum n'shrub and whatever you're drinking, Jack."

"Rum n'shrub," queried Jack. "What the devil's that?"

"Rum with a measure of shrub, would you believe," said Tony. "Dad got us onto it. It's popular with fishermen."

"Shrub's an alcoholic cordial from Devon made with herbs and spices," laughed Diane. "You should try it. My brother Graham says they sell loads of it here."

Tony sat up straight and tilted his head. "Listen, it's gone quiet inside. I bet Gloria's about to seduce the crowds with a song."

"Humph, Raymond's such a pig making her do that," said Diane, crossly. "Come on, let's all go in and give the poor woman a bit of moral support, and then Jack can treat us."

The Inn was packed out with patrons enjoying the Wild West Night. Every table and seat was occupied and the only standing room was just inside the door.

As the first notes rang out from the upright piano tucked away in a corner, standing punters moved back to make way for Gloria Withers, who entered the public bar from the passageway and seductively walked through the crowd, mockingly fondling the faces of men who behaved in a bawdy manner. Singing tunefully and heartily, she fanned her flushed face with a hand-held feathered fan, thrust forward her ample cleavage, threw back her head and swayed in time to the piano accompaniment skilfully played by her son, Roger.

When the song was finished, the cheers, wolf whistles and clapping went on for a full ten minutes, prolonging the agony of Gloria Withers, whose face, flushed by the heat, embarrassment, relief and the delight of success, resembled that of an over-ripe tomato.

"Well, I think we can safely say that was another triumphant night," boasted Raymond Withers, as he locked and bolted the front door of the Inn after Graham left, tucking his night's pay of three one pound notes, into his pocket. "It seems the holiday makers love me as much as the local folk."

"Well, it's hardly surprising, is it?" said Gloria, pinning up a stray strand of her brown hair. "You are a magnificent sight in all your cowboy getup."

Raymond gazed at his reflection in the full length mirror in the bar and looked himself up and down, from the boots and spurs on his feet gleaming beneath the chaps covering his long, slim legs, to the Spanish leather, double holster, around his portly waist, holding two shining guns. A sheriff's badge adorned his brown, leather waistcoat, beneath which he wore a red check shirt. Around his collar hung a bootlace tie, and tied around his neck was a red spotted scarf. The finishing touch to his outfit was a large brimmed hat which covered his greying hair. With a satisfied sigh, Raymond nodded to his reflection, removed his hat, and then sauntered across the bar to the nearest table and removed his boots.

"You're a damn lucky woman, Gloria. There's a lotta women who'd give their eye teeth for a bloke like me."

Gloria gave a feeble laugh which Raymond read as endorsement but in reality meant nothing of the kind.

"Where's Roger gone?" Raymond suddenly asked. "He always manages to disappear when it's time to clear up, the idle so and so. He knows we always let Graham go as soon as we've locked up cos the lad's got work tomorrow, meaning we need another pair of hands."

"Yes, but poor Roger has to be up for work tomorrow too," said Gloria, loosening the hooks on the bodice of her dress so that she could breathe more easily. "And I don't know where he is, but the last time I saw him he was chatting up one of the girls staying upstairs."

"Oh, he's a chip off the old block alright," laughed Raymond, slapping his thigh. "Oh well, best leave him alone then; you'll have these glasses washed in no time, anyway. Fancy a nightcap, Glore? I think I could do with one, I reckon I've not had the chance to drink more than half a bitter all night."

"Of course, love. You stay there and rest," yawned Gloria, stepping behind the bar, her long taffeta dress swishing as she walked. "What would you like, another beer, or do you fancy a whisky?"

"A large Jack Daniels, please and chuck in a bit of ice if it hasn't all melted."

As Gloria poured the drinks, Raymond removed his holster and laid it on the brass table top.

"Your song went down quite well, Glore, but you shouldn't let 'em clap for so long. While they're clapping they're not buying drinks and that's what this game's all about. And I think another time you might slap a few faces, you know what I mean, not hard like, more of a gesture than a real slap; that should get them wild."

"But don't you think they already get wild enough?" asked Gloria, wearily. "It must be bedlam for the neighbours and some of the men here tonight were quite rough."

"Our nearest neighbours, Glore, are in the churchyard and they won't complain. Hey, did you hear what that short, stocky chap who looked like a copper, said to me? You know, the bloke I mean, the one with the pretty little wife drinking Gold Label. Anyway, he wanted to know if me guns were loaded. I told him not to be so bloody daft. I'm hardly likely to carry loaded weapons and neither are my patrons. I told him to read the posters on the wall which clearly state all guns must be imitation or harmless replicas and I pointed out that if he looked close enough most folks had bloody plastic toy ones anyway."

"But your guns are real," said Gloria, exasperated, "and the posters only apply to our customers. Anyway, I think you'll find he's not a policeman but one of the chefs from the Hotel, who's renting the Old Police House, and the woman he was with wasn't his wife, she's a holiday maker staying at Cove Cottage."

Raymond snorted. "Don't be daft, Glore. I know what the chefs look like. One's short with a beard and a bald head and the other's a lanky bloke with freckles."

"And the man you mean was the short one with the beard," laughed Gloria. "Except he doesn't have a beard now because he's shaved it off and his bald patch was hidden beneath a cowboy hat. Anyway, it's an easy mistake to make, dear; thinking your guns might be loaded, that is, cos you've told him of your reputation as a first class marksman which is very well known, and of course the fact you are a prominent member of the *Good Shot Gun Club*."

"Yes, I suppose you're right," beamed Raymond, as his wife handed him his glass. "Before you sit down, Glore, be a love and go and get me best pistol. I fancy handling it just now. No need to bring the box, leave that and the ammunition behind cos I won't be doing any shooting. Not unless we have any intruders, ha ha ha."

Gloria nodded, placed her glass of Drambuie and milk on the table, and trudged along the passage between the bar and their living quarters.

As Raymond laid back his head, he heard the sound of the side door opening.

"Is that you, Colin?' he called, without leaving his seat, knowing his younger son was due home anytime from visiting family and friends in Yorkshire.

"Yeah, where are you, still in the bar?" answered a voice from the hallway.

Before Raymond had a chance to respond, Colin peeped around the bar door. "Course, I forgot, tonight was Wild West Night, wasn't it? How did it go?"

"Brilliant, as always," said Raymond. "Put your bags down, son, and pour yourself a drink, then come and tell me how everyone is back home."

Colin did as he was told and then sat beside his father. "Everyone's fine except Gran. She has a bit of a cold but it's nothing serious, and they all send their love. Where's Mum?"

Raymond put his feet up on the nearest stool. "She's just gone to get my gun. Did your Auntie Fay say whether or not she'll come and visit us this summer? I hope she will. I've not seen my little sister for over twelve months now."

"She said it all depends on..."

They heard a scream, followed by the clicking of heels on the hard floor of the passage. Gloria rushed in, her face ashen, and stood before them shocked and trembling.

"It's gone Raymond," she panted, shaking her head in disbelief. "Your gun. Your best gun. It's gone, box, bullets, the lot."

Chapter Fifteen

Towards the end of July the schools broke up for the summer holiday and on the last day of term Ned returned to the School House grateful to have several weeks to recuperate before he needed to start thinking about the Christmas term.

"You know, Stell, it's really depressing to think that when I go back to school in September I'll be an old man of fifty. Fifty! It's crazy, because apart from a few creaking bones and the occasional bout of forgetfulness, I don't feel any different to what I did twenty years ago."

"And you don't look much different either, but I'm glad you've mentioned your birthday, because I was talking to your mum this morning and she thinks you ought to have a birthday party and I agree with her. What do you think?"

Ned groaned. "Really, at present, I feel too weary to even think about it and I certainly don't want to get involved with lots of preparation work and that sort of thing. I'd like to give my poor old brain a rest first and have a few days with absolutely nothing to do or think about."

"But, Ned, you needn't think about or do anything. If you give it the okay then we'll do all the planning and so forth. Anyway, Elizabeth will be home soon, so that'll be something else to celebrate and I know she'd love to be involved with the arrangements. So do we have your blessing?"

Ned nodded. "Yes, of course, if that's what you want. Do as you please. But where will we have it? Here? I certainly don't want it at the Inn."

"Well, I was thinking perhaps we might hire the function room at the Hotel. That way we can invite lots of people and make it a really big do."

"Good grief, that'll cost a pretty penny, won't it?"

Stella shrugged her shoulders. "Don't know, but I'm sure whatever it costs it will be worth every penny."

"Okay, if that's what you really want, then go for it, but please make the event an open invitation to everyone and play down the emphasis on my birthday. I don't want anyone missed out and if we're not sticking to just family and close friends then that's likely to happen if invitations are sent out."

Beaming, Stella gleefully clasped her hands. "Brilliant, we'll do that then. Now while you put your feet up and rest, I'll just run round to Rose Cottage to tell your mum the good news and then I'll ring Rose. They'll both be thrilled to bits."

"I think you should go to the police and tell them your gun's been stolen," said Gloria Withers to her husband as they drank tea in the kitchen of the Inn. "It's been gone for over a week now and I can't sleep properly at night for worrying about who might have it. What if someone gets shot with it or it's used to rob a bank?"

"Don't be daft, Glore," scoffed Raymond. "You watch too many silly films. Whoever nicked it did so because they were in awe of me. Either that or they were jealous of my shootin' skills and thought without a gun I'd be snookered. Silly sods! It's pretty obvious a first class shot like me would have more than one pistol. Blimey, there are enough of the old beauties on the wretched beams alone to show that's the case. But to keep you happy, next time we have a Wild West Night I'll get our boys to look closely at our patrons' pieces. Subtle like, cos I reckon whoever nicked it did so on the last Wild West Night while he were here enjoying our hospitality. Cheeky sod! And without doubt, I also reckon he'll be back."

Gloria sighed deeply. "I suppose you're right because you didn't exactly keep its whereabouts a secret, did you? But I don't think whoever took it would be daft enough to ever set foot in here with it, and I think you ought to be more careful in future and keep all your guns that have ammunition under lock and key."

"Alright, I'll do that just to keep you happy," said Raymond, standing up and placing his empty mug on the draining board. "It'll be for the best anyway, because I forgot to tell you my little sister, Fay, is coming to stay for a while with the kids next month and we don't want her little treasures hurt, do we? They're a smashing couple of lads. They remind me of me when I was a boy."

"Oh, that'll be nice," said Gloria, a marked lack of enthusiasm. "Will Nigel be coming too?"

"No, her hubby can't get time off work, that's why Fay's coming to us, so that we'll be able to give her a hand looking after the kids. You'll like that, love, won't you? It'll be like having Roger and Colin as nippers again."

During the first week in August, Elizabeth returned home. Ned and Stella met her at Penzance Station, laden with luggage and thrilled to be back in her beloved Cornwall. Anne was still at work when Elizabeth arrived at the School House, but the two sisters made up for lost time later and sat chatting in the front room, past midnight and into the early hours.

"I feel as if I've been away for years," said Elizabeth, curled up in a fireside chair, "which is silly considering I came home for the Easter holidays. You must tell me all the latest news and then we'll get down to the nitty-gritty and discuss Dad's party."

"Ah, but there's a big difference between living in Cornwall and just popping home for a while," said Anne, admiring the bracelet Elizabeth had bought for her during her holiday. "You can't get back in the swing of things when it's just for two weeks, so in a way you must have felt a bit like an outsider every time you came home for a visit. Anyway, everything is much as it was at Easter, except Jamie and Linda are married now. The weather on their wedding day was really atrocious but then I told you that on the phone, didn't I?"

Elizabeth laughed. "Yes, and so did Mum. In fact Mum mentioned it in a letter as well because she wasn't sure whether or not she'd told me."

"Well, it was noteworthy, and although poor Linda was distraught at the time she was able to see the funny side afterwards."

"Good, and I'm looking forward to seeing the wedding pictures taken by your darling Danny."

Blushing, Anne ignored her sister's remark. "Right, now what else do I have to tell you? Let me think. I know, I'll run through everyone's news one by one. We'll start with Jane who is still working in the shoe shop. She doesn't have a boyfriend at present cos she found out, Stu, her last one, was a druggy. His unpredictable moods frightened her and now she's a bit wary of all males but I think it will soon pass."

"Poor Jane, but I'm not surprised. I didn't think much of Stu when she introduced me to him last Christmas. He seemed in a world of his own half the time."

"Hmm, absolutely, I thought the same. Anyway, Matthew next. He's still fishing as crew with Ron Trevelyan over at Polquillick." Anne giggled. "Would you believe, he has a motor bike now and we often hear him go flying down the road."

Elizabeth shuddered. "Ugh, that's terrible. I hate motor bikes. What happened to his dreams of owning a flashy car?"

"Well, he's a bit young for that yet; he's still only eighteen and I think you'll find it was Graham who said he wanted to have a flashy car, wasn't it? It doesn't matter anyway. Matthew does have a girlfriend though; she's Ron Trevelyan's daughter, but I don't think it's anything serious and they've only been going out for a month or so."

"I should hope it's not serious," said Elizabeth. "Eighteen is far too young to be thinking of settling down. Too young for a bloke anyway. What about the others?"

"Diane's still working for the Bristol and West Building Society, but Graham's jacked in his job at the travel agents and is now working as a trainee estate agent with Pennard and Rowe and he loves it, but he doesn't go out much as he's saving every penny he can because he's obsessed with the notion he must buy a house. He's even started to work at the Inn for a few nights each week to earn some extra money."

"But he's only nineteen," said Elizabeth, amazed. "Whatever makes him think he needs to buy a house? Does he have a girlfriend?"

Anne threw back her head and laughed. "No, he can't afford one."

Elizabeth tut-tutted and shook her head. "Dear, dear, and the others?"

"Well, Susan's still doing her office job in town, but she also works at the Hotel during the weekends and for a few evenings too cos she's saving up to buy a car. Did I tell you she passed her test?

Well, she has anyway, must be a couple of months ago now and first time too."

"Oh no, I really must start learning to drive soon. I can't believe I'm getting left behind by my juniors. Have you got a car yet?"

Anne shook her head. "No, there doesn't really seem much point when I work in Trengillion and can walk. I keep my hand in though and Dad has put me on his insurance so I drive the Escort if I need to go anywhere."

"Good, that's handy, so you can chauffeur me around if needs be. What about Tony and John, and the boys from the Inn. Any change there?"

"No, things are just as before. John's still working for Dave Richardson. Tony's still on his granddad's farm. Colin's still working as a mechanic, and Roger's still an electrician."

"Ah, but what about girlfriends?" asked Elizabeth. "They can't all be foot loose and fancy free, surely."

Anne laughed. "Oh, but they are, cos like all the other blokes around here, they're besotted with Suzie Pilkington. Suzie is everything we always wanted to be. You know, very, very pretty, slim, long legs, gorgeous hair even though it's red and she's brainy too."

"Ugh," said Elizabeth, pulling a most unflattering face, "I don't like the sound of her. Who the devil is she?"

"Thankfully, she's one of the students so she'll be gone in September, but actually it's quite entertaining to watch blokes drooling over her and it's not just local lads and fellow students; Susan told me, some of the Hotel's guests have been reprimanded by their wives for behaving badly when she's waited on their tables. Anyway, you'll see everyone soon as they'll all be at Dad's party, even the students, cos we've invited everyone."

"What even Lily and Greg, are they coming down?" asked Elizabeth, eagerly.

"Lily is. She's coming down for the week, but I'm sorry to disappoint you, Liz; Greg can't make it cos he'll be away then. He and Jemima are going on holiday. Lily tells me they're off to Spain to get engaged. I think it's really romantic, but I don't expect you'll feel the same, will you? Jemima's dad has a holiday home there with a huge balcony that overlooks the beach."

"Oh," whispered Elizabeth, feeling light-headed and dizzy. "So, tell me about the party. What are the plans?"

"It's going to be brilliant," said Anne, with unbridled enthusiasm. "You already know it's to be at the Hotel, don't you? Well, we've decided to make it fancy dress too, but we want it to be in keeping with the Hotel so we've decided on a Victorian theme. It was my idea, as you know I really liked it when the Victorian look was fashionable a few years back and I still have my granny shoes. What do you think? Mum and Gran both like the idea."

"Oh yes, "said Elizabeth, trying to suppress the pain brought on by hearing of Greg's impending engagement. "That sounds really good. I was wondering what to wear, but now I can wear my long black skirt and I'll only need to find a high neck white blouse."

"Mum's got several," said Anne, "and loads of brooches too. She even has a cameo one, cos Gran bought it for her birthday, but of course she'll be wearing that."

Chapter Sixteen

The residents of Trengillion were not the only ones looking forward to Ned's party. Mary Cottingham and Heather Jarrams, delighted that their hotel had been chosen as the venue, were both very enthusiastic, for the occasion would make a very pleasant change from the usual day-to-day routine of running a hotel. They were also very excited about the function room's décor and insisted that that aspect of the party be left solely to them, hence, they spent much of their spare time rummaging through junk shops looking for suitable accessories, ostentatious ornaments and thick curtains and fabrics which could be passed off as Victorian tablecloths. They even put an advertisement in the local newspaper asking for the loan of Aspidistra plants, real or artificial.

The students also, looked forward to the event, although for Suzie Pilkington and Poncey Pete the party had very little appeal for it was their evening to work, and although they would be at the party it would be in the capacity as waiting staff and they would be required to serve drinks and help with the food for the early part of the evening.

Heather informed all the staff working that evening that their costumes would be provided. The girls were to be dressed as maids and the boys, footmen. Suzie was not impressed.

"It's not fair," she said, late one night, throwing herself into a chair in the sitting room shared by the live-in students. "I don't want to dress as a dreary maid; I want to wear something glamorous. Black and white is so dowdy and Victorian maids used to wear those silly lacy hats, didn't they?"

"But you need to wear something subtle," teased Jack. "Bright colours would most likely clash with your red hair. Having said that, if you really crave colour you could always brighten up your outfit with a feather duster."

"Don't be so impertinent," screamed Suzie, throwing a cushion with perfect aim. "It's alright for you, you can wear anything you like or be anyone you like." A small cloud of dust rose as she thumped the arm of her chair. "In fact your horrid personality would very much suit that of a ghastly historical person such as Jack the Ripper?"

"Hey, that's a good idea, Suzie," said Jack, sitting forward in his chair and making light of her caustic comment. "Do you think you could nick me a knife from the kitchen, Crystal? When the Pots have their backs turned, of course?"

Crystal blushed; she knew Jack was only joking, but was unsure how to respond without sounding foolish.

Malcolm, however, saved her from embarrassment. "I could probably help you out there, Jack. Mum and Dad both work for a Repertory Theatre so they have access to all sorts of costumes. I've already got them to look me out something authentic and I'm sure they'd have something Ripper-like tucked away for you somewhere."

"Brilliant, things are really looking up," said Jack, slapping together his hands. "Thanks, Malc, you'll save me a lot of hassle if you can do that. I must confess, I don't have much imagination when it comes to dressing up. I did for a while think about being some chap called Gorran who was shot dead here, but I soon realised no-one would know who I was meant to be and I've not the foggiest idea what he looked like anyway."

"Gorran," said Dilys, wrinkling her nose. "Who the devil's he?"

Jack laughed. "Some bloke who used to live here donkey's years ago. Apparently he got some poor bird called Florrie Ham up the duff and her old man shot him dead."

"That's horrible," said Suzie, repelled by his jollity. "You're heartless, Jack. I can't see why you're laughing."

"Calm down. It happened a long time ago, sweetheart," said Jack, still hurt by her earlier put-down.

"I'm not your sweetheart," snapped Suzie, her face reddening with anger. "I never have been and never shall be."

"Does anyone else need help with a costume?" asked Malcolm, glancing around the room, attempting to alleviate the tension. "If you do just say the word and then my folks can send everything down in one big parcel."

Crystal and Dilys both asked for help, but as they had no idea what or who they wanted to be they said the choice could be made by Malcolm's parents. Malcolm therefore reached for a piece of paper and took down the approximate sizes of his fellow students.

"Get something for Grev too," said Crystal. "I heard him saying earlier he doesn't know what to wear."

Malcolm tapped the end of the pen against his teeth. "Okay, but what size do you reckon he is? I really ought to measure him. Where is he, anyway?"

"He said he was having an early night," said Crystal. "But I should think he's about the same as Jack. It doesn't matter too much though, does it? I mean, a fancy dress costume doesn't need to be a perfect fit and a safety pin here and there can put right any obvious discrepancies."

"Hmm, no, I suppose not," Malcolm said, duplicating Jack's measurements on his sheet of paper. When all names and statistics were recorded, he left the room to use the phone in the lounge bar.

Two days before the party, Ned's best friend of many years, George, arrived with his wife, Rose, by car from London.

Ned who was in the front garden when the car pulled up, was shocked when George stepped from the driver's seat and onto the pavement. "What the! Jet black hair! Whatever happened to subtle colouring?"

George growled as he closed the car door. "I was ordered to dye it like this for your wretched party. I look a right donkey. Thank goodness it'll have washed out by the time I go back to school."

"I don't know, I think it looks rather fetching," smiled Stella, who on hearing voices left the house to greet the guests. "Almost like having young George back."

"Except for the wrinkles," said Ned, tugging at his friend's cheek. "They're a bit of a giveaway. Anyway, it's great to see you both and we're delighted you could make it."

Stella linked arms with Rose and both returned indoors to put on the kettle leaving Ned and George to unload the luggage.

"Blimey, I thought you were only staying for the weekend," said Ned, as George opened up the boot. "You've enough luggage here for a month."

"Humph, well, the large case which you're about to pick up is full of nothing other than our costumes for your party. Rose has been flapping around for days to make sure everything will be perfect. She loves anything to do with period costume. Actually, I think she missed her vocation and should have worked in the theatre or for television. Personally, I would have preferred a pair of shorts, flip-flops and a T shirt but I take it that fancy dress was your Anne's idea."

"Yes it was. Sorry. I made the big mistake of leaving everything up to the females. Still, it could be a laugh, although it's far too hot for dressing up."

Desmond, work colleague of Jamie Stevens and best man at his wedding, was asked by Stella if he would operate the disco for Ned's party. Desmond happily agreed, especially as he would be required to play both music hall favourites and contemporary music, the mixture of which greatly appealed to him. He also decided to dress up, even though Stella had said he must not feel obliged to, and after consulting his wife, they decided to conjure up an outfit similar to that worn by Leonard Sachs on the television's old time music hall show *The Good Old Days.*

"Do I really have to wear this ridiculous hat?" groaned Ned, as he entered the sitting room of the School House, where his wife, two daughters and Rose were helping each other with chokers and hair ornaments.

Stella glanced over her shoulder. "Oh, but Darling, you look extremely handsome, and you'll be able to take off the hat once we're inside, which is a shame really."

"But I look such a prat," moaned Ned, glancing into the mirror. "I should be exempt from dressing up since it's my birthday. Anyway, I'll have to take the wretched hat off to drive otherwise there won't be enough headroom in the car, so it's hardly worth the bother."

"Ned, where's your party spirit?" asked Stella, a little dismayed by his lack of enthusiasm. "The top hat looks splendid and you look a real gent. Now where are your gloves and the cane?"

He pulled a pair of white gloves from the pocket of his coat and held them up for Stella to see. "Here, and I left the cane upstairs.

George had it last time I saw it and he was twirling it round like a majorette."

Rose giggled. "That'll be because he's intrigued as to how the girls do it. Our neighbour's daughter is a majorette, you see, and she makes it look so easy."

Stella tut-tutted. "Well, go back upstairs, Ned, and see if you can get it off him. I want to take a picture of you in your complete attire along with our lovely daughters before we go, and one of Rose and George too. In fact I think I'll take the camera with me as there could well be some very interesting spectacles this evening."

"And chivvy George up while you're up there," said Rose, slipping on her shoes. "He's taking far too long to get ready, even longer than me."

"Alright, but he was still in his dressing gown when I last saw him with my cane. What's he dressing as anyway? He wouldn't tell me."

Rose grinned. "Oh, you'll soon see. All I'll say is his outfit is similar to yours, Ned, but he has a cape and the difference will be in his make-up."

"Make-up," spluttered Ned, as he left the room for the stairs. "Thank Goodness I don't have to wear make-up. I hate dressing up as it is, and this get-up's most uncomfortable, but make-up would be taking it a step too far."

However, when George made a grand entrance into the front room of the School House dressed as Count Dracula, Ned changed his tune.

"Why didn't I think of that?" said Ned, tapping his best friend's fangs. "You look bloody brilliant, George."

Much to Ned's surprise, everyone in the Hotel's large function room was dressed to the nines, even the staff, and the décor made him feel quite humble.

"You really shouldn't have gone to all this trouble," he said, as they were greeted by Heather and Mary.

Mary beamed with pride. "If a job's worth doing, then it's worth doing well. That's our motto, isn't it, Heather?"

Heather nodded.

"Mine too, actually," agreed Ned.

"Anyway," said Heather, delighted with his approval, "it was too good an opportunity to miss, doing the place up, I mean. We've really enjoyed it and we've been overwhelmed with offers of Aspidistra plants. I didn't think people kept them these days, but we've managed to get a staggering eight."

Bob Jarrams, however, did not share his wife's euphoria. "Damned starched collar," he groaned. "God only knows where Heather dug this up. I reckon my neck will be red raw by the end of the evening."

"Ah, I drew the line there," said Ned, touching the collar of his polyester cotton shirt. "I said I'd wear a waistcoat, cravat and all the other paraphernalia but there has to be a limit when it comes to discomfort."

"Hmm, I wish I'd put my foot down too. God, this is uncomfortable. No wonder the Victorians were a grouchy lot."

Not all the men wore gentlemen's outfits, many opted for simpler options and dressed as paupers, yokels and street urchins. The women, however, chose as glamorous an outfit as their financial resources would allow, for all aspired to be the belle of the ball; consequently, the room was a sea of elaborate hairdos, bonnets and mob caps, and dress jewellery sparkled from every corner in the light of the crystal chandeliers.

Anne was speechless when she saw the turnout. "Where on earth did they all get their costumes from?" she asked Elizabeth, glass of punch in hand and equally impressed. "If it was the dress hire shop in town then their clothes racks must be empty. Having said that, I know Gran's been helping lots of people out. All the same this is quite overwhelming, isn't it?"

Elizabeth thoughtfully cast her eyes around the room. "Hmm, it is, but I don't know half the people here: either that or I don't recognise them."

Anne giggled. "Well, you must remember that chap over there carrying the tray of champagne glasses."

Elizabeth felt the colour rise on her face as she spotted the waiter in question. "Christ! It's Poncey Pete. You could've warned me he was back, Anne. Oh, this is too embarrassing!"

"Don't worry, Liz, he's forgotten all about you and last year's little dalliance. He's after Suzie now like all the rest."

"Humph! So where is this beautiful Suzie? I take it she'll be here."

"She should be because she's working tonight. Dilys told me she's really brassed-off because all the staff working are to dress as maids. The females, that is. The chaps are dressed as footmen."

Anne glanced around the room. "Ah, there she is. Look, over by the fireplace, with a tray of canapés. The chap she has her back to, dressed as Jack the Ripper, is Jack Smeaton, he's one of our students too."

"Hmm, he's quite dishy, but I find the blood stained shirt a bit of a turnoff." Elizabeth drained her last drop of punch and placed the empty glass on a nearby table. "Is Steve Penhaligon coming? Sue was telling me she's got him lined up as her next fella."

Anne shook her head. "No, sadly not. It's Mrs Penhaligon's birthday this weekend too and Steve had already planned to take her away for a couple of days when Dad's party first cropped up. I think it's really nice the way he looks after his widowed mum, especially since Alice married that up-country bloke and left the area."

"Could be a problem for Sue though. His mum might not want him to have a girlfriend if it's likely to lead to him leaving Trengillion like Alice."

"Oh no, Liz, it's not a bit like that. You weren't around when Alice got married, I know, but her mum was the one who pushed her into it. She says she wants all her children to settle down and be happy. She's not at all selfish, really, she's not. It's a pity she's never remarried herself though, cos she was no age when her poor Denzil drowned."

"Yeah, I remember Dad saying that a few years back. We must look out for an eligible husband for her: someone kind and considerate."

"Come on, let's get another drink and then I'll introduce you to Dilys and Crystal. They're the two girls over by the door dressed as Queen Victoria and Florence Nightingale."

Molly and the major hired a taxi to take them to the party along with their next door neighbours, Jim and Doris Hughes. The major had considered driving himself but as it was inevitable he would have a drink or two and as no-one else in his party held a driving licence, he decided a taxi was the best option.

"I feel we should be arriving by coach and horses," said Molly, as the taxi pulled up at the front of the Hotel and the sound of music drifted through the tall open windows of the function room. "I almost feel as though I am back in Victorian times. It's most eerie."

They climbed the steps and entered the Hotel through the large double doors whereupon they were shown into the function room by Eric the porter, enjoying every minute of the experience.

"I think," said Molly, as she entered the room and drank in the décor, turn out and costumes, "that this must be the venue for our Silver Wedding Anniversary next year. What do you say, Ben? Wouldn't it be splendid? We'd have to have a different theme though, the forties perhaps and wartime or even the roaring twenties. Oh, life is wonderful at present. I'm just so happy."

"Gertie, you don't have a drink, let me get you one," said Ned, as he mingled with the guests having returned the much-hated top hat to the back seat of his car along with gloves and cane.

Gertie gasped. "Oh no, I can't have another; too many calories. I had a tonic water earlier so that's enough for one day."

"What!" Ned spluttered, aghast. "For heaven's sake, Gertie, it's my birthday. I insist you have a drink and enjoy yourself, you look as miserable as sin."

"But I'm on a diet, Ned. I can't have more than twelve hundred calories a day."

"Says who?" asked Ned, exasperated. "Come on, Gert, let your hair down. I mean that metaphorically of course, your hair looks really pretty swept up in that style."

"But I don't think you realise how important it is to me to lose weight. I hate being round like a barrel and I long to be slim."

Ned slipped his arms around her waist. "Gert, you wouldn't be you if you were skinny. We all love you the way you are, the way you've always been. It's not as if you're unfit or unhealthy and need to lose weight for medical reasons, with you it's pure vanity. But I can say this with all sincerity, it's the Gertie inside that matters and that Gertie, our Gertie, is presently being smothered by a misguided crack-pot, obsessed with dieting."

Gertie released herself from his grasp and looked at her reflection in the huge gilt framed mirror hanging between two windows. Frowning, she opened her mouth to speak but then quickly changed her mind. Poncey Pete stood not far away offering guests chicken and mushroom vol-u-vents from a silver platter and they smelt tantalisingly good. Ned noted her hesitance and tilted his head to one side in a questioning manner. Gertie looked in the mirror again and gradually the frown vanished from her face and her painted red lips slowly curled into a smile.

Ned spoke. "A penny for your thoughts, Gert."

Gertie's eyes drifted from her reflection in the mirror towards Pete and the platter as both weaved amongst the guests. Her face broke into a broad grin. She took Ned's hand and squeezed it gently. "I don't know what it is about you, Ned, but I think you've convinced me. Percy and the boys have moaned about my diet from the very first day, and I suppose, to be fair, it's because it affects their lives, which I confess makes me very selfish. You're right, Ned. Life's too short to worry about my weight, and counting calories does make me unhappy. And so now, thanks to you, I can say my diet's well and truly binned."

Ned, taken back and amazed by his influence, gave the thumbs-up sign. "That's my girl, and good riddance to it."

Gertie giggled, unable to wipe the smile from her face. "Oh, it's ridiculous, I feel as though a huge weight has been lifted from my mind. It's brilliant, I can enjoy myself again."

She grabbed Ned by the shoulders and kissed him. "Thank you so much. Now while I snatch myself a vol-au-vent or two, Ned, I'll take up your offer of a drink, if it still stands, and have a sweet Martini with ice and a generous splash of sugary lemonade?"

When returning from the Gents, George came face to face with Jack the Ripper. Touching the fake blood on his cape, George laughed. "Seems you and I are in a similar line of business."

Jack grinned. "Yeah, looks like it. I didn't realise dressing up could be so much fun. I think this outfit was a great idea, not that it was me who thought of it."

"Hmm, I can agree with you there to a point, about dressing up, that is."

"You're not too keen."

"Not really, but then with me it's the teeth. I can't talk properly while wearing them, or drink either for that matter."

"So take them out."

George did as suggested and dropped the false, blood-stained, plastic fangs into the pocket of his waistcoat. "That's better. So how come you know the birthday boy? I don't think I've seen you around before."

"That's because I'm not local. I'm a student just down for the summer and I'm working here at the Hotel."

"Really. And are you enjoying it?"

Jack nodded. "Yeah, I work in the grounds which is right up my street. How about you. Are you from round here?"

George shook his head. "No, I live in London. We're just here for the weekend. The wife and I, that is. We came down especially for Ned's party. I wish we could stay longer but Rose has to get back for work on Monday because a colleague is in hospital and so they're a bit pushed."

"I see, and so Ned must be the birthday guy."

"Yeah, that's right. I've known him for years. We used to teach at the same school before he met Stella and moved down here."

Jack glanced around the room. "Which one is he? I know he's Anne's old man but I haven't a clue what he looks like."

"Hey, less of the old, he's younger than me."

Jack laughed. "Sorry, but you know what I mean."

"Yes, of course, that's him over by the window dressed like a Victorian gent."

Jack nodded. "I see him."

George leaned his arm on the white marble fireplace. "Impressive place this. Too big for a house though. I'm glad it now has a more useful purpose."

Jack nodded. "Yes, and I hear it has quite a history."

"Hmm, I've heard rumours over the years. Mind you, I expect much of it is over exaggerated. And as for that bloke in Canada who inherited this lot, what a lucky sod he is. He must be loaded now after selling it all off."

Rose appeared just as Jack opened his mouth to reply. "There you are George. I've been looking everywhere for you. "Time for a dance, I think."

"Whoops, sorry love." He turned to Jack. "Nice to have met you. I hope you enjoy the rest of the summer."

"Did you by any chance watch the cricket from Lords today?" Frank Newton asked the major after the two men had bumped into each other in the vestibule. "It was quite amusing."

"A bit," said the major, "but we had to pop into town so I didn't see it all. What was it that amused you?"

"Rain, would you believe. Rain stopped play for about fifteen minutes and it got the crowds on their feet cheering. It just seemed so funny. I mean, usually rain causes folks to groan when it stops play like that, but I reckon if there'd been a downpour today then instead of putting up brollies they'd have been dancing in the stalls."

"That's what I like about us British," said the major, nodding with pride. "We have a good sense of humour and there's a lot to be said for that. Mind you, I don't think I could sit out in the sun all day watching the cricket this year, it's far too hot even in Cornwall and it's always a damn sight worse in the cities, especially London."

Frank loosened the collar of his shirt. "I agree with you there. It's even too hot to sit in the garden for long in the bloomin' shade. I don't think there will be any record breaking veg at the village show this year either. My marrows are only half the size they were this time last year in spite of washing up water being poured on them umpteen times a day."

"God, I'm boiling hot," moaned Grev to Anne. "I mean it was awfully kind of Malc to get me this costume, and Sherlock Holmes is a really great idea, but it's ever so thick and I'm sweltering."

"Well, I think you can take off the caped coat and deer stalker now," smiled Anne, noting the beads of perspiration on his brow. "I see lots of men are losing their outer garments, some have even rolled up their sleeves. Tut, tut, it seems that Victorian etiquette isn't part of the package." Anne glanced around the room. "Have you seen my sister, Grev? I seem to have lost her and I've a feeling she's had one too many glasses of punch."

"Is that the pretty dark haired girl you were with earlier?" asked Grev, fanning his face with the hat on its removal. "If it is, I saw her a while back talking to your friend Susan and I must admit, she did look a bit sloshed."

"Oh, God, that sounds like Liz. Thanks, Grev, I'd better go and find her."

Anne found Elizabeth stretched out on the bottom step of the grand staircase quietly singing *Plaisir d'amour*.

"Elizabeth, what on earth are you doing out here?" she cried, taking her sister's arm. "Goodness only knows what the Hotel guests will have thought should any of them have had the misfortune to have seen you. Come on, back in with the rest of us."

Elizabeth raised her head. "But I can't, I'm waiting for the love of my life. I saw him, Anne, I really did. There was a sudden flash of light which dazzled me and when I looked up I saw him standing by the door in Dad's party room and he smiled at me and blew me a kiss. But then clumsy Queen Victoria knocked into me and I lost my balance and when I looked up he'd gone. That's why I'm out here. He must have slipped out the door and gone up these stairs, but I shall stay here until he returns and whisks me away on his shining white horse."

"A flash of light and a shining white horse!" muttered Anne. "Oh dear, Liz, what have you been drinking? No-one from the party would have reason to go up these stairs anyway because they only lead to the guests' rooms and my bosses' living quarters. Really, you are a nightmare. Come on, get up and then you can tell me what the god of your idolatry looked like?"

"I can tell you now, Anne. He's young and handsome. His hair is dark and he's wearing a frock coat and a burgundy waistcoat, and has a matching cravat around his lovely neck," said Elizabeth, dreamily.

"That sounds like Malcolm Barker," laughed Anne, relieved that her sister had not been hallucinating. "He's one of the students. Come on, I'll introduce you."

"One of the students!" gasped Elizabeth, part rising. "Oh no, that's terrible because it means he'll leave me in September."

"Oh God, please don't say we might have a re-run of last year. Remember that, Liz? You spent the first half of your summer holiday chasing Poncey Pete and the second half trying to avoid him."

Elizabeth stood, unsteadily. "But I didn't know he was going to be such a big-head, did I? Malccy Walccy's not a big-head, is he?"

"No, he's really nice," smiled Anne, leading her sister back into the function room. "He's the chap who got the students their costumes. His parents are both actors and members of a repertory theatre group."

Elizabeth, patted her sister lovingly on the back. "Wow! Lead the way, Annie. I'm not a bit bothered really about Greg and Jemima Puddleduck getting engaged. She can have him cos I love lovely Malcolm."

Malcolm Barker was genuinely delighted and amused to be introduced to the inebriated Elizabeth and within minutes of their meeting the two were smooching together on the dance floor.

"I don't believe it," said Susan to Anne, as they watched from the side-lines. "Liz has only been home ten minutes and she's landed herself a fella already."

The heat, the loud music and several glasses of gin and tonic caused Molly to feel in need of fresh air and peace and quiet, hence, as the major chatted to Frank about the Government's hurriedly passed through Drought Bill and the appointment of Denis Howell, Sports Minister, to take charge of said Bill, Molly slipped out through the front door of the Hotel and wandered around to the back of the building and the gardens beyond where she sat on a bench illuminated by light shining from the dining room windows.

The scent of the roses and tiny white flowers of jasmine twisting through the branches of a lantern tree, filled the night air and helped soothe her aching head. Molly closed her eyes, happy in her solidarity, where the only sound was the distant din of music from Ned's party and the high pitched squeak of crickets in the shrubbery.

From the conservatory door on the side of the Hotel, a figure merged into the darkness. Molly watched as it walked down the path and into the shadows where the only sign of life was the red glow from the end of a cigarette. Molly felt a pang of envy. She had recently given up smoking and was proud that she had not succumbed to temptation and started again, but she had to admit there were times, such as when she'd had a drink, that the temptation was stronger than others, hence she was glad when the smoker returned indoors and left her in peace.

Molly sat for a while longer until she felt obliged to return indoors aware the major may have noticed her absence. She rose from the bench and crossed the garden towards the path, but as she walked along the area where the smoker had stood her foot kicked against something on the ground. Molly bent to look at the item. It was a Rothmans cigarette packet. Assuming it was empty, she tut-tutted and picked it up with intention of throwing it into a bin. But when she peeped inside and found one cigarette remained she realised the smoker had inadvertently dropped the packet and not discarded it as litter. Whilst still walking, Molly put her nose to the packet and took a deep breath. Rothmans was her favourite brand. Convinced no-one wound know, she removed the cigarette and placed it between her lips, but as she fumbled in her bag, hopeful of finding an old box of matches, she heard a voice call from the top of the steps.

"Ah, there you are, Moll," said the major. "I wondered where the devil you were. Are you alright?"

Molly quickly spat the cigarette into her open handbag and crushed the Rothmans packet in her hand.

"Sorry love. Just looking for a hankie." She smiled, while pretending to look through the contents of her bag. "I only popped out for a bit of fresh air, I didn't think you'd miss me."

"Well I did. Come on, young Desmond's playing some good old fashioned music, let's have a dance."

She climbed the steps and reached for his outstretched hand. "You know, Moll, when at first I couldn't find you I thought you'd probably nipped out for a crafty fag."

Molly laughed, sheepishly. "Well, I can honestly say, hand on heart, that I've not smoked once since the day I gave up, in spite of temptation."

As they entered the vestibule Jim Hughes spoke to the major, and Molly, aware that she needed to lose the cigarette and its packet, seized the opportunity and excused herself on the pretence she needed to powder her nose. She entered the Ladies and dropped the cigarette and packet into the waste paper bin with a sigh of relief, conscious that she had nearly been caught red handed. But as she turned to leave she noticed hand writing on the packet. With curiosity she retrieved it from the bin. Written in black ink was *Florrie Ham, Polquillick.*

Chapter Seventeen

"I think," said Dick Cottingham, as he and the family cleared away the Victorian décor and scattered debris following Ned's party, "that we ought to have a pond out the back. Young Elizabeth Stanley suggested it to me last night. She says that dip in the meadow would be the perfect spot. She's always liked it out there apparently cos as we know the village youngsters used to play in the grounds as kids. I think it's a great idea. I'm not talking about anything too huge, just something that will be a feature and somewhere where the guests can stroll in the evenings. We could have a couple of benches to sit on and we might even be able to have a fountain in it. What do you think?"

Heather nodded. "I think it's a brilliant idea, although if we have another summer like this one and last year's too for that matter then I think we'd probably have guests jumping in."

"Perhaps we ought to have a swimming pool instead, right out the back by the terrace," said Bob, who was fond of swimming and tired of the heat.

Dick folded up the step-ladder and leaned it against the wall. "Well, that would be nice, but the trouble is it'd be unused for best part of the year and then of course, in the autumn we'd have trouble with falling leaves. What's more, constructing it would be a far more expensive than a pond and we'd no doubt need planning permission too."

Mary agreed. "It would have to be done in the depths of winter as well, because guests wouldn't take too kindly to having a building site out by the back terrace if it was done in the holiday season."

Bob laughed. "You're both right, of course. It was just wishful thinking on my part. I'll have to make do with the sea instead."

Heather picked up a broom and began to sweep up party poppers and litter from the floor. "Come on everyone, let's get this mess cleared up and then we can take a walk down to the meadow and see what we think. It pays to strike while the iron's hot."

They left the Hotel through the newly constructed conservatory on the side of the building and walked around to the back, down the original flight of granite steps and onto the terrace. This led them to the rectangular lawned area where benches were symmetrically placed on all four corners of the grass, each overhung with scented climbers, twisting through the lattice slats of rustic wooden arbours.

The lawns ended with a steep bank which edged the breathtakingly beautiful meadow - a blaze of colour in summer, where buttercups, scarlet poppies and ox eyed daisies nodded in the gentle breeze amidst long, waving grass.

Mary closed her eyes. "I think," she said, dreamily, "that it would be a shame to have a fountain, because although the sound of trickling water can be relaxing it would spoil the peace and tranquillity here where the only sound is the wind."

Heather nodded. "I agree. It would also negate the need of electricity here and keep the cost down."

Bob scratched his head. "Hmm, I'm happy either way. Filling it with water when it's done will be a bit of a problem though. I mean, this hosepipe ban's likely to last for a good while yet and if we're going to rely on rain water to do the job we might be in for a very long wait."

Mary laughed. "Oh, come on, Bob, we all know once the rain starts it won't know when to stop. It'll be full by Christmas, you see."

"I wish I could share your optimism, Mary," said Heather, fanning her face with her hand. "But it feels to me like it'll never rain again. Good weather seems to draw more good weather."

They climbed down the bank and into the field. "I assume this is the spot Elizabeth meant," said Dick, approvingly. "In which case, the lass is right. I think it would be perfect."

Mary frowned. "I wonder why the bank exists. It's quite steep."

"They probably had animals here at one time," said Bob. "Sheep most likely, and the bank may have been a ha-ha to keep the beasts out of the gardens and away from the house. It was common practice on country estates at one time and of course negated the necessity for a fence which might spoil a view."

Mary nodded. "Of course, silly me."

"You're right though, the bank is steep," agreed Heather, "so I think we'll have to have a flight of steps constructed. I mean, we can't risk guests falling down the bank and getting hurt, can we?"

Dick shook his head. "Certainly not and steps would be a nice feature anyway." He turned to address other family members. "Right, so are we all in agreement that we'd like a pond here?"

The vote was unanimous.

Dick rubbed his hands. "Brilliant, I'll give Dave Richardson a bell when we get back indoors and see if he'd be interested in doing it, and if so, when he can get started. I don't know about you lot, but I feel this was a good morning's work and when it's done, the project will prove to be a big success."

On Monday afternoon, as Gertie slipped on her sandals prior to cycling up to Long Acre Farm to visit her parents and deliver her mother's birthday present, she remembered Percy had brought home two crabs that morning and to her dismay she had completely forgotten to cook them. Gertie cursed; she knew Percy would be back from Newlyn, where he and Peter had taken their shellfish to market, before she returned from her visit and he would not be pleased if the job was not done.

Whilst drumming her fingers on the kitchen work top, contemplating her options, Susan arrived home from work.

Gertie sprang forwards and gleefully clasped her daughter's hands. "Brilliant, you're just in time, Sue. Please be a dear and cook some crabs for me. I should've done it earlier but I completely forgot."

Susan tossed her handbag onto the table and groaned. "Oh, but Mum, I'm already sweltering hot. It was boiling in the office today and I just want to relax in a nice cool bath."

"Oh please, Sue, please. I really must go and see Grandma. I should have gone earlier but the day has just flown by and I've not been idle all the time. I did work for a couple of hours this morning."

"But cooking crabs makes the kitchen all smelly, hot and steamy."

"I know, but if you're hot anyway it won't make any difference, will it? You can cook the crabs and then have a bath." Gertie tilted her head to one side. "Please, Sue. I'll make a chocolate cake tomorrow if you do."

Susan raised her eyebrows. "Will it be iced with real chocolate?"

"Yes."

"Dairy milk?"

"Yes, two whole bars of it."

"Right, you're on. And tell Grandma and Granddad I send my love and that I'll pop up and see them soon."

"Thanks, love," said Gertie, picking up her mother's present and opening the kitchen door. "And don't forget when you have a bath that you must have no more than five inches of water. Government's orders."

From the back doorstep, Susan watched her mother disappear around the corner of the house wheeling her bicycle with the birthday present neatly tucked inside the basket attached to the handlebars. Susan then went indoors, kicked off her sandals and peeled off her tights which had stuck to her legs like a second skin. From the cupboard she pulled the largest saucepan and stood it on top of the cooker, she then went back outside. In the shade stood an old plastic bucket containing the crabs. With reluctance she picked up one in each hand and ran back inside, placed them in the saucepan and poured water from the cold tap. One of the crabs moved as the water splashed onto its shell. Susan wanted to cry. She hated cooking crabs. It seemed so inhumane to cook them whilst they still showed signs of life. Once they were immersed, she returned the saucepan to the stove, put on the lid and whilst waiting for the water to boil ran up to the bathroom to get her make-up remover.

Sitting at the kitchen table she removed every trace of make-up, leaving her face red from the heat and the rubbing of the cotton wool. To cool down she splashed cold water on her face which wet her sweaty hair further leaving it lack lustre and lank. She caught sight of herself in the mirror and laughed. The crab water reached boiling point and the water ran over the side of the saucepan. Susan jumped up, turned down the heat and looked at the clock. It was half past five, hence it would be ten to six before she could get into the bath. To kill some of the time she attempted to clean the cooker top where the water had spilled, but the heat burnt her fingers and the steam made her eyes run. She picked up the newspaper from the table and sat down on the back doorstep. As she was reading her horoscope there was a knock on the door. Susan tut-tutted. Tony had no doubt forgotten his key again and was too lazy to walk round to the back door. She threw the newspaper onto the table and walked down the hallway ready to reprimand her big brother, but to her horror it was not Tony on the doorstep; it was Steve Penhaligon holding up a lunchbox.

"Hi, John left this in the truck so I thought I'd better drop it in because he'll need it tomorrow."

Susan's heart sank. "Oh, yes, umm, thanks, err, where is John?" she mumbled, painfully aware of her hideous appearance and the unappealing smell of crabs drifting along the hallway from the kitchen on a draught from the back door.

"Dave's dropping him back. They went to the yard to drop off some wood, you see, and left me with the van. After they'd gone I saw John had left this on the seat." He passed the lunchbox to Susan.

"Oh, I see," she said, wondering how Steve managed to look cool in spite of the heat. "Thank you, I'll give it to him when he gets back."

"Good, I take it you're Sue. John's little sister. I'm Steve Penhaligon." He held out his hand for her to shake.

Susan subtly wiped her hand on her dress and took his hand. "Yes, I did recognise you. I've sorta seen you around."

"Yeah, I expect you have. I've seen you too. John said I should join him and his mates for a drink at the Badge tonight. Why don't you come along too?"

"Well, actually I'll be there anyway. With my friends, that is. We like to pop in on a Monday night because it's a bit quieter than the weekend."

"Brilliant, I'll see you later then. Bye."

Susan closed the door and ran back to the kitchen with a bounce in each step. She looked at the clock, it was ten minutes to six and the crabs were done. She switched off the cooker and drained the dirty, scummy water down the sink. She then ran up the stairs to pour her bath and plan her wardrobe, for she wanted to look her very best for Steve Penhaligon.

That evening as Ned and Stella sat in the front room of the School House watching television, the telephone in the hallway rang.

Ned dragged himself up from the chair. "I'll get it, although I expect it'll be for one of the girls."

However, the call was for neither of the girls. It was Ned's step mother.

"Marilyn," said Ned, surprised, for she had never rung before, "how nice to hear from you. Is everything alright?"

There was a pause and then Marilyn spoke, her voice was soft and her words faltered on the other end of the line. "Well, no actually it's not and that's why I'm ringing."

Ned felt a sudden chill and alarm bells rang in his ears. "Dad. Is it Dad? Is he alright?"

He heard a distant, muffled sob before she answered, her voice trembling with every word she spoke. "No, he's not. He's gone, Ned. He had a heart attack this evening and was dead by the time the ambulance arrived. I don't understand it. He was fit and healthy for his age and he hadn't complained about feeling unwell." Her voice faded away until it was scarcely audible. "I must go. I'm too choked to speak now. So sorry, Ned. I'll ring you back when I feel more composed."

"Yes, yes, of course. Poor Dad," mumbled Ned, feeling tears prickle the backs of his own eyes. "Is there someone with you? You shouldn't be on your own right now."

"Yes, Jenny, my best friend's here. Give me a couple of hours, Ned, and then I'll ring you again."

Ned put down the phone and went back into the front room to relay the news to Stella. He then put on his jacket and walked round to Rose Cottage in a daze to tell his mother that Michael, her first husband, had died.

Molly received the news of Michael's death with surprising calm, and as the news sank in she told of the time when she had first met him and spoke each word with unbridled affection. For during the many years since they had first parted and battled through a painful divorce, she had learned to admit that the faults in their tempestuous marriage were not entirely due to Michael's unreasonable behaviour, and that she herself had without question helped fuel the fires that had destroyed their union, although at the time she believed she had done no wrong.

"I shall write to Marilyn," said Molly, surprised by her own composure. "It's too late to say I'm sorry to your father but it's not too late to make amends with her. Isn't it silly how it takes the death of someone to make you admit the truth? Poor Michael, I hope he didn't suffer."

"It's very magnanimous of you to say so, Mum," said Ned, "but don't be too hard on yourself. Dad found happiness with Marilyn before your marriage ended, and you mustn't forget you spent many lonely years in Clacton before you met the major."

The major rose and clasped Molly's hands. "Cry if it'll make you feel better, Moll, I'll not be offended. It's obvious you must have loved him once or you'd never have married him."

"No, I won't cry," whispered Molly, her smile weak. "Too much water has passed under the bridge. Poor Marilyn, she has no-one now. It's such a shame she never had children. I trust you'll be going to the funeral, Ned."

"Of course, and if you're okay I'd better get back cos Marilyn's going to ring again. I'll come and see you in the morning when I have more news."

Deep down, Molly knew Ned telling her not to punish herself was right, and she had forgiven Michael within a year of marrying the major. Her anguish, nevertheless, was caused by knowing she had never told her erstwhile husband she no longer bore a grudge and it grieved her that he was going to his grave never knowing of her penitence.

During the night she awoke having clearly seen Michael in a vivid dream, where both had said sorry for the grief they had caused one another in years gone by. Warmed by her exoneration, Molly slipped from her bed and from the window looked up towards the clear, dark sky and the last quarter of the moon shining above Trengillion. She smiled as a shooting star sped through the sky. "A soul," she whispered, "on its way to heaven." As she gently waved her hand, she realised that seeing Michael had not been a dream, but that he had come in spirit to say goodbye. With tears misting her eyes she crept downstairs, curled up on the settee and cried until she could cry no more.

Chapter Eighteen

On Monday afternoon, Raymond Withers' sister, Fay Walker, arrived at the Sherriff's Badge Inn along with her two children Johnny aged ten and Jimmy aged eight. Raymond met them at the door and promptly picked up his two young curly headed nephews, one under each arm, and spun them around.

"How are my two favourite deputies?" he asked, putting them down on the floor, where they staggered, feeling dizzy. "You bin a catchin' any cattle rustlers lately?"

"Sure have, Sheriff," said Johnny. "Why, our jail back homes full of them pesky rustlers and last week we hanged a couple of them blighters, didn't we, Jimmy?"

"Sure did," squeaked Jimmy. "We hanged the blighters."

Fay clapped her hands together and laughed.

"We've watched every cowboy film on the telly for a month now to get us in the mood for this holiday. Haven't we boys?"

"Sure have, Ma," said Johnny. "We've even got our own cowboy outfits, but we decided not to wear them for the journey as we came here by car cos it was too far for the horses."

"Why that's good," said Raymond, ruffling the two heads of hair. "You'll have to get into them clothes then mighty soon, cos it'll be time to open up the bar in an hour or so. Would you like a drink before we show you to your room?"

"Yeah, gimme a whiskey," said Johnny, "with ice but no soda."

Gloria, hiding in the shadows at the top of the stairs winced. It looked like being a very long summer.

Jack Smeaton took to his work in the Hotel grounds like a duck to water. He enjoyed being left to work alone and appreciated the fact he was deemed responsible enough to use his own initiative.

In a shady corner in a disused part of the walled vegetable garden, a flourishing elder occupied a large area, and as neither the fruits nor the flowers were used by the hotel, Dick Cottingham asked Jack to dispose of it so that in its place they could erect a greenhouse to shelter tender plants during the winter months.

With a pair of garden shears Jack cut away the foliage and clusters of small green berries from the branches and tossed them onto the compost heap. He then sawed off the bare branches and laid them out to dry in the sun to be burned another day. Around the stump that remained, he dug a large hole and then hacked at the roots and stump with an axe until all traces of the elder were removed from the earth. He then dug the area over with a spade and raked it level. Pleased with his efforts and the time in which he had completed his chore, he turned towards to the garden shed eager to take a well-earned break, but as he walked along the path he trod on the prongs of the rake and the handle sprang up and bashed him hard on the face. Jack winced, as the pain spread from his chin to his eye socket and in anger he kicked the rake in retaliation and sent elder branches flying in all directions. From behind he heard female laughter. He turned to see Dilys, much amused by his antics.

"Gertie sent me down to see what's happened to the flowers," she said, trying to suppress further giggles on realising Jack was not in the best of moods. "They aren't where you usually leave them in the utility room."

"That's because I haven't cut the damn things yet," snapped Jack, in obvious pain. "Dick told me to get rid of this sodding elder and I forgot all about the soppy flowers."

Dilys placed her hands on her hips. "Well, you'd better do them now then, cos Gertie wants them and she doesn't like to be kept waiting. In fact you'd better get a move on or I'll be in trouble for being out here for too long. She's always moaning and saying I'm slow."

Jack pulled a handkerchief from his pocket and wiped his watering eye. "Then you better help me. Go and get two pairs of secateurs from the shed. You can't miss them, they're on the table."

Dilys did as she was asked and then, without speaking, the students cut four bunches of flowers to put in rooms where new guests were due to arrive. Asters for two of the pink rooms, gold and white dahlias for a yellow room, and cornflowers mixed with white love-in-the-mist for the sky blue room. When the flowers were cut

Dilys went back indoors leaving the injured young groundsman to lick his wounds and take a long overdue tea break.

"Jack's made a smashing job of clearing the area for the new greenhouse," said Dick Cottingham to Bob Jarrams, later in the day. "I couldn't have done it better myself. He's even raked the earth level."

"Has he? Good, but how come he's got a black eye? I hope he's not been fighting. I sense that one has a bit of a temper."

"No idea and I must admit I didn't like to ask."

Mary, sticking photographs taken at Ned's party into an album, sighed. "I hope he's not been fighting one of the other lads over Susie Pilkington. I hear quite a bit of hissing and snarling when she's around."

Heather nodded. "Same here."

"Silly sods," tut-tutted Bob. "Anyway, whatever he's been up to, I think we can safely say we've been pretty lucky with this year's students. All three lads certainly work well, so no complaints there. How are the girls getting on, Heather?"

"Fine, they're all doing well, although Dilys is a bit workshy. I hope she's not causing poor Gertie any unnecessary stress."

"Do you think this place is haunted?" Dilys asked, as she idly gazed from a bedroom window overlooking the terrace at the back of the Hotel after returning with the flowers. "I do. I mean it must be, mustn't it, because lots of folks must have died here and big houses are always haunted, and I think the little secret room that goes down from under the floorboards in our room is really spooky. Crystal and me went down there last night after Linda told us about it. The funny old staircase is ever so steep and it's really scary. I bet lots of people have been trapped in there. Have you ever seen it?"

"No," said Gertie, wearily, "but Maggie Nan was hidden down there by the man who kidnapped her a few years back, so there was a lot about it in the papers at that time."

"What? Who's Maggie Nan? I don't know anything about that."

"Surely you've heard of Maggie Nan. She was a very famous fashion designer in the sixties." Gertie sighed. "No, I suppose you haven't cos she's never done anything since her ordeal. Poor old thing."

"Yeah, well, whoever she was doesn't matter unless she was murdered and is now a ghost. I still reckon this place is haunted, cos the one near us back home is and it's a bit like this with a big wing sticking out the back."

Gertie filled a vase from the tap in the en-suite bathroom. "How do you know it's haunted?"

"Because lots of people have seen a lady dressed in grey floating down the corridors at night and strange things happen which are really frightening."

"Such as what?" said Gertie, carefully arranging the flowers in the vase.

"Well, um, like plates and things falling off tables and things. You know, like poltergeists do. And folks say a dog barks at night even though the house doesn't have one and there aren't any other houses nearby."

Gertie stifled a yawn. "It's probably just made up stories to scare people. Is the house you're talking about open to the public?"

"Oh, yes," said Dilys, proudly, "and it gets millions of visitors every year because everyone hopes to see the grey lady. I've been several times but I've never seen her."

"What a surprise," mumbled Gertie, a hint of sarcasm in her voice.

"What was that?"

"Nothing, come on, this room's done but if we don't get a move on we'll not be finished the others before nightfall."

However, when they stepped into the next room where the wandering chair misbehaved, Gertie immediately noticed once again the Queen Anne chair was facing the window.

"Hmm, does the ghost at the big house near you move furniture around by any chance?" she asked, with a frown.

"Funny you should mention that," giggled Dilys, heading straight for the window, "cos it does. A cradle in the nursery is often at a different angle to the way the owners like it left and some people have even seen it rocking when there's been no-one in the room. I'd forgotten about that, but you've gotta admit it's really spooky. I wish

I was susceptible to spirits and suchlike. I'd make a fortune and have tremendous fun tracking the ghosts down."

"So what is it you're studying at university?" asked Gertie, suddenly warming to Dilys. "Anything interesting?"

The student laughed. "Maths, I'm brilliant at maths but pretty hopeless at anything practical. But then you've probably already realised that, cos you've gotta admit I'm rubbish at making beds."

"Hmm, but you're very good at talking and gazing out of the window," smirked Gertie, glancing at the chair to make sure it had not moved again. "Are you looking for anyone in particular?"

Dilys blushed. "Oh dear, it looks like I'm pretty rubbish at being subtle too, aren't I?" She giggled, guiltily. "But between you and me, I was looking out to see if I could catch a glimpse of Pete nipping out for a crafty fag, like he does."

Gertie smiled, as memories of her younger days came flooding back and the anguish incurred, caused by idolising lanky youths oblivious of her adoration.

In the afternoon, Dilys wearily climbed the stairs to the room she shared with Crystal and headed straight for the drawer in which she kept her confectionary, for even though she had just eaten her lunch she craved something sweet and chocolate she deemed would be the perfect solution. However, when she opened the drawer and ruffled through colourful wrappers containing individual sweets, she found her chocolate supply was non-existent. She cursed, recalling finishing off the last bar the previous morning.

Dilys looked at her watch, it was half past two and so there was plenty of time to go into the village to replenish her drawer with goodies from the post office. She glanced from the window. As usual the day was sunny and warm and already she was uncomfortably hot. She cursed, but had no choice, if she wanted chocolate she must walk into the village.

After washing her face and wiping her sweaty underarms with a flannel, Dilys changed into shorts and a T shirt, she then went back down the stairs and left the Hotel by the rear entrance. As she walked around the side and approached the front of the building she saw Malcolm in the car park opening the driver's door of his Mini Cooper, a bunch of flowers in his hand. Hastening her steps, Dilys quickly waved and called to him. "Are you by any chance going into the village, Malc?"

He turned. "Yes, I am. Why?"

"Any chance of a lift? I need to go to the post office."

"Yeah, of course, hop in. I'm not coming back for a while though cos I'm going to see Liz."

Dilys gratefully climbed into the passenger seat as Malcolm placed the flowers on the back seat. "That's fine. I don't mind walking one way but I find walking both ways tiring, especially after a hard morning's work."

Malcolm dropped Dilys off outside the post office and then drove back along the road towards the School House. Dilys sighed as he disappeared out of sight, wishing she too had a dedicated boyfriend, preferably named Pete, who would call on her bearing gifts and flowers.

After buying as much chocolate as she could cram into her spacious shoulder bag, Dilys walked back through the village. After passing the School House where Malcolm's Mini was parked alongside the kerb, she turned into the lane and sauntered down the hill.

At the bottom she left the road, slid beneath the fence and entered the woods where she followed the woodland path alongside the meandering stream.

Halfway through the woods, Dilys reached the ash stump. Glad of the opportunity to rest, she sat down and opened the biggest bar of chocolate.

As the first chunk dissolved in her mouth she again thought of Pete and sighed deeply. Her continuous efforts to win his affections had thus far been fruitless and she was beginning to run out of alluring ideas.

Dilys broke off another piece of chocolate wondering where Pete might be spending the afternoon. She then remembered hearing him say during breakfast that he'd probably be going to Penzance to have a rummage through any second-hand shops on the off chance of finding something antique-like which might appeal to his father.

A sudden loud bang caused Dilys to jump and grab her chocolate bar to stop it falling to the ground. She then sat rigid, too afraid to move, puzzled by the loud bang and its subsequent echo. She pondered as to its cause. Maybe it was just a car backfiring or perhaps it was something more sinister, like gunshot? She knew it could be either, for the road which ran by the Hotel's main entrance wasn't far away from the woods and the landlord of the Inn had several guns.

Dilys dropped her half-eaten bar of chocolate into her bag. From the branches of a tall sycamore two crows flew up into the air, their wings flapping noisily, causing dead twigs to fall by her feet. Dilys screamed, her nerves on edge, as she recalled hearing the story of Gorran Penwynton who had been shot dead in the woods by a madman from Polquillick seeking revenge for his wronged daughter. She whimpered. Was the bang she'd heard the ghostly sound of the gunshot fired by the murderer as he'd pulled the fatal trigger?

Dilys, her body trembling, shakily stood. She had to get out of the woods and back to the safety of the Hotel. Pulling her bag onto her shoulder she turned to leave but then paused. From the leaves of a tall holly tree, dripped droplets of crystal clear water. She stepped closer, confused, for it was too late in the day for dew and there had been no rain for several days, so how could there be moisture on the holly's glossy leaves? Impulsively, Dilys dipped her finger into the water and dabbed it onto her tongue. The water tasted of salt. Like tears. Dilys stepped back. Was she going crazy? Trees don't cry! Nearby, something shuffled through the dry leaves on the woodland floor. Dilys turned quickly, just in time to see the tail of a grey squirrel disappear in the undergrowth. Gasping for breath and with heart thumping, she ran, stumbling and slipping, tripping on brambles, and screaming as her hair became entwined in a low branch. All desires to see a ghost now extinguished from her mind.

When she finally reached the Hotel, shaken and breathless, she vowed never to walk alone through the woods again.

On Wednesday evening it was the village school's turn to organise the weekly barbecue on the beach. Usually the school would not hold fund raising events outside term time, but following a brief meeting between Ned, Meg and a handful of dedicated parents it was agreed at the beginning of the holiday that the opportunity to add money to school funds was too good to miss.

To Anne's dismay she was unable to attend the barbecue, for she did the evening shift at the Hotel on Wednesdays. Elizabeth, however, footloose and fancy free, was able to go escorted by the new love of her life, Malcolm Barker.

Anne arrived at work with a little less enthusiasm than usual, for her friends in the village had repeatedly told of the jubilant atmosphere created by clientele who supported the barbecues and therefore she was a little peeved that she would miss them all. But as luck would have it, Mary spotted her sombre mood and came to the right conclusion regarding the cause with very little prompting.

"Anne, dear, isn't it the school's turn to do the barbecue tonight?"

Anne nodded. "Yes, but it's rather put a damper on it for poor Dad, him having just lost his father."

"Dear, dear, yes, of course, in which case you should be there supporting him and your old school. I wish I'd had the foresight to think of it before. Come on, up you get. You must finish early and I'll take over from you. But don't worry, I'll make sure your pay is as normal and then perhaps next week we'll change your hours around so that you don't work on Wednesday nights anymore. Not during the summer months anyway."

"But…"

"No buts," said Mary, taking Anne's flat shoes from the cupboard. "I insist you go now and have a really nice time, and we'll see you as usual tomorrow lunchtime."

Anne happily put on her shoes. "Thank you, Mary, I certainly would like to be there."

"Then off you go, it's almost dusk already, but I'm told the cove looks really pretty at night with all the Christmas lights and candles twinkling. Hopefully you won't have missed too much."

Anne retrieved her bag from beneath the reception desk and ran down the winding drive towards the road, for she never dared go through the woods at night, not even in moonlight. The main road felt safer and the walk always seemed to be shorter at night than during the day, although Anne conceded that was probably because there were fewer distractions after dark as visibility was restricted.

She walked down the road as fast as she was able and occasionally ran a few yards to speed up her journey, hence, in less than ten minutes she was on the outskirts of the village where the street lights were glowing to light her way. Above, the night sky was darkening with each minute that passed and twinkling bright stars were gathering in large numbers across the cloudless sky.

When Anne reached the School House it occurred to her that her purse contained very little money and knowing there would be stalls to browse and food to purchase, she ran up the garden path in order to raid her savings tin.

The house was locked when she reached the back door so she took her key from her shoulder bag and let herself in, but as soon as she stepped inside and switched on the kitchen light, she sensed something was wrong. The hairs on the back of her neck rose and goose pimples prickled her otherwise warm arms as she quietly closed the back door and cautiously crossed the kitchen floor. A crash from the direction of the front room made her jump and realise her sixth sense had not been deceiving her. Instinctively, she put her hand firmly over her mouth to stifle her strong desire to scream, for she was very much conscious of the fact, that whoever was in the house must not know of her presence.

Once she felt composed she switched off the fluorescent light, quietly opened the kitchen door and looked out into the passage. Someone was in the front room; she could hear them moving around. Momentarily, Anne felt relieved, thinking perhaps one of her parents, or even Elizabeth might be in the house, but she soon realised that could not possibly be the case, for family members would not have locked the door, once inside, knowing other family members were still out.

Anne crept back into the kitchen and pulled the carving knife from the wood block on the window sill, she then tiptoed along the passage, conscious of every beat of her thumping heart echoing like a drum in her ears. When she rounded the corner and saw that the front room door stood slightly ajar, she froze and whimpered, praying the intruder could not sense her presence or her fear. Through the gap of the door, a light flickered and Anne panicked. Suddenly she was terrified and could contain her petrifaction no longer. She screamed at the top of her voice. The light instantly went out. The knife fell from her hand. She heard another crash and then felt a strong draught. Annoyed by her weakness she picked up the knife and ran into the front room waving her weapon and shouting. She switched on the light but no-one was there. The back window was open wide, the curtains were blowing in the breeze and over the floor the contents of drawers from the sideboard were scattered, the cushions from the three piece suite were piled in a heap and her parent's treasured writing desk lay on its side, with ink dripping from a broken ink pot onto the fireside rug.

Chapter Nineteen

The following day the village buzzed with the news that five houses had been broken into the previous night and various items stolen from each. It seemed that the thief, as with most burglaries, was looking for money and small items of value. However, in all of the Trengillion cases the thief had confined his search for valuables to downstairs rooms, hence it was assumed, either he had no lucrative market for jewellery, usually found in bedrooms, or he was unable to distinguish the difference between precious gems and paste.

On their return home from the barbecue, Frank and Dorothy Newton found the old biscuit tin in which they saved one pound notes for a rainy day, empty and lying on the kitchen floor along with the contents of drawers and cupboards. Jim and Doris Hughes lost a set of silver spoons. Meg and Sid Reynolds lost a silver candelabrum, a recent acquisition and Silver Wedding Anniversary present from their son, Graham. From the post office, valuable coins discovered on a sunken wreck were taken from a display cabinet, although no attempt was made to break into the post office itself, and at the School House, Ned and Stella seemed to have lost only a silver cigarette case, but conceded things might have been worse had Anne not disturbed the intruder. But the loss of the cigarette case did not worry them unduly; they were more concerned that, had he not fled, their daughter might have been harmed by the intruder or that the desk might have been damaged by its rough treatment. The desk, and Anne, however, both remained intact and none the worse for their experience.

The police found very little evidence as to the identity of the burglar. There were no fingerprints in any of the houses, so it was assumed he had worn gloves, and as all properties had been broken into through back windows, the probability of anyone having seen anything suspicious was very slim. Hence, the only piece of evidence that seemed obvious, was that the houses were targeted by someone who knew which people were most likely to patronise the barbecue, and he had seized the opportunity to act on what was a beautiful, clear night.

Molly and the major went round to visit Frank and Dorothy as soon as they heard they had been victims in the robberies, and after Dorothy had made tea for them all, the women went out to sit in the sun while the men stayed indoors to keep an eye on the cricket.

"Is Dorothy alright," asked the major, "she seems quite perky but I wonder if she's just putting on a brave face because it must be pretty unsettling knowing someone's been poking through your belongings."

"Well fortunately, it looks as though the thieving bugger went no further than the kitchen," said Frank, clearly annoyed by the affair. "If they'd gone through the bedroom drawers that'd have been a different story."

"I'm glad I took my usual precautions before we went to the barbecue," said the major, with justified pride. "I always insist we leave on a light or two when we go out in the evening and I switch the radio on too. It stands to reason no-one's going to break in if they think someone's home. I don't know what this country's coming to though. To think we can have theft on this scale here in Trengillion. I blame the Government of course, they're a right load of hoot-toots and hobbledy-hoys and it's about time they called an election. It's ridiculous trying to run the country with such a miniscule majority."

Frank smiled. The major blamed every negative occurrence on the Government.

"Is Frank alright?" asked Molly, placing her empty cup on the grass, "he seems quite perky but I wonder if he's just putting on a brave face."

"I think he's alright now," said Dorothy, "it was a bit of a shock when we got in last night, but we've only lost a few pounds and nothing sentimental was taken, although the intruder managed to knock over a picture of Frank with his first wife, Sylvia, and the glass got broke. I think that upset him more than the loss of the money, but I've assured him the photo's not damaged so we'll get another frame. How's poor Anne? It must have given her a dreadful fright, but what a shame she didn't get a look at the thief."

"Well, to be perfectly honest, I'm glad she didn't," said Molly, alarmed at the prospect, "because if she had then he may well have attempted to do something dreadful to her to shut her up. I'm just so glad he had the sense to scarper. If he'd have stayed, I dread to think what might have happened. Anyway, she's bearing up quite well. But what a to-do, I think this'll fuel up the major's dislike for the Government even more and I'm never likely to hear the end of it."

"David Steel's far too young to be leader of the Liberal Party, far too young," said the major. "Don't get me wrong, Frank, I've nothing against the lad, nothing other than his age. Why, I hear he's the youngest British Party leader ever. I don't know what the Liberals were thinking when they voted him in. Personally, I think they should have begged Jo Grimond to take on the job again, just for a couple of years 'til young Steel at least gets to a respectable forty."

Frank nodded. "I see John Stonehouse has gone down for seven years. I used to like the bloke but I went off him when he faked his own death a few years back."

"Yes, that was a peculiar affair," laughed the major. "The lengths some chaps will go to, to deceive, well, it beggars belief."

"I did enjoy Ned's party," said Dorothy, "and I never realised the Hotel was quite so grand. I bet it costs a few bob to stay there for a night."

"I daresay you're right, but I would imagine their overheads are pretty high cos they have lots of staff to pay, not to mention rates, electricity and so forth."

"Oh yes, it must cost an arm and a leg. I was very impressed by the food too, so the new chefs get my vote."

"Talking of votes, I see that MP chappie, John thingy, has been jailed for seven years," said Molly, shaking her head gently as she tut-tutted. "The major thinks he's a right scoundrel and I daresay he's right, but I thought it was rather sweet the way he tried to fake his own death just so that he could escape his true life to be with his sweetheart. Not that I approve of philandering."

"Oh, I can't agree with you there," said Dorothy, "it must have been very humiliating for his poor wife. I bet she wished he really had drowned."

"Your sweet peas are doing very well," said Molly, who whenever possible always strove to avoid conflict. "If they're looking that good next week you must pick some for the village show. I'm sure you'd win a prize with them."

"I was going to do just that," said Dorothy, "but to be perfectly honest, I'll be glad when they've gone over, I'm so tired of lugging out bowls of washing up water; it's getting very tedious."

Molly laughed. "I know, and I'm surprised the vegetables are edible considering the amount of soap they had sloshed on them this summer. Still, it can't last forever, I expect it'll be wet day after day soon, but of course it'll be far too late to rescue the veg and summer bedding."

"It's been nice not to have to mow the lawn though, hasn't it?" said Dorothy, surveying the yellow grass. "Although to look at it now you'd never think it could be green again. And look at the cracks, they're so unsightly."

"You know what, Dot? As soon as it cools down I'm going for a nice long walk. I've not been far since mid-June now and it was always one of my favourite pastimes."

"Talking of walks reminds me of something," smiled Dorothy. "I saw your granddaughter, Elizabeth, walking through the village last week with a young man and he wasn't Gregory Castor-Hunt."

"Ah, yes, the young actor laddie," said Molly, emphatically, "but it won't last, Dot, mark my words. It won't last."

Elizabeth, bored with her own company, decided to walk to the Hotel to meet her sister from work, that way it would almost be teatime when they arrived back at the School House and the bulk of the day would be over. For Elizabeth was getting tired of being on her own. It was all very well being a teacher and having long summer holidays, but if your friends were all working then it seemed rather pointless. But apart from her desire to pass away the time Elizabeth had another reason for meeting her sister; she felt Anne might appreciate company for the walk home, as she had quite understandably been a little edgy that morning following her ordeal the previous night and the lengthy questioning by the police.

Elizabeth left the house at quarter past five in the knowledge that Anne finished at six o'clock, and walked down the lane which ran into the valley away from the house. At the bottom she stopped, slid beneath the fence and followed the stream into the woods, away from the scorching sun and towards the trees, where she strolled along the well-worn, familiar path.

Half way through the woodland she looked at her watch. It was half past five. Realising she was likely to be early, she sat on the old tree stump to pass away the time and cool down. She was surprised, however, to find the minute her body made contact with the old wooden ash stump that her arms felt cold and goose pimples ran from her wrists to her shoulders. Confused by the sudden drop in temperature and feeling in desperate need of warmth, she rose and proceeded along the path rubbing her arms rapidly to quell the cold.

With each step she took the cold intensified and rapidly the once bright sunlight peeping through the trees began to fade. Afraid to continue, she stopped abruptly. A breeze had risen from nowhere and was rustling the leaves on the trees towering overhead. Elizabeth looked towards the sky which once blue, had now turned an ugly shade of grey; through it loomed a mass of threatening black clouds.

Elizabeth leaned her back against the rough bark of a horse chestnut tree and cowered beneath the long swaying branches. The chill on her arms deepened further and spread to every part of her body, while all around the strength of the wind increased to gale force and whistled through the leaves; each gust murmured, mournfully, pitifully; wailing and calling, voice-like, as though attempting to speak.

Elizabeth frowned and strained her ears but was unable to decipher any words. Finally, her legs gave way and she listlessly slid her back down the tree and crouched on the ground; her teeth chattering with cold and fear, until the wind, as quickly as it had appeared, vanished, and the warmth slowly returned to her numbed body.

When the sun was once more visible shining through the tree tops, Elizabeth rose to her feet. Her legs still felt like jelly. She pinched her arm to see if she was dreaming, even though she knew she was wide awake and had just witnessed a most peculiar occurrence.

Needing to sit down, Elizabeth made her way back through the woods to the old tree stump. There she sat to evaluate the sudden storm and the mysterious voice in the wind. As she sat a leaf fell from the holly tree onto her lap. Elizabeth carefully picked it up and laid it on the palm of her hand. "Mattie," she said, puzzled as to why that name had come into her head. She stood up, crossed to the tall holly tree and touched its trunk. "Mattie," she said again. "But who was or is Mattie?" And although the tree didn't answer, she sensed her presence in the woods had triggered off the eerie incident as though to warn her of something of which she had not the slightest notion.

Elizabeth felt confused as she stood to continue her journey. She needed to find out more, but knew she could tell no-one of her experience because of its unbelievable nature. But then she realised she was wrong. There was someone in whom she could confide. Her grandmother, Molly.

Elizabeth heaved a sigh of relief, left the stump and walked towards the woodland path. As she passed the elder she looked at her watch. It was still half past five.

The students and live-in staff at the Hotel had their own sitting room in the rear wing; it was not very big and at one time would have been a bedroom, but the students liked it. It was somewhere to unwind and discuss their hopes and dreams for the future and any other subject, topical to the passing day.

On one such evening, when all had finished work except Malcolm who was on the bar in the residents' lounge, Grev asked if any of the gathered few knew the history of the Penwynton family.

"Ah, I'm glad you've brought that subject up," said Jack, "we were talking about it the other night but you missed out because you'd gone to bed. I've been rather intrigued for ages though as to why you bear the name Penwynton when you quite obviously aren't one."

Suzie looked up from the latest edition of *Vogue* and glared angrily at Jack. "Don't be so aggressive. Your tone implies he's not worthy of carrying the Penwynton name and I find that offensive."

Jack ignored her. "I know some of the history because Anne and her mates told me about the family when I was in the Badge on Wild West Night. It's quite interesting. Do you want to hear it?"

"Of course, if it's not too much trouble," said Grev, timidly.

Jack shrugged his shoulders, annoyed that his nonchalant attitude had aggravated Suzie when it was intended to impress her. Nevertheless, he managed to adopt a more caring tone and proceeded to reiterate the legend as told to him by Anne as though he were an expert on the subject.

"I see," said Grev, thoughtfully, when Jack had finished and the information received began to sink in. "I don't suppose you know what happened to the baby the servant girl had, do you?"

"It died," said Jack, bluntly, annoyed that Suzie had resumed reading her magazine instead of listening to his adept storytelling. "Why, surely you don't think that you might have descended from it, do you?"

Grev shrugged his shoulders. "I don't know. I don't know what to think. All I know is I've got a damn stupid name and I want to know why."

"But surely the people to ask are your parents," said Dilys, opening a bag of Liquorice Allsorts. "My folks know their family history going back yonks."

Grev bit his bottom lip. "I can't, they're both dead, you see, and have been since I was six. They died in a car crash one day when I was at school."

"Oh, you poor lamb," said Crystal, sympathetically. "That's terrible. So were you brought up by your grandparents or an aunt and uncle?"

Grev shook his head. "None of them. I believe all my grandparents were already dead, either that or they didn't want to look after me, and I don't have any aunts and uncles because Mum or Dad didn't have any brothers or sisters, so I've got no-one and I've spent most of my life living in orphanages or with foster parents."

"Blimey, Grev, I'm sorry mate, that must have been pretty tough," said Jack, genuinely penitent. "So you don't know anything about your past at all?"

"Well, not much, but that doesn't matter, it's the name that's baffling me. You see, I do know that Penwynton isn't my real family name. It's what Dad changed it to, but for the life of me I can't think why."

"Could you explain a little better," said Suzie, having finally tossed her magazine to one side to absorb all information.

"Well, there's not really much to tell except that Dad changed the name before I was born so I really was christened Grenville Penwynton. Then, when I was ten, one of the older kids in the orphanage was reading an article in a newspaper about a fashion designer who'd been kidnapped. I wasn't a bit interested in the story but it was pointed out to me that she'd been found at Penwynton House in Cornwall, so I read all about it to see if it shed any light on me and my name, but of course it didn't. Anyway, last year I was eighteen, so the authorities found me a bedsit and got me a job so that I was able to stand on my own two feet, which was rather nice, I must admit, but then in April, of all the rotten luck, I got made redundant. At first I didn't know what to do and then I decided to leave Cambridge and come to Cornwall to see if I could find out anything about Penwynton House and to find casual work at the same time. I slept rough for a time because I couldn't afford lodgings and that was over Falmouth way. You see, I didn't know where to look for this place because I couldn't remember the name of the village. Then one day I saw the name Trengillion on an advert for the Sheriff's Badge Inn and it jogged my memory, I knew then where I had to come and arrived on the night they were having a barbecue in the cove. I asked someone about Penwynton House and they told me it was a hotel now, and then my luck changed, I saw an advert in the post office window and the rest's history."

"Hmm, some story," said Suzie. "But are you sure your father changed the family name? I mean, if you were only six when he died, then when did you find out?"

"Mum told me," said Grev. "It's one memory I do have that is crystal clear. I asked her why I had such a big name when all my school friends had simple, easy to remember names and she laughed and said it was because I was entitled to it and so was she. But it didn't make much sense then and it still doesn't."

"Hmm, so out of curiosity, do you know what your family name was before your father changed it to Penwynton?" asked Jack. "Not that it will probably be of any relevance."

Grev looked slightly embarrassed. "It was Bugg. The family name was Bugg. I know that because I have a picture of Dad taken when he was a boy and his name is written on the back. Hugh Bugg aged seven. It's pretty horrible, isn't it? The name, I mean. But there you have it."

"What! Good heavens," screeched Dilys. "It's worse than horrible, it's ghastly. I could never marry a chap with a name like Bugg."

"It would be a little off putting," agreed Crystal. "What was your mother's name, Grev?"

"Betty," he replied. "I think she was Betty Taylor before she married Dad because my middle name is Taylor."

"Christ! Grenville Taylor Penwynton, what a mouthful," laughed Dilys. "But there's your answer. Who'd want a name like Betty Bugg? The answer to your conundrum is quite obvious, Grev. Your mother refused to marry your father unless he changed his name. In which case he must have been crazy about her to take such a drastic step"

"Maybe," said Grev, a little offended by her scorn, "but that still doesn't tell me why he chose the name Penwynton and why I was christened Grenville."

Elizabeth was pleased to find her grandmother alone, sitting at the kitchen table reading *Woman's Own*, when she called at Rose Cottage the following day, for the major had gone into town to pay in a cheque at the bank.

Molly looked up as her granddaughter peeped round the door. "Elizabeth, come in. How lovely to see you. Would you like a coffee? I was just thinking about having one."

"Yes please, and may I have one of your sweeteners in it. I'm trying to give up sugar but not having much success."

"Hmm, weight-watching are you? In that case you'll not want a slice of my fruit cake. Shame, because I only made it yesterday and it's really nice."

Elizabeth grinned. "Well, actually I am weight-watching, but that's because I've put on a few pounds since school broke up. It's the long holiday to blame. I get bored and eat for something to do, having said that, I'd love a piece of cake, please."

Molly removed the lid from an old biscuit tin in which she kept her cakes. "I thought you might, and if you're feeling lonely you know you can always pop round and see Granddad and me, not that we're the most scintillating of company, I suppose."

"Oh, don't say that. I like your company and so does Anne. In fact, I daresay you're fun compared with some grandparents."

"Hmm, maybe. I only ever knew one of my grannies and that was my mother's mum. She always insisted we each had a cup of tea when we went to visit so that she could read the leaves. I suppose that could be why I'm addicted to tea. Dad's mum, sadly died before I was born. Still, I expect I've told you that before."

Elizabeth nodded. "Well, I'm here to see you today, although I must admit it's because I would like some advice."

"Advice," said Molly, stirring the coffee, "something everyone likes to give but no-one wants to receive."

"Hmm, sometimes maybe, but that's not the case with me today."

Molly handed Elizabeth her coffee along with a generous slice of cake. "So, what is it you want to know?"

"Thank you. Well, it's a bit odd really and you'll probably think I'm barmy, but I witnessed a most peculiar thing in the woods yesterday when I was on my way to meet Anne after she finished work."

Molly's eyebrows raised. "The woods. Really, please go on. I'd like to hear what you have to say."

Elizabeth told Molly the events just as they had happened, leaving out nothing and without exaggeration. Molly listened, her eyes sparkling, thrilled to learn that someone else shared her ability to hear voices in the woods.

"But what does it mean?" asked Elizabeth, after Molly told of her fondness for Mattie's tree. "And who is, or was, Mattie, do you think?"

"I don't know," said Molly, excitedly. "I really don't know, and would you believe, I've wandered all around the churchyard here looking for a grave bearing that name on several occasions, but I've never found anything. Of course, she may have lived before gravestones were commonplace or have come from a poor family who couldn't afford one."

"Or she, may have been a he," said Elizabeth, effusively. "Mattie can be the nick-name for Matthew as well as Matilda."

"Good heavens, that possibility never even crossed my mind," said Molly, amazed by her lack of thought. "How silly. I've always imagined Mattie to be female but I've no evidence at all to back that up. What a clot I am, I shall have to search the churchyard again for any Matthews, but I think it may well be fruitless as there will no doubt be several men with that name."

"You really believe Mattie existed then?" said Elizabeth, dreamily, "how fascinating. But who do you think was calling his or her name?"

"I don't know, but I like to think it's probably a case of some lost soul trying to find another lost soul. Can you remember if the voice you heard sounded male or female?"

Elizabeth shook her head. "No, it'd be impossible to guess, and at the time it never really struck me as being either because the most poignant thing about it was the sadness expressed. I also felt at the time it was trying to warn me of something but in retrospect I'm pretty sure that was just wishful thinking."

"We have a bit of a puzzle then," smiled Molly, gleefully. "We don't know the gender of Mattie, or even if the person calling was perhaps Mattie his or herself, and we've no way of finding out either. Nevertheless, I wouldn't be at all surprised if it's not part of the vibes I'm picking up. I told Dot something was going to happen this summer and at that time I didn't quite know what, but I sense it stronger now. There's definitely something going on and Mattie's tree will turn out to be part of the puzzle and I wouldn't be surprised if the damaged elder growing near to Mattie's tree and the remains of the ash haven't something to do with it either."

"Whatever do you mean?" asked Elizabeth. "What influence can Mattie's tree possibly get from an elder?"

Molly took a sip of coffee. "Please don't tell your mum or dad I told you this or they'll be cross, but the spirits of elder trees are alleged to be vindictive, so when a tree is destroyed or damaged then the spirits naturally want revenge. The poor ash next to Mattie's tree, as we know, was badly damaged in a winter storm and was felled because it was dangerous. Unfortunately the elder was also damaged when the unfortunate ash crashed to the ground following the strokes of the axe man's axe. Hence, it was man that caused the damage to the elder. So in the eyes of the elder mother, she would see it as an act of vandalism and that may well have brought about bad luck."

Elizabeth leaned back in her chair, shocked. "I didn't notice the elder was damaged, in fact I've never really taken much notice of it at all, but surely you don't believe all that stuff, Gran. I mean, a tree's a tree and it can't have a spirit, can it?"

"You heard voices didn't you, Liz? So judge for yourself. But there's much more. Legend has it that if elder wood is used to build a house then the people who live there will feel hands tugging at their arms and legs. The burning of elder is said to bring evil into a home, especially here, in Cornwall, where it's believed to burn elder in the hearth will bring the devil himself to sit on the chimney."

"Don't Gran you're giving me the creeps. I'm glad it's summer and it doesn't get dark until nine."

Molly laughed. "There's still more. To sleep beneath the elder will bring about dreams of death, and to dream of elder denotes impending sickness. And if anyone is unfortunate enough to accidently fall asleep beneath an elder tree then he will be overcome with horror and delirium. What's more, witches are supposed to hide beneath the branches. I see you've finished your coffee, would you like a glass of elderflower champagne?"

Elizabeth giggled. "And what will that do? Turn me into a toad or craggy old crone?"

"Neither," smiled Molly, "it's just good to quench the thirst. Having said that, beware of elderberry wine, as it was used by the old dears in the film *Arsenic and Old Lace* to bump off unsuspecting folk."

Chapter Twenty

Five days after hearing of the death of his father, Ned, with Stella, prepared to leave Trengillion for the funeral in Kent due to take place the following day.

At first, because of the robberies, both were a little reluctant to leave the girls to fend for themselves, but after reassurance from Molly, the major, and friends each stressing they would all be close at hand should the girls need any moral support, Ned and Stella prepared to leave without any misgivings.

Stella shook her head in a disapproving way as Ned put their suitcase in the boot of the Ford Escort. "We can't go up-country with the car looking like this," she said, running her finger through the grime. "It's filthy and looks a disgrace."

"Nonsense," said Ned, impishly writing his name beneath Stella's streak. "The muck's protecting the paintwork. Anyway it's patriotic to have a dirty car, shows we're not wasting water and so forth."

"I know, but…"

"Stella, that's enough," said Ned, adamantly. "We're not cleaning it and that's that. Christ, there have to be some benefits to be had from this wretched drought, and I reckon two of them are not having to clean the car or cut the grass, and to be perfectly honest that's fine with me. Now, have we got everything?"

Stella tut-tutted. "I think so. I've even got a bottle of squash in my bag cos we're bound to get thirsty on the way, but I've not made any sandwiches cos the butter will melt."

"We'll stop several times anyway because I'll want to stretch my legs and no doubt you will too, we can get a bite to eat then."

Stella nodded.

Ned slammed shut the car boot. "Right, let's say goodbye to the girls and then we can get off."

As they drove through the village they passed Gloria Withers with her two young nephews carrying a kite. The Stanleys waved and Gloria waved in return, thus causing Ned to express to Stella his admiration for Gloria regarding her dedication to the two young lads, when already she had a very full schedule with the everyday running of the Inn.

"The Vicarage is going on the market next week," said Graham to his parents when he arrived home at Coronation Terrace after a day's work, "and we're handling it. I went down there today with my boss. It's in a poor state of repair and needs quite a bit spent on it, but it'll be smashing when it's done."

"It was getting in a bad way when I was a girl," said Meg, thoughtfully. "There always seemed to be builders in patching it up, so I'd imagine it must be a lot worse by now, especially as it's been standing empty for four years since Dad moved out. I can't understand why the church has taken so long to try and sell it, but I hope whoever buys it doesn't make any drastic changes. The place has loads of character and it would be criminal to destroy that."

"Don't you want to buy it, son?" laughed Sid, "You usually want every house you see."

"In my dreams," laughed Graham, tugging his shirt out from his trousers. "The asking price is sixteen grand so it's a bit out of my reach, but then everything's out of my reach until I've saved a lot more. Why don't you buy it? You should, Mum, for old times' sake, after all you were brought up there."

Meg smiled. "Now why would we want to leave here? This house has everything we need and we know the place inside out, besides I came here as a bride."

"But you rent it," said Graham, amazed by his mother's lack of ambition. "It's a Council house and at your age you should have your own place."

"Maybe," said Sid, "but if we did want to buy our own place then it would have to be somewhere a little more modest than the Vicarage, as nice as it might be."

"Has there been much interest in Sea Thrift Cottage?" asked Meg, keen to change the subject. "I meant to ask you the other day when I saw it advertised in the Free Gazette."

"Yeah, a few people have looked at it but I don't think anyone's put an offer in yet. Why, would you like to buy it? It's a lovely location and surprisingly spacious with lots of potential and magnificent sea views. I think you should go for it."

"You sound like a parrot," laughed Sid, "the way you reel off estate agent's repetitive jargon. Anyway, stop nagging. Your mother and I have talked of moving on several occasions over the years but have always reached the same conclusion that it's best to stay put. What's more, I'm a bit too old to get a mortgage now. We've missed the boat, so that's the end of it."

"Yeah, I suppose so. Anyway, what's for tea? I'm a bit pushed for time cos I'm working tonight."

"Oh, I didn't realise that," said Meg, jumping from her chair and turning towards the kitchen. "I thought you had the night off."

"I did, but Ray phoned me at the office and asked me to work. Friday nights are always busy because for so many holiday makers it's their last night, so he reckons it'll need four of us on the bar 'til the season quietens down a bit. And Gloria is often quite late getting on the bar now cos she has to put Johnny and Jimmy to bed after she's finished cooking the basket meals."

"Poor Gloria," tut-tutted Meg, "she has more than enough to do without looking after her nephews. What does Fay, their mother, do all night?"

"She likes to sit on the stool at the end of the bar," said Graham, "and she reckons if she's not on it at opening time then someone else will pinch it, so that's why Gloria sees to the boys. Mind you, in a way I think Gloria quite likes it, and it gets her away from Raymond for a while."

"So who looks after the boys while Fay's in the bar boozing and Gloria's doing the cooking?" asked Meg.

"They watch television in the family sitting room. It's not far from the kitchen so Gloria keeps an eye on them 'til she's done and the waitresses pop in from time to time too, to make sure they're alright."

When Graham arrived at the Inn, as predicted, Fay Walker sat at the end of the bar drinking Pils Lager, enjoying her break knowing her boys were in good hands, for she would be the first to admit, they were unruly, untidy and at times, downright disobedient. She had her fingers crossed therefore, that their Auntie Gloria's calming influence might rub off on them and she might return to Yorkshire at the end of her holiday with two angels instead of two young thugs.

Gloria meanwhile had her work cut out, but as she had spent many years tidying up after Raymond, Roger and Colin, having two extra pairs of shoes scattered about the place and clothes strewn over the floor was nothing new. She was, however, not used to children with bad manners, hence it was an uphill struggle to teach Jimmy and Johnny the basics and to say please and thank you.

As Gloria closed the bedroom door, leaving her two young nephews sleeping, she stifled a yawn to hide the fact she was shattered. For everyday she had had the boys in her constant care, her only reprise being during the lunchtime opening when she was required to cook the basket meals, and the only time during the day when their mother, Fay, looked after the boys herself and took them to the cove where she lay on the beach sunbathing with her head engrossed in a romantic novel leaving the boys to do as they pleased. But for all her tiredness, Gloria did not complain. She felt sorry for the boys and felt it was her duty to make their holiday as enjoyable as possible, hence in the afternoons, when usually she would rest, she took the children to the Rec where they played with a ball, flew a kite, played on the amusements or picked blackberries from the surrounding hedgerows.

"I'm coming to work near you next Monday, Anne," said John, that same evening, as they sat with friends around the picnic table on the cobbled area in front of the Sheriff's Badge Inn. "We'll be starting to build the Hotel's pond then. Well, not exactly build it, more like digging out a big hole."

"I thought you might be involved," said Anne, sweetly. "Bob's dead chuffed that you can do it so soon. He thought we might have to wait for months."

"Well, it's worked out just right really, cos we finished a job today but we can't start the next one for a fortnight or so cos the bloke who we'll be doing an extension for is away, so Dave's thrilled that your pond will fit into the gap perfectly."

"Brilliant, well, I must pop down and see you during some of my breaks. Will you be digging it out by hand?"

"Not likely," laughed John, "not in this heat. Have you seen how big it's going to be? It's huge so we'll be using the digger. We've got some building work to do as well. Your bosses want a flight of steps built into the bank, a path laid around the pond and a stone wall as well. It should look really nice. I'm not sure what I'll be doing yet but there'll be four of us on the job because we've got to get it done as quickly as possible of course so we can start the next job on time."

"That pond was my idea, apparently," giggled Elizabeth, "not that I remember saying so to Mr Cottingham, although I do vaguely remember talking to him. It's weird, Dad's party night all seems a bit of a blur. I can't remember half of it."

"Humph, that's because you drank too much," said Anne, recalling the moment she had found her sister sprawled out at the foot of the grand staircase.

"But I didn't drink too much," said Elizabeth, defensively. "I had two or three glasses of punch and a couple of vodka and oranges. That's all."

"That punch was really strong," said Jane. "I only had one glass and avoided it after that, but then I'm not keen on spirits anyway, except for gin that is."

"You were well gone," laughed John, waving his finger at Elizabeth. "It's a pity your sausage roll missed Poncey Pete though and just as well it hit poor old Dilys and not one of the older guests."

"What!" squealed Elizabeth, "please tell me you're joking?"

John shook his head. "No, I'm not. Several of us were standing in the corner around the table where the food was laid out and Ponce walked by with his nose in the air, like he does. That annoyed you and so you threw a sausage roll at him, but I don't think he even noticed."

"Oh, for God's sake, Liz! You really must behave when in places like the Hotel," said Anne, horrified to learn of her sister's behaviour. "I hope to goodness no-one noticed."

"Don't worry, Anne," said John, reassuringly, "they didn't. Though a few heads turned to see what we found so funny, but by then it was all over."

"Was this before or after I met Malc?" asked Elizabeth, nervously, wishing she could remember everything.

"Before I should think," said Susan, snuggled up closely to Steve Penhaligon, "because once you'd met him the two of you became inseparable."

Elizabeth groaned. "Oh, God, whatever must he have thought of me, if he noticed?"

"Don't worry," said Diane, "I think he was far from sober. Well, he was by the end of the evening, I can't vouch for when you first met. Anyway, where is he tonight?"

"Working," said Elizabeth. "He always works on Tuesday, Thursday, Friday and Sunday nights, plus some lunchtimes too of course."

"So, if it's not too indelicate a question, do you think you'll see him any more once he goes home?" asked Diane.

"No, I shouldn't think so," sighed Elizabeth, in a matter-of-fact manner. "Once he gets back all he'll care about is his acting career. I mean, he talks of very little else now, so by then it'll be the only subject on his lips."

"That's good," said Jane, much cheered, "it won't be the same if we all start going off and getting married and stuff."

Anne wrinkled her nose. "Oh, that's weird. Weird, I mean, to think that one day we might all be married and perhaps living miles away from each other. I don't think I like the idea of that at all."

"I wonder which of us will marry first," said Diane, stroking her ring finger. "Or more to the point, which of us will be the last. Now that really would be sad; to be the only one left alone."

"Oh, that's terrible," said Anne, saddened at the prospect. "It would be dreadful to be left on the shelf if everyone else was married."

"You won't be left on the shelf, Anne," chuckled Tony, "I reckon you'll end up with Poncey Pete."

The boys laughed at Anne's indignant face.

"Whatever makes you say that?" she spluttered.

"I think," said Susan, before Tony had a chance to answer, "that we should make a pact. A pact that says we'll never desert each other and if possible we'll live in Trengillion for the rest of our lives like our parents have; because I think it's lovely the way they've all known each other for ever."

"But we can't vow never to leave Trengillion," said Elizabeth. "Cornwall yes, but Trengillion is far too binding."

Diane nodded. "I agree and I think to make sure no-one is ever compelled to live a lonely life, we should also vow that any of us left unmarried by the year, say, 1990, they will have to marry any other member of the pact still unmarried."

"That's barmy," laughed Tony, spilling his beer, "but I like it."

"But what if siblings are left?" said Anne, "or worse still two blokes or two girls?"

"Oh, we'll cross that bridge when we get to it," giggled Susan. "Anyway, 1990 is forever away. Come on, let's join hands and everyone repeat after me..."

"…but we're not all here," squealed Elizabeth. "What about Lily, Greg, Matthew and Graham?"

As she spoke Graham appeared, looking for empty glasses.

"Just in time, sit down quickly," commanded Susan.

"What!" exclaimed Graham. "I'm working, Sue, and I don't have time to sit down like you lot."

"It'll only take a minute," said Susan, shuffling along and pulling him onto the bench. "Now, as Elizabeth quite rightly pointed out we're not all here, so I put forward the motion that we speak on behalf of our friends in their absence. Does everyone agree?"

The response was unanimous.

"Right, then once again everyone repeat after me: I do solemnly swear to never leave my native Cornwall."

They joined hands and amidst much laughter repeated Susan's words. She then continued with: "And I vow that should I be still unmarried in the year 1990, then I will wed whosoever in the pact shall also be left unmarried."

Much to the amusement of other drinkers both inside and outside the Inn, the youngsters repeated Susan's words and then fell about laughing until the tears ran down their faces. And then Graham, completely baffled by the bizarre occurrence, returned to the bar nonplussed to continue his work.

Chapter Twenty One

Day after day of hot sunshine meant bliss for the many holiday makers who chose to stay in the British Isles for their summer vacation. Likewise, the heat was welcomed with open arms by shops, restaurants, cafes, hotels, pubs and ice cream salesmen alike, especially in Cornwall, where many businesses relied heavily on tourism, and the larger than average influx of visitors meant a bumper year which would help boost incomes and maintain a sustainable living during the long months of winter.

Farmers and firemen on the other hand were distressed by the far reaching dryness. Parched, arid soil meant the crops failed and on scrubland gorse fires became a regular occurrence. Gardeners across the county faired a little better and were able to maintain life in their flowers and vegetable produce with the aid of waste water from baths and washing up bowls. This was welcome and encouraging news for the organisers of the Trengillion Village Flower Show, which always took place on the third Saturday in August, and because British summers were usually unreliable, the event was always held in the village hall. In 1976, however, because of the hot dry summer, it was decided by the committee to hold the event in the village field known as the Rec, where it was hoped it might attract even more support than usual. The date was August the twenty first.

On the morning of the village show, Grev Penwynton, who had the whole day off work, decided, as the weather was beautiful again, to walk into the village and down to the cove for a dip in the sea. During breakfast, Crystal, taking a short break from her early shift on the reception desk, agreed to join him, but as she would not finish work until lunch time she insisted he go on without her and she would join him later in the day. Grev was thrilled. Crystal was a real beauty and he felt very lucky that she was prepared to spend the afternoon with him, and he planned, should the day go well, to suggest popping into the Badge for a drink and a basket meal in the evening, for he knew Crystal was fond of scampi, as he had heard her say so to Dilys.

Grev cheerfully changed his clothes and put his bathing trunks on beneath his jeans. He then put a towel and a clean pair of underpants into his rucksack and zipped his wallet safely in the side pocket. He, and everyone else, had been a lot more security conscious since the burglaries, for although they knew it was most likely the work of an opportunist who was no longer in the area, there was always the chance a local person might have committed the crimes and still be at large, although the locals claimed that could not possibly be the case as they all knew and trusted each other implicitly.

Grev left his room and ran down the narrow staircase to the floor below. He then went to the next flight of stairs which led to the ground floor. Before he left the building by way of the back door, he ran along the passage and peeped into the vestibule where Crystal was talking to Eric the porter. On seeing him, she waved and promised to catch up with him as soon as she was able.

Once outside the Hotel, Grev walked around to the front and stopped to ponder in which direction to go, for both routes appealed to him. The driveway he liked for it was pleasant to walk on the grass verges overhung with hydrangeas dripping with pink, blue and creamy white flowers. The woods on the other hand, would be cooler and considerably quicker. Grev opted for the latter, even though he knew, if Crystal would not finish work for several hours, then time was of no importance.

Whistling happily he crossed the gravel driveway and walked towards the trees where he slipped through a gap between the rhododendron bushes; inside Bluebell Woods he then followed the well-worn path winding beneath the trees en route towards the stream. Grev was in exceptionally high spirits, for not only was his prospective meeting with Crystal an occurrence he looked forward to immensely, but he'd had a dream the previous night; a dream, which although a little weird, had warmed his heart and given him a feeling of belonging. For Grev had dreamt his body had been clasped and cherished, his brow stroked by loving hands and his cheeks kissed by the lips of his long dead mother.

By the stream he stopped and threw a twig into the shallow water, he watched as it floated away bouncing around stones and tussling with the vegetation that hung over the water's edge. When the twig was out of sight he continued on along the valley towards the village.

In a clearing, he stopped to admire wild honeysuckle dripping with flowers, its scent pungent and pleasant. Grev reached up and pulled off a spray, imagining it placed in Crystal's honey blonde hair. He sat on the old tree stump and buried his face deep in the flowers to breathe in the scent. A rustle in the nearby shrubbery caused him to look up. Hopeful that he might see a fox or a badger, for he was a keen animal lover, he lay down the flowers on the tree stump and went to investigate, but in his haste he tripped and fell over the gnarled roots of a tall tree and fell headlong, flat on his face onto a patch of loose earth.

Feeling dazed, he slowly pushed his hands against the earth to ease himself up, but whilst doing so his eye caught sight of something bright and shiny in the undergrowth. Grev knelt, leaned forward and picked up the object. It was a spoon, a silver spoon. Puzzled, he ran his hands over the spot where the spoon had lain. Something else was there, something else made of metal. Grev pushed aside the loose earth with his bare hands. When a candelabrum came into view he jumped up in alarm. For surely it was not treasure he had found but the items stolen from Trengillion houses on the night of barbecue.

Grev panicked, unsure what to do. Voices in his head told him to flee for his life. He felt a hand tugging at his arm but on turning around saw no-one was there. Instinct told him to run, but he was unsure whether or not he should leave the stolen things where they lay or gather them together and take it with him to phone the police. Before he had a chance to make up his mind, he heard a laugh. A mocking, heartless laugh, which emanated from behind the thick bush of ivy directly in front of him. Grev stepped back. His heart sank. He felt a sudden sensation of doom and knew he should have heeded the warning of the voices. He turned and tried to run, but to no avail. Fear numbed his legs and anxiety thwarted his ability to speak or call out. With heart thumping, he watched as slowly the glossy, green, ivy leaves quivered and parted on the bush in front of him and then through the foliage a bright, gleaming object emerged. Grev, his face as white as a sheet, stood motionless; his eyes transfixed onto the barrel of a revolver. He felt his heart pounding inside his breast, and beads of sweat trickle from his brow. Trembling, he heard a click and then he fainted, simultaneously, a ghostly voice from nowhere, cried out in anger and despair.

Crystal Hart finished work at twelve o'clock. Anne, who had been dropped off at work by her father, had taken over from her on the reception desk and so Crystal was free now until lunchtime the following day.

In the room she shared with Dilys, she changed into her skimpiest bikini and then put her jeans and T shirt over the top. She thought about Grev. He was a sweet, dear boy, but it was Jack Smeaton she was crazy about and had been since she had first clapped eyes on him. Jack worked in the grounds so she was never sure when he was working or when he had time off, hence she was always prepared for that chance meeting wherever and whenever it might be. She laughed as she closed the door. Why did things have to be so complicated? She was crazy about Jack, but he seemed to have eyes for no-one but Suzie Pilkington. Suzie on the other hand thought herself to be above them all and poor Dilys was wasting her time even thinking about Pete.

Crystal left the Hotel by the back door and then walked round the front and onto the drive. If she had been with friends she would have gone through the woods, but as she was on her own she thought it unwise. One of the students where she studied had been attacked when walking through woodland near the university last term and so she was always on her guard. Besides, she had on her new sandals and thought they might get dirty on an earthy path.

In the village Crystal met Susan carrying a large wooden crate of vegetables. Crystal was intrigued and so stopped to ask Susan where she was going with her edible cargo.

"The Rec," said Susan, standing the box on a garden wall in order to wipe the perspiration from her brow. "Our Tony grew these up at Granddad's farm. It's the Village Show today, you see, and he's entering them in their various categories. He brought them home last night but I'm not sure how I've managed to get roped into carrying them instead of him. Still, that's nothing new."

"Sounds like my brother used to be," laughed Crystal. "Always laying down the law and asking favours which he seems to think I should bow to. Mind you, he was always very good in return and frequently topped up my pocket money when I was still at school. He's married now though so I've gone down a bit in his order of priorities."

"I can't imagine Tony getting married, or John either for that matter. It'd be weird not to have them around, but I suppose it'll happen one day."

"Well, you never know you might be married and gone before them," smiled Crystal. "I saw you in the Badge the other night with a chap who looked rather besotted with you."

"Really! Did he?" giggled Susan, amazed to find herself blushing. "That was Steve and I must admit I'm absolutely crazy about him, but it's early days yet. Are you going somewhere nice?"

"Only to the beach," said Crystal, waving the bag containing her towel. "I'm meeting Grev there cos we thought a dip in the sea would be a good way of trying to cool down a bit."

"Grev," said Susan, with eyebrows raised, "do I detect a budding romance there?"

"No, we're just friends," said Crystal. "He's got the day off and mentioned he was going to the beach, so I said I'd join him when I finished work, which I did at lunch time. I can't wait to get in the sea, I'm sweltering hot."

"I know, this weather's pretty draining isn't it? I don't think I'll ever moan about being cold again after this summer. Anyway, I must go, see you at work tomorrow."

Crystal crossed the road after Susan's departure so that she could walk in the shade, she then continued on her way towards the beach. Outside the Inn, Colin Withers was tinkering with the engine of his Triumph Herald. She greeted him warmly and he watched her as she walked until out of sight.

On reaching the cove, Crystal cast her eyes around looking for Grev. She was surprised and a little annoyed that he was nowhere to be seen. Thinking perhaps he might be in the Gents or even have gone up to the Inn for a pasty, she removed her T shirt and jeans and then sat down on the beach to await his appearance. Ten minutes passed by, and still she was alone. She felt cross. Surely the likes of Grev Penwynton could not have stood her up? Feeling friendless and rather foolish, she stood and cast her eyes again across the beach; it was then she saw Jack emerging from the sea, dripping wet. Her heart skipped a beat when he looked in her direction and waved. She felt her face turning red as she waved back, and as he walked towards her, the absence of Grev Penwynton instantly became a matter of no importance.

"It's good to see a familiar face," said Jack, sitting down beside her. "Are you here on your own?"

"Yes," she said, hoping he didn't detect the quiver in her voice, "it certainly looks that way."

"Do you fancy a bite to eat? I'm starving and was planning to pop up to the Inn for sausage and chips. It'll be my treat."

Crystal was dumbstruck. "Well, well, yes, that would be nice," she stammered. "I've not eaten since breakfast."

Jack jumped up and then pulled Crystal to her feet. "Good, come on then. Food first and then we'll do a bit of serious sunbathing. We can't be going back to our respective universities next term without a perfect tan."

Crystal slipped her T shirt back over her bikini top as Jack fetched his towel from a different spot on the beach and then dried himself vigorously. She would have slipped on her jeans too, but she had good legs and thought it a shame to cover them.

"So, what do you think of this place?" asked Jack, as they ate their basket meals on the cobbled area in front of the Inn. "I think it's fantastic and I'm enjoying the summer far more than I ever thought I would."

Crystal quickly swallowed a mouthful of scampi in order to respond to his question. "Same here, and I really like the people I work with too, they're all very friendly."

Jack growled. "Hmm, except for stuck-up Suzie. God, what a self-centred, self-opinionated, vain bitch she is."

Crystal wanted to jump for joy and clap her hands with glee. She figured Suzie must have re-buffed his advances yet again, leaving the way clear for herself.

"She is a little stuck-up," said Crystal, demurely, "but she's very pretty too."

"Humph! Looks aren't everything," snapped Jack, picking up a sausage with his fingers, "and she's certainly no more attractive than you."

Anne Stanley was about to finish work when Poncey Pete emerged into the vestibule. Anne smiled sweetly as he looked her in the eye over the desk.

"We're going to see *The Omen*, tonight," he casually said. "Do you fancy coming too?"

Anne was rather taken back; she could not believe her ears. Was Pete really asking her out? What should she say? And if she said yes, what would be the reaction of her friends, especially Elizabeth and the boys from the village?

"Well, hmm, err, it's very sweet of you to ask, Pon, Pon, Pete, I mean Pete, and it's, err, a bit short notice, but damn it, yes, why not? I'd love to go."

Pete frowned, baffled by her muddled response. "Good. We're going in my car. That is you, me, Jack, and whoever Jack decides to bring along. What time do you finish today?"

"Hmm, anytime now. When Linda gets here around five o'clock."

"Perfect, I'll pick you up at six."

"But you don't know where I live," said Anne. "I live ..."

Pete scowled. "Of course I do. You live in the School House with your parents and that really weird sister of yours. Remember, I was here last summer too."

"Oh, yes, silly me. Alright then, I'll see you later."

Pete nodded his head with a satisfactory gesture, turned on his heels and left the vestibule.

As Anne left the Hotel through the main entrance, Bob Jarrams pulled up at the bottom of the steps in his car. "Would you like a lift, Anne? I'm just popping into the village to post a letter."

Normally Anne would have been more than happy to walk, but as she was going out, time was of the essence, so she accepted the lift eagerly and climbed beside Bob in his car.

"Suzie says *The Omen* is really scary," said Crystal, as they left Pete's Corsair in the car park beside the library in Helston and walked down Meneage Street towards the cinema. "She saw it in London apparently before she came down here. Dilys on the other hand said it's not scary one bit, but I think she's just trying to sound brave and fearless."

"Dilys, brave and fearless," laughed Pete, momentarily stopping to admire his reflection in a shop window. "She's a right cowardy custard. Remember when she tagged on behind us one Wednesday as we walked back through the woods after a barbecue and that owl hooted? The soppy cow jumped out of her skin and squealed like a pig."

Crystal frowned. "Don't be mean. Poor old Dilys is just over sensitive. She told me that she thinks the woods are haunted."

Anne giggled. "Haunted! I've walked through the woods hundreds of times and I've never witnessed anything remotely ghostly."

"Exactly," said Jack, "I reckon she says crazy things like that just to draw attention to herself, after all she fancies you rotten, Pete."

"Yeah, well, I can't blame her for that."

"She told me that she saw a holly tree crying," blurted Crystal who immediately regretted speaking out.

"She what?" Pete said, momentarily stopping in his tracks.

Anne frowned. "Was she sober at the time?"

Crystal nodded. "Yes, it was one afternoon so she'd not been drinking. She said water was dripping from the tree's leaves and they tasted salty, like tears."

"I tell you, she's crazy," said Pete. "Crying trees indeed!"

Jack laughed. "Absolutely, and let's face it, any fear she has of unpleasant happenings can't be genuine. I mean, it's pretty obvious she's used to horrific sights cos she sees one every time she looks in the mirror."

"That's horrible," said Crystal, turning red with anger, as the two boys fell around with laughter. "She can't help it if she looks, umm, if her face, umm if…"

"… if she looks like the back end of a bus," interrupted Pete.

"Hey, that's a pretty derogatory comment," said Jack, hands on hips, pretending to be serious. "You can't go around insulting buses like that."

Anne said nothing and looked on, indecisive as to how to react. She was surprised therefore and a little cross with herself when she realised she was smiling, and before they reached the cinema, her smiles, stimulated by the jollity of her companions, turned into infectious laughter. Hence when the four young people arrived at the cinema they were in very high spirits and did not take the film quite as seriously as they might have done had the prelude to the evening got off on a more serious footing, and Crystal in particular was impressed by her ability to watch a horror film and not be left a quivering wreck.

In the middle of the night, however, things seemed a little different. Crystal lay awake for hours haunted by Damien's cherubic, yet sinister face, and she was convinced there were at least three Rottweilers snuffling around the room. Therefore, she was a little heartened when she realised the snuffling was Dilys breathing heavily in the bed by the window, and after deep concentration, she was finally able to substitute the face of Damien with that of Jack and live again the moment when he had kissed her.

Chapter Twenty Two

"So where did you go last night," Elizabeth bluntly asked Anne, as the sisters sat down for breakfast. "You were fast asleep when I got in but I could see you'd been out cos your favourite skirt was lying on the back of the chair and your room reeked of perfume."

"I went to the pictures," said Anne, casually spreading butter on a slice of toast. "I'd have told you, but it was a last minute arrangement and I didn't know where you were."

"The pictures! I see, so who did you go with?"

"Just people from work," said Anne, sensing an imminent bout of interrogation. "We went to see *The Omen*, which in retrospect was quite terrifying, but it didn't seem so at the time. I'm surprised I was asleep when you came in, because I didn't think I'd slept at all with no-one in the house. Anyway, you and Malcolm must go and see it when he has a night off."

Elizabeth, not one to be deterred, put her head to one side. "Any particular people from work?" she persisted. "Anyone I might know?"

"Hmm, yes," said Anne, hesitantly, as she reached for the marmalade jar. "Crystal, you remember her, she was Florence Nightingale at Dad's party. Then, hmm, there was Jack, as in Jack the Ripper and hmm, then hmm, Pete."

"Ha-ha, I knew it!" said Elizabeth, triumphantly. "So which one was yours? Jack or Pete? Please don't tell me it was Pete. That would be too embarrassing."

"Hmm, well, yes, it was Pete who asked me, but I think it was just to make up the numbers because he'd agreed to go with Jack and he knew that Jack would be taking someone. I don't expect we'll go out again, so you can take that look off your face."

"But you should go out again, Anne, although not necessarily with Pete. You can't sit forever waiting for Danny. I mean be serious, it's not going to happen, is it? Danny's a dear, dear friend to you, I know, but he's never going to be any more than that, is he? Promise me, that if err, Pete asks you out again, you'll go."

"You can be very cruel at times, Liz," said Anne, feeling tears prickle the back of her eyes. "But yes, if Pete asks me out again then I may well go, though not for any reason other than last night was a good laugh."

Elizabeth reached over and patted the back of Anne's hand. "Make the most of the lads while they're here, Anne, after all they'll be going back before long and then we'll probably never see them again."

"I've got the day off today," said Anne, not wishing to pursue the subject further, "so why don't we go out, just the two of us, although we can't go very far because Mum and Dad have the car."

"That's a brilliant idea, we could walk over the cliffs to Polquillick and have lunch there," suggested Elizabeth. "I could do with a bit of exercise because I've been really lazy since I got back home and I won't be seeing Malc today because he works all day on Sunday."

"Okay, and we'll call in on the way and tell Grandma what we're doing, cos if she comes round and we're not here she might start to worry."

"What a nice idea," said Molly, who, with the major had just arrived back home from church. "I've not been out walking myself much lately because of the heat, but at least there's usually a bit of a breeze on the cliff tops. Anyway, if you feel it's going to be too much to walk back, please don't hesitate to ring, and then Granddad will pick you up, won't you Ben?"

"Of course," said the major, hanging his jacket on the back of a kitchen chair. "I'll run you over there too, if you like."

"That's very sweet of you but we must definitely walk one way," said Elizabeth, "and so we'll most likely take you up on the offer for a lift back."

"Well, you know where the phone box is in Polquillick, don't you?" said Molly. "It's by the church. Now run along before it gets to the hottest part of the day and don't do anything silly."

Elizabeth and Anne arrived in Polquillick just after midday, both hot and gasping for a drink.

"Are we going to the pub or shall we go to the café?" asked Elizabeth, as they rested on a wall in the shade of a cottage.

"I think I'd rather go to the café," said Anne, "it's nice there cos it looks over the cove and we can sit under one of the big brollies. Besides, I don't really want an alcoholic drink this time of day and I always feel guilty if I ask for a soft drink."

"Yes, but the landlord here doesn't make derisory comments like crazy Raymond Withers," said Elizabeth. "He's got far more sense. I'm not fussed either way where we go, the café is bound to be packed and I expect the pub will be too."

Anne rose from the wall, casually looked down the road and pointed. "Gosh, look over there; there's a bloke by the chapel who's the spitting image of Greg."

Elizabeth quickly leapt from the wall and looked to where Anne was pointing. "Where, where? She demanded. "I can't see him."

Anne rested her hand on her hip and tilted her head to one side. "That's cos there's no-one there now, and really the person I saw looked more like Danny, but I said Greg just to test your reaction. So, you're still smitten with him then. I thought you were."

"I'm not," said Elizabeth, angry that her impulsive behaviour had betrayed her.

"Yeah, I believe you: thousands wouldn't. Come on, let's go to the café, I fancy one of their banana milk shakes and then I'm going to have fish and chips."

"What! Fish and chips, but think of all the calories in that," said Elizabeth, spanning her waist with her hands.

"Oh, don't be silly, we're supposed to be having a fun day out. Besides, the walk here must have burned up loads of calories and if you want to we could always walk home to burn up more."

Elizabeth pulled a face. "Well, I don't know about that. I think I'd rather just have a day eating very little tomorrow instead.

As luck would have it they arrived at the café as a family were leaving and so were able to get a table straight away beneath a large red and white striped sunshade and near to the railings overlooking the beach.

"I love it here," sighed Anne, sitting, as she gazed onto the sand below. "I'm surprised that no-one in Trengillion has had the foresight to open up a cafe or tea shop near to the beach. It would be a little gold mine in the summer if they did."

"Hey, that's a good idea," said Elizabeth, picking up the menu. "Cove Cottage would be ideal because it has quite a big front garden so people could sit out there in the good weather or go inside if the weather's grim."

"Wow, yes," enthused Anne. "Why don't we start our own little business, we could be rich by the time we're thirty."

"Well, for a start we don't own Cove Cottage or anywhere else near the beach for that matter, and then there's the fact I have my chosen career in teaching to pursue and you like your job at the Hotel."

Anne giggled. "You're right. I'd hate to leave the Hotel. I'd miss the people I work with terribly. I love them all."

"So you do love Poncey Pete," teased Elizabeth, cheekily. "I knew it."

"Don't be silly. You know what I mean. I love them collectively, not individually, except perhaps for Grev. He's very special."

Elizabeth raised her eyebrows. "Special, in what way?"

Anne wrinkled her nose. "Well, it's difficult to explain, but he's special in as much as I want to mother him, look after him and protect him from a world which has not shown him much love." She sighed. "Really Liz, he's such a dear, sweet boy and I'm sure he'd never hurt a fly."

Elizabeth giggled. "Complete contrast to Ponce then."

When the waitress came to take their order Anne gave her a quizzical look. "I feel I know you from somewhere," she said.

The girl nodded. "Yes, you do know me and I know you. I'm Cissie Trevelyan, Matthew Williams' girlfriend. I was at your dad's birthday party with Matt, but I had my hair in a bun then, so I suppose I looked a bit different to now."

"Of course," nodded Anne, who seldom forgot a face. "Did you meet my sister, Elizabeth at the party? She's going to start teaching at your school here in September."

"Really, I'm pleased to meet you," smiled Cissie, politely nodding and offering her hand to shake. "We didn't actually meet at the party but I remember seeing you with a handsome hunk. So, you'll be replacing Mrs Naylor who retired last month after a staggering thirty three years at the school. She'll be quite a hard act to follow."

Elizabeth scowled. "Oh, don't say that, I'm nervous enough as it is."

Cissie smiled. "I'm only kidding. She was good though and much loved too but I think most folks are looking forward to seeing a fresh face and kids adapt pretty quickly to change."

Elizabeth sighed, clearly relieved. "Did you go to the school here?"

"Yes, I did, and so did my parents, grandparents and great grandparents. You'll like it and I think the kids are all well behaved, although we did have a bit of vandalism a couple of nights ago, but that will have been older boys with nothing better to do."

"Vandalism!" said Anne, surprised. "Where was that?"

Cissie lowered her voice. "In the churchyard, of all places. One of the gravestones must have been hit with something mighty hard cos it's badly cracked now and the corner has broken right off. What's more, I'm told something smelly like creosote has been tipped all over the actual grave and it's killed the grass. I keep meaning to go and take a look but I never seem to find the time."

Elizabeth gasped. "Good heavens, what a horrible thing to do. Have you any idea whose grave it was?"

Cissie glanced over her shoulder and leaned forwards. "The infamous Wilfred Ham, so I'm told," she whispered. "Infamous, because local history has it that he shot a posh bloke from over Trengillion way, donkey's years ago. Apparently he was never charged with the murder though cos he had an alibi and he always denied it anyway, but then he'd hardly have boasted about it, would he? Cos if he had, it meant he'd have been strung up."

"Wilfred Ham. He must have been Florrie Ham's father then," said Anne, feeling a pang of excitement. "How strange. Whoever could have done it?"

"Well, like I say," said Cissie, confidently, "we think it were vandals."

"Or someone bearing a grudge," said Elizabeth, sharing her sister's intrigue. "But who could that be after all these years?"

John Collins left the family home in Coronation Terrace on Monday morning after breakfast for work and wandered down the lane between the school and the School House having decided to walk for a change. Normally Dave or one of the other lads picked him up in the van, but as the latest job was to be at the Hotel, he said he would walk instead, for he fancied the opportunity to wander through the woods, something he had not done for several months. When he reached the bridge, he slipped under the fence and followed the stream into Bluebell Woods.

He happily whistled as he walked the woodland path beneath the trees where sunlight glinted through the swaying branches and onto the trickling water, his notes in harmony with the bird song drifting through the dappled shade.

John, a keen nature lover and true countryman, lapped up the beauty of the morning and delighted at the birdsong; at the same time he was hoping that during the course of the day he would see Anne.

By a bend in the stream, near to the stump of the old ash tree, his head brushed against a dangling strand of honeysuckle, entwined through the thorny branches of a hawthorn bush. Its scent stopped him in his tracks; the smell was irresistible and he could not pass it by without taking a quick sniff. He closed his eyes to take in the strong perfume and then turned to resume his journey, but as he did so something caught his eye: a shoe, and he was mystified as to why it should be lying there in the woodland near an elder bush and part hidden by a mass of tangled ivy. Intrigued, John left the path to investigate but when he reached the shoe and bent to pick it up, he found it appeared to be caught on something and could not be moved. John stooped to see what the problem was. When he saw the shoe was attached to a foot he broke out into a cold sweat.

Managing to compose himself, he peered into the mass of dense leaves but could glimpse no more than two legs wearing faded jeans. Nervously, John crept around the bush hoping he might see better on the other side. His search revealed a head covered with a mop of dark hair. John moved closer, baffled as to who the person might be. Was it a tramp sleeping, or a drunk perhaps who had been unable to find his way home in the dark the previous night and was now resting? John crept a little closer and knelt beside the figure whose head was face down in the undergrowth. Slowly and carefully he turned the head. His effort revealed a young face: cold, white and lifeless. John's lips quivered and tears welled up in his eyes. Gently he stroked the pale face and brushed dirt from the blood-stained cheeks. He let out a cry of frustration. There was no question as to the person's identity. He was one of the young lads who worked at the Hotel. The one known as Grev Penwynton.

Chapter Twenty Three

Unaware of the dramatic events unfurling in the woods and at the Hotel, Elizabeth, after Anne had gone to work, tidied the house ready for the return of Ned and Stella later in the day. She then took a writing pad from the desk in the front room and walked down to the beach to write to her old teaching friend in Sussex; for the two girls had vowed on parting after their holiday abroad that they would keep in touch and it was Elizabeth's turn to write.

The tide was way out when Elizabeth reached the cove so there was plenty of room on the beach, but since she had nothing to sit on she walked across the sand and shingle to the rocks at the foot of the cliff beneath Chy-an-Gwyns and there sat with her legs dangling over the side of a large boulder.

Elizabeth opened the writing pad and bit on the end of her pen. She was not really in the mood for writing, at least not to Gabby, for her friend was unfamiliar with the everyday life of Trengillion, hence there seemed very little to say. Nevertheless, Elizabeth put pen to paper and wrote her address on the top right hand side of the page, followed by the date, she then attempted to begin her letter, but before she had written even one line she noticed a glaring mistake, instead of writing Dear Gabby, she had inadvertently written Dear Greg. Elizabeth sighed deeply. Why could she not get Greg out of her head? He was engaged to Jemima and she had Malcolm, so there was no reason at all why he should be on her mind. But he was. Constantly. For never a day went by without her hoping to hear the engagement had never occurred and they had parted and gone their separate ways.

Elizabeth glanced across the beach; everyone looked blissfully happy. Perhaps it was the glorious weather causing their contentment and beneath the smiles and laughter they really were only moderately gratified with life or even downright miserable. Elizabeth doubted it. Most of her friends seemed content and would not wish to swap places with anyone, nevertheless, she questioned the depth of her own happiness and conceded to a point she was satisfied with her life, but something was missing and she could not fool herself as to what that something was, for quite simply it was Greg. He was something to her that Malcolm could never be and there was nothing at all she could do to change the situation.

Elizabeth looked at the sheet of white paper on her lap. Damn it, she would write Greg a letter, not with the intent of posting it, but just to make her feel better, thus she began.

My dearest darling Greg,

I wonder if I told you how much I loved you it would change anything in your life. I wonder if you would break off your engagement to Jemima and come rushing home to me. I wonder if you could ever love me enough for us to spend the rest of our lives together. I wonder if you even think of me at all.

At the moment I'm sitting on the beach in Trengillion, at the foot of the cliffs beneath Chy-an-Gwyns. I'm supposed to be writing to a friend but it's not easy when all I can think of is you. Now that I'm home everywhere I go I see your face. I hear your voice in the wind and through the crashing waves of the sea. I see you climbing trees in the woods, and hear you laughing on the beach.

When next we meet you'll probably say you've set a date for your wedding, I'll smile and say I'm glad for you, but my sincerity will be false, my heart broken. And later when I get home I shall cry myself to sleep.

A sudden commotion on the beach caused Elizabeth to stop writing and look up. Someone appeared to be relaying news worthy of many dramatic gestures, and the arm waving had the necessary effect because the receivers of the news put hands to mouths and looked shocked. Intrigued, Elizabeth wished she were a little closer so that she might get some indication as to what the kerfuffle was about, but she was well out of earshot and not concerned enough to edge closer in order to cavesdrop.

Elizabeth attempted to continue with her letter but the spell was broken. She read that which she had written and burst into laughter. "Greg would run a mile if he received this," she told two tiny crabs visible through the shallow water of a rock pool near to her dangling feet.

She tore the page from the pad and pushed it into the pocket of her jeans but immediately decided that was a bad idea, for as likely as not she would forget to remove it and her mother would find it on wash-day. Elizabeth took the paper from her pocket, screwed it up and tossed it into the rock pool with the crabs. She watched as the ink smudged and her words became illegible; she then jumped down onto the wet sand, fished it from the water and pushed it into a deep crevice between the rocks with the tip of her pen. Once happy she could not be accused of dropping litter she started a new letter and correctly began with Dear Gabby.

Jane Williams repeatedly looked at the clock in the shoe shop where she worked and each time sighed with dismay, for the hands on the clock seemed hardly to have moved since she had arrived for work at half past eight and she knew only too well that once the shop closed at half past five then the time would fly by. Her anxiety regarding time was due to the fact that she was going out in the evening, for Ben, one of the two chefs working at the Hotel, had asked her the previous day if she would like to go with him to the pictures to see *The Omen,* the film which everyone in Trengillion under the age of forty was talking about. Jane had been delighted with his invitation and made no restraint in showing her enthusiasm, for she was tired of having no regular boyfriend and although after she had first split with Stu, on discovering he took drugs, she had vowed she wanted no other, but the monotony of having a mediocre social life was wearing a bit thin. For unlike several of her friends who had jobs they really enjoyed, Jane found shop work tiring and boring, hence it was devoid of any of the excitement other jobs might have.

As she unpacked a carton of winter boots ready for the autumn trade, she wondered if it was not too late for a change in career and whether she ought to train for something like hairdressing as her mother had. For her mother, Betty, had her own hairdressing salon at the back of the family home, Fuchsia Cottage, and Jane knew she loved every minute of her work, for both the social side and job satisfaction.

The shop doorbell rang as she stacked the large boxes on the floor; she looked up as a family walked in and sat on the seats provided. Jane approached them with a smile but knew what they wanted; school shoes no doubt for the new term in September, and the children, just as she had done as a child, would say every pair of shoes they didn't like hurt their feet and only the less practical seemed to fit perfectly. Wearily, Jane went through the routine of selling her wares and when the children, as predicted, rebuffed her good intentions, she made up her mind there and then it was time for change; she contemplated whether or not she might ask Ben if there were any vacancies at the Penwynton Hotel, for there always seemed to be a buzz of excitement there.

Bluebell Woods was closed to the public after the body of Grev Penwynton was discovered, and the staff and guests of the Hotel were detained and questioned by the police in order to try and establish his last known movements. No-one was told the cause of Grev's death and it was too early to say for how long he had been dead, hence speculation was rife.

Crystal Hart was more devastated than most by the news, for it did not take her long to realise the reason Grev had not met her on the beach as planned was because he was probably already dead, or worse still, dying. She was riddled with guilt for not having at least checked to see if he was alright when she returned to the Hotel to change prior to the trip to the cinema. But she had been so overwhelmed with Jack's attention and the impending outing that poor Grev's welfare had never entered her mind at all.

Anne likewise was distressed by the tragic news, although unlike others who could talk of nothing other than the possible cause of death which had not been disclosed by the police, her only thoughts were that she would never see him again. Mary Cottingham told Anne, whom she had invited into her office, that Grev had been missing the previous day, but they hadn't been too concerned as they thought it possible he might just have vanished as readily as he had first appeared.

"But he would never have done that," sobbed Anne. "He loved working here, he told me so, besides he had nowhere else to go."

"Yes, I can see that you're right," said Mary, sympathetically, "but we couldn't have gone to the police and reported him missing after such a short space of time. Heather and I agreed we'd leave it 'til today and then if there was still no sign of him we'd try and do something about it. I'm sorry, Anne, truly I am. This has to be the most dreadful day of my life."

Ned and Stella returned home early on the Monday evening to the news that young Grev Penwynton had died. Both were shocked, especially by the state of Anne who sobbed uncontrollably as she told the story from her point of view.

"I expect there'll be a third now," whispered Stella, as the news sank in, "for some strange reason death always seems to go in threes."

"Oh, don't say that," sobbed Anne, "the deaths of Grandpa and Grev have been very close to home, I can't bear the thought of losing anyone else."

"While on the subject of Grandpa," said Ned, desperate to say something to ease his daughter's pain. "I know this is hardly the right time but he left you both some money in his will and quite a substantial amount too."

Anne looked up. "Grandpa left us some money."

Ned nodded. "Yes, you are each to have five thousand pounds when the estate is finally settled."

Anne's eyes again filled with tears.

Elizabeth flopped down in a chair her legs having turned to jelly. "Five thousand pounds!" she gasped. "I didn't realise Grandpa had that sort of money."

"Well, he did have a well-paid job," said Ned, "but according to Marilyn he opened a savings account for each of you on your birth and topped the money up frequently over the years so that on his death you would both get the same. You see, he always felt guilty that he had left Grandma and me to fend for ourselves. I guess it was his way of saying sorry."

A little later, when Anne felt more composed, she and Elizabeth, both still overwhelmed by the generosity of the grandfather whom they seldom saw, left their parents to go to Elizabeth's room where they wanted to discuss their new found wealth and the demise of Grev Penwynton.

"I think," said Anne, sitting on the floor and leaning against Elizabeth's bed, "that I shall take a leaf from Graham's book and invest my money with a building society, so that one day I'll be able to buy a house. How about you, Liz, what will you do?"

"I don't know. I'll probably do the same. Having said that, I might use some of the money to pay for driving lessons and then buy a nice car. I don't want to rely on the bus to get me to Polquillick for too long as it'll be horrible hanging around on wet, cold mornings."

Stella, weary from the journey in the heat and in no mood for cooking, made a round of sandwiches each for Ned, the girls and herself. The girls ate theirs in Elizabeth's bedroom, and Ned and Stella took theirs into the sitting room intent on relaxing and putting up their feet. Before they had finished their supper, however, there was a knock on the door and, as it opened, a familiar voice called out, "Coo-ee, it's only me."

"Come in, Mum," shouted Ned, "we're in the front room."

"Sorry to bother you but I've brought you six bottles of elderflower champagne," said Molly, taking the bottles from her basket and placing them on the table before sitting down on the settee. "I made three batches in all and the major and me are getting a bit fed up with it, because it'll need drinking soon or it'll be as flat as a pancake. Having said that, these bottles still have plenty of life left in them. Anyway, how did the funeral go? Poor Marilyn! She's been in my thoughts for days now."

Ned sighed. "It went as well as a funeral can go and was certainly very well attended. In fact the church was packed. Marilyn's really cut up, naturally, but at least she has some very good friends to help her through the rough bit. I felt sorry for her too, but then I never did dislike her as you did."

"Oh, please don't say it like that, Ned," pleaded Molly. "You make me sound so callous and uncaring and it wasn't Marilyn I blamed, it was your father. Well, perhaps I blamed her a little but whichever, I forgave them both years ago." She sighed deeply. "It's sad, I know, but well, these things happen, don't they?"

Ned smiled, rose without speaking and left the room. When he returned, seconds later, he held in his hand a small velvet covered jewellery box which he handed to his mother. Molly looked at the box clearly puzzled. "What's this?"

Ned sat down. "Open it and see."

Molly carefully raised the lid, mystified as to what the box might contain. She gasped, much surprised, on seeing a brooch she instantly recognised resting on cotton wool. It had belonged to her first husband's mother.

"But, I don't understand," she said, lifting the brooch from the box. "Why have you brought this home?"

"It's for you," said Ned. "It belonged to Dad's mum and she left it to you in her will cos she always liked you. But apparently Dad was too proud to admit her disapproval at the marriage breakdown and so he kept it locked in a box containing his mother's possessions beneath the bed. And then suddenly, out of the blue last week, he showed it to Marilyn and his very words were: 'I must send this on to Moll. It's rightfully hers. Remind me to get it in the post, Marilyn.' He never got round to posting it though, cos he died the following day."

"I always used to admire this brooch," whispered Molly, watching as the emeralds reflected the light from the standard lamp. "Michael's mum, your grandmother, wore it to our wedding. I can see her now in her chocolate brown suit. It was a perfect fit and complimented by emerald green accessories. She was a very elegant woman with impeccable style and taste."

"I bet you looked very elegant too," said Stella.

Molly threw back her head and laughed. "At the time I certainly thought I did. I made my own dress of course. It was made of cream chiffon, calf length, shapeless and draped with row upon row of beading. And my headdress! Well, it was two thick strings of pearls on a band which went round my head and it had three large feathers rising from the right hand side. But then it was the Roaring Twenties and Flapper fashions were all the rage with the young."

"What year was that?" Stella asked.

"Nineteen twenty four and I was twenty years old. I have some old photos somewhere. I'll show them to you sometime when I can remember where I've put them."

Ned looked amazed. "Good heavens, Mother, fancy you keeping your old wedding pictures. I always imagined you burned them years ago. How come I've never seen them?"

Molly sighed. "Because they were too painful to look at. In fact I was often tempted to throw them away but never could. Besides, a lot of work went into that dress."

Molly looked down at the brooch in her hand and then carefully pinned it onto her blouse. She then stood to admire it in the mirror but her vision was blurred by the veil of tears welling in her aching eyes.

Chapter Twenty Four

The following morning, when Anne arrived at work, she heard that the police, who at first had refused to reveal any information whatsoever about John's gruesome discovery in the woods, had finally, after gathering together a substantial amount of evidence, released a statement regarding the death of Grev Penwynton. Their brief announcement revealed that his death was to be treated as murder and the cause was a single gunshot wound to the chest inflicted sometime during the morning of Saturday August the twenty first.

The news that Grev had been shot travelled fast and furious around Trengillion, where villagers, still reeling from the recent burglaries, were disillusioned further still by the knowledge that there was a murderer in their midst. And no-one was more alarmed than Gloria Withers, who, on hearing the news in the post office, ran home at a speed which surprised even herself.

Arriving at the Inn, Gloria flew through the side door and ran along the passage calling to Raymond.

Raymond on hearing his name put his head around the kitchen door. "I'm in here, Glore. What's all the panicking about? Calm down, woman, you look in a right state."

Gasping for breath, Gloria leaned on the door frame and attempted to speak. "That lad," she panted, "the one from the Hotel. I've just been in the post office and Milly told me that the police say he'd been shot. Shot, Raymond shot. Oh, please, please tell me it can't be the case, but do you think it was your gun that killed him? Please tell me it wasn't."

The colour drained from Raymond's face. Shakily he reached for a chair and sat down.

"Oh, Christ, I hope not," he muttered, his face devoid of colour, "I hope not. This is terrible, Glore. You were right, I should have gone to the police when it first went missing. Now they'll probably trace it back to me and I'll be in deep trouble. Blimey, they might even think I shot him."

Gloria stepped forward and knelt by his side. "I thought the same. But all is not lost. You must go to the police now and pretend you've only just found it's gone. Say that when you heard the news about the Hotel lad you went to make sure your guns were all safe and found your favourite one missing and its ammunition too. That way they'll not be able to reprimand you, except perhaps for not having it locked up securely in the first place. Then if it was your gun the killer used, you'll be in the clear. I know it's dishonest, Ray, but whatever we do now we can't bring the poor kid back. I'll tell the boys what you're doing so they won't put their feet in it; after all they're the only ones who know it's been stolen."

Raymond patted Gloria's head. "Alright then, I'll do as you say, but for God's sake don't tell Fay, will you? I don't want her worried."

As she hung out the washing in the back garden of Rose Cottage, Molly heard Doris over the boundary fence, beating a rug with the head of a broom, and so after she had pegged out the last item from her laundry basket she crossed to the fence and peered through a gap where the neighbours often conversed.

"Coo-ee, Doris. Have you heard the latest news?" called Molly, tapping on the fence to attract her attention.

Doris put down the broom and acknowledged her friend's call.

"What news is that?" she asked, brushing dust from her floral pinafore.

"About that poor young lad from the Hotel," said Molly, tut-tutting to emphasise the gravity of the news. "Apparently the poor soul was murdered. Shot dead by a ghastly gun. The major just told me; he heard about it in the post office, you see, and now he's gone round to see Frank and Dot to tell them. Isn't it dreadful?"

"Good heavens! Come round for elevenses, Molly, and then you can tell Jim as well as me, all that you've heard."

Doris and Jim Hughes lived at Ivy Cottage next door to Molly and the major. Doris had lived in the house all her life, and Jim had moved in when the couple had married in late 1967, twelve months after Jim had lost his first wife, Flo, to whom he had been married for over fifty years.

Jim lay down a newspaper and rose from his chair when Molly entered the room. "Any news about the lad?" he asked, "the one found dead in the woods. The expression on your face tells me there probably is."

Once seated, Molly proceeded to tell her neighbours as much as the major had divulged to her; they listened with an air of disbelief and then sat in silence to let the unsavoury news sink in.

"I don't like the sound of this at all," said Jim, when he finally found his voice. "By all accounts it's a dreadful thing to happen but I can't help but think it wouldn't have happened at all if the poor lad had had a different name. I mean, to be called Grenville Penwynton for whatever reason, and then for him to lose his life like this, it's too uncanny for words. It's almost as though the first Grenville has come back, reincarnated, to remind us of his fate. Not of course that we know what happened to him after he left."

"Oh, come on, Jim, I think you're talking utter poppycock, if you don't mind me saying so," said Doris, puffing out her cheeks. "Reincarnation indeed! I don't believe in that sort of stuff as you well know, and if I did I wouldn't think it likely that Grenville Penwynton would come back with the same name for his second life. That would be too far-fetched."

Molly kept quiet during the disagreement as she thought it unwise to take sides with either of her neighbours, and so instead she manoeuvred the conversation around until it pointed in the direction as to who might have pulled the fatal trigger. The debate, however, reached no satisfactory or even feasible conclusion, so while Doris put on the kettle for coffee, Molly and Jim turned to the second most topical subject of the day, the drought.

The following day, Stella received a phone call from her mother who was very excited because they had had a firm and very good offer for their house up for sale in Surrey and they wondered if she and Ned would mind if they popped down to Cornwall for a couple of days to see if they could find a property to buy. Stella, thrilled at hearing some good news for a change, told them they would be welcome whenever they chose to make the journey. It was decided, therefore, since time was of the essence because their buyers wanted as quick a completion as possible, to leave for Cornwall the following morning.

"It'll be funny having two lots of grandparents in the village," said Elizabeth, when Stella told her the news. "Do you think they'll buy one of the new houses? I hope so, cos they're nice and near."

"Well, they may well have to," said Stella, "cos I can't think of anything else in the village for sale, can you?"

"There's the Old Vicarage," said Elizabeth, "but I suppose if you're retired you'd want somewhere smaller than that."

Stella laughed. "Much smaller. Dad loves his gardening but I think that would be much too much for him now. I hear it's in quite a poor state of repair too, and Mum and Dad want a bit of comfort in the autumn of their years, not the prospect of living on a building site."

"How about Sea Thrift Cottage?" said Elizabeth, after brief consideration. "That's for sale, isn't it? Pennard and Rowe are selling it according Graham because he's told us all about it and it's really lovely up there on the cliffs."

Stella slapped her forehead. "Good heavens, why on earth didn't I think of that? It'd be right up their street and it's got wonderful sea views too. I'll give Meg a ring and see if she'll ask Graham to bring home a set of the details tonight as I'd love to see just what it has to offer. I've only ever been inside the kitchen and living room, but it struck me as being quite roomy."

"I like the name," said Elizabeth, dreamily. "I think it's very pretty and really quaint, but then I suppose that's because the name makes me think of thrift. There's lots of it growing on the cliffs near Chy-an-Gwyns, and we used to bring you home bunches of it when we were children. Do you remember?"

Stella nodded. "Of course I remember, and you pressed some too, along with other wild flowers and stuck them into a scrap book for me. Do you remember that? I still have it of course. It's amongst my treasures from your childhood."

Elizabeth giggled. "Yes, I remember. Where is it I'd like to look at my old handiwork?"

"It's in the bottom drawer of the chest standing in the hallway, along with the old photo albums."

Elizabeth found the old scrap book and sat back to shuffle through the thick grey pages, where wild flowers, the colours of some of which were as vibrant as the day they were pressed, lay beside Elizabeth's neat, childish handwriting.

"It must be ten years since I did this," she said, "yet it seems so very recent. When I start teaching at Polquillick School in September, I shall get the children there picking and pressing wild flowers, so that they too have something to look back on."

"That's a nice idea," agreed Stella, "now I must give Meg a ring about Sea Thrift Cottage before I forget."

"And I'm going to the Hotel to tell Anne about Grandma and Granddad having sold their house," said Elizabeth. "The poor girl needs to hear something to cheer her up."

Chapter Twenty Five

Anne found it very difficult to comprehend the death of Grev Penwynton; she even blamed herself, for had she not been so enthusiastic about him having employment at the Hotel, she conceded he might have moved on elsewhere and lived a long and healthy life.

In an attempt to boost morale, Mary Cottingham, concerned for Anne's welfare, tried to keep her receptionist as occupied as possible, hoping by doing so, it might help divert her mind away from young Grev's plight. Therefore, when Elizabeth arrived at the Hotel to convey the good news regarding the potential sale of their grandparents' Surrey home, she found Mary on the reception desk and Anne nowhere to be seen.

"Your little sister's upstairs with Linda," smiled Mary, correctly reading Elizabeth's puzzled frown. "We've a chambermaid off sick today and quite a few people checking out, so their vacated rooms need a thorough cleaning. Anne and Linda are helping the girls out by doing all the beds, but you're more than welcome to go up and find them."

"Oh, I see, thanks," smiled Elizabeth, "I'll do that then. The reason I'm here is because I thought Anne could do with hearing some good news, so I wanted to tell that Grandma Hargreaves rang this morning to say they have a buyer for their house. They're hoping to move down here, you see."

"Oh, that's wonderful news. I take it they'll be your grandparents who live in Horley then. Anne told me how you used to guess the number of coaches on trains there when you went to visit as children."

Elizabeth laughed. "Did she? Yes, I'd forgotten that, but now you come to mention it, I recall it seemed quite good fun at the time, but then I've always liked trains. Anyway, may I go and find Anne? That's if you can give me some idea as to where she might be?"

Mary glanced at a list of guest departures and arrivals lying on the desk. "Well she could be in any of six rooms, I'll write down the numbers for you."

Once done, Mary handed a sheet of paper to Elizabeth. "They're all upstairs. Rooms six and eight are on the first floor and rooms nine, eleven, fourteen and sixteen on the second. They're all numbered so you can't miss them."

"Shall I knock before I go in?" asked Elizabeth.

Mary shook her head. "No need; today's departures have all checked out, so only our girls will be in the rooms. Please feel free to browse while you're up there. I'd like to know what you think of them, and there's plenty of time as the new arrivals aren't permitted to check in until after two."

"Thank you," said Elizabeth, leaving the vestibule, "and if they look stressed, the girls that is, not the rooms, I might even give them a hand."

"Please do," said Mary, "the more the merrier and I'm sure Dilys at least would appreciate that."

On the first floor, Elizabeth checked room six and found it clean and ready for the next guests. Room eight likewise was looking bright and fresh. She climbed the stairs to the top floor, the door of room nine was slightly ajar, she peeped inside and saw a woman whom she did not recognise vacuuming the floor. Confident that she had not been seen, Elizabeth quietly pulled the door shut to avoid detection so she didn't have to explain who she was and why she was there.

Outside the door of room eleven, Elizabeth listened for any sounds within; all seemed quiet and so she opened the door and peeped inside. To her surprise, the room seemed dull in comparison with others she had viewed. The walls were covered in heavy embossed wallpaper incorporating several shades of blue. Dark brocade curtains hung on either side of the two windows and a large multi coloured square carpet almost covered the floor, but where it did not reach, the bare boards were stained with a dull, dark varnish. Puzzled as to why number eleven should be decorated in such an old fashioned way, she stepped inside but was instantly startled by the presence of someone sitting in a chair facing towards the window. She could not see a face, but a head of dark hair was clearly visible above the back of a chair. Elizabeth hastily retreated, hoping her intrusion had not disturbed the guest. As she quietly closed the door, she heard laughter coming from further along the corridor and she was relieved when she saw Anne and Linda emerge from one of the rooms carrying a large basket of dirty laundry.

"Lizzy," said Anne, surprised. "Whatever are you doing here?"

"Looking for you," said Elizabeth, moving away from door eleven, lest her voice should disturb the guest for a second time. "Mary sent me up because I wanted to tell you Grandma and Granddad Hargreaves have a buyer for their house and they're coming down tomorrow to look for one here."

"Wow, that's brilliant," said Anne, gently clapping her hands, "absolutely brilliant. We'll have to get Graham to find them a really nice house."

"Well, actually, I suggested to Mum they might like Sea Thrift Cottage," said Elizabeth, proudly, "and so Mum was going to ring Mrs Reynolds to get Graham to bring home a copy of the details for us all to look at."

Before Anne could answer, the woman with the vacuum cleaner emerged from room nine chuntering beneath her breath.

"Hi, Val," said Linda, aware of the cleaner's very short fuse. "All the beds are made now. Gertie and Dilys are just finishing off fourteen and Trish is in number sixteen vacuuming, so you've nearly finished."

"Thank goodness for that," grumbled Val, wiping her brow on the back of her hand. "I'm bloomin' starving and I need a fag." She then stepped towards room eleven and put her hand on the brass knob.

"No," cried Elizabeth, "there's some..." her voice trailed away as Val opened the door, revealing a bright room painted white and complimented with a rich turquoise.

"What's the matter, Liz?" asked Anne. "You've gone awfully pale."

Elizabeth moved towards the door. "Err, nothing."

Anne took her sister's arm and pulled her into the room. "Come on in and have a proper look. I think this is probably my favourite room. What do you think, isn't it beautiful?"

Elizabeth nodded but was too numbed to speak. The room was completely different from how she had seen it just minutes beforehand. The walls were painted white; the plain curtains were velvet. A large rug lay on a cream coloured, fitted wall to wall carpet. Everything in the room had changed except the chair, the Queen Anne chair, it was still by the window facing the back gardens, but unlike earlier, it was empty.

The students, reminded of Grev's fate every time they went into their sitting room, were still confused by his untimely death, for like everyone else they could see no possible motive for anyone to take the life of a harmless individual such as their work colleague, and the fact that he was a stranger to the area who would have done nothing to antagonise anyone, in their young eyes made the mystery a bigger puzzle than any they had ever been confronted with before.

"Perhaps it was an accident," suggested Suzie, as the students sat in their room at the end of a very busy day. "You know, someone could have been target shooting or something and poor Grev just got in the way. You've told me that the bloke from the Badge has some real guns and belongs to a gun club, so it might even have been him or one of his mates. I mean to say, if that was the case, then he or whoever it was wouldn't come forward to confess, would they."

Jack shook his head. "No, it couldn't have been Ray. Poor Grev was killed at lunchtime on Saturday according to the cops and Ray was in the pub then cos we saw him, didn't we Crystal?"

Crystal nodded but was too full of remorse to speak.

Suzie frowned. "Actually, I'm sure the police said he died on Saturday morning, not lunchtime, so he could easily have done it and been back by opening time."

"Why are you so keen to incriminate poor old Raymond?" asked Pete, clearly annoyed. "You don't even know him. Anyway, he would never be careless enough to shoot anyone. Besides, I'm sure he does his shooting practice out the back of the Inn or at his club, so why on earth do you reckon he'd bother going all the way down to the woods?"

"Okay, so maybe it was deliberate," persisted Suzie.

"Oh, don't be daft," snapped Pete. "Raymond's all mouth and he wouldn't really hurt a fly. Besides, what possible motive could he have and how would he have known Grev was going to be in the woods anyway. Grev only decided to go to the beach during breakfast, we all witnessed that."

"Perhaps he really was a member of the Penwynton family and someone thought if he was able to prove it he'd contest the will and get hold of the dosh," suggested Dilys, unwrapping the last toffee in her bag.

Feeling exasperated, Pete looked heavenwards. "But we've already established that can't be the case. Anne said the baby that the servant girl had had, died and I'm sure Anne wouldn't have got her facts wrong, even if her sister is an airhead."

"That's a dumb idea anyway, Dilys," said Suzie. "There are obviously no Penwyntons left in this country, let alone this village and that's why it was inherited by someone overseas."

Dilys stopped chewing. "Meaning?"

"Meaning, because no Penwyntons live here then there is no-one around to feel threatened by Grev and his unexpected arrival and therefore no motive to kill him. Think about it. The people who inherited the estate live abroad and so wouldn't know anything about Grev and his name, hence they would have no reason to think he might contest the will."

Jack beamed. "Good point, Suzie."

Suzie glowered at him but didn't respond verbally.

"Well, I think it's very worrying," said Crystal, rising to retire to bed, "because if there doesn't seem to be a motive then the murderer might well be some trigger-happy nut who'll shoot anyone just for the fun of it. Are you going to bed now, Dilys? Please do, cos I'm tired and I don't fancy being alone in our room right now."

"Yeah, alright, but I'll have to go and make my Horlicks first."

"Can't you go without it for just one night?" pleaded Crystal.

"No," said Dilys, throwing her empty sweet packet into the waste paper basket. "I'd have difficulty sleeping without it. But if you hang on here for a minute, I'll call for you on the way back from the kitchen."

"No, on second thoughts I'll come down with you," said Crystal, crossing the room to where Dilys stood. "I think I might even have a mug too. I feel dreadful over all this and I can't sleep properly with my brain weighed down with guilt."

In the Hotel's walled garden, Jack picked up a severed branch from the deceased elder and examined it. The wood snapped with ease and so confident it was quite dry, he fetched newspaper from the shed, screwed it up tightly into balls and formed a heap onto which he carefully placed some of the elder.

After licking his finger and holding it up into the gentle breeze to establish from which direction the wind was blowing, he lit the bonfire knowing the westerly wind would blow the smoke away from the Hotel and down towards the fields in the valley. He then sat on an upturned wheelbarrow, took a piece of chewing gum from his pocket, popped it in his mouth and watched the flames slowly consume the wood.

Shortly after, Chef Ben emerged carrying two large cardboard boxes. "Ah, it's you with a bonfire, is it? I could see the smoke from the kitchen window. Chuck these on, lad; we've just had a delivery of veg but something's leaked in the box and made it a bit smelly so it needs disposing of quick."

Jack took the boxes from Ben's hands and threw them into the flames without speaking.

"How are the runner beans coming on?" asked the chef, "must be nearly ready by now."

Jack glanced towards a row of garden canes supporting the red flowering beans. He shrugged his shoulders. "According to Dick another couple of days should do it. We water them every night with cans but he says they're still behind. I wouldn't know though cos I've never grown anything before."

"No, I suppose not. They could do with some real rain to give them a good soaking, having said that everything's dry and dusty and needs a damn good wash. Got any fags on you?"

"No, more's the shame. I left them in my room. They're in my jacket pocket. I keep thinking I'll go and fetch them but I can't be bothered, this heat is so tiring."

"Yeah, still, that's probably a good thing cos I want to give up anyway. Must get back then; it's hotter out here than it is in the bleedin' kitchen. See yer."

Jack watched Ben leave the garden and close the gate. He then turned back to the fire. Some of the branches beneath the crisp, blackened cardboard boxes, had burned away. The boxes fell apart and dropped through the smouldering elder when Jack poked them with a garden fork.

Looking at his watch, Jack saw it was time for his tea break. Eager to return indoors and away from the heat, he picked up the remainder of the branches and carefully placed them on the bonfire. To his surprise a sudden gust of wind dramatically caused the fire to snap, crackle, hiss and spit. Jack stepped back as smoke blew in his face, burned his eyes and made him cough. He moved away but it followed him in whichever direction he ran and in panic he tripped on an edging stone, fell and grazed his knee. Jack cursed as he stood up, half expecting to see Malcolm furiously fanning the flames with bellows, but no-one was present. Jack scratched his head, puzzled, for the slow moving clouds in the clear blue sky above indicated there was very little wind.

Down in the meadow, the excavation of the pond was complete and around the edge of the large hole, the earth that had been removed was banked up ready to be levelled and made into a pathway. Because Bob and Dick were keen to have fish and Heather and Mary were eager to have aquatic plants and especially a water lily, the pond base sloped dramatically to give both a deep and a shallow end, and around the edge, solid earth formed a margin shelf to hold pots containing shallow water plants.

Swirling clouds of grey smoke from Jack's bonfire drifted slowly across the walls of the garden and down towards the meadow where Bob and Dick, both keen to see the progress of the pond, watched, as John Collins and Steve Penhaligon jumped into the hole after the final scoop of earth had been removed and then walked, holding buckets, across the bottom to pick up any large stones and sharp objects, prior to the addition of a layer of sand which would provide a soft base for the huge pond liner lying in waiting on the meadow grass.

In the shallow end, John stooped to pick up a bone protruding through the compressed earth. With little interest he dropped it into his bucket but then instantly saw another. He stooped again. However, when he touched the bone and tugged it he found it was larger than the first and much of it still beneath the ground. He called to Dave Richardson, his boss, and asked him to throw down a shovel.

Annoyed by the hold-up he then started to dig around the stubborn bone.

"No, stop, stop," shouted Bob, running along the side of the bank. "Hang on, lad, I'm coming down."

Bob jumped into the hole, ran over to the bone, knelt and looked at it closely. He then searched through the objects in John's bucket, pulled out a piece of slate and carefully scraped the earth away from around the base of the bone. John and Steve curiously looked on, promptly joined by Dick and Dave, equally inquisitive.

"Christ, Bob, you don't think it's human, do you?" asked Dick, noting the look of excitement on Bob's face.

"Not sure yet, but I've a sneaky feeling it will be," said Bob, continuing to scrape away the earth.

When a little more of the bone was visible it was clear that there were in fact two bones lying side by side. With a thoughtful nod, Bob shuffled along the ground and started to scrape away the earth in a different spot. It was not long before a curved piece of bone appeared in the earth. Bob scrambled to his feet when it was obvious that he had revealed a human skull. The other men looked on in disbelief.

"I think we'd better give the police a ring," said Dick, shocked. "How long do you reckon that poor blighter's been down there?"

"Hmm, job to say at this stage, but from what I can see it must be a fair few years," said Bob, wiping his brow. "The experts will be able to be a lot more accurate than me, of course."

Steve knelt to examine the find closer. "How on earth did you know there was gonna be a skull there?"

"Archaeology was a hobby of mine when I lived up-country," said Bob, a look of satisfaction stretching from ear to ear. "At first it was just a haunch but when I identified the bones as the radius and the ulna I guessed there had to be more. Funny really, it's the first time I've ever excavated a skeleton. I've seen it done of course, but I never actually found one myself."

John sat down on the margin shelf, his face was as white as his T shirt.

"Blimey, do you think there's going to be a whole skeleton buried there then?" he stammered. "I mean, surely I can't have been unlucky enough to have found two bodies in such a short space of time."

Bob patted John's shoulder. "I expect so, unless of course it was dismembered before burial. But don't worry, lad, there's no way you'll have known this chap, he must have been buried there for God knows how many years: probably even before you were born."

Chapter Twenty Six

Not many doubted the identity of the skeleton found in the meadow belonging to the Penwynton Hotel. The suggested name on the lips of everyone familiar with Trengillion's history was of course Grenville Penwynton, and when it was revealed that the remains were that of a male in his early to mid-twenties and that he had been dead for around one hundred years, it proved their speculations to be correct. Jim Hughes took in the news with a saddened heart.

"So they were right all along then. All the rumours passed down through the servants' quarters about Talwyn's cruelty towards Grenville were right, except the dreadful woman went one step further than any of us had ever imagined and killed the poor lad. It seems so wrong that her descendants should ever have got a single penny of Penwynton money. It's wrong, very, very wrong."

"But Talwyn's children, Gorran and Kayna, were Penwyntons too, Jim," said Stella, who broke the news to Jim when she and Ned called round to see him knowing he was keen to hear of the latest developments. "George was their father, after all. But I know what you mean about the corruption of it. It's just a pity all this didn't come to light before the death of Charles, that way he may have chosen to leave his money and the estate elsewhere."

"But the Reeves family would probably have contested it if he had," said Ned. "Because when all's said and done, they were his next of kin."

"But why do you think she killed Grenville?" asked Jim, unable to make any sense of the situation. "She must have hated him very much, and how for that matter, did she do it? I mean to say, it'd not be an easy job for a woman, would it? And how the devil did she get him down to the meadow to bury him?"

Ned felt great pity for the elderly man, who was clearly troubled. "The motive for murder would no doubt have been the same as for the cruelty, Jim, to do him out of his inheritance. As for the method, I would guess, perhaps she poisoned him first to render him helpless.

And if that were the case, the dreadful deed may even have taken place in the meadow, meaning it would negate the necessity to move the body. For when all's said and done, I think it likely that Talwyn was a buxom woman. That's how I envisage her anyway."

Stella nodded. "Possibly, and I suppose the sight of her digging poor Grenville's grave, would have been well hidden from the house windows by the bank." Stella sighed. "The evil woman obviously planned it very carefully."

"Are they definitely sure it's Grenville?" asked Doris. "I mean, just because the remains found are a hundred years old and male, doesn't actually prove it's him. It could be anyone from that era."

Ned reached out and patted Doris' hand, conscious she was probably thinking of her niece who was murdered in the 1950s. "Yes, they're sure it's him. Apparently there was a stick pin found with the body which must have been attached to a cravat once but which has long since rotted. That's how they've identified him because he's wearing it in his portrait which hangs in the art gallery."

"Still doesn't prove it was him" said Doris, obstinately. "Someone else could have had one just the same."

"Possibly," said Ned, "but I doubt it. We believe it's quite unusual. According to Anne, the pin is of a robin sitting on a silver cane inset with diamonds and a ruby for his breast."

"Is that right?" said Jim, his spirit slightly uplifted. "Well that'll no doubt be worth a pretty penny, so at least something has escaped Talwyn's thieving hands."

Ned sighed. "Well, sadly, although most of the diamonds are intact the ruby is missing and I believe the stick itself is quite badly distorted."

Connie and Tom Hargreaves arrived at the School House shortly after Ned and Stella returned from visiting Jim and Doris, and before they had even stepped inside the door, Connie asked to see the details of Sea Thrift Cottage. For Stella's brief description over the telephone the previous day, of the house and its location, had whetted her appetite to a degree where she was desperate to see it.

"I thought you might be enthusiastic," smiled Stella, filling the kettle, after taking the details out from behind the clock on the sideboard, "and for that reason I've already made an appointment for you to see it this evening, that's if you're not too weary."

"Too weary, good heavens, no. I've been sitting on my backside all day. Your father might be feeling a bit stressed though. It can't be much fun concentrating on driving in this heat."

"I'm alright," said Tom Hargreaves, stretching, to ease his back, "and believe it or not I'm as keen to see this cottage as your mother. It sounds too good to be true, sea views and so forth and ideal for pottering around and over the cliffs."

"Don't get too excited," said Ned, "it can get pretty windy up there, as there'll be nothing between you and the Atlantic when the winter gales start to blow. Having said that, I don't mind the wind but I know it drives Stella mad."

The wind was not blowing when the family stepped from Ned's car after he had parked in the driveway of Sea Thrift Cottage; the evening was still; the sea tranquil and the air pleasantly scented with the fragrance of a climbing rose rambling its way through the wild hedge surrounding the property.

"My spine feels all tingly," whispered Connie, wringing her hands together, "it's an even nicer spot than I dared imagine."

"It's more isolated than I expected," said Tom, casting his eyes in all directions, "and a little further back from the cliff than I thought it'd be, but then that's probably a good thing, otherwise we'd have ramblers walking past our gate all the time in summer. What's that house over there? I don't think I know it."

"Yes, you do, it's Chy-an-Gwyns, but the west facing elevation you can see is completely different from the side we see facing us at the School House. The Castor-Hunts who live there would be your nearest neighbours here, along with May and Pat Dickens on the farm," said Stella pointing to Higher Green Farm on the right, "but they'll probably be gone soon as they're going to retire when the farm gets a buyer."

As they spoke, Bertha Fillingham on hearing voices, emerged from the cottage to greet them. After shaking hands and passing the time of day, she showed Connie and Tom around her home while Stella and Ned waited outside in the garden, seated on a bench and enjoying the peace and quiet.

"I wouldn't mind living up here," said Stella, watching butterflies flitting from one flower to another on a large mauve buddleia. "It's so peaceful with just the gentle sound of the sea. At least it is now. I don't expect it'll have quite the same appeal on a miserable wet, winter's day."

"Yeah, but let's face it, nowhere is very appealing in bad weather, is it? Having said that it'd be quite cosy tucked indoors up here listening to the wind howling outside and heavy raindrops lashing against the window panes."

A tap on one of the upstairs windows caused them to turn their heads. Through the glass Connie Hargreaves waved and then gave the thumbs up sign.

"It looks like it has bowled Mum over," laughed Stella. "I knew she'd love it; I just hope to goodness Dad likes it too because he'll have the devil of a job to dissuade her from wanting to buy it if she's hooked."

Ten minutes later Tom called Ned and Stella indoors to join them all for a cup of tea.

"We're buying it," said Connie, excitedly, as they entered the kitchen. "It's just perfect; we both love it and I've not been so happy for years."

"We're not even going to insult Mrs Fillingham with an offer," said Tom, taking a seat at the kitchen table. "It's worth every penny of the asking price and we've done alright with our place back home. So in the morning I'll give the agents a ring and tell them."

"Please, call me Bertha," said Mrs Fillingham, pouring tea from a stainless steel teapot. "I hope we shall be friends when you move down here. I feel like I've known you for ages already."

"I know what you mean," smiled Connie, unable to wipe the happy grin from her face, "it's like that with some people, and when we are happily settled here I hope you'll come and visit us often."

"I'd love to," whispered Bertha, her voice a little choked, "that way I'll always feel I didn't desert our happy home, but instead put it in the care of friends."

News of sinister happenings in and around the Hotel brought Danny down for a brief visit at the weekend and after hearing details of the events from his parents and viewing the excavation site of the pond, he went round to Penwynton Crescent, the new development where his cousin Linda and her husband, Jamie were happily ensconced in their new home.

"It seems to me that the old Hotel's getting a lot of free publicity at the moment," he laughed, as Linda handed him a coffee. "Great stuff! Our folks really ought to cash in on it further though and dream up a ghost or two."

Jamie laughed. "Well, believe it or not, there was one a few years back. A newspaper bloke called Teddy Tinsdale managed to get his image on a snap taken by Elizabeth Stanley two weeks after the poor sod had died. Having said that, no-one has seen hide nor hair of him since, so it's assumed his ghost scarpered to another world after the chap who'd murdered him got nicked by Dad."

"Oh yeah, I remember hearing about that now. It was while our folks were negotiating for the Hotel, wasn't it? Well, if it'd boost trade I could always doctor up any photos to back up claims of ghosts; it'd be quite exciting."

"I don't think trade needs a boost at the moment," said Linda, amused by her cousin's flights of fancy. "Mum told me this summer's been really good because of the weather; in fact they're having to turn people away."

"Oh, shame. Still it's something to bear in mind if ever there's a lull and we go back to having the usual wet summers."

"How long are you down for?" asked Jamie.

"Only the day really. I shall have to be on the road by eight tomorrow morning and I only got here last night. I really came to see for myself the hole where they found that Grenville bloke. Not so sure I wanna see where they found the other poor sod though. Does your dad have any idea what that was all about, Jamie?"

Jamie shook his head. "Not really, being retired he doesn't have any more information than anyone else."

"Well, I guessed that, but I wondered if his instincts focused his thoughts in any particular direction."

"How's Carol?" asked Linda, knowing Jamie was tired of people asking about the thoughts of his father.

"Who? Oh Carol, yes, she's history," laughed Danny. "Got a new girl now, Patty. She's stunning and one of the reasons why I have to get back."

"Yes, I'm sure she is," smiled Linda, "but I don't expect she's the marrying kind, is she?"

"What! Well, of course not. I'm not looking for a wife. Life's great. Why on earth would I want to get hitched to some bird and have to spend the rest of my life with her? I'm having far too much fun."

"Because if you're not careful you'll wake up one morning and find you're a lonely old man," said Linda, didactically.

"Right," said Danny, rising to his feet. "If you're gonna start nagging, I'll go and find Anne. Mum tells me she's not working today so I'll have to go and look her up. Any idea where she hangs out?"

"She lives at the School House, which, would you believe, is near the school," said Jamie. "You can't miss it, the name is on the gate."

"You know you're breaking that poor girl's heart," said Linda, with hesitance, as he headed for the door.

Danny turned. "What! Don't be daft, how can I be doing that, we're great mates."

Linda sighed. "Because she's potty about you, you numbskull. Didn't that sink into your silly head when she reacted so badly on your introduction to the erstwhile Carol? Really, Danny, you must be blind."

"But...no, you're pulling my leg."

"I'm not," said Linda, emphatically. "It's obvious for anyone to see. Isn't it Jamie?"

Jamie nodded.

Danny sat down on the arm of the settee. "But Anne and I live in different worlds. She loves it down here and would never leave and I love my life in London. Blimey, I couldn't be here for more than a week, I'd be stifled by too much fresh air, and the constant twittering of birds would give me a headache. We get on brilliantly, Anne and I, but when it comes to lifestyle, well, we're chalk and cheese."

"I know that," said Linda, gently, "and that's why it's so sad. When you see her, try and be a little less full of your own importance and open your eyes. That way, maybe you'll treat her differently and with a little more thought. She's a dear, dear friend and a smashing girl and I don't want to see her hurt."

After all of the students had seen *The Omen*, a number of strange occurrences began to happen, usually after darkness fell. Dilys and Crystal returned to the room they shared one night, switched on the light and saw, spread across the ceiling, the eerie black shadow of a huge spider. Once their screams had faded away, a close inspection of the light bulb revealed a plastic spider glued firmly onto the glass. The following evening, Suzie Pilkington, who had a small single room, pulled back the blankets on her bed and came face to face with a picture of a snarling Rottweiler, torn from a magazine. Two days later, after pork had been on the Hotel menu, Pete found a pig's trotter in his bed. The following day, Jack was woken in the early hours by a foul smell and found a stink bomb resting on his pillow, and Malcolm was woken on several occasions by someone clicking the latch on his door as though about to enter the room.

The students blamed each other for the tricks and pranks and it was even suggested that the chefs, Bill and Ben might be taking revenge for the cheek they received from the youngsters on a daily basis.

A few days after the discovery of Grenville Penwynton's remains, Jack was listening to Radio One and singing *Devil Woman* along with Cliff Richard, whilst trying to think up a trick to play on Malcolm, for he was convinced the young actor was responsible for the stink bomb on his pillow and revenge was called for. Jack always had the radio on when he worked unless he was in close proximity of the Hotel and its din might disturb the guests, but on this occasion he was working alone in the walled garden, gathering runner beans for the evening menu.

Jack racked his brains to think of a ploy and when he saw the old scarecrow standing amongst the peas an idea came to his head. He would make a dummy priest, like the one in *The Omen*, drape it in black material, hang it from Malcolm's ceiling while he was out with Elizabeth and then spear it with a garden cane. Delighted with his idea, Jack picked the beans with gusto and took them to the kitchen. He then returned to the garden, borrowed the scarecrow's head and slipped it into his room along with a garden cane.

In the evening he put his plan into action and hung the dummy from the light in Malcolm's room after he had gone out to meet Elizabeth. Jack then went to the Badge for a pint as previously arranged with Pete. When he returned to his room Jack switched on his radio, but the night time signal was poor and the fact his batteries were very low did not help. Frustrated by the crackling, hissing and low volume, he removed the batteries and placed them in his shoes as a reminder to get new ones from the post office the following day. He then climbed into bed and tried to keep awake so that he might hear Malcolm return to the room next to his and witness the response to his trick. The beer he had consumed, however, soon sent him off to sleep and he heard nothing for several hours until he awoke for no apparent reason.

As he lay in the dark, Jack remembered his prank and wondered if Malcolm was back. Curious as to what the time might be, he sat up in bed and reached for the bedside lamp to look at his watch. But when he pushed the switch, nothing happened and the room remained in darkness.

"Sod it," grumbled Jack, thumping the bed clothes, "something else not working."

Too idle to get out of bed and switch on the main light, Jack lay back on his pillow and listened for any sound from the next room, but all was silent. He sighed; it looked as though his efforts had been in vain. He snuggled back down beneath the covers and closed his eyes hoping for sleep to return, but the room felt stuffy in spite of the open window. Suddenly, there was a click followed by a crackle and a hiss. Jack opened his eyes, cautiously peeped over the top of his sheet and looked across the room towards the chest of drawers by the door. On top stood his radio, lifeless because it contained no batteries, but there were lights on the tuning dial and muffled voices, some foreign, some English, coming and going as the radio appeared to be tuning itself in. The voices stopped abruptly and Jack froze as music began to play. Quiet, but familiar music; slow, sombre and eerie. And then began choral voices chanting in Latin. It was the theme music to *The Omen*.

Jack buried his face in his pillow and put his hands over his ears, but the music played louder and he could not escape it. He lay trembling with fear as every note and every word vibrated in his ear drums. His head throbbed and he felt dizzy and sick. Then finally it stopped. Jack lifted his head and watched as the light on the dial flickered and went out. The room was then silent.

With a surge of courage, Jack leapt out of bed switched on the main light and looked at the radio. As expected, it was dead, lifeless and the old batteries lay in his shoes. Jack shivered. He knew it could not be a prank. Afraid and confused, he reached for his dressing gown hanging on the back of the door. As he slipped his arms into the sleeves, through the stillness of the night, he heard the sound of footsteps approaching along the passage. Jack leapt back into bed. The central light hanging from the ceiling, spluttered, the bulb popped and went out. From the open window, a strong breeze chilled him to the marrow. The temperature in the room dropped to little more than freezing. Jack's teeth chattered with cold and fear as he heard the door in the next room slam shut, followed by an almighty crash as the sash window in his own room dropped shut. Jack opened his mouth and screamed, simultaneously with Malcolm in the room next door.

Chapter Twenty Seven

Elizabeth, with time on her hands and feeling a little lonely as her sister, Anne, and boyfriend, Malcolm, were both working, decided to take a stroll over the cliff tops towards the Witches Broomstick, something she had vowed to do often since her walk to Polquillick with Anne. The morning was glorious when she left the School House and walked down the road towards the sea; there was not a cloud in the sky and already the heat from the sun had pushed the temperature into the eighties.

When she reached the cove she stopped and looked across the beach to the sea where numerous people were taking refuge in the cool, tumbling waves. Momentarily, she wondered if it might be a more sensible option to join them, but decided against it, for the deaths of two people bearing the name Grenville Penwynton made her want to be alone and not on a crowded beach where her thoughts would be hindered by piercing screams and joyful laughter.

Before she reached the Witches Broomstick, she stopped to sit and admire the view and relish the beauty of the Cornish coastline. Beside a clump of thrift, past its best, she stretched out her long legs on the dry grass, removed her sunglasses and cast her eyes out to sea. Not far from the cliffs, Ron Trevelyan's boat, the *Lillian Ruth*, bobbed on the gentle waves, as the fishermen aboard it hauled crab pots from the crystal clear turquoise sea softly rippling beneath the boat's gunnels. Elizabeth waved when she recognised Matthew's brown fishing smock and his long, thick, sand coloured hair. He had grown into a handsome young man and would no doubt break several hearts before he settled down.

Elizabeth lay back on the grass, replaced her sunglasses, closed her eyes and pulled the wide brim of her straw sun hat over her face. It was too hot to walk on any further so instead she decided to content herself with a doze in the sun and listen to the cry of gulls, the murmur of the sea and the occasional moo from Pat Dickens' dairy cows grazing in a nearby field. She thought of Grev, a young man she had barely known, but whose death had affected her sister badly. She thought of Grenville Penwynton, unknown to them all, yet somehow familiar because of his tragic life and premature death. She also thought of the strange occurrence at the Hotel, when for some unknown reason she had the ability to look back into the past. Nevertheless, for all its intrigue, she had told no-one of her glance into the turquoise room as it had been in days gone by; not even Anne or her grandmother, Molly. For some reason she felt her experience was something only she should know of, hence she kept quiet. It was her secret.

Lying in the sun, Elizabeth soon felt drowsy. Her eyelids flickered and she was on the verge of drifting off to sleep when she heard a female voice calling her name. Slowly, Elizabeth sat up, removed her sunglasses and attempted to adjust her eyes to the sunlight. Through a blur she saw Tabitha Castor-Hunt walking through the tussocks of grass towards her, both arms waving.

"I thought it was you, dear," said Tabitha as she reached Elizabeth's side. "For although I couldn't see your face I recognised the dress." Tabitha sat down on the grass. "It's lovely to see you again and I'm so sorry I couldn't get to your father's birthday party, but I really did feel rough. Such a rotten shame though, because Lily and Willoughby both said it was a wonderful do. How are you keeping? You look well."

"I'm fine," said Elizabeth. "I'm enjoying the weather and trying to keep myself occupied until I start my new job next term."

"Yes, I hear you're to teach at the primary school in Polquillick. How nice for you and I bet your parents are delighted you're home. I know when I saw your father some time ago he said they all missed you dreadfully, but of course they would never stand in your way if you chose to work up-country. I know I miss my two and so of course does Willoughby. Still, perhaps one day they'll be back nearer home. I didn't really expect Lily to stick at nursing like she has. I thought it was just a fad, but she's always been the caring type and she's taken to it like a duck to water; I'm really glad. Choosing the right path in life is something that not everyone is fortunate enough to do."

"So true," said Elizabeth, smiling broadly. "For years Anne wanted to be a nurse but when she was fifteen it dawned on her she couldn't stand the sight of blood, so that was the end of that dream."

"Ah, but she's very fond of her job at the Hotel, isn't she?" said Tabitha, shading her eyes from the sun with her hand. "She was telling me earlier in the year, when Lily was home, how she loves every minute of it and there's a lot to be said for that. But it must be a little depressing at the Hotel at present. I mean to say, it's dreadful to have two deaths discovered in such a short space of time and I hear it was poor John Collins who found the body in both instances. They must have been very unpleasant experiences."

Elizabeth nodded. "I know, poor John; he always was the quieter of the twins but now he's even quieter."

Tabitha sighed sympathetically. "Oh dear, it'll take a while for him to banish it from his mind, but he will eventually. The weather can help a lot when things are grim, good weather I mean. The sun's a great healer because it makes one feel good."

"I always feel good when I'm up here," said Elizabeth, gently stroking the grass. "There's something magical about the breeze on the cliff tops and the sound of the sea below. You're very lucky to live at Chy-an-Gwyns."

"I know, dear and I could never leave here. Bertha Fillingham will miss the air up here too, if she sells her house."

"Oh, but she will sell, because she has a buyer," said Elizabeth, with a laugh. "Mum's parents are going to buy it. They had a look round the other day and instantly fell in love with the place, especially Grandma, although I think Granddad was pretty smitten too."

"Really, that's wonderful," said Tabitha, genuinely pleased. "It's always a bit of a worry when a nearby house sells and there's a change of neighbours, not that Sea Thrift Cottage is that close, but if your grandparents are to be our new neighbours then we won't have any problems. Willoughby will be pleased too. Anyway, I don't know about you, but sitting here is too hot for me and I could murder a cup of tea. Would you like to come back to the house and join me? We could sit in the shade of the old apple tree. It's been my favourite spot this summer."

"I'd love to," said Elizabeth, rising to join Tabitha who was already standing. "There was a chap in the Badge the other night who must have fallen asleep in the sun wearing sunglasses, because he had large round white patches round his eyes and looked like a panda. It had us in fits of laughter, but now I always dread the same thing might happen to me."

As they walked to Chy-an-Gwyns, Elizabeth told Tabitha about *The Omen*, which she had seen a few days earlier with Malcolm. Tabitha listened with interest, amused by Elizabeth's descriptions of the *scary* bits.

"Would I be right in thinking Gregory Peck is in that film?" smirked Tabitha.

"Yes, that's right, he was the main character."

Tabitha giggled, girlishly. "I thought so. He used to be my pin-up back along. In fact I named our Greg after him. But don't tell Willoughby; he believes I chose the name in memory of a dear uncle. A bit naughty of me really, but still, what does it matter?"

Elizabeth felt her face burn as it always did when Greg's name was mentioned. She found it a very annoying infliction, especially as she tried hard to believe and convince herself that she cared for him only as a friend and that Malcolm was the love of her life.

When they reached Chy-an-Gwyns, they went in the back door and into the kitchen. As Tabitha put on the kettle Elizabeth glanced around the room. It had been decorated since her last visit and on the dresser stood a picture of Willoughby taken when he was a young man. Elizabeth wanted to look away but her eyes were drawn towards it, for the young Willoughby was the spitting image of his own son, Gregory. Elizabeth felt her face flush again.

"Gosh, it's so hot," she muttered, conscious that Tabitha might notice her bout of embarrassment.

A door opened and closed in another part of the house followed by the sound of approaching footsteps echoing along the polished hall floor. Outside the kitchen the footsteps stopped and a head peeped round the door.

"Ah, there you are, Tabbs, I thought I heard you come in," said Willoughby. "Oh, hello, Elizabeth, I didn't see you there."

"Hello, Mr Castor-Hunt."

"Tabbs, I've just had the most extraordinary phone call from Gregory and you'll never believe what he had to say. He's broken off his engagement to Jemima. He wouldn't say why, in fact he wouldn't say much about it at all. It's most odd, isn't it? I thought he was besotted with the girl."

"If you'll excuse me," said Elizabeth, shocked and feeling faint as well as flushed. "I'll pop outside and sit under the apple tree. I need somewhere to cool down."

Since the day John had stumbled across the body of Grev, the students and inhabitants of Trengillion had avoided walking through the woods alone. Common sense prompted this initiative and the police made similar recommendations, for although the weapon used to shoot Grev had been established as belonging to Raymond Withers, the fact that it was in the hands of a brutal murderer meant its whereabouts were unknown and there was always the possibility the killer might strike again, although a motive for the seemingly unprovoked attack still remained a mystery.

Suzie Pilkington needed to walk into the village to buy a stamp and post a letter she had written to her parents, but since she had no car and the walk along the drive took considerably longer than the woodland route, she felt the woods was the only worthy option. Time was of the essence, because one of the guests had invited her out for the evening and she needed lots of time to make herself look her very best. The guest, she believed, was considerably wealthy: the sort of chap her parents would no doubt approve of. Rumour even had it that he was a self-made millionaire.

Against her better judgement, Suzie left her room and the Hotel by way of the main entrance, even though staff had been asked to use the back door only; but Suzie considered this request discriminatory, for she knew full well that Anne Stanley always used the main entrance so that made the whole issue unfair nonsense.

Suzie jumped down the steps two at a time, and as she hastily stepped onto the gravel driveway, she heard a car door slam shut in the car park. She looked back. From the driving seat of a white MGB, an elegantly dressed, middle aged woman carrying a small attaché case, emerged. Suzie swore beneath her breath, recollecting Dilys' boast that she had recently met Danny Jarrams who had driven down in the same car model when he had briefly visited the Hotel. Suzie was still seething over the occurrence, especially as, at that time she had been unaware of his visit and his relationship to Heather and Bob Jarrams. Furthermore, the situation was made worse by Dilys' continuous gloating. Still, thought Suzie as she tossed back her head and slipped between the rhododendron bushes, what would she want with a decrepit *has been* anyway, who was without doubt the wrong side of thirty and probably nowhere near as wealthy as the other group members who had continued to pursue careers in music.

Without once looking back over her shoulder, Suzie ran into the woods. When she reached the stream she followed its contour through the woodland, dense in places and deathly quiet except for the sound of her own feet snapping on twigs underfoot and the murmur of trickling water. On reaching a honeysuckle bush her pace slowed down, for she knew she was somewhere near the spot where Grev's body had been found. The sight of a police cordon confirmed her views and she passed on with caution, keeping out a watchful eye for anything untoward around her. When the sight of daylight at the end of the woods came into view she heaved a sigh of relief. Voices, however, stopped her dead in her tracks. Voices drifting through the trees from behind. Panicking, she fled from the woodland path, scrambled up a bank and hid behind the prickly leaves of a holly bush where her feet crushed an empty Rothmans cigarette packet lying on the ground. With disregard she kicked the packet beneath the hedge and listened intently as three people walked by chatting about the drought and threat of standpipes up-country.

Suzie heaved a sigh of relief, realising they were innocent people taking a stroll. Able to relax, she wiped perspiration from her forehead and attempted to compose herself. As she replaced the damp handkerchief in the pocket of her jeans she became aware of someone or something nearby panting and snuffling. Suzie crouched lower and then quietly giggled, much relieved; for not far from where she hid, a Jack Russell was digging in the earth. He stopped, pricked up his ears when one of the walkers called his name and then ran off eager to catch up with his mistress.

Suzie laughed and when all was quiet, she stood up, brushed the earth from the back of her jeans, ran her fingers through her hair and proceeded to walk back towards the path. But then something caught her eye. Something was shining from the spot where the dog had been digging. She crossed to take a look. A silver cigarette case lay on the earth near to what looked like part of an old sack. Suzie knelt down, brushed aside the earth and pulled at the hessian. More objects came into view. A candelabrum, spoons, a silver vase, a watch and various items of precious metal. Suzie went cold. Was this what Grev had found? The cause of his death? She quickly pushed the loose earth back over the objects and marked the spot with the old cigarette packet. She then hurriedly continued on her way to the village, intent on calling the police from the phone box as soon as she reached the post office.

The following day, the police confirmed the items found by Suzie in Bluebell Woods were the objects stolen on the night of the school's barbecue. Furthermore it seemed that all items reported missing were there except for the one pound notes taken from Frank and Dorothy's biscuit tin. The police also revealed that following the discovery of Grev Penwynton's body, a search of the nearby vicinity found earth there had been disturbed, but at that time there appeared to be no apparent reason for the earth's disturbance. Therefore, on account of this new evidence, it looked as though the stolen objects might have been moved by the thief from the said vicinity after and because Grev had discovered them. This brought about a sense of relief to the inhabitants of Trengillion, for if Grev's murderer had a motive, then he might not strike again unless provoked so to do. Nevertheless, Trengillion's residents and the police alike were completely baffled as to why someone should take the risk of burgling houses in the first place, if the items he stole were of no interest.

Inside the Sheriff's Badge Inn, Gloria Withers bathed her two young nephews and put them to bed for the very last time, and then, as she had done on every evening since their arrival, she read them an adventure story written by Enid Blyton. For Gloria firmly believed that very young children should not be exposed to gratuitous violence, especially if said violence involved guns. But at the same time she accepted that little boys needed adventure, action and excitement, and so she chose to read the books she had read to Roger and Colin during their childhood, and Johnny and Jimmy loved them.

When she closed the book on the very last page, she kissed their brows and wished them pleasant dreams. She then crept quietly from the room and closed the door. In the hallway she stooped to pick up their dirty shoes with the intent of taking them to the utility room to clean them, wondering as she did so, if her weeks of dedication during which she had attempted to change her nephew's outlooks had succeeded. Hence, she was gladdened when as she turned to go she heard a small voice say: "I don't want to go home, tomorrow, Jimmy. I love Auntie Gloria."

"I don't want to go either," said Jimmy, "and I don't want to be a bad cowboy with nasty guns anymore. I want to be like the children in Auntie's books and have lots of adventures."

Gloria smiled. "Mission complete," she whispered.

"Liz, would you like to go with me to the art gallery tomorrow?" asked Anne, one evening as the sisters sat watching television. "Mary said to take you along. I'm going there to pick up the old painting of Penwynton House."

Elizabeth turned to face her sister clearly puzzled. "What in Dad's car? Will it fit? I'd always imagined Penwynton paintings to be quite big."

"Hmm, yes, it is," said Anne, "so I'll be taking the Hotel's van. Mary was going to do it herself but she seems to think I need to get out more, so asked me to do it for her. What do you say?"

"Yes, I'd love to go," said Elizabeth, thrilled by the prospect of a day out. "What time are you going?"

"Around nine, so you won't have to get up at the crack of dawn."

"Yeah, that's fine. But why does Mary think you need to get out more? Has she, like me, noticed you've been a bit down lately?"

Anne stared blankly at the television screen. "I don't know, but the death of poor Grev certainly hasn't put me in very high spirits."

Elizabeth frowned. "No, there's more to it than that. You've been gloomy ever since Danny's last visit. What's wrong? Is he going to marry one of his dumb blondes or something?"

Anne shrugged her shoulders. "How should I know? I'm not his minder. He can do what he wants."

Elizabeth leaned forward and looked her sister in the eye. "What's happened? What's he done? Come on, Anne, you can tell me."

"Nothing," insisted Anne, deliberately looking away. "Nothing at all. I don't know what you mean."

"Then why are there tears in your eyes?" persisted Elizabeth. "For heaven's sake, Anne, tell me what's wrong."

Anne wiped her eyes on the sleeve of her cardigan. "He told me that we'll always be good friends, but never anything more. There, now are you satisfied?"

Elizabeth sat bolt upright. "Oh, no, I'm so sorry, Anne. Really I am. When was this?"

"When he was down last week. He came round to see me, Liz, when you were all out. He was ever so sweet. He said he didn't want me to get hurt and that my friendship meant a great deal to him, but that was all it was. All it could ever be. He said he wasn't the settling down type and that he could never live in Cornwall and that I'd never be happy in London. In a way, I know he's right, but now I feel really silly and life seems, well, so empty now. He's spoiled my dreams; each and every one of them."

Elizabeth slipped from the chair, knelt at Anne's feet, raised her arms and cuddled her."

"But at least he's been honest with you, Anne. And although he may have been a little tactless, at least you know where you stand now. I did warn you though, didn't I?"

Anne nodded. "Yes, and if I'm honest with myself, I knew you were right. But I feel so deflated now - so devoid of hope. I mean, in reality I guess I always knew we had no future together - would never be anything more than friends - but at least I could pretend things might turn out differently. I can't do that anymore now and it hurts; it really hurts."

Elizabeth smiled. "You must pin your hopes a little lower, Anne. Your fascination with Danny is and always has been because he's famous and has a glamorous lifestyle. There are plenty more fish in the sea and a lot of them much easier to catch."

Anne half-smiled. "No, it wasn't just because he was famous, Liz. He made me laugh and, well, you know, he just made me feel happy."

"And he'll still do that, Anne, but as a friend. Come on, cheer up and dream about Poncey Pete instead."

Anne laughed as Elizabeth took a handkerchief from her sleeve and wiped away her tears.

"When Malcolm's gone home, Anne, we'll go out lots and lots and find you someone worth a hundred Dannys: someone who'll love you and cherish you for the rest of your life. He's out there somewhere. We just need to find him."

Chapter Twenty Eight

Anne and Elizabeth left Trengillion after breakfast the following day for the art gallery. Mary had told Anne not to rush back, but instead to enjoy the morning out with her sister and take a look around the gallery, for she knew Anne was a keen artist and appreciated seeing the work of others.

Inside the gallery's rectangular reception area, the girls were greeted by a middle aged, bespectacled woman who looked the epitome of a stereo typed custodian. Her dress was old fashioned, drab and plain, her greying hair twisted tightly into a small, neat bun, and around her neck dangled a pair of gold rimmed spectacles attached to a beaded chain. Her manner, however, was welcoming and she spoke with genuine warmth and undeniable enthusiasm.

"My name is Madeleine Penaluna," she whispered in a soft Cornish accent. "The Penwynton painting is awaiting your inspection prior to my instruction for it to be wrapped. Come this way, please."

The two girls followed Madeleine along a dark passage to a room where hundreds of paintings were stored, and in a corner the painting of Penwynton House stood on the floor, resting against a gloomy brown wall. Madeleine switched on an overhead light which shone directly onto the painting. Anne felt a tingle spread through her body as she leaned forward and touched it.

"It's beautiful," she gasped, her hands clasped, awestruck. "It'll be so good to see it back in its rightful place on the grand staircase. Oh, how I wish we could have all the old paintings back, but I'm afraid they're a little beyond the Hotel's budget yet."

"Meanwhile they're perfectly safe with us," said Madeleine, with pride. "Would you like to see the other Penwynton paintings while you're here? They're all on display in the great hall. Of course the one of poor Grenville, God rest his soul, has been widely viewed of late, especially by the police. Mrs Cottingham says it's the one she would like to purchase next, as it seems only right that the poor soul be returned to his home."

They followed Madeleine down yet another dimly lit passage and into the great airy hall where generations of Penwyntons lined the high walls.

In the doorway Madeleine paused. "Actually, I must correct my comments regarding the Penwyntons. Not all are here, you see. Regrettably the portrait of Grenville's half-brother Gorran is away for repair work."

"Repair work?" Elizabeth was puzzled.

Madeleine looked uncomfortable. "Yes. Sadly, last week the painting fell from the wall and the frame was rather badly damaged. I've no idea how it happened. No-one was here when it fell, you see, as it must have happened during the night." She sighed. "It was me that found it the following morning. Fortunately the picture itself was not harmed; the frame bore the brunt of its impact with the floor."

From a back room a telephone bell rang and a young girl appeared to inform Madeleine someone wished to speak to her.

Madeleine looked relieved. "I'll only be a moment. Please take your time and have a good look around."

The girls watched as Madeleine left the room, they then walked around the great hall and viewed the pictures with reverence. Penwyntons going back to the time of the first Henry born in 1720 lined the dark walls. Penwyntons, their wives and their children. Neither girl spoke until they reached the west wall where the portrait of Grenville hung beside his brother Cedric. He was dressed in clothing almost identical to those worn by Malcolm Barker for Ned's birthday party, and on a brass plaque beneath the painting it stated the picture was painted to commemorate Grenville's twenty first birthday.

"I feel quite giddy," said Elizabeth, when she found her tongue. "I mean, to think this is the poor chap whose body was found in the meadow. It doesn't seem possible, does it? I mean, it's uncanny, and look at that cravat pin he's wearing; it must be the one found in the earth. Isn't it beautiful?"

"Yes," whispered Anne, her head tilted to one side, "but I must say that if the ruby in this picture is true to size then I'm very surprised it wasn't found with poor Grenville's remains."

"Well, perhaps Talwyn took it from the pin before she buried him. After all, it would be worth quite a lot of money."

"I don't think that would be the case," said Anne, thoughtfully. "Because surely it would have been worth far more still in the pin. Having said that I suppose she'd not have been able to sell the pin complete because it might have been recognised by the jeweller. If it was made especially for Grenville, that is."

Next to Grenville hung the portrait of Cedric, father of the last of the Penwyntons, Charles, and alongside him was a picture of Charles himself and his twin sister.

"Where's Talwyn?" said Anne, suddenly. "We must have missed her."

Elizabeth shook her head. "I suppose she'll be somewhere alongside her husband, George."

Anne looked back. "Hmm, we must have walked straight past them both. We did miss a few, didn't we, when we spotted Grenville?"

The girls walked back across the polished parquet floor until they came face to face with Talwyn.

"Oh, she doesn't look as evil as she's reputed to be," said Elizabeth, surprised and a little disappointed. "In fact if anything she looks sad."

"Humph, well it was probably painted after her ghastly son, Gorran was killed," said Anne, dispassionately. "I mean, according to legend she was devoted to him."

Elizabeth frowned. "Yes, I suppose so." She turned to face her sister. "I think the damage to Gorran's portrait sounds rather fishy. What do you think?"

Anne shrugged her shoulders. "I can't see why you think it's fishy. I mean there's nothing strange about a picture falling, surely." She pointed to an empty space on the wall. "And I suppose that's where he was hanging."

"Hmm. It's a real pity he's not here because I should have liked to have seen what he looked like."

When the girls arrived back at the Hotel, Elizabeth left Anne as she was not due to finish work for several more hours; she walked home through the woods. Once back at the School House, she found no-one was in and so decided to walk down to the cove. Outside the

Inn she saw Jack Smeaton sitting with Poncey Pete at the picnic table, both eating sausage and chips.

"Hi, Lizzy Wizzy," called Pete, as she passed by. "Do you wanna a chip?"

She tried to ignore him. "No thank you."

"Go on, you know you want one really."

Elizabeth turned to face them. "Shouldn't you two be at work?"

Pete laughed. "No, got the half day off; so has Jack. We're going swimming in a minute. Do you want to join us?"

"You should never swim when you've been drinking or after a meal," said Elizabeth, primly, turning to walk away. "It's dangerous, and you've obviously done both. You ought to know better."

"Oh no, you've been ticked off by teacher," laughed Jack, wagging his finger at Pete. "Who's a naughty boy then?"

"Shut it," said Pete, ramming a sausage into Jack's mouth. "Lizzy Wizzy doesn't want me hurt cos she loves me, don't you Lizzy Wizzy?"

Elizabeth scowled as Jack bit into the sausage hanging from his mouth. The other half he laid down on top of the chips in the basket almost hidden beneath a thick layer of tomato ketchup. With difficulty, due to uncontrolled laughter, he began to chew the sausage, but when he attempted to swallow it he began to cough, wheeze and choke, and his face turned blue. Pete panicked and jumped back in alarm. Elizabeth rushed forward and slapped him hard between the shoulder blades. Jack fell forward as the slap forced minced up sausage to fly from his mouth across the table and onto the cobbles.

"What you doing choking on sausage, you silly arse," shouted Pete, his voice trembling. "You scared the life out of me."

"There was something in it," croaked Jack, his green eyes watering as he rubbed his neck. "Something hard."

He slid off the bench and poked the chewed up sausage lying on the cobbles with a fork. To his surprise, amongst the pork, he found a small red stone. He screwed up his face, clearly puzzled. "Blimey, how did that get in there? I'm surprised it didn't break my bleedin' teeth."

Pete scowled. "What is it? It looks like a bit of glass."

Jack picked up the object and wiped it clean with his paper serviette. He laughed. "It is glass. I'm a good mind to go and tell Dead-eye Dick to be careful what he puts in his sodding sausages. I could have choked to death."

Elizabeth smiled. "But he and Gloria don't make the sausages, do they? Having said that, I suppose you ought to say something so they can tell their butcher. Anyway, are you alright now?"

"Yes, I'm fine," said Jack, wiping his nose on his towel. "But I don't think I want anything else to eat. Come on let's go for a dip."

Pete looked at the red glass. "You're not going to say anything then?"

"No, can't be bothered. Come on, let's not waste our afternoon off work. I'll race you to the beach."

Pete picked up his glass and quickly gulped down the last dregs of lager. "Okay. Bye then Lizzy, you know you can join us if you want to."

Elizabeth watched as they disappeared out of sight, and then she turned to leave, but as she stepped away from the table, the piece of glass caught her eye. She picked it up and examined it closely. It was small, oval in shape with one side flat and the other curved with no rough edges. She laid it on the palm of her hand; in the beam of the sun's rays it shone and sparkled like a precious stone.

John's words passed through her mind when he spoke of the day and described events leading up to and when Grenville's remains had been found in the meadow. Amongst the bones lay the misshapen stick pin, identified as belonging to the missing heir; a representation of which she had herself witnessed that very morning on her trip to the art gallery with Anne. Elizabeth looked again at the stone. Could it possibly be the missing ruby? But surely if it was it would never have found its way into Jack Smeaton's sausage. Elizabeth laughed. The notion was absurd. It was no doubt just a worthless piece of glass which had fallen from a necklace or bracelet of someone making sausages at the butchers; but all the same she thought it best to hang on to it, just in case. Elizabeth dropped the red glass into the pocket of her jeans and headed towards the beach where she sat on Denzil's bench well away from the two students, already in the sea and noisily splashing each other.

Chapter Twenty Nine

Following the death of Grev Penwynton, the police in Cornwall asked for the help of the Force in Cambridge to try and establish whether or not Grev had any living relatives, and eventually, after an extensive search, they traced a great aunt living in Hunstanton, Norfolk.

On hearing the news of her great nephew's death, Miss Lavinia Bugg made a reservation over the telephone for a room at the Penwynton Hotel, which she was very fortunate to get, as only minutes before her call, Mary Cottingham received notification of a room cancellation due to a sudden bereavement in the family concerned. Delighted that a room was secured, Miss Bugg left her Norfolk home for the journey to Cornwall, by train, and Mary herself, greeted the elderly lady in reception on her arrival by taxi from the station.

After showing Miss Bugg to her room, Mary invited the new guest into her office to discuss the passing of Grev Penwynton and his funeral arrangements.

"I shall of course pay all the expenses and after the interment I should like to hold a little farewell buffet for the poor lad," said Miss Bugg. "I feel so utterly guilty over the whole affair. If only I'd known the circumstances I would have done something earlier. Family feuds are an evil thing, Mrs Cottingham, and I'm thoroughly ashamed of myself, but what the poor lamb did not have in life he shall have in death and I shall make sure he has a fine memorial stone so that he shall not be forgotten."

"I take it then that you propose to have him buried here in Trengillion," said Mary, surprised.

"Yes," said Miss Bugg, primly, "there is nowhere else for him to go. Nowhere he would have said with hand on heart 'this is home'. He died here and I hope for that short time that he was happy here."

Recalling his appreciative smiles, Mary gave a little nod. "Yes, I think he was happy here. He was well liked by other members of staff and got on well with the guests and of course we all liked him too. By we, I mean my husband, sister, brother-in-law and of course myself."

"That's good to know," sighed Lavinia Bugg, relieved by information received. "That helps me feel a little better."

"Please don't think me impertinent, Miss Bugg, but may I ask the cause of the family feud, or would that be too indelicate?"

Miss Bugg threw back her head and laughed. "I think in the circumstances I owe you an explanation and believe me Mrs Cottingham the whole affair will sound very trite, very trite indeed." She paused and took in a deep breath. "You see, our family name, as you are of course aware, is Bugg. It's not a name I am ashamed of or embarrassed about, nor should I be; but Hugh, Grenville's father, was when he met Betty Taylor. Betty, if you'll forgive me for saying so, was, although polite and pleasant, frightfully common. She had no breeding and was ignorant to boot. Her one claim to fame was that she might be a descendant of the Cornish Penwynton family, for her grandmother, who was born out of wedlock, claimed this to be the case. But of course it was never proven one way or the other. Anyway, I digress. Betty Taylor took a strong dislike to our name, you see, even though Hugh explained it was Olde English and certainly did not mean what it implies, but she remained obstinate and informed Hugh that if he wished to marry her he would have to change his name by deed poll, and because the fool was besotted with the little minx, that is what he did, hence my hostility towards her."

Mary opened her mouth to speak but she thought better of it and Lavinia continued. "I was disgusted by the name change and told my brother, James, Hugh's father, their behaviour was intolerable. Sadly, I never saw my brother again after that day. You see, Mrs Cottingham, my brother James was dying and I didn't know. No-one knew. He'd already lost his wife, so he cared about nothing and certainly not an issue as trivial as a change of name by his son." Lavinia Bugg bowed her head. "After the death of James, I had no desire to contact my nephew, Hugh, but I knew he had married and changed his name to Penwynton. I also knew that he had a son who had been christened Grenville, because apparently they had seen the name linked to the Penwynton family and liked it. A few years later,

I heard that Hugh and Betty had been killed in a car crash, but to my shame I made no attempt to enquire about the welfare of the child, for I assumed he would be taken care of by the Taylors. Had I known Betty's parents were no longer living, I would of course have made contact. At least I think I would, but I can't even swear, hand on heart, that that would have been the case. So you see, Mrs Cottingham, at the end of the day, to use that dreadful phrase, I am no better than anyone else. In fact if anything, I am far worse and I shall have to live with my guilt for the rest of my life."

"Oh, dear, how dreadful," said Mary, sympathetically, facts churning around in her mind. "But may I ask just one more question, Miss Bugg? You see I'm curious to know if there was any truth in the claim made by Grev's mother that she might have descended from the Penwyntons. I know quite a lot of the family history, you see, and wonder if there might be a clue in her name. Do you know what it was? I refer of course, to the name of Betty Taylor's grandmother."

"I believe it was Louisa," said Miss Bugg, thoughtfully. "In fact I know it was. I remember, you see, because Louisa was my dear mother's name, not that that has any bearing on the case. Does that help you in any way?"

"I'm afraid not," said Mary, shaking her head as bygone Penwynton family names rushed through her mind. "Louisa isn't a name I can link with the family at all. There may be some truth in Betty Taylor's claim, but if there is then I just can't see it."

"Told you so," said Dilys, on hearing the story of Grev's father's name change. "It stands to reason no-one's going to marry a bloke with a ghastly name like Bugg, especially if she's called Betty. I mean, Betty Bugg. Yuck!"

"Shush," hissed Crystal, aware that Miss Bugg was within earshot. "You really are an idiot, Dilys. I don't think she heard, but if she had you could well have been out of a job."

"Doesn't really matter now though, does it," spat Dilys, angry because Pete had told her to get lost. "It'll be time to go home soon, thank goodness."

Unlike the hotel, the stable block had not been refurbished, although it had been made safe should anyone wish to take a look inside. The reason for its lack of attention was because neither the Cottinghams nor the Jarrams were able to make up their minds as to what the buildings could best be utilised as. When first Penwynton House had been purchased, the possibility of the stables being used to house horses was the obvious choice, but as neither family had any knowledge of the animals, the idea of stables was soon dismissed. The next proposal was to use the buildings for storage, but Mary and Heather both agreed to do so would be a waste of space, for the buildings would inevitably in no time become brimfull of junk. Hence, the stables stood forlorn, and nine years on looked much as they had done for generations. It was Linda who eventually came up with inspiration for a suitable use. She suggested the buildings be converted into accommodation for seasonal workers, thus leaving the one-time servants' quarters free to be converted into budget rooms for paying guests. Mary, Dick, Heather and Bob were delighted with Linda's suggestion, for during the hot summer months they had turned guests away because they had no vacancies. Hence, immediately after they unanimously expressed their enthusiasm, they asked an architect to view the stables prior to drawing up plans and applying to the council for the necessary permission.

A copy of the proposed plans arrived in the post the day after the arrival of Miss Lavinia Bugg and Mary proudly put them on display for staff to see and voice any relevant comments. Anne viewed the plans with enthusiasm. The twelve stables were to be converted into six self-contained bedsits, each with a small bathroom and a kitchenette. Six of the twelve stable doors would become windows and the other six fitted with new stable doors with a window pane on the top section. And the central area overlooked by the stable bedsits, where once horses would have been exercised, were to be paved around a central flower bed, thus making a courtyard where hanging baskets and tubs of flowers would give a Mediterranean touch to what in future was to be known as Penwynton Mews.

"It's lovely," said Anne, after studying the plans during her tea break. "And as the structure won't change it'll still look very much as it does now. But what's going to happen to the adjoining coach house? I see it's not on the plans."

"We're not sure," said Mary, "we'll probably use it for storage or as a garage, either way the stone work will all be made good and cleaned up to be in keeping with the accommodation."

"I feel quite envious of future students," said Anne, wistfully. "What fun they'll have in their own self-contained environment. When the present lot see this I wouldn't be surprised if it doesn't make them want to come again next year, that's if it will be done by then of course."

"If we get planning sorted quickly then it'll easily be done," said Mary. "Bob's already had a word with Dave Richardson and he said he'll be delighted to do it. He and his lads have worked well on the pond, so it'll be nice to have them doing this little project."

Anne agreed whole heartedly. She liked having her old friends around and the renovation of Penwynton Mews would be something to watch develop in the dark, dull days of winter.

"That outfit you wore for Dad's party was very authentic," said Elizabeth to Malcolm, as they spread out a blanket on the beach in the glorious afternoon sunshine in preparation for sunbathing, the day after the picture of Penwynton House was finally hung back in the Hotel. "In fact I'd say it was almost identical to the attire Grenville is wearing for his portrait that hangs in the art gallery."

"The Rep's costumes are good," said Malcolm, lazily lying down on his back. "I suppose if they have to make them, there's not much point in failing to get facts right and going into fine detail. And of course in the Victorian era, there wouldn't have been the choice of clothing like there is today."

Elizabeth sat down beside him. "Hmm, I suppose not and as you say, if a job's worth doing then it's worth doing well. I go along with that. It's one of Dad's favourite sayings, although it used to irritate me enormously when I was a kid."

Malcolm laughed. "Common sense usually irritates children, but you'll be fully aware of that, teaching youngsters as you do."

"Yes, I know. I wonder what my new pupils will be like. The kids at my last school were terrific and I was actually sorry to leave them, even though I'd not known them for long. I seem to have done a lot of chopping and changing recently and soon you'll be gone too."

Malcolm stretched up his arm and ran his fingers through her curls. "Will you miss me?"

"Of course," she whispered, clutching his hand and kissing his fingers. "You've made this summer special and I'll never, ever forget the time our eyes first met and the romantic way you smiled and blew me a kiss, even before we'd been introduced."

Malcolm frowned. "What! I think you must have dreamed that, Liz. I'd never clapped eyes on you 'til the minute your little sister introduced us."

"But I remember it distinctly," said Elizabeth, annoyed by his obstinacy. "There was a flash of light and then I saw you standing, just feet away, near the door. You caught my eye, smiled and then blew me a kiss. And then at the very same time clumsy Dilys knocked my arm; I was distracted and when I looked up you had gone. After that I went looking for you and when I saw Anne and described you and your outfit, she pointed me in your direction and introduced us both. You must remember that, for God's sake. It was only a few weeks ago!"

Malcolm sat up and grabbed her by the shoulders. "Hey, calm down, Liz. If that's the way you remember it then it wasn't me you saw, because when you were introduced to me by Anne, I had only just that minute arrived at the party as I'd worked in the residents' lounge bar up until nine. I should have had the whole night off, of course, but Brian, the bloke who always comes in on Saturdays, was held up while shopping with his wife in Plymouth so I covered for him till nine."

"What! Are you sure? But, you, I …"

"Absolutely sure."

Elizabeth's face turned white as she thought of the pictures in the art gallery and the portrait of Grenville Penwynton. She looked at Malcolm and then closed her eyes. Was it possible that it may not have been Malcolm who had bewitched her with his smile, but in fact had been the ghost of Grenville Penwynton? With her eyes closed tightly she tried to recall the incident, and the memory, faint at first, gradually returned. She saw the sudden flash of light. A mystery it seemed at the time, but could it possibly have been a reflection of the ruby and diamonds shining from the stick pin adorning Grenville's cravat. Elizabeth relived the smile; the kiss, and the expression on the face of her admirer, and then she realised, the eyes were wrong, the style of hair was wrong and so was the shape of face. She shuddered; her vision had not been Malcolm at all.

Confused, Elizabeth opened her eyes and gazed out to sea. In retrospect, she recalled the man she had first seen standing by the door had a cravat around his neck, but without question Malcolm had worn a bow tie and a waistcoat. Also the frock coat Malcolm wore had been a deep shade of burgundy, but the coat worn by the person she had first encountered was unquestionably brown. Elizabeth felt sick. So many strange things had happened since her return. The voice calling in the woods; her vision of a room at the Hotel in a bygone era; the piece of red glass, possibly the ruby from Grenville's cravat, which had curiously found its way into her possession. All these things had occurred since her sighting of Grenville Penwynton, who had acknowledged her ability to see beyond the grave with an airborne kiss and a smile.

Elizabeth chose to say nothing of her thoughts to Malcolm. He had been very good to her during the summer months and she had no wish to offend him with her suppositions.

"Are you alright, Liz? You've gone awfully pale."

She patted his arm affectionately and smiled. "Yes, yes, I'm fine and I expect you're right about Dad's party. I mean, let's be honest, I had had one too many glasses of punch and it was quite strong."

Malcolm reached out and kissed her hand, yawned, and then closed his eyes; the combination of the sun's warmth and the two pints of lager he'd drunk at lunchtime, gradually sent him off into a deep sleep.

Chapter Thirty

As August drew to a close so the weather changed and on Bank Holiday Monday the much longed for rain arrived along with a very strong north wind. Downhearted playgroup organisers expressed their dismay; it was their turn to organise the final barbecue the following Wednesday night, but they knew if the weather did not change then the event might have to be cancelled. However, their luck was in, the weather did improve and the event went ahead as planned, although holiday makers were fewer than for previous weeks as the new school academic year was fast approaching.

Anne no longer worked on Wednesday evenings and had not done so since Mary Cottingham had sent her home on the night of the school's barbecue, hence every week, the barbecues became the one night when the youngsters of Trengillion were able to get together for a social evening along with new found friends and acquaintances, where they danced on the beach to music blaring from a cassette tape player, ate hot dogs and burgers and chatted and reminisced about days gone by.

"Has anyone bought the Vicarage yet?" Susan asked Graham, as they sat on up-turned fish boxes drinking lager from cans. "Mum asked me yesterday but I said I'd not the foggiest idea."

Graham shook his head. "No, loads of people have looked at it, but it wants lots of work done cos apparently it's got dry rot in places. A lot of people think the garden's too big as well."

Anne looked shocked. "Nonsense, how can a garden be too big? I'd love to live in the Vicarage; the location is gorgeous. I like big houses and big gardens. In fact, next to the Hotel I think the Vicarage is the most exciting property in Trengillion."

"Oh, and Chy-an-Gwyns," said Diane, glancing up at the house prominently situated above the cove. "I think a house on the cliffs would be my dream place."

"Absolutely," said Elizabeth, vigorously nodding her head.

"Yes, but the main reason you like Chy-an-Gwyns is because of who lives there," teased Susan.

"But he doesn't live there, does he?" said Elizabeth, crossly. "He's stuck up-country somewhere in some dreary solicitor's office."

When she realised what she had said she blushed.

"I only said that to test your reaction," giggled Susan, snuggling up to Steve. "I must admit I'm very surprised by your response."

For the rest of the evening Elizabeth was very quiet and said she wasn't in the mood for dancing when the others sprang to their feet on hearing the lively music of Abba's new release *Dancing Queen*. Anne noticed her melancholy mood which at first she had attributed it to the absence of Malcolm who had volunteered to work in place of a colleague who was sick. However, her earlier response to Susan's light hearted tease regarding Greg threw doubts in her mind as to whether Malcolm meant anything at all.

As the evening drew to a close, people drifted away home or to the Inn for a drink in the warm and dry, for the night air felt chilly and there was a touch of light drizzle in the air. Anne wanted to join her friends at the Inn, but Elizabeth claimed to have a headache and said she wanted to go home. Anne was torn between joining her friends and escorting her sister home to try and find out what was wrong, for she did not believe for one minute the declaration of a headache bore even the tiniest amount of truth.

"I'll come home with you," said Anne, making a spur of the moment decision. "I think I've had enough to drink anyway and I have to be at work for half past eight tomorrow."

"You don't have to," said Elizabeth, a little off hand. "I shall probably go straight to bed anyway."

Anne linked her arm through that of her sister. "That's alright, but what's wrong, Liz? I know there's something, you can tell me."

"I know I can," said Elizabeth, close to tears, "but the trouble is you'll probably think I'm potty. So many weird things have happened this summer and I'm not sure you'd even believe me if I told you."

Anne frowned. "Such as what? I know the death of two Grenvilles has been a bit odd, but what else have you seen or heard?"

Elizabeth smiled. "Well, don't say I didn't warn you, but I think I saw a ghost on Dad's birthday night and not just any old ghost either, I'm pretty sure it was Grenville Penwynton. In fact I know it was him. You see, he was just as in the portrait at the art gallery. The same clothes, the same hair and everything. I'm convinced now it wasn't Malcolm at all who smiled and blew me a kiss, in fact it definitely wasn't because Malcolm told me so, so it has to have been Grenville's ghost and I find that a little alarming."

Anne's steps slowed. "Really! That's scary. And I suppose his face didn't gel properly at the time because you were so drunk."

Elizabeth paused. "Yes, although in retrospect I recall thinking at the time when you introduced me to Malcolm that something wasn't quite right about him, but then you know I'm pretty rubbish at remembering faces anyway and it was after all only a fleeting glance; but seeing either Malcolm or Grenville by the door is the only part of the evening I do remember clearly."

"So what do you think he wanted? I mean, he must have wanted something from you because no-one else has ever reported seeing his ghost or any other ghost for that matter, so it must have singled you out in particular."

"I've no idea," said Elizabeth, with a feeble laugh. "Perhaps I'm just susceptible to ghosts like Dad and Grandma. Remember Teddy Tinsdale? He turned out to be on a photo I took, although I must admit I didn't see him at the time, but then I wasn't looking at the window, I was looking at you lot. On the other hand, and I know this sounds daft, I think Grenville probably used me to clear up this mystery and it was he who put the notion into my head about making a pond so that his remains could be found. It must have been something like that cos to be perfectly honest I'd never even thought about a pond before Dad's birthday."

"Come on," said Anne, suddenly. "We're dawdling and this drizzle's getting quite heavy. Let's continue this conversation at home in the warm with a hot drink."

The girls ran along the road, dashed up the garden path and retrieved the door key from beneath the doormat since both had forgotten to take their own. Neither of their parents was at home as they had gone to the Inn after the barbecue for a drink with Meg and Sid, so the house was in total darkness. In the kitchen they switched on the light and Anne reached for the kettle to make coffee, but as she did so they both heard a crash and froze.

"Ever had that feeling of déjà vu?" squeaked Anne, nodding towards the door leading to the hallway.

Elizabeth clutched her sister's arm. "Surely we can't have another burglar. I mean to say, lightning isn't supposed to strike twice in the same place, is it? Besides, he didn't want what he nicked last time, did he?"

"Come on," whispered Anne, feeling a gush of bravery. "There are two of us this time. Let's see if we can catch him. We'll creep up on him, rush in and hit him over the head."

"What with?" Elizabeth asked, her voice hushed.

Anne giggled, nervously. "The rolling pin. Hang on while I get it from the cupboard and you grab yourself the milk saucepan from the shelf."

With weapons in hand, the girls quietly opened the kitchen door and crept into the passage. As before, torch light flashed through the small gap of the sitting room door, slightly ajar; but the girls were undeterred and continued along the passage. Outside the door, they stopped.

"Ready?" whispered Anne, "one, two, three, go."

The girls ran into the room, arms raised above heads with weapons ready to strike, but the intruder was too quick; he sprang to his feet as Elizabeth flicked on the light switch; both girls gasped as the illuminations revealed they were left facing the barrel of Raymond Withers' gun.

"Well, you crept in pretty quietly, didn't you," snarled Jack Smeaton, with an exaggerated laugh. "How unfortunate for you both."

The brave expression on Anne's face melted away to be replaced by a look of utter disbelief as she glanced from the desk lying upside-down on the floor, to her sister hoping for guidance. But Elizabeth's face was momentarily frozen; paralysed by shock, fear and confusion.

"You," said Anne, taking the initiative. "I can't believe it's you. What on earth are you looking for? I mean, if it was you that broke in before then you didn't want what you took then because you dumped it all in the woods."

"Well, I could hardly take it back to the Hotel, could I? Not with you nosey bastards prowling around. Anyway, what I want is my business, but your interruption has caused me a bit of a problem. Sit on the settee, both of you, put your hands behind your heads and keep your mouths shut."

With the gun pointing at them, the sisters nervously did as ordered and from the settee they watched as Jack knelt on the floor and pulled a packet of Rothmans cigarettes from the pocket of his jeans. Using only one hand he slipped a cigarette into his mouth, lit it and then blew smoke in their direction to taunt them. Laughing, he reached out towards the desk. Anne stifled a sob. Thinking of Grev she realised once Jack had found what he was looking for then, unless a miracle happened, their lives would be well and truly over. In desperation she looked pleadingly at Elizabeth, but Elizabeth also was at a loss as what to do. But then the most extraordinary thing happened. On top of the sideboard a fizzing noise emanated from the six bottles of Molly's elderflower champagne. The girls both heard it but Jack seemed neither to hear the fizz nor sense anything happening. The fizzing continued for a good minute; growing louder as the bubbles increased in volume and rose steadily up the bottle necks until all six were brim full. Then, pop! Dramatically, the champagne erupted and a succession of loud bangs, like gunshot, filled the room, as all six corks flew up into the air and hit the ceiling with a series of loud thuds.

"What the…" shouted Jack, losing his balance and tumbling backwards.

But the girls were too quick. They took their chance, leapt up from the settee, pounced on him knocking the gun from his hand onto the floor. They then rolled him over and sat firmly on his back.

"Take your tights off, Anne," commanded Elizabeth.

"What! Why?"

"To tie him up," snapped Elizabeth. "Hurry up, he's really strong."

Anne did as her sister said and quickly removed her tights; they then bound Jack's hands firmly together, rolled him over and sat on his stomach.

"Right, that's got you, you hateful brute," shouted Elizabeth, as she slapped him hard across the face. "I'm going to reach for the gun, Anne, and then while I'm pointing it at him I want you to go into the hall and phone the police."

But the next part of the plan was not necessary, for as Anne headed towards the door they heard laughter emanating from the kitchen. All was well. Their parents were back from the Inn.

Several hours later, after the police had gone and Jack Smeaton likewise, the Stanley family sat and tried to make sense of the evening's activities.

Anne was very subdued and sat tearfully on the settee safely snuggled up to Stella, while Ned paced the room asking the girls questions they could not answer.

Elizabeth sat on the floor, flustered and breathing deeply, for Jack Smeaton's actions had stirred up her emotions to a degree where she could not think straight nor explain her unrelenting anger. She sat grating her teeth noisily; her eyes transfixed on the desk, now standing up again after Jack's manhandling and back in its rightful place with the drawers intact.

"It's the desk," said Elizabeth, vehemently, after thinking things through. "It has to be the desk. Even when we had caught him red-handed, Jack was still trying to find something in it."

"But it's just a writing desk," said Stella. "There's nothing of any value in there, we all know that."

"On the surface, yes, you're right," said Elizabeth, pointing at the piece of furniture, "but deep inside it must hold some sort of secret."

She crawled across the floor and looked underneath. She then removed all the drawers and ran her hands along the back.

Ned frowned. "Surely you don't think it has a secret compartment and even if it does, how would the likes of Jack Smeaton know about it?"

"I don't know," snapped Elizabeth, frustrated by her inability to find answers. "I don't know. I'm just following my instincts."

She ran her hands around the inside area where the drawers fitted, but found nothing. She then examined the area between the top where it opened out to give a platform for writing on, and the section above the top drawer space.

"Look, there is a lost area between these two points. That means there's more than enough room for a secret compartment."

She ran her hand all around once more but no obvious catches or bolts were detectable. Annoyed and frustrated she banged her fist against the top of the drawer space and instantly they all heard a distinct click and a shelf appeared from the lost space.

"Good God," gasped Ned, kneeling by Elizabeth's side. "You're right, Liz. Is there anything inside?"

Elizabeth slid her slim hand inside and fumbled around.

"Yes."

From the desk she pulled out a sheet of very old paper; she unfolded it carefully. Written repeatedly across the page was the name Grenville Penwynton.

"It's as though someone has been practising his handwriting," said Stella, looking over the shoulder of Ned who held the yellowing paper. "Which in retrospect I realise someone must have done to write the phoney note saying he was leaving, which of course we all now know he didn't write because he was dead, if you know what I mean."

"There's something else," said Elizabeth, retrieving a velvet bag. She handed it to Ned, while she continued to search for anything else. Inside the bag was a pocket watch, made of gold and engraved with the name Grenville Penwynton.

"Good God, this must be worth a pretty penny," said Ned, standing to hold the watch beneath the light. "No wonder young Smeaton was keen to get his hands on it."

"And there's no doubt now that Grenville was murdered by his step mother, Talwyn," said Stella. "This desk must have been used by her and she stashed away these things knowing it's unlikely they'd ever be found."

"But, I still don't see how Jack knew about any of this," said Anne. "He couldn't have known about the pocket watch and as you say, Dad, that's the thing he'd most likely have been looking for."

"Just a minute, there's something else," said Elizabeth, excitedly. "It's tucked right away at the back."

She pushed her hand into the far corner.

"It's something solid; damn it, I can't grasp it properly."

As she spoke the shelf dropped a little lower and the item she was seeking was clearly visible.

"It's a book," said Elizabeth, her hands trembling as she attempted to open the cover. "Oh my God, it's a book and I think I know exactly what it's going to be."

She opened the cover carefully and on the first page clearly written in neat handwriting was the name Talwyn Louisa Penwynton.

Chapter Thirty One

"I'm going to call the police," said Stella, rising to her feet and heading for the door and the telephone in the hallway.

"No, no, please Mum, not yet," pleaded Elizabeth, grabbing her mother's skirt. "We must read it first, after all it might just contain old recipes or something like that."

Stella paused with her hand on the door knob. "Yes, and that may well be the case. But the desk also concealed a valuable watch which no doubt was the reason young Jack felt the need to ransack the place for a second time, and so the police need to be told as it's evidence."

"But, Mum..."

"I agree with Liz," said Ned, rising to take Stella's arm and guide her back to the chair. "After all I'm sure we're all very interested to hear what Talwyn has written, if anything, and the book being in the hands of the police at this time of night isn't going to do anything other than give the old bill a possible insight into the mind of a psychopath. As for the discovery of the watch, well, that can certainly wait a little longer too."

Stella nodded. "Okay, yes, I can see you're quite right." As she sat back down, Elizabeth turned over a few of the pages. In places the writing had faded, but not enough to make it illegible. "There are several pages of text," said Elizabeth, scrambling into an armchair. "I'll read it to you and that way we'll all learn together whatever there is to be learned."

And so she read the following:

Sometimes the best intentions in life go wrong, as in the case of me and my stepson, Grenville, who lost his mother when he was just two years of age. Charlotte, his mother, of good blood and a member of the Grenville family, died following the birth of Grenville's younger brother, Cedric.

It's funny that of the two Cedric was the stronger, almost as though he had taken from his mother every last bit of strength she possessed, for it is said she was not a robust woman, although I am told no finer horsewoman ever rode the boundaries of the Penwynton Estate.

Because of his love of riding, hunting, fishing and shooting, Cedric soon became the obvious favourite of his father and my husband, George. George had very little time for Grenville; he showed him only a modicum of affection and gave him no incentive to stand up for himself and be a man. I stood back for many years not wanting to interfere with the bringing up of the two boys, after all, they had their nanny, an adequately educated woman, but even she made it obvious that Cedric was her favourite. Besides, it was not my place to interfere, for I had two children of my own, Gorran, my son and Kayna, my daughter.

As the four children grew older, Grenville, it seemed grew weaker; he showed no interest in any of his father's pastimes and instead immersed himself in books. In one fit of rage, George said the boy was an embarrassment to him and he even threatened to disinherit him. It was at this stage, although I did not for one moment believe George would execute his threats, that I decided to step in; I adopted an attitude of firmness with all the children, but especially Grenville, hoping by doing so it might help to strengthen him, but my harsh words did nothing to help the situation and only fuelled up the tongues of the servants who labelled me a tyrant.

But alas, that was only the beginning. Gorran, my own flesh and blood, never liked his half-brother, Grenville, and for much the same reasons as their mutual father. This unfortunate situation, therefore, led Gorran to seize any opportunity that arose, to instigate a fight, knowing full well he would emerge the victor. On one such occasion the matter escalated out of hand. George and I were away for the weekend with Cedric and Kayna and because of our absence many of the servants were given a day off. When we returned, Gorran handed me Grenville's pocket watch and informed me he had fought his half-brother and killed him that very morning and his body lay buried in the meadow beyond the gardens at the back of the house. Gorran foolishly believed his father would congratulate him on his foul deed, but I knew this was not the case, George may have seemed a harsh man, but I knew deep down there beat the heart of gold. Besides, he is a law abiding citizen and would have insisted the police be informed, which would have inevitably led to my son being tried and hanged like a common criminal. I could not let that happen. It would have destroyed George and the well-respected name of Penwynton, even though I know it was not the Penwynton blood which flowed through the veins of Gorran that made him a felon. My son had inherited his wayward disposition from my maternal grandfather's family whose bad blood inflicted its evil on male family members who had the misfortune to be born with those penetrating green eyes.

And so I did the only thing possible. I forbade Gorran to say anything regarding Grenville's death to his father and I quickly practised writing in the style of Grenville, I then wrote a simple note pretending to be he, saying I had gone away to live a more uncomplicated life and asking that no-one try and find me. I left the note on George's pillow.

I was right regarding my analysis of George's caring, for he searched high and low for his missing son, but of course it was all in vain, for the poor boy lay rotting in the meadow, something of which I am reminded every time I look from the windows at the back of this house.

Meanwhile, things at home went from bad to worse, my dear, devoted maid, Matilda, of whom I was very fond, lost the charm and the vivacity I associated her with. She became distant, seemed disconsolate and then one day I found her weeping. At first she would not tell me the reason for her gloomy temperament, but then it all came out; she was with child; Grenville was responsible and she believed he had left the family home because of her and her condition and she was distraught, for he told her he loved her and would stand by her and she had believed it with all her heart. What could I say? No doubt he spoke the truth when he expressed his love for her, for I can say, hand on heart and with all sincerity, he was not one to deceive, nor one to utter a falsehood. Not like I, who had to lie and deceive to cover up the wrong doings of my own worthless son.

In an attempt to ameliorate, I offered Mattie a substantial amount of money and suggested she and her poor widowed mother leave the area and start a new life where they could bring up the child without having to worry about money. For I knew I could not tell George; he would not understand and it would only give him more reason than he had in by-gone days expressed, to declare his son to be a lily-livered coward who had disappeared because he could not face up to his responsibilities.

I let Mattie go with a very heavy heart; I longed to tell her the truth, but of course I could not. She thanked me for my kindness and said should her child be a girl then she would name her Louisa, my middle name, a name of which she often expressed great fondness.

I told George she had left our services and the area with her mother, and that at least was the truth. Cedric put them on the coach destined for Truro where I had arranged temporary accommodation until they decided on their final destination; where that eventually was, I know not, for I never heard from Matilda again. But thankfully in the woods I have a reminder of her. A tree; a little holly tree which she asked me to cherish. She and Grenville often met by an ash tree in the woods, and one day whilst awaiting his arrival she spotted a tiny holly seedling growing on the woodland path. Aware that the seedling would be either trampled on whilst tiny or felled if it grew and obscured the path, kind-hearted Matilda asked Grenville to transplant it, which he did. It now stands almost two feet in height and I cherish it with all my heart.

As the long months passed by, George finally accepted that Grenville had gone and was unlikely ever to return home again; thereafter he threw himself into his work and named Cedric his heir. Meanwhile in the kitchens, accusations against me were prevalent; the servants believed I had driven Grenville away and Matilda also and they despised me for it. My own son, Gorran, however, relished the absence of his half-brother and became very self-assured and aggressive. He made enormous effort to please his father in the hopes that one day he might be named the heir to the estate, should his other half-brother, Cedric, fall from grace.

And so the months turned into a year and August the twenty first, the first anniversary of Grenville's death was fast approaching, or as poor George believed, we were nearing the anniversary of his son's disappearance. To mask this milestone, Gorran, in an attempt to demonstrate his caring nature, suggested to his father a shooting weekend on the pretence that it might take his father's mind off the selfish and cowardly act of his absent half-brother. George thanked

Gorran for his kindness and plans were put into progress for the big event.

Meanwhile, I discovered that another of the servants was with child and that accusations of Gorran being the unborn child's father prevailed in the kitchens. When I approached Gorran and asked him if it were true, he laughed in my face, flatly denied it and said the girl was a lying whore. But deep down I knew he was deceiving me, for had I not with my very own eyes, seen him emerge from the stables with the wronged girl on several occasions? My only action therefore was to dismiss the girl, a chambermaid named Florrie Ham, promptly for her own safety; an act which turned the servants against me furthermore. In this case I did not offer the girl money even though the child she bore might be my grandchild, my reason being there was always the slight possibility that Gorran may have spoken the truth. Furthermore, to do so would have endorsed her claims, should she have chosen to incriminate the family in any way.

And then, as if matters were not already intolerable enough, Gorran, who had taken to drinking heavily, threatened to tell his father the truth behind the absence of his son, Grenville, and my part in covering up his disappearance, should I not assist him in organising the demise of his living half-brother, Cedric, heir to the Estate. This for me was the final straw and I was faced with only one option, for George must never, never know the truth. Hence, on the weekend of the anniversary shoot, I dressed myself in men's clothing and took myself to the woods and there, from behind a tree, I did take the opportunity when it arose, and I shot my own son, dead. It was August twenty first; a date I shall never forget. The date on which both Grenville and Gorran died just one year apart.

To this day I feel deep remorse; remorse for not having done more to protect Grenville and remorse for not having stood up to my own son. But I believe I am safe from accusations of any unlawful wrong doing, for whispers in the servants' quarters suggest it was the father of the servant girl I dismissed that fatally wounded my dear Gorran. And although I am still accused of driving Grenville away, I feel I can live with that. For it is better to be thought guilty of cruelty than of murder. But until the day I die I shall endure the pain of guilt, for my conscience punishes me daily and will not let me repose without vexation. For each time I go into the room, in which *once Grenville had slept, I feel his presence and imagine him sitting by the window overlooking the gardens and the meadow where he now rests, I pray, in peace. But at least my daughter, Kayna is untarnished by my bad judgement and hopefully she and her descendants will live on to be virtuous, worthy citizens and not discredit the good name of Penwynton.*

"Now I know why Talwyn had such sad eyes in her portrait," said Elizabeth, as she gently closed the book. "What a terrible, terrible time she must have had."

"This will all be a bit of a shock for Jim," said Stella. "He, like everyone else has always believed Talwyn to be an absolute monster and as it is, she was anything but." She cast a pitiful glance at the book resting on Elizabeth's lap. "I'm so glad that has turned up so that the truth can be told at last. It's a shame Charles Penwynton's not still around though, because he must often have wondered what really happened to the uncle he never knew."

"Do you think," Anne mused, "I mean, do you think it's possible that Talwyn's maid, Mattie, was the mother of Grev's great, grandmother and that he really did have Penwynton blood? After all his great aunt admitted it was his mother's claim to fame and it certainly looks as though she might possibly have been right."

Ned nodded his head. "Yes, it certainly adds up; but what mystifies me is why that lad Smeaton should have been looking for the book, that's if he was. How on earth did he know it was there?"

Elizabeth shrugged her shoulders. "Goodness only knows. Jack's behaviour makes very little sense."

Ned leaned forwards. "Pass me the diary please, Liz. I should like to see it before we phone the police."

Elizabeth stood to pass the book to her father. As she released her grasp two cards fell from the back pages. Anne quickly knelt and picked them up. When she saw they were old photographs the colour drained from her face. One picture, as the neat writing on the back told, was of Kayna; the other was Gorran. She held up the latter for her family to see. Gorran was the spitting image of Jack Smeaton.

The reason for the resemblance between Jack Smeaton and Gorran Penwynton became apparent as the days unfolded. Anne found out when she went to work the following day and Mary Cottingham, who knew the history of the Penwynton family, called her into the office following a visit to the Hotel by the police.

"What a to-do, eh, Anne?" said Mary, as Anne sat down on the opposite side of the desk.

Anne nodded. "Yes, but I'm struggling to get my head round it at present. It all makes very little sense."

"Hmm, well I'm sure things will seem a little clearer when I tell you that Jack, I'm amazed to discover, is a descendent of the Penwyntons."

"But that's ridiculous. I mean, I know there's a strong resemblance between him and Gorran because of the old picture, but I don't see how, I mean. Oh dear."

Mary laughed. "Let me explain. For a start, Jack doesn't come from Loughborough at all, as he said." Mary laughed sardonically. "He's actually Canadian, would you believe? Although of course he has English blood, or should I say, Cornish? But whichever, he's never been to Leicestershire in his life. Having said that, I believe the university he attends is somewhere north of Leicester."

Anne frowned. "Well I suppose that at least explains his peculiar accent. So all along he must have been trying to disguise his Canadian tongue to avoid suspicion. How very crafty, but why? I'm really intrigued, Mary. Please tell me how he can be a Penwynton."

Mary leaned back in her chair and unconsciously twiddled a pen around in her hands. "Jack, I am told by the police, is the great, great, great grandson of Talwyn Penwynton, nee Nancarrow, and the great, great grandson of Kayna, Gorran's sister. His grandfather was Bernard Reeves, who, if you remember your history, inherited the Penwynton Estate on the death of Charles."

Anne nodded. "I'm with you so far."

"Good. Well according to Jack, a story has passed down through the Reeves family saying that Geoffrey Reeves, Kayna's son, had a memory of seeing his grandmother, Talwyn, reading a book which made her cry. He, Geoffrey, was in the drawing room at the time he witnessed this, hiding from his brothers and sisters with whom he was playing hide and seek, and Talwyn went into the room, not knowing he was there, hidden behind the curtains. Apparently, when she heard the chatter of children's voices in the hallway, she quickly put the book away, but to do so she had to take out the drawer and the little boy was mystified by this. Geoffrey never had a chance to examine the desk himself as it was always kept locked. And then when he grew up he emigrated to Canada and got married out there. Geoffrey never returned to England again, but his tale was passed on down through the generations, so when Jack's mother, Bernard's daughter, suggested Jack come to England to further his education, he seized the opportunity with enthusiasm; the main purpose of his visit being to try and find out if the desk and the book that made his great, great, great grandmother cry, really did exist." Mary stopped twiddling the pen and laid it down on the desk. "When Jack saw our advert in a student magazine asking for seasonal staff he couldn't believe his luck and the rest of the story you know."

"So, do you think he knew then, what happened all those years ago?" asked Anne. "I mean to say, did Jack know about Grenville's disappearance and the way Gorran died? I know he heard the stories when he was here, because he asked about Penwynton history, and we told him one night in the Badge. He was fascinated and hung onto every word, which makes a lot of sense now. But do you think he knew before then?"

Mary sighed deeply. "Apparently, he didn't know the truth. You see, family rumour suspected there was more to Grenville's disappearance than they knew of, but they had no idea just what it might have been. That's why Jack was keen to get to the bottom of the matter and he was convinced the truth lay somewhere in your parent's desk."

"And he was right," sighed Anne, as tears welled up in her eyes. "How weird. To think no-one ever found it in all these years. So was it Jack who killed poor Grev? And if he did, what possible reason could he have? That's something I don't understand."

Mary nodded. "Yes, I believe Jack has confessed to Grev's murder and it was because poor Grev stumbled on the stolen property hidden in the woods. But whereas when Suzie found it she was able to tell the police, Grev was unfortunate inasmuch as Jack was there in the woods at the time intending to bury it properly, as he'd not had a chance to do so before. And before you ask, Jack stole articles he didn't want to make it look like the work of an accomplished burglar, as he didn't want to draw attention to the fact his only target really was your parents' desk."

"Oh God, how creepy, and I nearly caught him twice," said Anne, with a shudder. "But what's even worse then, is Grev died just because he happened to stumble across stupid unwanted stolen property. That's just so unfair and so unlucky."

Mary half-smiled. "Yes, very unlucky, and I find it a little odd also, and disturbing too, that Gorran killed the first Grenville Penwynton and his sister Kayna's great, great, grandson, Jack, killed our Grenville Penwynton."

"Hmm, and also, our Grev died exactly one hundred years to the day after the first Grenville."

Mary looked surprised. "Is that right?"

Anne nodded. "Yes, both were killed on August twenty first. Grenville in 1876 and Grev in 1976. I find that really eerie." Anne shivered. "Mary, do you think the two were related? The two Grenvilles, I mean."

"Yes I do, and it's because of the name, Louisa. Miss Bugg told me that Louisa was the name of Grev's great, grandmother, so she, undoubtedly, was Mattie's illegitimate child."

To pass the time, Elizabeth decided to tidy her room and whilst doing so she came across a pair of jeans which had fallen down the back of a chair. As she picked them up, the red stone which she had placed inside the pocket, dropped onto the floor. She stooped down and picked it up and then crossed the room, where from the top drawer of her dressing table she pulled out a large magnifying glass. She then took stone and glass to the window for a closer look. To her amazement, the stone was perfect. Perfect in shape, flawless and clear.

Elizabeth bit her bottom lip. It sounded daft, but could this little piece of red glass possibly be the missing ruby and it had found its way into Jack's sausage in an attempt to choke him? And if so, why? Elizabeth laughed, but as things stood she was prepared to believe just about anything.

She glanced across the room. Things were almost straight and what wasn't done could wait until later; because if the red glass was a ruby, *the* ruby, then it was far more important to establish that fact, than it was to finish tidying her room. Elizabeth sat down on the bed to think. If her memory served her right, the stick pin had been returned to the Hotel after the police had finished with it; therefore the Hotel was the place to go.

Crystal was on the reception desk when Elizabeth walked into the vestibule. She looked pale and tired.

Elizabeth smiled awkwardly. She knew, through Anne, that Crystal had been besotted with Jack and had been out with him several times since they had seen *The Omen*. She attempted to be bright and breezy. "Hi, I don't think you know me but I'm Anne's sister."

Crystal half-smiled. "Well, we've not been introduced but I do know who you are. You're Malcolm's girlfriend. He talks of you a lot."

"Does he? Oh, dear Malc." Elizabeth glanced around. "Have you any idea where I might find Anne?"

Crystal nodded. "Yes, she's up in the office with Mrs Cottingham."

"Oh, do you think she'll be long?"

Crystal shrugged her shoulders. "No idea. Shall I ring up and say you're here?"

"Hmm, I don't really know. I don't want to disturb them. Having said that, what I'm here about might be important, and so, yes please."

Crystal rang the office. She smiled as she put down the receiver. "Mrs Cottingham said to go up. Do you know your way?"

Elizabeth shook her head. "Sorry, but no."

Crystal pointed towards the grand staircase. "Go up to the first floor. You'll find a door marked office at the end of the corridor next to the family's living quarters."

"Thanks."

Elizabeth went up the staircase and passed beneath the newly installed painting of Penwynton House. At the end of the corridor she found Anne waiting with the office door open. Anne gave her sister a quizzical look. "What brings you here?"

Elizabeth didn't answer and looked sheepish as both girls went into the office where Mary Cottingham sat behind a large oak desk. She too had a quizzical expression on her face.

"Sorry to interrupt," said Elizabeth, "but I've something you might like to see. I should have shown it to you before now but at the time I assumed it couldn't really be what I now think it is."

Mary raised her eyebrows. "I'm intrigued. Whatever is it?"

From her pocket Elizabeth took the stone and laid it down on the desk. "I think this just might be Grenville's missing ruby."

Mary leaned forwards and picked it up. "It certainly looks about the right size, but I don't understand. Where did you get it?"

Elizabeth half-smiled. "You're not going to believe this, but it was in a sausage Jack Smeaton was eating. He was at the Badge, you see, several days ago now. In fact it was just after Anne and I had been to the art gallery to pick up the painting. Anyway, Jack was sitting outside with Ponce, I mean Pete, and they were drinking and both had basket meals. I spoke to them cos they called to me. They said they were going swimming after their lunch and I said that was unwise as they'd obviously been drinking. It was really weird because while we were talking Jack start to choke and eventually he spat out chewed up sausage and this stone."

Anne leaned back. "Yuck, do you mean to tell me that stone's actually been inside Jack's mouth?"

Elizabeth nodded.

Mary opened up a drawer in her desk and took out a small padded envelope. From it she tipped the stick pin onto the palm of her hand. Elizabeth and Anne both leaned forwards as she carefully lowered the stone into the small gap on the robin's breast. It was a perfect fit.

Anne slapped the palm of her hand across her forehead. "But, I mean, why, how. Oh, this doesn't make any sense. How on earth could that ruby have found its way into Jack's silly sausage?"

Elizabeth shrugged her shoulders. "I've not the foggiest idea and I think that's a question that no-one will ever be able to answer."

Before dawn broke on the morning of Grev Penwynton's funeral, Gloria Withers was woken by the sound of Raymond getting out of bed and leaving the room. Assuming he was going to the bathroom, she turned onto her side and tried to get back to sleep, but when he had not returned after ten minutes, she sat up, concerned that something might be wrong, for Raymond never arose until after she had taken him his first cup of tea and a slice of buttered toast.

Hearing no evidence of his imminent return, she slipped out of bed, put on her dressing gown and slippers and went to find him. To her surprise, she found him in the snug bar, standing on a stool taking guns down from the old wooden beams.

"Oh, for goodness sake, love, surely you're not going to start cleaning them all now; not at this time of the morning, it's not even light yet."

"No, I'm not cleaning them," said Raymond, throwing down one after another into a cardboard box on the floor. "I'm taking them down and they're going to stay down. It's time for change you see, Glore. It's time for change."

He stepped down from the stool and moved it along to the next beam.

"Would you like a hand?" asked Gloria, very confused by his out of character actions. "Many hands make light work."

"Well, I've nearly finished now, but I'd love a cuppa if you'd care to make one. I've been awake for hours, you see cos I couldn't sleep."

Gloria obligingly left for the kitchen and returned shortly after with two steaming mugs of tea and a plate of biscuits on a tray, just as Raymond threw the last gun into the box.

"All done, Glore, what do you think?" he asked, stepping down from the stool and taking his mug of tea from the tray. "Looks better already, don't it?"

"Hmm, it's a little bare, but I suppose we'll soon get used to it," said Gloria, still in a dazed state.

"Well, it's not going to stay like that. I thought we'd hang a few old fishing nets from some of the beams in here and in the public bar too. We'll buy a few miniature crab pots as well from Percy. You know, the withy ones he makes for visitors, they'd look really good either side of the fireplace. We're going to go for a nautical theme, you see, Glore, after all we have a fishing cove here and we should exploit that fact; it's what the holiday makers like."

"Yes, hmm, but I thought…"

"We'll have to change the Inn's name of course," interrupted Raymond. "I mean, it can't be called the Sheriff's Badge Inn if it's full of fishing stuff, can it? Besides, there'll be no bleedin' sheriff in here, that's for sure. Having said that most of our locals call it the Badge anyway, so rather than confuse matters I think we'll just change the name to The Badger, so they can still call it The Badge, clever eh, Glore? Bit of word play and all that. We'll have to have a new board made, but that's no problem and we'll have a nice picture of a cute badger in it. You'll like that, Glore, cos you like cuddly animals, don't you? And I was thinking perhaps we'd get one of those glass fronted cabinets containing knots to put on one of the walls and a few crab shells wouldn't come amiss. Of course, I'll obviously not be wearing my stupid cowboy outfits anymore. They can go on the ruddy fire for all I care. From now on it'll be smart shirts and a tie like that Frank bloke who used to be here. I might even wear a posh waistcoat on special occasions. What's more we're gonna take on a full time member of staff. I think that nice girl, Jane would be ideal. You know who I mean, Pete and Betty Williams' daughter. She asked me the other day if we had any vacancies cos she's fed up with shop work. She'd be a great asset to us. She's a pleasant girl and I know you like her."

Feeling lightheaded, Gloria sat down. "But, but, I don't understand. What's brought about this sudden change?"

"Guilt Glore," said Raymond, his lips quivering. "Guns are symbols of violence and I can't sleep properly at night knowing my gun killed that poor lad. It's almost as though I pulled the bloody trigger myself. No, things have gotta change, Glore, and nothing you say will change my mind. I shall resign from the Gun Club today and donate all these awful weapons to them, after which you'll never, ever see me with a gun again. They'll be burying that lad today, Glore. Burying him, and it's all my fault."

To Gloria's surprise he then put his head in his hands and wept; something she had never before seen him do in all the twenty nine years she had known him.

Chapter Thirty Two

"Molly, Ben, come quick, please. It's Jim, he's not breathing," sobbed Doris, as she stumbled through the back door of Rose Cottage.

The major leapt from his chair, took Doris by the arm and with Molly following, all hastened next door to Ivy Cottage.

In a chair by the window, Jim sat, his head bowed and both hands resting on an open newspaper spread across his lap. His tired eyes were half closed; his lips frozen in a half smile and his face a picture of contentment. The major bent forward and felt for a pulse but he knew it was too late.

"He's gone, Doris," whispered the major, turning to take her hands. "There's nothing we can do for him and he didn't suffer. He's at peace; I'm so sorry."

As Doris fell into the major's arms and sobbed, Molly glanced down at the newspaper. Her lips trembled. "It looks as though he'd been reading Sid's article about Grenville Penwynton and Talwyn's diary," she said, softly. "I hope the shock wasn't too much for him."

Doris attempted a smile but her mouth was reluctant to co-operate. "No, it wouldn't have been. He was really heartened to hear that Grenville hadn't run away, but surprised like the rest of us to hear Talwyn had written a diary. The last thing he said to me was how he was looking forward to reading Sid's article in the paper. That's why I wasn't with him when he died. I went outside to hang out the washing and ended up dead heading my dahlias. I didn't want to disturb him, you see, because I knew it meant a lot to him. But I should have been with him when he died, I can't forgive myself for that."

She sat on the settee and cried whilst Molly and the major tried to comfort her. "It would've been his birthday next week and he'd have been eighty seven, so I suppose he's had a good run and he was pretty active right to the end, still doing the garden and so forth." She sat up straight. "I must compose myself, he'd want me to do that.

Anyway, Flo will be able to look after him now, so he'll not be lonely."

The major closed Jim's eyes and drew the curtains; he then made a phone call on Doris's behalf and as he did so he attempted to push aside the painful memories which always came back to haunt him whenever bereavement reared its head.

A week later, Elizabeth sat on the swing that had been in the back garden of the School House since she and Anne were children. It was the last day of the school summer holiday and the following morning she was due to start her new job teaching youngsters at the primary school in Polquillick. She felt both excited and apprehensive about taking up her new position. She knew the village of Polquillick of course and had been there many times, but she was not acquainted with any of the locals other than the landlord of the Mop and Bucket and his wife, and Matthew's girlfriend who worked in the cafe.

She thought of her friends, all happy in their respective occupations and one or two with partners whom they would most likely marry. She thought of Malcolm. He and the rest of the students had finished their work at the Hotel the previous weekend and returned to their respective homes in order to spend a little time with their families before preparing for the forthcoming academic year.

Elizabeth thought of the night she and Malcolm had met, and how, because of that first brief encounter, she had thought it to be love at first sight. But always she had known there was something wrong, something missing, and the reason was, it was not Malcolm who had charmed her with a smile and a seductive kiss, it was without doubt the ghost of Grenville Penwynton, troubled, so she believed, by the arrival of Jack Smeaton at the one-time family home: Jack, with his green eyes and his looks identical to Gorran. Elizabeth smiled. Was it possible in her Grenville saw a kindly soul who would help him achieve justice?

Elizabeth felt a slight chill; there was definitely a nip in the air. She pulled her cardigan tightly around her chest and folded her arms. Soon the leaves would be falling from the trees heralding autumn, to be followed by the long dark nights of winter. Elizabeth liked winter nights. There was something comforting about curling up in a chair beside an open fire listening to the wind outside whistling down the chimney and the rain pitter-pattering against the window panes.

"When I have my own house," she told a bumble bee hovering over the snow white Japanese Anemones standing amidst Michaelmas daisies in her mother's weedless flower bed, "I shall have a fire there too. I couldn't possibly live in a house with only central heating to keep me warm, it would be too boring."

She laughed; realising her sentiments were very much like those of her grandmother, but then in many ways, she seemed to be getting more like her grandmother with every passing year.

The back door of the house opened and Anne emerged from the kitchen holding several sheets of paper in her hand.

"The postman has just brought a letter from Lily," she said, waving the pages in the air, "and guess what?"

Elizabeth felt her heart sink. "Greg and Jemima are back together," she answered, her voice faltering. "Oh well, I suppose it was inevitable."

Anne, her face twisted into a smirk, laughed. "No, no, not at all. Admittedly, you're on the right track, but your conclusion is far from correct. They're not back together at all. He and Jemima have well and truly split up for good."

Elizabeth hoped Anne could not hear her heart thumping, but her sister was too busy laughing.

"What's more," she continued, "he's coming home, Liz. Greg's coming home. Lily told me not to tell you, but apparently it was when he heard you were to teach at Polquillick that he broke off his engagement and then asked if it was possible for a transfer to Cornwall. He's due back at the end of the month."

By the middle of September the Hotel's new pond was finished, and Bob and Dick, through laborious determination, had managed to fill it to the brim with rain water by catching every drop possible in receptacles all around the Hotel.

The result was stunning. Alongside the curved edge, a slate path wound and twisted beside a row of freshly planted fuchsia bushes, and a small wall, just the right height for sitting on, ran alongside two stretches of the path. At either end, stood pergolas, each with climbing roses, honeysuckle and clematis newly planted at the base of their posts. And inside, sturdy benches sheltered beneath the rustic constructions.

On Mary's insistence, Anne left the reception desk to take a look at the finished work; the pond, it was decided, would be planted up and filled with fish the following spring, thus leaving time for it to settle during the long winter months.

Anne found John loading the cement mixer on the back of the truck and clearing away the last bits of building materials. He smiled broadly when he saw he had a visitor.

"So what do you think, Anne?" he asked, wiping his hands on his grubby T shirt. "Does our work meet with your approval?"

Anne clasped her hands in gratification. "It's beautiful, although this was a lovely spot anyway." She sat down on the wall and gazed into the water, her head tilted to one side. "You know, it's silly but I find the pond quite fascinating even though there is nothing in it but water."

John left the truck and crossed to her side. He sat down. "There is something in it, Anne. Your reflection."

"Oh yes, and I can see yours too," giggling, she leaned forwards. "I never realised water could be quite so enthralling. In fact I think when I have a house of my own, I shall definitely have a pond and you must build it for me, John."

"There's nothing I'd like more than to build you a pond, Anne, except maybe perhaps build you a house. A magnificent house as grand as any mansion and a place where you could hang your paintings in the hallways and grow your favourite flowers in the gardens."

Anne gazed at his reflection in the water as he looked at his watch and then stood up. She was very surprised by his statement, though not so much for the disclosure itself but for the sincerity with which it was said. As his words sank in, she turned her gaze from his reflection in the water and looked towards John himself standing beside her on the newly laid path. She blushed, for what she saw was not the boy whom she had known for as long as she could remember, but a young man with a look in his eyes she had never before seen.

"Are you going to the Inn tonight?" she asked, aware that her face was flushed and her voice had a quiver. "Elizabeth and I are. It should be a lot quieter now the children are back at school and the holiday season is over. In fact, it'll be just us locals again."

He nodded. "Yes, I'll be there, so see you later then."

Anne watched as he crossed the grass, jumped into the truck, waved and then drove off towards the old stable block. She bit her bottom lip. "Anne Collins," she whispered, with a girlish giggle. "I rather like that name. How blind and silly I've been all these years, wasting my time dreaming of Danny."

She rose from the wall, and meandered back through the gardens towards the Hotel. By the time she reached the reception desk her eyes were shining and a broad grin stretched across her face from ear to ear.

"So how do you like our new pond, Anne?" asked Mary Cottingham, intrigued by the look on Anne's face.

Anne smiled, dreamily. "I think it's absolutely beautiful, Mary. Enlightening even, and I know it'll be a very dear spot and close to my heart for ever and ever."

On the last day of September, one hundred years and forty days after his death, Grenville Penwynton was finally laid to rest with other members of his family in the churchyard at Trengillion. The funeral was attended by a great number of people in spite of the rain which had fallen throughout much of September.

Anne and Elizabeth attended the funeral along with family and friends and after the interment they crossed the churchyard beneath their umbrellas, to the new part where Grev Penwynton and Jim Hughes lay side by side, not far from George Fillingham.

"Mum always says deaths go in threes," said Anne, tears welling in her eyes as they always did when she thought of Grev. "But this summer, since you've been home, we've had four. Grev, Granddad Stanley, Jim Hughes and of course Grenville. I hope that doesn't mean we're starting a second three."

Elizabeth smiled. "Well, I don't really think we should include Grenville, after all he has been dead for a hundred years."

"Hmm, yes, I suppose you're right." She swapped her umbrella from one hand to the other. "What do you think will happen to Jack, Liz? I know he did wrong and he should be punished severely, but there was something about him I liked. Oh dear, if only the world was devoid of trouble and strife like it always seemed to be when we were children."

"I should think he'll get life," said Elizabeth, slowly shaking her head. "And quite rightly so, for when all is said and done, he committed murder and that can never be justified. What a poor, stupid fool he was."

Anne paused. "Well, yes, but I don't think he came here intent on killing anyone, he just wanted to find Talwyn's diary and learn the truth. Silly boy. If only he'd told us who he was and what he was after, then the mystery could have been solved without bloodshed and he would be free to return to Canada with the diary and the watch. It's all very sad and made worse because unfortunately he obviously has the bad gene referred to by Talwyn which runs from her grandfather's side of the family; and he has the green eyes too."

"Lots of people have bad genes and are tempted into doing wrong," said Elizabeth, "but anyone who finds themselves in that position should fight against it, cos when all's said and done the difference between right and wrong is pretty obvious, isn't it?"

Anne shook her head. "No, it's not that simple, Liz. A person can be born with an affliction such as an unsightly birthmark or a withered arm, but all the willpower in the world won't change that fact and I believe it's the same from within. A flaw of character is an affliction like an ugly scar only on the inside and I don't think anything short of brainwashing or hypnotism will ever do anything to change an imperfection such as that."

"Maybe you're right, but there was more to Jack's case than that anyway," said Elizabeth, passionately. "Jack angered the elder tree mother when he cut down the elder at the Hotel and burnt it. Also, because of his looks and who he was, he angered Grenville the minute he arrived at the Hotel. Having said that we'll never know for sure if his misfortunes can be attributed to his genes, Grenville's angered ghost or caused by the destruction of the elder, but I think it was probably a bit of all three."

Anne smiled. "But Jack destroyed the elder on the instructions of Dick Cottingham, so surely he can't be blamed for that. I think you're taking folklore far too seriously, Liz, although I do agree with your theory regarding Grenville, as nutty as it might sound to us more down-to-earth beings."

"I've just realised," said Elizabeth, running her hand over the corner of a broken tombstone. "It must have been Jack who desecrated the grave of Florrie Ham's dad and for no just reason it now appears. I bet the Ham family are relieved to know their predecessor wasn't a murderer after all."

"Probably, but Jim Hughes always said the family were pleased about Gorran's demise, so in the vicinity of Polquillick, no doubt, the Hams weren't too quick to deny it, except of course to the police."

Elizabeth laughed. "Come on, it feels cold and dismal out here. Let's join the others in the Badge. I've a feeling with the large media gathering here today and the good turnout by the locals that we could be in for an impromptu wake. What's more, John Collins will be wondering where on earth you are."

"What do you mean? John is …"

"Oh, Anne, don't be so secretive," said Elizabeth, taking her sister's arm. "I'm not blind, you're dotty about each other, any fool can see that and your union is in the stars."

In the late afternoon the rain ceased briefly and Elizabeth took the opportunity to slip quietly from the Inn, unseen by anyone, and walk round to the churchyard, for she wanted to speak to Grenville alone, without the presence of others who might think her mad. Elizabeth walked along the gravel path to the far end of the graveyard where the memorial stones of many Penwyntons towered above the tops of more modest graves. By the mound of fresh flowers she stopped, bowed her head and whispered: "Did I do all that you wanted of me, Grenville? Was it your wish that your remains be found and the truth be told? I'm sure it was, just as I am sure it was you I spotted at my father's party. And as for the ruby, I'm sure it was no accident that Jack Smeaton nearly choked on it. You were seeking revenge, weren't you? And who can blame you. But justice has been done now and you can rest in peace."

Elizabeth knelt by the grave and whispered a little prayer. When she stood, a sudden gust of wind arose from nowhere and whipped around her feet. She pulled her coat collar tightly around her neck and tried to keep her balance as the strengthening wind buffeted against her body and rain droplets dripped onto her shoulders from the fluttering leaves of a tree overhanging Grenville's final resting place. On the mound of freshly dug earth, colourful flowers shivered in the breeze until a multitude of petals broke free and danced in a circle above her head. Elizabeth watched, spellbound, speechless, as the wind dropped as quickly as it had risen and the petals fluttered to the ground where they fell in formation on the wet grass and spelled out the words *be happy*.

Mesmerised, Elizabeth stepped forward to touch the quivering petals, but as she stooped they rose again, twisting and twirling amidst fresh raindrops falling from the heavens. Like snowflakes the petals floated and danced above her head, circling the trees, fluttering and flittering through the branches. Elizabeth laughed, the petals wanted her to be happy. She jumped up and tried to catch them as they swirled around her head, but they were too quick and rose high above the trees. She span on the spot, determined not to lose sight of their antics as they drifted back down to eye level and fluttered along the gravel path like a swarm of bees.

Elizabeth ran after them. By the lich gate they hovered. Some-one was walking through the gate and into the churchyard. A young man. A tall, handsome young man. Elizabeth stopped running and stood perfectly still, watching as the petals danced around him in formation above his head. And then with a swish and a swirl they gently fell like confetti and momentarily rested upon his shoulders. Elizabeth gasped as they suddenly rose again and formed one last pirouette before they drifted away towards the tower of the church, brushing against the red leaves of the Virginia creeper, each petal fluttering as though waving farewell.

Elizabeth turned as Gregory Castor-Hunt stepped forward onto the gravel path. As he approached her he reached out and affectionately touched her cold cheek. She clasped his wrist as he took something from the inside pocket of his jacket. Grinning he casually shook his head and frowned in a quizzical yet amused manner. "I've not the foggiest idea how this came to be in my possession, Liz, but it was on the window sill of my room when I awoke one morning. But how it got there doesn't matter. Elizabeth Stanley, you can't possibly know how happy reading it made me feel."

Standing snuggly by her side he placed a piece of paper into her cold hand and whispered, "Receiving it was like a gift from heaven."

Elizabeth frowned, puzzled and dazed. As she unfolded the sheet of paper, a chill dashed down her spine and goose pimples rose on her arms, for on it, words written in her neat handwriting stretched across the crumpled page. It was the letter she had written and drowned in the rock pool on the beach.

She gasped as he gently slipped his arm around her waist and kissed her damp hair; with tears trickling down her cheeks she cast her eyes to the skies and watched as the last petals disappeared, like magic, into the heavens.

THE END

Printed in Great Britain
by Amazon